CW01081022

UNEXPECTED EVA

THE TRIPLE TROUBLE SERIES - BOOK 3

VH NICOLSON

For all the superheroes cleverly disguised as stepfathers, this is for you. This is for mine.

AUTHOR'S NOTES

Please note this book comes with a content warning. This book is intended for over 18s.

My books all come with the guarantee of a happily ever after but sometimes the journey to get there can be a hard fought one. The main focus of my books is love, romance and happiness.

Please keep that in mind. Also there is lots of humor too.

However, just in case you aren't sure, and if you are a sensitive reader then please proceed with caution, here's a content warning list.

Triggers: abusive relationships, absent parents, alcohol addiction, emotional assault, physical assault, divorce, emotional abuse, abandonment.

For Content Warnings & Tropes of All My Books, Please Scan the QR Code Above.

Playlist

Sunshine - TIEKS
Dress On - Justin Timberlake
Kaleidoscope Dream - Miguel
Talking to the Moon - Bruno Mars
Love Nwantiti - CKay
Purple Rain - Prince
Tell Me Something Good - Ewan McVicar
Shut Off the Lights - Bastille
Rendezvous - Craig David
Remember (Acoustic) - Becky Hill
Be Alright - Dean Lewis
#Beautiful - Mariah Carey ft Miguel

CHAPTER ONE

Eva

Curving my body around the never-ending circular tables littered throughout the extraordinary ballroom, I'm on a mission to make it to my seat without being noticed.

I'm surrounded by hundreds of cheerful people.

Cheerful people I can*not* be bothered speaking to this evening.

Hitching my floor-length ball gown up at one side, being careful not to snag the delicate ink-blue silk on my towering gold heels, I'm suddenly stopped in my tracks. *Shoot.* Too late, didn't make it... And what's her name again?

Eh, oh, crap, hmm, think Eva, think.

"Hello dear, it's so wonderful to see you. How are you?" The cheery silver-haired woman smiles brightly.

"Evening. I'm great, thank you; how are you and the family?" I try my best to hide my confusion and flustered appearance, deep down hoping she does, in fact, have a family. A tiny smidge of memory slides in. I know her name; it's on the tip of my tongue. Is it Carol? Something beginning with *C*, I know it.

"Oh, they are wonderful, darling. Thomas is a top criminal lawyer now, and his wife, Matilda, is simply divine. She's also a lawyer. They've bought one of the Victorian mansion houses down Cherry Gardens Lane. You know the ones?" She raises her voice over the chitter-chatter around us, glancing to her left and right to see if anyone heard her momentary boast. She clearly wants everyone to know how successful her son is.

Cecilia? Is that her name?

Nope, that's not it either.

I'm at a loss.

"Yes, I know those homes. They are beautiful at that end of town."

The nineteenth century mansions down Cherry Gardens Lane are stunning. There are ten in total. Each one is unique, otherworldly, and big—dream goals big. Many of them can't be seen from the curbside because they're heavily guarded by surrounding trees, high stone walls, and solid wooden gates.

Our little town of Castleview Cove may be small, where everyone knows everyone, but those homeowners are a mystery to me and most of the residents of Castleview.

Owned by affluent businesspeople and celebrity types, they float into town for the weekend and then drift back like ghosts to their high-powered city jobs during the week.

The old-timers of the town do not approve of them at all, nicknaming the new town people *incomers*. Silly stuck-in-a-time-warp fuddy-duddies.

A couple of the homes have been inherited from townspeople of old, passed down from generation to generation. When that happens, the remodeling begins.

It's wonderful to see the old decrepit mansions undergoing renovations, giving them a new lease on life, injecting new blood into our unique little community.

Rumor has it two pro golfers have purchased homes down Cherry Gardens Lane, but I'm yet to catch a glimpse of one in town. And my brother-in-law, Hunter King, also a pro golfer, doesn't count. He and my sister, Eden, built a brand-new all-glass home that sits up high on the hill overlooking Castleview Cove. Sometimes I just happen to be *passing by*. Any excuse to kick back on their deck, a hot steaming cup of tea in hand, and lazily drink in the view. It's beautiful and a far cry from the playpark I can see from the upper window of my little three-bedroom townhouse.

From Eden's house, though, you can see the entire town. The castle that sits prominently on top of the hill keeping watch, and the golf courses that span for miles, blanketing the landscape.

Our tiny Scottish town feels magical, like it's breathing in the sea salt air, exhaling spellbound particles, casting us under her charm.

It's a truly captivating place, one I have lived in my entire life, save from when I attended dance school to become a dancer. It's littered with ancient ruins and buildings; some date as far back as the eleventh century. Every twist, nook, and cranny is another discovery waiting to be uncovered. It really is something special.

Those homes down Cherry Gardens Lane, though, they are special. Intriguing.

I've always wanted a little sneak peek or tour of one. It's a shame I don't know anyone that lives down that road, apart from my father's friend, Knox Black, but I would *never* ask him. He's strictly off-limits. *Although I wish he wasn't.*

A sudden whoosh of recollection hits me.

Ah, got it!

The woman standing in front of me is Christie. Christie Burns. I knew it began with a *C*.

They live in the next town over. She ran the local Sewing Bee group with my mom when I was around eight years old. Thomas, her son, always tagged along with her; pulling my pigtails was his favorite pastime. He always did have the ability to wind me up something stupid. He's no longer a silly little boy, but a lawyer, no less. Thomas has done well for himself.

Pointing toward the stage, informing Christie the charity auction is about to begin, I shift around the dainty woman.

"Oh, it was lovely to see you, Eden. Please tell your mother I'm asking about her."

I bite my tongue and fake a smile.

It's Eva, you silly woman, not Eden.

One thing that annoys me about being a triplet—people mix us up. Although my sisters, Ella, Eden, and I are not identical, it has been known on occasion, like now, for people to get us muddled. We are fraternal triplets, like vanilla ice cream with different toppings.

Yes, we all have blond hair and yes, we look similar but we are very different in terms of styles and height. Eden is a continuous bundle of youth and laughter, while Ella is our sassy sexy platinum goddess then there's me. The homemaker. I'm the tallest in our trio and my style is more eclectic than them both combined. While Eden loves nothing better than a trip to the shops to buy more Disney apparel and Ella loves the whole biker chic, leather pant look, I'm more bohemian in style and love a mooch around a vintage clothing store. And it's normally a quick in and out, unlike Eden, I'm not a fan of shopping around dozens of clothes shops.

Also, Eden is only five foot two and I'm five foot ten. Clearly, not identical triplets.

Goodness knows how Christie thinks I am Eden.

Finally breaking away from Christie, I mosey over to my designated table. Politely greeting everyone with a small hello, I slide into my seat for the evening and make myself comfortable.

I'm relieved to be taking the weight off my feet for the day. They are already throbbing and the night hasn't even started yet. I'm wearing what my sisters call sitting shoes—too uncomfortable to walk or dance in, simply sit in and look pretty, although even that is too painful.

I push the sky-high gold heels off my feet and give my aching toes a wiggle in the cool air beneath the table.

Enjoying the welcomed calm in contrast to my busy day of school runs, teaching dance classes, cooking, cleaning, and washing, I relax into my chair.

I ferried my two boys off to my parents' for a sleepover for the entire weekend.

I do not know what I will do with myself for one whole day and night tomorrow. It's been months since I had any downtime. Although my ironing pile is massive, I'm pretty sure it was waving at me earlier, trying to grab my attention.

Sipping my crisp glass of champagne, I sneak a glance around the room in awe. No matter how many times I've been in this ballroom, it never ceases to amaze me.

It's stunning, decorated in luminous white with a contrasting navy-painted ceiling. Recessed into the ceiling are hundreds of fairy-style lights. It's dazzling and makes the ceiling look like a clear, starry night. White furnishings cover every inch of the room. Elegant white chairs, white flowers, white table covers, white everything, even the floor, which I thought was a brave choice. However, given the five-star hotel's clientele, it's not as if they have rowdy hen parties here every week. No sirree.

The Sanctuary Hotel and Spa is luxurious. Breathtaking. Expensive. Designed for the elite. When the golf championships are in town, this is where all the celebrities stay. You can't get within an inch of the security gate without being frisked.

When Ewan and I were planning our wedding, I had always dreamed of entertaining my wedding guests here, but it was a way out of our budget. Instead, we rented a large pavilion-style tent within the grounds of my parents' sports retreat. It was beautiful, but a far cry from the extravagance of this magnificent space.

The over-the-top auction items up for grabs this evening mirror the extravagance of the ballroom. Those items draw people in from near and far for tonight's yearly pissing contest —er, charity auction—and seated around the table, I only recognize half the people to the left and right of me. This could be a long night.

Me, Eden, and Ella literally pulled straws to decide who would represent our dance school, The 3 Sisters Dance School, or as we like to call it, *T3SDS*.

I lost.

Having recently decided to move our studio to bigger premises, we agreed only one of us would attend this year as we are saving like crazy to make that happen.

It will most likely be a few years before we can afford to move, but we've set our intentions. Therefore, sacrifices need to be made, and at two and a half grand a ticket for tonight's event, even one ticket was pushing it. Although it is all going to charity. How can I get annoyed with that?

Hours later, I've relaxed into the evening; surprisingly I'm enjoying it. I've made polite conversation with an older gentleman to my left, who I have learned is named Edward. He hasn't said a single word to his wife next to him since I sat down; the poor woman looks bored to tears. In between my new elbow buddy's never-ending sea of words, I've listened to the auctioneer's noisy chanting and hammering.

With each auction item, the bids, mainly from the men, get more and more elaborate. As I said, a pissing contest. Next, they'll be whipping out their dicks to compare who has the biggest.

"Going once, going twice, sold! To the gentleman at the back." The auctioneer slams his gavel down hard against the wooden podium, then points his oversized, battered wooden hammer toward him. "Number thirty-eight. Congratulations. You just won yourself a luxury all-inclusive week, right here, at The Sanctuary Hotel and Spa, courtesy of the owner, Knox Black," the auctioneer's nasally voice chants across the ballroom.

Not caring who won the item, I remain facing toward the stage area and softly clap.

I zone out, daydreaming.

Every year my little Scottish hometown hosts this charity auction in aid of the local children's hospital, Lily's, which supports children with life-shortening illnesses.

I love everything the auction stands for, its purpose and the incredible cause the money raised goes toward, but I miss being at home snuggled up with my sons.

A smile breaks free from my lips momentarily at the thought of them. Hamish and Archie. I thank my lucky stars and feel a wave of gratefulness; they are both happy and healthy.

They've both gotten so big this past year. Archie, who's seven, is going to be tall, just like his daddy, but with ice-blond hair like me when I was younger. He's shot up another three inches in height, and I've yet again had to restock his wardrobe.

Archie's a cocksure little lad, an infuriating little monkey at times. He knows what he wants, and he knows exactly how to get it. Negotiating and bartering are Archie's strengths. That's where my weakness lies, and he knows it. It's exhausting. I reckon he's going to be on the debating team at school someday. I can feel it. God help us all. Although he could maybe help me argue a case to pass a law for all upcoming divorcing moms to receive six months off, like a sabbatical, but paid to give us time to reevaluate our lives and heal.

I need that.

Then there's my little Hamish. He's my darling three-year-old boy who's utterly adorable, loveable, and playful. He giggles endlessly and smothers me in kisses daily. He's a mirror image of his father—dark-haired with big brown eyes. He loves playing in the mud and would eat worms for breakfast if he could. No matter how hard I try to dress him, he won't have any of it. He's fiercely independent and thinks he knows best when it comes to dressing himself.

I failed to stifle my giggles when he ventured down the stairs the other morning, not dressed in the outfit I laid out for him, but dressed in a pair of frog-green rubber boots on the wrong feet, red shorts on back to front, a bright-yellow sweater, and to complete the look, a pair of swimming goggles, and matching blue-and-orange swimming float. He wore it proudly, like he was modeling the finest waistcoat. Classic Hamish and oh so beautifully innocent. My boy.

There is no way I would have survived the last twelve months without their distraction, their love, and their cuddles. My two boys are my everything.

Although I'm not sure I've been the best mom, struggling to keep my frustration and tiredness levels hidden. Snippy and shouty is what Archie has started to call me. I thought it would make a good name for a cartoon show. When I suggested that to Archie, he rolled his eyes, informing me how uncool I am.

Since my husband, Ewan, and I agreed to separate—well, I asked him to move out and then finally persuaded him we should divorce—I've been a cranky bitch.

My sisters can vouch for that too. I wasn't exactly myself earlier this year when Ella and Fraser, her husband to be, needed me. I was selfish and self-centered in their time of need. I have apologized profusely. Fraser understood and explained how divorce can make you feel and act out of character. He gets it. And Ella being Ella, she was forgiving and loves me unconditionally. It's just as well because I have needed them more than ever recently.

I've also been helping Eden and Hunter out with their new triplet baby boys too. Mainly out of guilt to show my sisters I am here for them and truly sorry for my recently mood swings. Separation and divorce has brought out the worst in me at times. But I'm trying to be more level-headed. As time has gone by I seem to be getting my moods under control and no longer feel like I'm on an emotional roller coaster

I'm still mad though.

Mad at myself.

Mad as a hatter at myself for not spotting Ewan's need for help with his alcohol dependency earlier. And mad at myself for not being able to save our marriage.

I failed.

Failed at marriage.

Failed to keep our little family together.

Filing for divorce at twenty-eight years old, a broken marriage under my belt before the age of thirty, was *never* a future goal for me. I'm high up the failed marriages leaderboard. *Score.*

Now it's just me and my two boys, and even though I feel disappointed at myself that I couldn't make my marriage work, for the first time in a long time I feel happy. I'd almost forgotten what that felt like.

My mom said I should give myself a pat on the back.

I survived separation; I survived the lawyer meetings; I survived Ewan flipping out when I produced our divorce papers. He's still yet to sign them, but I survived.

I made it.

I did also shed an ocean of tears.

For losing my childhood friend.

Said farewell to our love.

Waved goodbye to our marriage.

But it made me question everything once we finally separated.

I'm not sure we were ever as tight as I thought we were.

Within three weeks of us separating, Ewan found someone new and started dating Ruby Thomas from five doors down the street.

Was he loyal and faithful to me?

Were they together before? With us living so close together?

Probably. I may never know, and I'm too proud to ask Ewan. I actually don't want to know if he cheated on me. That would be a step too far for me after he broke my heart the way he did.

Maybe that's why he stopped having sex with me. He was getting it from someone else. Or maybe it was the alcohol. Because he always chose that over me and our boys.

I don't feel jealous or upset that he's already moved on.

I feel... fine.

It seems like such a nondescript word, but I am fine.

I'm good and finally getting back on my feet.

I'm tired though, as my two boys, running a business, and teaching extra dance classes to cover Ella's unexpected time off and Eden's maternity leave, are taking its toll. I need a vacation. Stat.

Hence why I didn't want to come here tonight. I'm here to represent the business, nothing else. But I need more sleep and sunshine. Oh God, yeah, now that does sound lush. Maybe I should book a vacation? My boys would love a water park somewhere warm. Mentally, I make a note to ask my sisters when that would suit them for me to have a week off. A gentle buzz of excitement thrums through me at the prospect of a vacation with my boys. It's exactly what we all need.

An enormous *bang* from the auctioneer's gavel startles me, instantly pulling me from my thoughts. I jump, throwing my hand to my heart. I let out a small yelp and a flutter of laughter drifts around our table.

"Sorry, I was lost in my own little world there." I shake my head. Reaching out, I clasp my champagne flute and take another little sip of the sparkling liquid. This is only my second glass tonight. I don't want to waste my day off tomorrow by nursing a hangover. Being honest, I could take or leave a drink.

"Up last," the auctioneer bellows. "Twelve kizomba dance lessons for two people. Privately tutored by none other than our own local expert dance teacher, Eva Wallace. Who I believe is with us this evening." I clench for a moment at the use of my maiden name. That may take some time to get used to again. I reverted to it before my divorce is final. It's not legal yet, but it will be.

I watch the auctioneer curve his hands above his eyebrows, seeking me out in the crowd.

Making my presence known, I wave my hand in the air.

"Ah, there's the exceptionally talented Eva from the world famous T3SDS. Eva and her sisters really have taken social media by storm. Ask Eva for her autograph while you can because those girls are changing the face of dance, ladies and gentlemen." He claps a semicircle around himself, indicating others to join in.

Well, this is embarrassing. Although he's not wrong. Social media has been the best thing to happen to us. Dance routines are totally our bag and we have grown a massive following online.

A gentle wave of appreciation echoes across the ballroom as my ears catch some complimentary comments. *Their parents must be so proud. We should book private lessons, Geoffrey. Look at her figure. Has she not recently separated from her husband?*

Ouch.

Ignoring the last comment, I sit up a little straighter in my seat, push my shoulders back, and hold my head high, all while displaying a dazzling smile.

I'm always the businesswoman.

"Ladies and gentlemen, to get this underway, I'm starting

the bids at one hundred pounds. Who will give me one hundred?" The auctioneer's brows shoot up.

And that's it, the bids go up by tens. Before I know it, those twelve intimate kizomba lessons are sitting at five hundred pounds.

"C'mon, ladies. You know you want these lessons. Kizomba is considered being *the* sexiest dance in the world. We all want to know how to move our hips, now don't we?"

A faint titter of laughter breaks out.

"Six hundred," someone shouts, and that's it. The bids go higher yet again.

What the hell? People are crazy here tonight.

Urging the bidders on, the auctioneer's chanting becomes more frantic. "C'mon, we are up to one thousand pounds. Who wants to learn a fusion of dance steps and how to synchronize those hips, baby, with the beautiful Eva here." Everyone bursts out laughing, including me. He's a great salesman; I'll give him that.

Kizomba is such a sexy dance. It's one of my favorites. Sultry, erotic, elegant. It combines many dance styles; like the auctioneer says, it's a fusion of footwork and flirting. I have always thought if I got the *right* dance partner, then I'm pretty sure I would orgasm on the dance floor from this dance alone.

It connects you together like no other type of dance. It's sensual and provocative; it creates tension with every smooth wave of your hips.

I hope I get to teach a couple who love each other and want to connect on a new level. I've watched so many couples eye-fuck each other to this erotic dance, then watch as they run off the dance floor to fuck each other's brains out; it's that powerful. The ultimate foreplay.

The bids rise again. Wow.

"Two thousand pounds. Are we done? Going once, twi—"

"Ten thousand."

A loud audible gasp ripples through the seated guests.

Aw, shit, I know that voice.

The auctioneer stalls.

"Did I hear that correctly?" His eyebrows pull together. "Ten thousand pounds?"

"Yes," the voice calls all the way from the back of the grand room.

A low hum of hushed tones gasp, gossip, and conspire all at once. All eyes in the room turn to the voice that makes my stomach loop the loop.

Every. Single. Time.

I slowly turn in my seat to face the infamous man that has flooded my dreams for the last couple of months. My eyes lock on his dark orbs.

Knox Black.

CHAPTER TWO

Eva

Knox's eye color matches his name.

Black.

And they're looking right at me.

He's so handsome, suave, and sophisticated.

Dark.

He oozes power and dominance like no other man on the planet. It's unnerving. Sexy. Commanding.

He extraordinary and always manages to make me feel on edge. He has the ability to make me feel like I belong to him. I can't explain it.

For a moment, it feels like it's only us. His dark eyes never leave mine as he confirms his bid again, making my heart pound in my chest. "Ten thousand pounds."

From the left of me I hear a faint whisper. "He must have a new woman in his life. I wonder who the lucky lady is."

Oh, well, isn't that just perfect? Teaching him. Watching him eye-fuck someone else under my instruction is *not* what I had planned when I donated the lessons.

"Right," the auctioneer bellows across the microphone,

startling me yet again. Knox's gaze doesn't let up. It's me who finally breaks our trance. I look back at the auctioneer. "Ten thousand pounds, it is. Going once, twi—"

"Twelve thousand," a jovial voice I also recognize calls out from the other side of the elegant room.

Snapping my head back around, I see Knox's son, Lincoln, with his hand raised in the air, the other casually tucked into the pocket of his dress pants as he leans lazily against the back wall.

Eh, excuse me?

Whispered words dance across the vast space once more.

Knox instantly retaliates with his counter bid of thirteen, and then the two of them ping-pong incomprehensible amounts of money back and forth.

My brain can't accept what's happening.

Captivated along with everyone else in the room, we all bounce our heads between the two most handsome dark-haired men I have ever seen in my life, watching on as father and son play a virtual game of power tennis.

The auctioneer struggles to keep up with them as the bid reaches twenty-five thousand.

Twenty-five thousand!

But Knox doesn't stop there. "Thirty thousand plus another fifty to help toward the construction of the new ward for the hospital. Done." His deep velvet voice sends warm ripples down my spine.

His words are final. Lincoln shakes his head, blazing a knockout smile across his lips in my direction. He knows he lost, but he doesn't care. It's almost as if Lincoln was trying to prove a point to his father. About what, I don't know, but I intend to find out.

"Good gracious," the auctioneer stutters. "Eighty thousand pounds. Sold." *Slam* goes his gavel. "To Knox Black. What a way to end the evening."

A tremendous roar of claps, whistles, and whoops begins and all I can do is simply sit there stunned with my mouth gaping open like a fish out of water.

Eighty thousand pounds.

What just happened?

Nervously, I capture my bottom lip between my teeth, flitting my eyes around the room. Lincoln's eyes find mine. He smiles, then throws me a cheeky wink. Pushing his back away from the wall, Lincoln struts toward his father.

Where Knox is dark and quiet, Lincoln is bright and playful. He is only three years younger than me and I remember him from high school and the beach parties we local kids used to have in the bowl of the cove on warm summer evenings.

Knox and his ex-wife were teenagers when they had Lincoln. Lincoln's mother is no longer in the picture and I've never thought to ask what happened to her. I wonder if my father knows.

I watch both Knox and Lincoln exit the ballroom together.

Unsure of what to do, I quickly tuck my feet back into my uncomfortable heels, accept the looks of gobsmacked congratulations around the table for raising so much money on my auction item, then excuse myself.

Making my way to the exit door, I feel hundreds of sets of eyes on my every move.

Looking braver than I feel, I flip my long caramel locks over my shoulders. With my head held high, I exit the grand room and exhale a deep breath as I almost throw myself into the corridor.

Holy cow, that was intense.

Distracted now by the familiar raised voices along the corridor, carefully teetering on my heels, I follow them.

"What the hell do you think you were doing, Linc?"

Knox.

"Do you like her, Dad? I like her. *Really* like her. Be honest with me."

Knox does like me. I know this already. Knox disclosed his feelings for me last year, when I was still married, instantly following up his confession with an over-the-top apology, informing me he had overstepped the mark. He didn't make any advances on me. He was respectful and has kept his distance since then.

But Lincoln likes me too?

What the hell?

Did Knox bid to have dance lessons from me so he could get close to me? Eighty thousand pounds seems extreme.

"No. We've discussed this, Linc; she's off-limits to me. Now drop it, son."

"No way. You bid eighty thousand pounds to have private lessons with her." Lincoln laughs. "You need to explain."

I continue toward them.

"And you just bid twenty-five thousand."

"I wanted to see what you would do, if you would push. You did. I've seen you checking her out."

"It's for the hospital."

"Is it? I personally would like to get to know her better. *Do* you like her? You should admit it if you do. Now that Ewan's no longer in the picture, she's fair game. And what about Tabit—"

Words leave my mouth before I can stop them. "Why are you two talking about me like I can be bought? You may have paid eighty thousand pounds, but I have never felt so cheap in all of my life." They both jump at my unexpected presence.

"Shit." Knox sighs under his breath.

Lincoln welcomes me with yet another wide smile. Gosh, he's handsome.

But when Knox swivels on his feet to face me, his eyes fixed on mine, my insides liquefy, and a tornado of flutters batter wildly in my lower stomach. He's even more captivating.

Knox creates strange emotions I have no control over. I have never felt this way, with anyone, including my husband, er, ex-husband to be.

"I'm sorry, Eva," Knox apologizes. "I never want you to feel like that. Please forgive the crassness of our conversation."

"You bid eighty thousand pounds for twelve dance lessons that cost only five hundred pounds. I'm confused. What was that about exactly?"

I point back in the room's direction. My eyes dance between the two of them.

"I think he's staking his claim." Lincoln grins.

"Enough now, Linc." Knox scowls through a tight jaw.

Staking his claim?

"Huh?" I pinch my brows.

"Go, Linc," Knox instructs.

"I hope to see you around, Eva." Lincoln bounces past me jauntily with his trademark cheeky smile. That guy is annoyingly cheerful twenty-four seven.

"So?" I bug my eyes out, waiting for an answer.

Silence. I watch Knox's throat bob up, then down.

Gosh, he's so, just so, *masculine.*

"I got carried away. I'm sorry. I didn't mean to offend you. I do genuinely want to learn how to dance. That dance in particular." He looks nervous as he loosens the top button of his crisp white shirt.

"You want to learn how to dance the kizomba? Since when?"

I genuinely want to know.

He's thinking.

"I've watched you before. I've seen you teach it."

Watched me.

"When?"

"When I've visited your father at his sports retreat. When

we meet at the back entrance sometimes, next to your dance studio. Then."

"Oh."

"I'm always captivated."

"Oh."

"By you." A smirk pulls his mouth to the side.

I lick my lips, my mouth suddenly parched. "Could you not have booked lessons with me directly, instead of paying eighty thousand pounds for them? Or forty thousand per person, depending on which way you look at it. Who are you bringing?"

"It's for the hospital. And it will be me. No partner."

"Oh." I'm lost for words. Oh seems to be the only one I can sound out.

Just him.

I audibly gulp.

"Your father tells me you're now divorced."

His change in subject throws me. "Eh, yeah, well, not yet, but I will be soon."

"Are you okay?"

"Yeah." I faintly smile. "I'm slowly getting used to the feeling of being happy again."

He nods.

"How are your boys?"

"Fine. They'll be fine." I squeeze my tiny evening purse in my hand.

"Where are they tonight?"

Why is he asking? "Staying all weekend with Mom and Dad."

Knox bobs his head. I notice then exactly how close he is to me. Did he move or did I move? I don't know. What I do know is that he is only a foot away from me now.

"You look beautiful tonight, Sunshine." His deep voice rumbles low in his chest as he examines me, sweeping his eyes across, over, up, and down. I feel his gaze flood every inch of my body.

"Sunshine?"

He nods. "You light up every room you're in. You're like sunshine in human form."

That's beautiful. Thoughtful. "Oh."

I don't think I've ever had such a long conversation with Knox in my life. He's quiet most of the time, an onlooker. He watches everything. He doesn't waste words and makes every one count when he does speak. He doesn't suffer fools gladly, nor does he have time for idle chitchat. I would call him broody, but I think he's more thoughtful and profound.

"You never called me about the business proposition I have for you, Eva." I shudder as he draws out my short name through a soft exhale.

Ella and I bumped into Knox on the beach a few months ago while he was walking his dog, Sam. He said I was to call the hotel reception and book an appointment to discuss a business proposal. I had forgotten all about it.

"I've been busy. Sorry."

"I'll make it worth your while. The dance school, that is." Beneath hooded eyes, he zones in on my lips.

I clear my throat.

"I'll remember to call you." I breathe out, increasingly aware he's now mere inches from me. My chest heaves up and down with expectation. Of what, I don't know.

"You light up my soul, Sunshine. It's like a fucking blazing inferno burns inside of me when I'm near you." His confessions rolls off his lips.

Knox leans in unexpectedly. He runs his nose up the side of my neck, into the curtain of my caramel locks; his lips lightly ghost my ear.

I've dreamed about this moment.

I close my eyes as my resistance to him fades away.

"What are you doing?" I gasp, feeling every hard inch of him beneath my thin, silky dress when he presses his firm body against mine.

"Something I've wanted to do for a very long time. I told you last year. I want you," he growls into my neck. "You smell like heaven."

Oh God.

My skin flushes and my heart beats like a drum. He was as serious back then as he is now. His confession of longing to taste me has never changed.

Last year at the Spring Fling Ball, he expressed his desire for me. It was yet another event Ewan couldn't be trusted to attend, especially with a free bar, so I went with my sisters and friends.

Knox doesn't dance with anyone. But he asked *me* to dance. Pressed flush together, he threw a curveball. As we drifted across the dance floor, he confessed to me how I was the most beautiful woman in the room. How he wanted to taste me, but I was forbidden fruit. His forbidden desire. None of his words shocked me. He's always watching. Watching *me.*

He's never subtle, not to me. To everyone else I think he is, but I sense him everywhere.

"If you were mine, everyone in that room would know it. You come to these events by yourself. Ewan never appreciated you. Or your body. Your beautiful body fucking speaks to me, calls my name. I feel you everywhere in my veins. When you're around, I can't fucking think straight. You're an intoxicating goddess and a terrible distraction. I have bad thoughts about you, ones I shouldn't have, and I make stupid decisions when you're around."

I whimper at his admission. I don't think I'm intoxicating; I think it's the other way around.

"Like bidding eighty thousand pounds to dance with me?" I gasp.

"Best fucking money I've ever spent, if it means getting closer to you." His hot breath surfs across my goose-bumped skin before he pushes me up against the wall behind.

Well, this evening is not what I expected. It's way better.

"Eva. Tell me. Do you think about me?"

I can't deny it. "Yes. I dream about you sometimes."

Crap, I think they laced my champagne with truth serum.

"That right?"

"Yeah." I pant like a bitch in heat.

"Do you want me as much as I want you?"

"Yes." I'm not playing games. Screw it. If anything, the past year has taught me that life is too damn short.

"I know you do. I see it. I see *you*. The way your skin flushes around me. I know you want me. Your mind might deny it, but I can read this fucking sexy body of yours and it wants mine."

"It does. I do." I moan.

"Do you care that I'm fifteen years older than you?" he mumbles against my skin. I want him to kiss me.

"No, and it's only fourteen. I'll be twenty-nine in a few months. Forty-three isn't old. You've not long turned forty-three, right?"

Although that's not what I told Ella all those months ago on the beach. I told her he was too old for me. I was denying what my body desires, but I do want him.

"You pay attention. Good girl." He plants a soft kiss on my nape. "You should be with Lincoln; he's closer to your age," he says as if he's mumbling reasons we shouldn't be together to himself.

I shudder. "I don't want him."

"He'll hate me." He thrusts his hips into mine. I can feel how hard he is for me. His thick length is undeniable. He's big—bigger than, well, Ewan. That's all I have to compare him to.

"I don't want to cause trouble between you two."

"I'm a shitty dad." He kisses my neck again. "Fuck, I can't resist you."

"Then don't."

"I'm also your father's friend."

"He never needs to know."

"It's wrong." But he doesn't move away from me.

"I don't care."

"I'm a bad man for wanting you."

"I want you to be bad, Knox. I'm always the good girl. I want to be bad with you."

"Fuck," he exhales against my skin.

I'm clearly not thinking straight this evening. I think my deep desire for intimacy is doing the talking for me.

Knox lays a path of gentle kisses across my nape, toward my delectable spot behind my ear. It's another of my weaknesses.

I let out a frustrated groan as he flicks his rough tongue again and again over my sensitive skin, biting, kissing, licking, soaking my panties in the process. Warmth spreads between my legs and I'm aching for him to touch me *there*.

I let out another loud moan.

"Shhhhh. This is a classy hotel." A deep chuckle leaves his throat. I don't think I've ever heard Knox laugh before, and I kind of like it.

His hand drifts across my clavicle, gently stroking the silk of my dress as he heads south, between my cleavage. Skirting across my stomach, he goes lower.

He stops, teasing me, before he slips his hand inside the thigh-high slit of my dress and skims his large hand over the thin, now-soaked lace of my panties, then traces his fingers across my throbbing pussy.

I groan, feeling his powerful erotic touch. He surely must feel how wet I am for him.

"Oh God, Knox, I need you." It's been so long since anyone has shown me any affection; my body needs the release, and I want him to be the one to do it. I want him to shake off the last year. I want to feel free and desired once more, to feel joy and to be fucked right, like I know Knox will. He'll look after me.

"Stay with me tonight, Eva."

I snap my eyes open to find him staring back at me with deep, apprehensive eyes.

"Okay."

He gifts me a rare knockout smile and I practically melt into him.

He's gorgeous.

I want him.

For one night only.

That's all I need.

No one ever needs to know.

It's just one night.

Right?

CHAPTER THREE

Eva

Without another word, Knox threads his long, thick fingers into mine, and leads me along the pristine white-paneled corridor of his hotel. Every door is painted jet-black. It screams innocence meets devil—him and I, like thunderstorms and clear skies. A faint warm glow from the silver spotlights overhead illuminates our path, welcoming us, as each one automatically flickers on as we pass by.

I have no clue where he's taking me, but I don't question him. My feet are carrying me, but I'm not sure my brain is making them work. On autopilot, I feel like I'm floating in a weird bubble, as if twice removed from my body.

Am I actually doing this?

I've never been with anyone else apart from Ewan.

A thousand doubts zoom through my brain.

What about my C-section scar with Hamish? And the slithers of faint silver stretch marks above it?

And, oh, God, what about the fact I had to be cut down below when I had Archie and had to have an emergency vacuum assisted delivery?

Ewan always reassured me and said because I was stitched inside and out, I now have what he called a designer vagina, and he informed me I felt as tight as a virgin.

I didn't exactly have it easy in the birthing of children department. Hence my utter fear of childbirth.

I'm not having any more babies. Nope, not doing that. Never again. Nuh-uh.

Knox senses me tense. "Hey, are you sure you want to do this?"

I flick a tendril of hair off my face. "Mmmmm."

He stops us in our tracks, then faces me directly.

"Talk to me, Eva."

I can't look him in the eyes. I'm not exactly inexperienced. Ewan and I always had a healthy sex life in the beginning. But I've never been intimate with another man. That scares the living shit out of me. Is there such a thing as one-night-stand etiquette? If so, I don't know the rules. I bet Knox does this kind of thing all the time. He's experienced.

Aw, crapatooee. What am I doing?

Knox tilts my face up, demanding an answer with his cavernous eyes. So dark you can't tell what part is iris or pupil.

I internally cringe. "It's, I, I've only ever been with one man. And I've had two babies."

"Right, and?"

"I know I have an okay dancer body, but it's not what it used to be since I had the boys." I fiddle with my evening purse.

"And do you actually think I give a shit about any of that, Eva? Because I don't."

Knox reaches out, moves in close, and for the first time, what I feel like I've waited a lifetime for, he plants a soft kiss to my lips and holds me there. It's gentle.

Reassuring.

Unexpected.

And beautiful.

He leans back slightly.

"You don't have to come home with me, Eva."

He holds his gaze.

Oh, we're going to his house? I kind of assumed he'd take me to one of his hotel suites here.

He continues in his deep velvet tone. "But I will look after you if you do. I will pay homage to your glorious body. I want to memorize everything about you."

"Oh-kaaaaay."

"Is that a yes?"

"Yes," I whisper.

He offers a sudden smile. "We can always just cuddle."

I snort. "Cuddle? Why do I get the impression you are not a cuddler?"

His smile drops. "There's a lot you don't know about me, Eva."

Does Mr. Dark and Aloof like cuddles? *Interesting.*

"Show me then, Knox. Show me all of you."

Like he's been waiting for me to say that, he closes his eyes and on a deep inhale, he turns on his heels, guiding me through the maze of corridors.

Rounding the next corner, Knox instructs me to wait where I am, and he'll be back to get me in two minutes. I watch him disappear out of sight through a heavy door at the end of the corridor.

Before I know it, he's back, appearing from a secret white pocket door on the opposite side of the wall I'm leaning against.

"Oh, that's magic." I smile.

"There's lots of these throughout the hotel."

"It's like Harry Potter," I say in a hushed tone.

"I know," he whispers back against my ear, causing a gentle flurry of goosebumps to break out across my skin.

I teeter through the doorway.

Like a pair of conspirators, he slides the pocket door shut again, as if it doesn't exist behind us. He ushers me straight through the steel and concrete staff corridor, out the other side, through the fire exit door into the cold November Scottish evening.

Without hesitation, Knox removes his black suit jacket, then gently places it over my shoulders. He's a true gentleman.

I push my arms into it and pull it tightly around me, enjoying it as the scent of him and his transferred warmth wrap around me.

I almost fall backward as I catch sight of his black McLaren P1, shining under the floodlights that line the hotel roadside. It purrs away, waiting to pounce into action. Like a lioness in heat seeking her king.

"Are we going in this?" I gasp.

Knox nods.

Way to go keeping *us* on the down-low.

"It's beautiful. I've always wondered what it would be like to drive."

I often see Knox and sometimes Lincoln driving the squat car around town and it sure does turn heads. It's an attention-seeking peacock. The sound of it alone screams *look at me.*

Knox opens the passenger butterfly door for me. As elegantly as I can, I squeeze myself into the minuscule two-seater cockpit and drape my inky-blue silk dress across my knees, being careful my pin-sharp heels don't scratch any part of this beautiful piece of engineering.

Knox softly glides my door down and it clips shut with a low *clunk.*

I can't help the *wow* that comes out of my astounded mouth as I smooth my hand over the carbon fiber dashboard.

He slides into the driver's side and instructs me to put my

harness on. This sports car doesn't have a standard seat belt. Why would it? Nothing Knox does *or* has is standard.

"Ready?" His eyes sparkle my way. Well, I think they do. His eyes are so dark in the shadowy space of the car, the only highlight of light I can see in his eyes is a tiny spotlight reflection from the faint interior light beneath a thick layer of his dark lashes.

Once strapped in, Knox gives the accelerator a confident push and the car comes alive. Low, growling, dominant. We take off down the sloping road that skirts the entire hotel perimeter. As soon as we hit the country road leading back down to Castleview Cove, Knox really opens her up and lets her fly around the sweeping bends. I can't contain my squeal of excitement as the car pops and growls, kissing the curves of the narrow roads leading down into the cove.

I feel Knox checking me out.

Watching my enjoyment.

Once we hit Castleview, he slows down, and the car glides into our small seaside town.

A euphoric smile finds my lips as I turn to look at him. "Wow, this car is awesome. Three point eight twin turbocharged V8 engine. Top speed of two hundred and seventeen miles an hour and naught to sixty miles per hour in two point five seconds. And will set you back almost a million smackaroons. This car is wild, Knox." Doing two things at once, he watches the road while also gaping at me, snapping his head back and forth.

"You like cars?" he exclaims.

"I freaking *love* cars. If I had all the money in the world, I would have so many cars. One in particular."

"Which one?"

"I'm not telling you. It's silly and completely out of my reach. But a girl can dream."

He doesn't push me for an answer as he cruises through our sleepy town with only the roar of the car to keep us company.

Knox breaks our comfortable silence. "Do you want to grab a bag of clothes and your things?" He clears his throat.

Is he nervous too?

I've never seen Knox look anything other than confident. Sure. Steady. Strong.

"If your boys are away all weekend, I would like you to stay with me all weekend, Eva. That's if you don't have any plans."

He looks across at me again.

"I only have the ironing to do. My life is *that* exciting." I tuck my lips into my mouth before I answer. "I'd like to stay with you all weekend," I whisper.

He rewards me with a suggestive wink.

Holy shit, this is turning out to be the best weekend *ever*.

Maybe this single mom thing is going to be okay after all.

Then a thought hits me. What if Ewan is at Ruby's, his new girlfriend from five doors down? What if he sees me?

It's too late to ask Knox to pull over as the car prowls onto my quiet street lined with dozens of family-friendly homes. His car stands out like a fully clothed nun at a nudist convention.

I wished I lived elsewhere, but the little three-bedroom townhouse was all Ewan and I could afford when we got married. Then when Archie came along unexpectedly, we spoke about moving, and then Hamish arrived. Then my sisters and I got busy with the dance studio and now the 'interim' house I seem to have grown into has become my home.

I don't have the money to move now, so it will have to wait until my divorce is settled as I may have to buy Ewan out, and that will set my plans back a few years.

As I stare at the disarray of skateboards, bikes, and injection-molded plastic toys littering the front garden, I kick myself internally, wishing I tidied up before I rushed out of the house earlier.

"Sorry," I whisper.

"For?" Knox looks at me, his brows bow low.

"My untidy garden."

Knox flicks the interior light on. "You have two active boys. Boys make a mess. A lot of mess," he says matter-of-factly.

He knows because he raised Lincoln. Pretty much single-handedly.

"I'll be as quick as I can." I reach for the car handle. Knox stops me by gently laying his hand on my wrist.

"Don't bring too many clothes, Sunshine. You won't be needing them for what I have planned."

I blush. Full-on summer berry-colored blush.

"You're shaking." He blinks.

I bounce my head slowly. "Yeah. I'm nervous. I've done nothing like this before."

"What, had sex?" he says deadpan.

"No! A one-night stand."

"I told you, it's not a one-night stand, Eva. I'll look after you. I promise. I've wanted to get you alone and spend time with you for so long. You intrigue me." He runs his pointer finger across his bottom lip with his other hand. *So sexy.*

"Also, if I knew you did this all the time, we wouldn't be here. I know you don't sleep around."

"Do you?"

"You were married to Ewan for years and, as far as I'm aware, tonight is the first night out you've had in months."

How does he know that? "Golf with my dad this week, Knox?"

"Yes. I knew you were attending the ball this evening. I didn't know your boys would be away all weekend though." His face twitches, concealing his smirk. "Now go get your bag. And bring your bikini."

I frown, questioning.

"Because I have a pool in my home. You can have a swim tomorrow if you'd like. To relax."

My brows spring up.

That sounds like bliss.

This is becoming so real now.

He continues holding on to my wrist.

"I'll be five minutes. Stay in the car," I instruct him. It'll keep Ewan guessing if he has spotted us. Because it could very well be Lincoln. He drives this from time to time too.

I flip the butterfly door up and elegantly push myself out of the low car.

And I'm still wearing his dress jacket. I wrap it around me again, pull the collar up to my nose, and inhale as I run toward my house. It smells of him. Expensive. Thrilling. Tantalizing.

I'm back in Knox's car with my little overnight bag I filled at high speed with my sleepover essentials. Not one for makeup, I skipped that; I did, however, bring all my facial lotions and body potions for my beauty routine. Skin care is life. Oh, and perfume, 'cause, you know, I want to smell nice for him and I packed a few pieces of clothing for leaving on Sunday.

I had to dig deep to find some sexy panties.

If I'm embracing this new single mom life, I need to pay a visit to the lingerie shop. Could I be a sexy single mom? Nope, drop the sexy. Regardless, I still need new underwear, like yesterday. I might actually do some online shopping tomorrow. I have all day tomorrow to do that. Sounds like heaven. Although Christ knows what Knox has planned for us. Whatever it is, I'll be naked by the sounds of it. I maybe didn't need to bring underwear at all.

I conceal an excited giggle.

Being in his car.

About to drive to his house.

Being with him *finally*.

After all this time. Dreaming about him. Remembering him

holding me on the dance floor last year. Being close to him. And if my body reacts to him from a few dirty words and a simple skim over my panties, then God knows what I'll be like when we do get down to business. I haven't had sex in what feels like a million years.

Ewan and I stopped having sex about a year ago. His chronic heavy drinking meant he couldn't get it up and with no appetite for sex whatsoever, our relationship dive-bombed quickly. I thought I was the problem at first, but it was the alcohol. It ruined everything between us.

Knox's eyes gravitate toward my driveway. "I like your VW Campervan."

I find it difficult to stifle my smile. I'm proud as punch of its restoration. It's taken me years to get my gleaming metallic-green beauty up to show quality. I only take it out on special sunshine beach days. It's my precious cargo and half the time my boys treat it like a fun park. I'm very particular about when we use it.

"I love her."

"Her?"

"Yes, Olive."

"Because she's green. Olive. I like it. She's a bit like you."

"Yeah?"

"Unique. Quirky. Hippie at heart."

I stare at my pride and joy. I suppose we are the same.

He called me unique. That makes my heart flutter with delight.

It really has been too long since I have had any type of male attention. I'm getting excited by someone calling me unique.

But it's Knox who said it. And he's not just anyone.

"What would you call this car?" he inquires, his voice rich and textured.

"Raven," I answer without hesitation.

Amusement flits across his usually serious features.

I explain myself. "Dark, mysterious." I think of the right word. "Powerful. But playful once you learn how to work it."

I use this moment to take him all in as his bold, black eyes bore through me. I must remember to ask him what ethnicity his mother is because he has her olive skin tone and dark features.

He's assertive. Quiet. But kind. He was so tender when he kissed me with those beautiful, full dark-pink lips of his. His ebony scruff and goatee are trimmed with precision. As is his hair, which is shaved into a high skin fade on either side with a wave of luscious swept-back black locks styled perfectly on top.

Every single touchpoint of his life screams expensive. From his suit, his watch, his car, shoes, you name it. It's quite intimidating.

"What are you thinking?" he asks, breaking me from my lucid daydream.

"How your car is kind of like you. Dark, mysterious, powerful." It's exactly like him. "Are you playful?" I side-eye him, wondering what he does for fun and to unwind. All I know about him is that his work dominates his life. He plays golf with my dad. *Yikes.* And then he spends an infinite amount of time at his hotel resort and spa.

He arches one perfectly manicured, thick brow but doesn't answer.

He's deeper than the ocean as I see his brain working overtime.

I want to unpeel all his layers and discover what's inside the enigma that is Knox Black.

"You all set?" Knox pushes the car into gear as he firmly wraps his strong fingers around the black leather steering wheel with his other hand.

"Yeah. Don't be too loud when you leave here. Ewan is dating Ruby from down the road."

"Fuck him." He does the exact opposite of what I ask,

pressing the accelerator hard. The exhaust roars, then pops, ending with an echoing loud *bang* as he takes off down the empty, dark street.

"You are so naughty." I laugh.

"You're about to find out how naughty I can be."

Maybe he is playful after all.

I can't wait to find out.

"We're supposed to be keeping you and me a secret."

Knox juts his chin out in annoyance.

Knox

Fuck, fuck, fuck. What am I doing?

Bringing Eva back here to my home? For the entire weekend?

Spend the night with me.

My thoughts slipped out of my loose mouth. Very out of character for me.

I seem to have lost all sense of self.

But I want her. So fucking bad.

I never bring women here to my home. It's too personal. When I do share an evening with a female, always Tabby, I ensure she stays at my hotel suite back at The Sanctuary. I don't let anyone into my private life. Not even Tabby.

But Eva.

She's the exception.

Someone who shines the brightest light into my darkest places.

I feel it. Feel her everywhere.

It's like something sparks within me when she's around.

I want to tangle myself around her, keep her safe, and fuck her brains out all at the same time.

I find it so fucking confusing.

I've been permanently hard for her since I touched her in the corridor of my hotel. When I fetched the car, I called my head of security, Dylan, instructing him to remove the hotel security footage of Eva and me from that moment, until the moment we exited through the concealed doorway.

No way do I want anyone replaying that footage with my hands inside her dress as I skimmed my fingers over the wet lace of her panties. Fuck me.

She's wet for me. I felt it. I know what I do to her. It's what she does to me too.

It's some freaky shit between her and me, and I don't know what the fuck happens around her, but I can't see, hear, or think straight.

She's an enchantress.

Sensing her unease as the electric garage door shuts behind my parked car in my ten-car garage, I reach out to take her hand. "Welcome to my home."

"Your house is enormous." She looks around the garage in wonder. "And we aren't even in the house yet." She smiles. "Wow. Look at your car collection." She eyes my multitude of expensive toys.

She's so carefree and shares how she feels. She loved me going fast in the car earlier, never holding back her elation and joy.

She's refreshing. Speaks her mind. I could do with a lesson from her on that.

I reach up and run my thumb across her plump bottom lip. I can't stop touching her.

I've never felt attracted to anyone as much as I am to Eva.

"You're beautiful when you smile." She's beautiful all the time. I'm a sucker for her deep dimples.

She shyly dips her turquoise eyes.

I unbuckle myself with haste, lean over the center console between us, cup her face, and pull her lips toward mine, being careful not to startle her too much. The last thing I want to do is scare her with my eagerness. I know the only way to calm her. Orgasms. Mind-blowing orgasms. Make her feel good.

To forget everything but remind her who she is—a sensual, radiant goddess.

Slowly at first, I let our lips explore one another before I push my tongue into her highly fuckable mouth that tastes like sunshine—refreshing and warm. She relaxes at our intimate connection.

She doesn't know how captivating she is.

Ewan never treated her right. I used to study him at the mixers and events her parent's hosted at their sports retreat. He took her for granted, ignoring her most of the time. Didn't see how utterly mesmerizing she is. What an extraordinary mother she is to those boys, and don't get me started on the dancing.

I could watch her for hours.

Her permanent radiance dazzles me.

While my son, Lincoln, has this super cheerful buzz about him, Eva's is subtle, bewitching, charming. She bathes the surrounding space in a cloud of calm luminescence.

I swear to God she's fucking cast a spell on everyone around her. Spellbound. When you're around her, you can't look away from her. She holds your attention. It's some magic supernatural shit. I watched the gentleman seated next to her all evening chatting away to her. He couldn't stop. She has this undeniable power over you where you want to speak to her all the time. And she listens to everyone, taking it all in. She pays attention; she cares.

She has this external magnetic field that I'm drawn to. I can't help myself around her. It's incredible, but fucking confusing. She's hypnotic.

I shouldn't want this woman. This extraordinary woman with a glorious body, sinful legs I would like wrapped around my ears, and a fucking smile that does things to my sensibility I can't explain. It's like a murmuration of starlings swirling in my stomach when I'm around her.

What is that?

It's wrong, but it feels oh so fucking right.

Then there's her age. She's fourteen years younger than me, closer to Lincoln's age. And fuck, he confessed to liking her tonight. I shouldn't be doing this. What a shitty thing to do to your own son.

But she said she didn't want him. She wants *me*.

And then there's her father, Charlie. We're friends—close friends—and business buddies. We play golf every week together and sit together on the Castleview Business Circle, the board that markets local businesses. He likes me. Trusts me. So why am I risking my friendships, my reputation, and my incredible relationship with my son?

There are so many people to consider.

I feel my balls shrink back inside my body as trepidation rips through me. There are many reasons we shouldn't be together.

None of it makes sense to me, but I want her. Need her. Have to have her.

Maybe I just need this weekend to fuck her out of my system.

Like the thing you can't have, that you longed for. Then you finally get it, and it's not as exciting as you thought it would be.

Maybe that's what I need to do. Fuck her and forget her.

The only thing close to any type of relationship I've ever had was with Lincoln's mother, my ex-wife. It's the closest thing to love I've ever felt. But I was young and didn't know any better.

I instantly slam the door on my archived thoughts. I don't want to think about *her* now. She's unworthy of my time.

And then there is Tabitha, or Tabby, as she likes to be

called. Thank the heavens above she wasn't at the charity auction tonight.

We've been having casual sex for the past three years. She wants more from me, but I'm not interested. Because of *her*. Eva.

But Eva was married. I'd lost hope. She's now free. Getting divorced. Finally.

I would never take what wasn't rightfully mine. But she feels like she should be.

Mine.

On paper, Tabby and I are the perfect match. Same age as me, beautiful. Domineering. Driven. Old-school wealth. Heiress to the local whisky distillery. Her father will be on his death bed before he hands it over to her. She's a liability. Someone who likes a fancy title but is work shy. If she pulled her weight, we would be a business powerhouse couple together.

But I don't want that.

I haven't wanted Tabitha for months.

I want a whole different type of woman.

I want this one. The one that's currently sucking my fucking tongue into her mouth like her life depends on it. If she sucks my dick in the exact same way, then I'm in danger.

Massive fucking danger.

I can feel it as she whimpers, then runs her delicate hand up the back of my neck and pulls me forcefully to her mouth with perfect pressure.

She wants me. I fucking knew it.

She wants this.

And she has for a while.

And here's me thinking I'm the one in charge, but now I'm not so sure.

"Let's go inside the house, Sunshine." I gasp between what feels like a life-changing kiss.

But we don't stop kissing. I never want this feeling of firsts with her to end as we connect in ways I've fantasized about.

She said she dreamed about me, too.

It's the words I've longed to hear.

She grins against my mouth. "I really enjoy kissing you, Knox."

I love how open and honest she is. It's invigorating.

"You can kiss me all weekend if you like it so much." Our tongues slip against one another.

"Sounds good to me." She chuckles, a sweet melody to my ears.

"Let's get out of here. We're steaming up the windows." I can't stop kissing her plump lips.

"That's hot. I can't remember the last time I made out in a car." She leans out of our steamy kiss, her face now flushed.

"Me either," I lie. I do. It was a *long* time ago. Lincoln was the by-product of that brief hiccup. A hiccup I wouldn't change for the world. My son has been the best thing to happen to me. But I never made out in another car again. Until now.

As we both slide out of my low car, Eva lets out an *oh my God*; it's emphatic and genuine as she spots the car nestled over in the far corner of my garage.

Her mouth gapes wide in the shape of an *O*. She's frozen to the floor, ogling the metallic-blue vehicle. How does she know what that is?

"Please tell me I'm dreaming," she says eventually. "Is that a Shelby Cobra 427 Super Snake? An actual Cobra or a kit?"

"It's an actual Cobra," I respond, astounded that she even knows what she's looking at. When she said she likes cars, she was telling the truth.

She drops her navy overnight bag on the floor. Out of shock, I think. Tentatively, she takes her time moving toward the most expensive car I own.

She reels off some statistics. "Four hundred and eighty-five break horsepower. Seven liter V8 engine. Only one genuine, original 1966, left in the entire universe."

Eva knows her stats.

She takes in a huge gasp of air. "Is this it? It can't be? Can it?"

I don't know if she is asking me or speaking to herself, but I answer.

"The one and only."

"I... I... I think I might faint," she mutters, astonished. "This whole time, my dream car is sitting in your garage. Here. In Castleview Cove. I think I'm hallucinating."

This is her dream car. I shake my head, baffled. "How the hell do you know so much about cars?"

And how does she know the specifications of my ten-million-pound investment?

"I love cars. I watch this American dude on the television. *The Revamp...*"

"*Champ.*" I finish her sentence.

Well, what do you know?

"It's the only television program I watch," I tell her.

Managing a five-star resort is a full-time job and then some. I don't have time to binge series after series, but that is the only one I make time for.

"I love it," she stares wide-eyed at my supercharged beauty.

"The program or the car."

"The car, silly," she scoffs. "Look at her." She spreads her arms wide, then clutches her hands to her chest.

I don't know what I expected Eva to be like, but she's a complete surprise. I take her in as she stares with hearts in her eyes, standing in her blue silk evening gown, wearing my dress jacket which is a billion sizes too big for her, and she's talking about cars. Now that is a turn-on. She's smart, refreshing, gorgeous, and we share the same interests.

It's just a coincidence, Knox. Stop overanalyzing this. Two nights. Just two nights.

"Have you ever driven her?" Her inquisitive face stirs something in me.

"Yeah, a couple of times."

"Wow. What does she sound like?"

"Beautiful."

I don't know if I'm talking about her or the car at this point.

"Best Friday night. Ever," she whispers to herself, smiling widely.

It's about to get a whole heap better, gorgeous girl.

"If it's dry tomorrow, we can take her out," I suggest. What am I saying? We've said we are supposed to be keeping us a secret; we shouldn't be seen together. And now I've labeled the gender of my car too.

"It's supposed to rain tomorrow. Typical Scotland. You cannot take her out in the rain. Does she have a name?"

"No."

"That's a travesty. She needs a name, Knox." I love the way she says my name in her soft and soothing voice.

"Name her then." *What the hell am I saying?*

"Me? You want me to name her?" She points at the resplendent supercar.

"Yes." I dip a quick nod.

"Well, that's easy. Lydia. That's what I would call her if she was mine. It's Greek for—"

"Beautiful one." I know what that means.

"How do you know that?"

"My mother is Greek."

She blinks at me with realization. "Ah, that's where your Mediterranean features come from?"

I bob my head.

"You're very handsome, Knox."

"And you are the most beautiful woman I know."

She is.

She wraps her arms around herself, bows her head, then quickly snaps it back up again and looks directly at me. "Thank you."

I hold my hand out, gesturing for her to take it, picking up her overnight bag as I walk toward her. I guide her through the side garage door leading into my house.

I'm actually doing this.

CHAPTER 4

Eva

As I think back over the last few hours of my bizarre evening, I remember how I longed to see inside a home on Cherry Gardens Lane.

Well, at midnight on a bitter cold Friday night in November, I'm standing in one. Exactly what I wished for came true.

And it's... I'm not sure I have the words for it.

Extraordinary?

Splendid? Nope, that's not it.

Magnificent? That's not it either.

Palatial? Yes! That's it.

Edge to edge luxury.

I'm in awe.

And I feel utterly out of place in this palace Knox lives in.

"Do you live here alone now?"

"Yes. Sometimes, when Lincoln is too lazy to walk the extra three hundred yards to his own house farther down the garden, he stays in his old room. But it's just me."

"Wow. How many bedrooms does this have?" I tiptoe farther into the large kitchen area, clicking my heels delicately against the sparkling black tiled floor. It's like an ebony sea of glitter against the stark matte-white kitchen units.

"Only nine. I converted two into a large office."

"Nine," I whisper to myself.

The whole footprint of my compact house would fit into the kitchen and dining area alone.

"I love your kitchen." I eye up the sleek white cast iron Lacanche induction cooker. Those things cost at least ten grand. How do I know this? Because I want one, that's why.

My parents were far from hard up when I was young. They put all three of us through dance school, and now they own the top sports retreat in Scotland for pro athletes, but this, this is next level wealth.

"Do you like to cook?" Knox glides around his kitchen with relaxed confidence. He takes two champagne glasses down from an overhead cupboard and then a bottle of champagne from the integrated wine cooler.

He pulls a glass tray of fresh strawberries from the fridge. He's refined and sophisticated as he moves with dominant ease.

Not knowing what to do with myself, I continue to stand in the middle of this overwhelming space, my arms crisscrossed around my body. I'm warm, but I don't want to take Knox's jacket off. It smells too good.

"I do, yeah. I'm an excellent baker too. My nana taught me. My mom's mom. Eden and Ella were never that interested, but I loved spending time with her. She was a great baker." I smile at the memory of my cuddly nana. She was a short, white-haired woman. The only way to describe her was round. And jolly. She was as wide as she was tall.

"I can't remember the last time I used the cooker," he says, watching me as he removes the foil from the top of the dark-green bottle of champagne.

"That's a travesty. Your cooker isn't living out its gastronomic purpose."

"You'll have to show me how to use it properly this weekend, then." Expertly, he untwists the cork cage. With precision, he slowly turns the bottle and with a low hiss, then a dramatic *pop*, the cork breaks free from the bottle, with Knox's firm hand capturing it.

"Okay." Why am I so nervous? I should act like the strong woman I am. Not some silly teenage girl, like I feel tonight. And I bet Knox has been with some remarkable women.

He certainly can't be short of offers from the many glamorous women who frequent his hotel and spa. He's gorgeous. One of the most sought-after bachelors in the county.

Why has he never settled down with anyone?

I only ever see him with Sam. His black Labrador is always by his side, even in the hotel.

"Where's Sam?"

I've watched Knox many times as he saunters along the beach. I love to watch him exercising Sam. His strong golden arms give off some serious arm-porn vibes. His all year round Mediterranean tan, although now I know why, makes me wonder what the rest of him is like underneath all of those designer clothes he wears. And his suits. Don't get me started on the suits. He's a Greek Adonis in a suit. Literally.

He always seems lost in thought as he walks the beaches. He's a solitary character. Almost reclusive. He's not one to speak about people or even spend much time around anyone. He's careful about who he associates with. He reminds me of that title of the Phil Collins' album my dad used to listen to all the time when we were growing up, *Hello, I Must Be Going.* He's exactly like that. Been here, done it, now I'm off.

I've only ever seen him out at the Vault nightclub in town a handful of times with a couple of his old school buddies. Every time, I knew he was watching me. It was subtle. But there.

He's always *there*. On the outer parameters, observing.

He shakes me from my thoughts. "Sam will be up the stairs,

sleeping. He's a grumpy old man now. He needs his sleep." He holds his hand out and beckons me to him. "Come."

I tip-tap my heels across the immaculate shiny floor. He leans into me and pushes his dress jacket down my arms, then throws it across the white sparkle granite countertop of the gigantic kitchen island.

Unexpectedly, he loops his powerful arms around my waist and summons my eyes up to his. He's so tall and I want to climb him like a tree.

"You don't have to be nervous around me, Eva. You know me."

"I do, but it's because it *is* you." I lay my hands flat against his chest.

Time stretches between us as he contemplates. "I've wanted to kiss you for such a long time."

"Me too," I whisper.

His eyes shimmer in the light. "I want you, Eva."

His confession does things to my heart I can't even explain. It feels happy.

"How long?"

"Too long."

That didn't answer my question.

"Eva, you being here tonight. I never expected this. What about..."

I push my pointer finger against his lips. "Don't. Let's have this weekend. Together. Just us. Two nights. Okay?"

His eyes crinkle at the sides.

Knox bobs his head slowly up and down, agreeing with me. I think.

He's a deep thinker.

I want to know what's going on beneath that hard exterior he wears.

You actually never know what's going on with him because he really is a man of few words. Tonight is the most I've ever spoken with him in at least ten years. That's how long my dad's been playing golf with him and since Knox took over The Sanctuary from his father.

His father, Gregor, still sits on the hotel board, but the everyday running of the hotel and spa is Knox and Lincoln's responsibility.

"Champagne?" he asks me eventually, still holding on to me.

"Yes, please."

That's not what I expected him to say. I expected him to go all domineering and lay down the law with me, saying he wanted more than two nights.

I thought he would fight for me. Maybe. Oh, I don't know.

Do I even want that?

Hell, yeah. I think maybe I do.

"Up." Knox slaps the granite worktop, instructing me to hop on top.

Once I'm settled, he gently coaxes my legs apart; casually, he stands between my thighs.

Knox picks up a strawberry and takes a bite.

I watch in fascination as he stares straight at me. Removing the remaining strawberry from his mouth, he offers me the rest and feeds it to me.

No one has ever fed me strawberries before. It's sensual.

Billionaire feeding fest.

His gaze dips to my mouth when I bite down. My lips brush against the tips of his fingers as he holds the top of the red berry fruit.

I push my tongue out slightly, licking my lips to catch the fresh juice. Quickly, I remove the top of the soft sweet fruit from his grasp, then suck his finger into my mouth. Knox's eyes dilate, turning dark, fixated by my erotic action.

My eyes never leave his as I roll my tongue around his tip, before pushing his finger out of my mouth.

"Tastes nice." I sit up straighter, confidently, feeling more like myself.

Hypnotized by my lips, he shakes his head to bring himself out of his trance.

"Champagne." He passes me the fine glass flute. I reach for it, but he steals a sip, sets the glass back down, quickly leans into me, then forces my mouth open and fills my mouth with bubbles. It's unexpected. I have to swallow fast.

Oh gawd, how is that so much of a turn-on?

He cups my face, drifting his hand down my throat possessively, squeezing my neck a little as he ravishes my mouth with his tongue and lips. And I groan as my body wakes up from its yearlong hibernation.

He entwines his lean fingers into the back of my hair and pulls me in to his mouth in a full-on hard and delicious kiss.

This changed gears quickly.

It's demanding. Passionate.

Forbidden.

His tongue expertly searches mine as the remnants of the fizzy bubbles dance between our mouths. A small trickle of champagne that escaped our fizzy kiss slides down the edge of my mouth. Knox laps it up with his tongue.

But I want his lips. I grab his face and direct his lips to mine again.

Our tongues lick one another, tasting, twisting together.

In one of the most heated kisses of my life, I pull his body toward me, holding him in place. Because I want all of him. I've been waiting for this moment. I run my fingers through his dark locks. Our breathing becomes hot and heavy. Gasps and sighs of enjoyment escape our mouths. We're all clashing teeth and hot breath. A pleasurable throb between my thighs begins as I move my pelvis back and forth against his aligned hips, urging him to relieve the pressure I feel building. As if knowing what I want, Knox pulls me closer to him, digging his fingers into my hips, letting me feel his hard length against my center.

Creating our own symphony of pleasure, synchronized, we moan.

"How much was this dress you're wearing?" Mumbling, he flicks his tongue against mine.

"No idea, it's old. I'm not that worried about it." I gasp through our illicit kiss that's making me so wet. I want him inside of me. Now. But I know he's going to make me wait. Play with me.

"Fuck it. I'll buy you a new one." He grabs the high slit of my dress and tears it with such force, he splits the whole thing in two from thigh to strap, leaving me perched on top of the quartz countertop in my barely-there navy lace panties. They're the sexiest ones I own. And that's the sexiest thing I've ever had anyone do to me.

Ewan liked my body, loved sex, but not that much he tore my clothes off.

Knox's dark eyes examine my naked skin. "No bra?"

"Don't wear one that often. Don't exactly need one." Not after breastfeeding two babies, anyway.

"They are the perfect fucking size. You have a breathtaking body, Eva."

He cups his large hand around my breast, then squeezes it. Dipping his head to my sensitive peak, he sucks it into his mouth, lashing his tongue around and around.

He moves fast.

My nipple grows hard as he gives it a teasing bite and pulls it between his teeth, causing a ripple of complete joy from my nipples into my sex and I silently beg him to touch me. *There.*

"Oh, God." I gasp and fling my head back.

He pulls my other arm out of the spaghetti strap of my now ruined dress.

Not that I actually mind. The last time I wore this dress

Ewan spoiled my evening by getting completely wasted at the bar of my cousin Emily's wedding. Then he started a fight with the best man. Worst. Night. Ever.

I had a lot of explaining to do, a lot of covering up. Something I spent my time doing during most of our marriage —making excuses for him.

My new beginning starts now. That dress can burn in hell for all I care.

"I have stretch marks and a C-section scar," I blurt out, now fully aware of my nakedness.

"Where?" Knox lifts his head from my breasts.

"There." I point to the long pink line above my pubic line. He then watches as I trace my fingertips across the faint silver ones below my belly button, too.

Knox looks me dead in my eyes with serious determination.

"I don't know what you see, but those tell me who you are. Your story. They tell me you gave birth to two healthy boys. Your body did an incredible job keeping them safe, and you grew two miracles inside of you. You have a beautiful body. You're lean, slender. You look after yourself. That's what your body tells me, Eva."

My story.

Who exactly is Knox Black?

Just wow.

He dips his head, then lays a runway of gentle kisses down my body, paying special attention to my scar. He kisses it with such tenderness. My heart can't handle it, and all the hairs across my skin stand at attention. For him.

Lower he goes and I might die if he doesn't touch me *there*, soon.

"I have something to tell you."

"Not now. Enjoy, Eva." He breathes against my pale skin.

I'll let him discover *it* himself then.

Knox sweeps the edge of my barely-there lace thong panties with his deft fingers, then slowly, teasingly, removes them.

I raise my hips to help him. He removes my tattered dress from under me, then peels my towering heels off, too.

"Lie back please, legs up."

He said please.

I do as he asks, lying back against the cool granite kitchen island. If it's freezing, I don't feel it because my skin is burning for him and I'm desperate to know what comes next.

I watch as he drops my dress into the concealed trash can. He hooks my panties onto one of the kitchen cupboard door handles, then turns the lights down low to a dusky warm aura.

And he still hasn't noticed.

Focusing his attention back to me, he scans my body laid out for him like an all-you-can-eat buffet.

His eyes survey every inch of my body.

"Spread your legs wider for me, Sunshine," he commands.

Here we go.

I open up for him. Showing him all of me. Showing him how wet I am for him.

I tilt my head forward slightly to watch his reaction.

And he stares.

His mouth gapes suddenly. He tilts his head to the side inquisitively. Squints his gaze, trying to get a better view of what he thinks he can see. But his brain doesn't quite compute. *Yet.* He moves in closer. Zoning in on exactly what I wanted to tell him about.

"What the...? Is that...?"

"Yes, Knox. It is."

"A fucking clit piercing. *You* have a clit piercing?" He drags his hand down his face.

"Yes. A vertical hood clit piercing," I whisper.

"Oh, Sunshine." He does nothing to hide his excitement as

he palms his enormous bulge over his black tailored dress pants.

"How long have you had it?"

"About a year." I may as well be honest. "When things started heading south between me and Ewan, I thought it would help our relationship because he lost interest in me. But it didn't. By the time it healed for us to have sex again, we were over. I've never, eh, had anyone play with it."

"Just me?" He points to himself. All the while his eyes haven't left the curved steel clit barbell that dons a shimmering opal quartz crescent moon on the top.

"Yes. Only you." I cover my face with my hands. "Oh my God, will you stop looking at it, Knox?" I've never had anyone eyeball my bare pussy for this length of time before. Thank the Lord for regular laser treatments.

"Holy fuck. I might blow too quickly and embarrass myself in front of you. This is the sexiest thing I have ever seen."

"Yeah?" I chuckle.

"Hell, yeah. I'm gonna make you feel so good, Sunshine."

I'm ready.

Knox circles the kitchen island slowly, stalking me, deciding what he's going to do first. With efficient fingers, he removes his silk tie, unbuttoning his shirt as he prowls, allowing me the first peek of what lies beneath that pristine fabric.

And he's beautiful. Full-on cut from marble beautiful. Chiseled, sculpted abs with divots so deep they look black against his olive skin. A small island of dark hair scatters his chest and it's trimmed to perfection. It paves a faint path downward.

Painfully slow, he puts on a show for me, unbuckling his soft black leather belt, letting his trousers dip a little before he unbuttons his dress pants and they disappear to the floor from my view.

He's in no rush. It's the ultimate torture.

His navy snug-fit boxers hang low on his hips, showcasing his incredible *V* that's instructing me to look lower, begging me. My eyes drop and I take in the smattering of manscaped goodness that disappears into his boxers, all clothed in cotton and hiding from me.

I stare at his impressive long and thick length that's popped out of the top of his boxers. It makes me salivate just thinking about wrapping my tongue around him.

Knox notices. "He wants you, Eva."

"*I* want *you*, Knox."

"You've got me."

He stalks along the side of the expansive island to where my face is, bows down, presses his soft lips against mine, and dips his tongue into my mouth, causing a flood of happy zings all over my body. Leisurely, he smooths his fingertips over my skin, from my neck, down the smooth valley of my cleavage, drifting lower, lower, and lower again, across my belly until he brushes them over my pussy.

I gasp.

He applies a little pressure. Unabashedly, I moan. His talented fingers gently part my swollen lips. Straight for the money shot, he circles my wet flesh and thrusts a finger inside of me. Deep. My back curves off the sparkling quartz countertop beneath me.

"Oh, Knox," I breathe.

"You're so wet for me, aren't you, Sunshine?"

"Yes," I hiss.

"What do you like, Eva? Tell me," he whispers to me.

"Do whatever you want to me. I don't care."

He groans wildly.

He moves his incredibly skilled fingers in and out of me. My excitement coats his fingers as he goes deeper with every stroke.

I suddenly have a thought. "Can anyone see in?" I tilt my

head toward the wall of glass on the other side of the room. All I can see is us.

"No."

"What about Lincoln?"

"He's on the night shift. He's overseeing one of the bar refits. He won't be home until the morning," he mumbles against my neck.

He follows my gaze.

I can't take my eyes off our reflection. "Look at you."

"Look at us."

We look great together. He's lean and tall. So goddamn tall. But I'm so pale compared to him. Like I'm glowing.

"*Chiaroscuro*," he says with a slight accent.

"Hmm?" I turn back to him in curiosity.

"It's Italian. To describe dramatic contrasts. Light and dark. Me and you."

He's quite intense.

"You're incredible, Eva."

Knox slowly removes his fingers from my wet pussy, then rubs my excitement over my sensitive, pierced bud.

"Holy shit," I hiss, grabbing the back of his hand to keep him there.

"That good?"

"Yes! Again."

"Impatient." Knox chuckles.

It's a sound I love already.

"It's been so long, Knox. And I've been waiting for you," I say with confidence.

His dark, puzzled eyes hold mine.

He blinks.

I do too.

Something changes between us. The air suddenly becomes thick with lust. Want. Desperation.

He smashes his lips against mine, simultaneously leaping

up onto the kitchen island like a lithe panther that's been desperate to pounce.

He nudges my legs wide with his strong thighs, panting, moaning, and groaning into my mouth as he explores my body. As deep as our tongues allow, we fuck each other's mouths with deep penetrating flicks and twists. Curling around each other like a bird of paradise courtship dance.

He clutches my hips and thrusts his huge erection between my legs, right over my clit piercing, and I gasp as I feel a firework of pleasure burst from my clit into my now burning core.

"Oh, that feels amazing." My piercing usually feels quite good when working out or crossing my legs, but nothing like this. He's unleashed its potential. Finally.

My heart batters in my chest like a troop of gladiators marching into battle.

Knox lays a path of searing kisses down my body. Nibbling and biting as he heads south.

Reaching for the champagne flute, he trickles the fizzy champagne into my belly button, then sucks, laps, and licks it all away.

He pours the cool pale golden liquid over my nipples and continues to torture me, licking every drop before he lays his tongue flat against my skin and licks all the way up my chest and throat. He devours me with his mouth.

I push my hips into his.

"Some fun before I take you to my bedroom." His lips leave mine.

He smiles.

He should smile more. His entire face sparkles with mischief when he does. He's gorgeous.

Sitting back on his heels, his eyes explore my body, leaving no inch untouched. He takes his time, inhales a deep breath, and takes a small mouthful of champagne.

"Stop teasing me," I pout shamelessly.

He makes a low hum sound from the back of his throat, and it's laced with a hint of humor as he swallows.

Continuing the anticipation, he splashes champagne down my already wet folds but the chilled bubbles do nothing to cool down my now hot-for-him pussy.

Knox bows down, kissing my inner thighs one after the other, slowly moving toward my center, making me squirm with impatience.

I feel him cover my entire pussy with his phenomenal mouth and I about come undone there and then. His hot breath sighs against my wet flesh as if he's in heaven. I am too.

Shoving his massive hands under my backside, he cups both cheeks, lifts my hips, and does the most surprising thing; he licks me from my back entrance to my clit piercing and I gasp at the unexpectedness. I have never been touched or licked back *there* before.

He continues to hold my hips up as he flicks his tongue back and forth, over and over between my clit, my core, and back entrance, making me gasp and buck my hips into his face with the intensity of it all.

"Make me come, Knox."

"You will come when I tell you to," he admonishes.

I hate being told what to do normally, but Knox can boss me about all he wants. I actually want him to.

Lowering my hips, his skilled tongue continues pleasuring me. He inserts two of his long thick fingers into my pussy, finding my deep sensitive spot; at the same time he plays with my clit ring.

"You are soaked, Sunshine."

"Oh, that is fucking lovely," I call out, grabbing on to his hair as I feel a rush of pure wet heat in my core.

"I've barely touched you." Our eyes meet as he looks up.

My body responds to him like an explosive chemical

reaction. It's unreal. I'm about to burst. I'm burning up and it's wonderful.

Oh, my God. I'm here. In Knox Black's house. Naked. In his kitchen. And he's eating me out like I'm a Michelin star meal.

"Keep doing that, or more, or whatever," I say breathlessly with a nervous laugh at the absurdity of how my evening has turned out.

And he does, grinning against my wet flesh. His tongue flicks, becoming quicker, wilder. His fingers slide in and out of me at the same time. My pleasure builds fast, so suddenly, moving through every inch of my body.

"Come now, Eva," he demands.

Knox tugs on my clit ring, sucking it hard, and I clench, trying to hold on to this feeling before I let it all go and a mind-blowing orgasm hits me hard with an intense force. I rasp a deep moan out loud. Knox does too, as I thrust my pussy into his mouth and hold his head between my thighs in a viselike grip. My pussy flutters around his fingers still held deep inside of me.

I call out Knox's name, like I own him, like he's mine and I'm his in my euphoric moment. Everything goes black for a second, a reflection of him.

My heart beats fast in my chest. Sheer elation of *feeling* again.

The clit piercing—best decision ever. It's heightened all my tiny nerve endings.

It's pure pleasure and I feel blissful as Knox continues to slowly finger fuck me, gently bringing me down off my high.

I release his head between my thighs.

Knox kisses my clit, making me jolt. "Good, Sunshine?"

"Better than good." I sigh. "The greatest orgasm, ever."

Amusement dances in his eyes.

He likes that. But it's true.

"Really?" he asks for confirmation.

"Scouts honor. It was out of this world," I whisper.

"You were never in the Scouts." He continues kissing my hot skin as he heads north.

"Nope. But still the truth." I enjoy his featherlike kisses.

"Taste." He pushes his fingers into my mouth.

Oh, my God. He's doing everything to me I have never done before. All with unapologetic confidence and dominance.

I lick and taste myself on his strong digits. My combined curiosity and horny devil inside gets the better of me, and I don't mind it at all.

"Do you taste how sweet you are?" He removes his fingers.

I nod, speechless.

I frame his face with my hands as he reaches me. "Thank you. That was pretty special."

"Like you. Special." He bites his bottom lip.

"And you, Knox."

We stare at each other.

"Something is changing between us," he breathes, his eyes full of desire.

He knows I feel this *thing* between us too. It's indescribable.

"Of course things have changed. You just finger fucked me and ate me out like a champion. I'll never be able to look at you the same way ever again."

"Clit ring. Same."

"I like it," I confess, wrapping my legs around his waist. "Make love to me now, Knox."

He flinches, leaning back slightly.

"Oh shit. I said the wrong thing. I didn't mean love. I should have said fuck me. I need you inside of me. Fuck me, Knox," I say, trembling a little between fear and desire.

Deep in thought, his brows lower.

Did I blow this? *Bugger.*

I've never done this one-night stand thing before.

Note to self: don't use the word *love*.

His jaw tics as he clenches it tight.

He pauses, a moment to think, then dips suddenly, proceeding to kiss me with savage lust.

"Bedroom. Now." He jumps down from the island. He pulls his wallet out of his inside jacket pocket.

"Am I being paid for tonight?" I jest.

"Condoms," he confirms.

Christ, I am crap at this. Of course!

He sits me up, then proceeds to lift me into his bronzed arms. I wrap my legs around him firmly.

Chest to chest, he walks out of the fine kitchen and dining area and into the darkened hall. I spot the sweeping staircase lined by glass panels leading up into the darkness above.

"You can't carry me up there. I'm too heavy."

"Watch me," he challenges, and he cups my ass cheeks, skimming my pussy lips teasingly.

I'm desperate to see around this awesome space he's carrying me into, but I want him more.

Knox finally enters his bedroom at the end of the long hallway, gently laying me down on his swimming pool-sized bed. "You're as light as a dandelion seed in the wind, Eva. I lift heavier at the gym."

I giggle. Fucking giggle.

Knox flicks a switch by his bedside, illuminating his sacred space and him. I want to look all around; however, my eyes can't tear themselves away from his sculpted body.

I hold my hand out in invitation, spreading my legs wide.

Come get me, Knox Black.

He pushes his boxers down his lean hips, and I get a full frontal view of his thick length, standing at attention between his legs.

My bold eyes examine his hard, glistening cock.

Whatever he's selling, I'm buying.

And I was right. He manscapes. Nice.

"Getting a good look?"

I'm not embarrassed. "Let me appreciate this moment. What size shoes do you wear?"

A flash of humor crosses his face. "Twelve."

"Figures." He's massive. Thick. Hung. Like a monument I should worship.

Knox fists his ever-growing cock and I watch with fascination as he strokes himself back and forth.

He allows me to enjoy this moment.

"It's not a spectator sport, Eva. Grab my wallet," he instructs. "I have four condoms. That's all you'll get me for tonight. Tomorrow I'll need to go out for more."

Four times. *Hallelujah.*

"Don't you have any more in your bedside drawer?" I ask, flirting with him as I pull the foiled packets from his black Italian leather wallet with his initials embossed in gold. *Suave scoundrel.*

"I never bring anyone back here. This is my private space."

I look up.

"But *I'm* here."

"I know."

Interesting.

"I want you here." He continues fisting himself with hooded eyes. "I need your body in ways that make no sense to me, Eva."

Warmth flutters in my abdomen.

"You feel it too, Sunshine. I know you do."

He's right. I want him to dominate me.

Moving fast, I sit up and tear open the condom with my teeth.

For the first time, I touch him as I roll the condom down his hard, thick cock.

A deep, raspy groan leaves his throat at my gentle touch.

I lie back on the bed, pulling his hand, urging him to me.

"Fuck me, Knox." I whisper. I want this.

"Spread your legs. Wide." He stares at my wet flesh. "Show me what's mine."

I do as instructed.

He crawls over me.

Eyes locked. Athletic chest to fair one, our naked bodies press flush together.

I spread my legs wider for him. In one swift expert thrust, he enters me, and I gasp at the pleasurable invasion, enjoying his hot, hard body molded to mine. There is nothing I can do to hide my excitement from him. I'm so wet.

Knox holds still, allowing me to adjust to his thick cock. His jaw ticks, eyes clenched shut, nostrils flared.

His eyes fly open. "I've been waiting patiently for you, Eva."

"I know." I think I've always known.

His mysterious dark eyes search mine.

"The wait is over, Knox. Don't hold back. Do it," I tease.

On my instruction, he moves. Slowly at first.

Our eyes never leave each other as he slides in and and out of me. It's intense. Close. Intimate.

More intimate than it should be.

Knox pushes my arms over my head and threads his fingers in mine.

Lifting himself up slightly, leaning up on his forearms, he thrusts into me, clenching his fingers around mine.

His eyes burn with intensity.

All hesitation and control gone, the tension in his features slide away as he gives himself to me, revealing how badly he wants me.

There are no words needed as we connect in a way I've only ever dreamed about.

He kisses me with desperation as the unyielding desires we have for one another sizzles like an electrical current between us.

Fingers entwined, I lock my legs around his waist, digging my feet into his ass, urging him to fuck me deeper.

"You are so fucking tight, Eva."

"I have a designer vagina," I reply huskily.

"Oh, fuck," he hisses through a tight jaw. "You're the mom that listens to hard-core rap music on the way to pick up the kids and yoga classes, aren't you? And the woman that looks like a bohemian angel, fucks like a porn star, and has a goddamn clit piercing. I think you're trying to kill me with all of your erotic surprises."

I burst out laughing.

He moves faster and I'm totally here for it.

He lets go of my hands and I use the opportunity to unlock my legs, grab his ass, and dig my nails into his rock-hard flesh. Pushing him into me, I drive my heels into the bed to give me more leverage. My tits bounce with every deep thrust.

Leaning right back, he squeezes my hips and fucks me senseless.

I clench my core muscles to grip him tighter.

"You have to stop doing that." His eyes bug out.

I love playing with him. He's so serious.

"Why? What will happen?"

"You'll miss out on one of the best orgasms you'll ever have because I'll come too quick. Stop right now, you devil woman." He keeps thrusting in and out, circling as he does.

"Ooooo, that's so good." I arch my back and let out a long moan.

Knox flicks my clit ring, and it sends a beautiful wave of pleasure straight to my core.

He does it again and again. I meet him thrust for thrust. Sensing my impending orgasm is on its way, he says, "You're close. I can fucking feel you clenching my cock."

"Yes!" I hiss.

He picks up the pace, hammering into me at lightning

speed. I tilt my hips slightly. The head of his cock hits my magical spot deep inside. Between Knox playing with my clit ring, his cock hitting my G-spot and watching his divine, godly Greek body move in and out of my wet heat, I can't hold off any longer.

Relentlessly, Knox drives into me and my second orgasm of the night erupts through my body. A shock wave of hot liquid fire blazes as I fall over the pleasure precipice and a wave of incredible joy zooms through my whole body.

I come undone and the release I feel is otherworldly as a kaleidoscope of powdered paint bursts behind my eyes.

My moans of pleasure echo through the expansive house as I call out Knox's name over and over.

I've never had an orgasm that felt like it touched every part of my body before. Until now. My body is buzzing.

The sexual tension that's been building between Knox and me for hours, days, months finally dissipates as I let him fuck me through my orgasm.

Like a back draft of fire, we've been concealing our need for one another, our feelings confined. The excessive heat between us has been climbing and all we needed was a tiny puff of oxygen to ignite our ferocious combustion.

And I feel it.

My orgasm doesn't stop; it rises again. In yet another first, Knox edges me quickly into another wave of pleasure.

"Look at me," he commands. "Look at me when you come, Eva."

His muscles move as if dancing across his skin in the dimly lit room, highlighting his hard, glorious muscles.

I watch Knox with bated breath as he fucks me with primal, fast, and furious intention.

"Come for me," he growls.

He toys with my clit ring, then flicks it, and I have to grasp the soft sheets around me to stop from lifting off the bed as I jolt and yet another orgasm tears through me.

Sparks fly between us.

My pussy convulses all around him, milking him as we come together.

And my heart stops for a breathtaking moment. My eyes never leave his.

He groans out my name, and I can't stop watching him as he holds himself deep inside my body.

"Holy ffffuuuuuuuuuuck," he gasps, jerking the last of himself into me before he lets out a long groan in pure ecstasy.

Unable to move, he holds himself still. "I don't want to move. You feel so good, baby," he pants.

I want him to stay right here, too.

Descending together, we're a sweaty mixture of messy breathlessness.

He lowers himself to me, sealing us skin to skin, and delicately kisses me, tracing his thumb across my cheek.

"You're perfect, Eva." He peppers kisses up and down the length of my neck before muttering words I don't understand. It sounds Greek, but I can't be sure. I don't care. I love it all and I've never felt so worshipped in all my life.

His priority was my pleasure, and boy, did he give me it.

He slowly slides himself out of me.

"Don't move." He holds me with his eyes.

I couldn't even if I wanted to. My body feels completely boneless.

I watch as he quickly walks into the adjoining bathroom of his giant bedroom to dispose of the condom. As he comes back, he then lays his divinely sculpted body over me again.

Eye to eye, he cups my face with his huge hands, then kisses me.

He seems to enjoy kissing, and he's freaking good at it.

"I've been fantasizing about this moment," he says between kisses.

My heart tinkles like a wind chime on the breeze.

"That was beautiful, Knox."

He covers his mouth with mine. I wrap my arms around his neck and run my fingers through his ebony locks. He flips us over.

It's late now, but I feel wide awake as we tangle ourselves in one another. I slide my hips down a little and that's when I feel his glorious cock hard for me again.

I roll my hips. My wet pussy touches his naked length. I slide back and forth, letting his cock swell between my slick folds.

Deepening our kiss, he grabs the back of my head with his enormous hand and groans into my mouth as we slip and slide together.

With his other hand, he cups my ass, then glides a finger down between my ass cheeks. He dips the tip of his finger into my pussy. I feel him circle his finger around my back entrance with my own excitement and I moan 'cause it feels nice.

"You like that, Eva?"

"Yeah, I think so," I whisper.

"Have you ever?" He circles it delicately.

"No."

He pushes the tip of his finger in slightly.

I inhale.

His lips twitch against my mouth. "One day, I will take this ass," he says with confidence.

But I'm only here for two nights.

He slides his hands up my waist, grabs my hips, and pushes them down hard, thrusting himself between my swollen folds, and his cock rocks against my clit ring. My whole body lights up as a jolt of excitement shoots through me.

"Ready for round two?" he growls.

My nipples pebble with desire against his skin as he continues to tease my pussy.

"You're an old man. I don't think you'll manage an all-nighter."

He spanks my ass. "Be quiet, you devil woman."

I gasp at the unexpectedness of the sting.

His cock rubs me back and forth.

"You like that too? Hmm, interesting," he mumbles.

Casual sex, ass fingering, spanking. Next, I'll be begging him to tie me up.

"Grab a condom. I'll fucking show you what old looks like."

He spanks my ass again before we have the best sex of my life.

Again and again.

CHAPTER 5

Knox

Only having had a few hours of sleep, I let out a pleasurable groan as I stretch myself out in my large comfortable bed, feeling more satisfied than I have in years.

All my fantasies came true last night.

With Eva.

Even when the condoms ran out, we explored each other's bodies with our tongues, hands, and mouths. All night.

She's fucking breathtakingly beautiful.

And fun. I had fun. For the first time in years, I felt like me.

Being with her was even better than I imagined.

She's so sexy and that dancer's body of hers can contort into all sorts of positions. Some were a first for me. How she didn't dislocate a hip I will never understand.

I'm more obsessed with her now than I was before.

Eva wrapped herself around me as she drifted off to sleep last night and I loved every single hot minute of it.

What the fuck is happening to me?

I groan again and pull my hands down my face.

I was wrong to think this could only be a two-night thing

between us. There is no way I can forget Eva. Not after what we did together last night in my bed.

Never. I was lying to myself that she could be a one and done.

Yeah, that was never going to happen.

I roll over in my giant bed to discover I'm alone.

I catapult up and look around.

Shit, did she leave?

Leaping out of the bed, I swiftly pull on my boxers and run down the stairs, calling Sam to wake him up. Not that he'll hear me. At thirteen years old, my furry friend is almost deaf now.

As I enter the kitchen, I stop in my tracks, shocked to find Lincoln standing in the fridge's doorway, drinking directly from the orange juice carton.

Shit, shit.

I look around.

Where is Eva?

"Morning. You're late getting up today, old man," Lincoln teases as he continues scavenging about in my fridge, unaware of my confusion. "Could those be something to do with it?" He points to the tiny lace panties hanging from the kitchen cupboard handle. "And that?" He then points to the leftover champagne and strawberries. "And your two-thousand-pound suit is lying on the floor."

Triple shit.

Thank Christ I put her dress in the trash can, or that would have exposed us.

"It's none of your business, Linc."

He laughs. "It's good to see you're finally trusting Tabby enough to bring her back to your home. It's only taken you three years." He closes the refrigerator door and heads straight for the breadbox. "Is she upstairs?" he whispers. "Her bag is still here." He points with his head toward Eva's bag that sits heavily on the kitchen floor.

She hasn't left.

"Eh, yeah," I lie, trying to figure out where the hell she is.

I pick up our clothes strewn across the floor, placing Eva's panties inside her bag.

Lincoln grabs a croissant from the breadbox, then strolls across the room, making himself comfortable on one of the white and chrome leather bar stools at the kitchen island. The kitchen island I made Eva come on last night.

I groan.

"You alright?" Lincoln stuffs a piece of the crescent-shaped buttery pastry into his mouth.

"Yeah, I'm good. Tired." I yawn. I am tired. It's been a very long time since I pulled an all-night sex session.

"I'm sure Tabby has something to do with it." He grins widely. "Sam's outside having a pee, by the way."

I nod.

Lincoln throws me off with his next line of questioning, "Do you think you'll marry Tabby? She wants to marry you. I can tell. She's all swoony, flirty, and shit around you all the time." He bats his eyelashes, raising his voice into a high-pitched tone, clutching his chest. "It's adorable. Although I haven't seen her in a while."

"Oh, stop it." I'm never marrying Tabby. "And stop drinking from the carton. What have I told you about that?" I scold him.

He ignores me, taking another slurp.

"I think you should get more serious with her. You deserve to be happy, Dad. Isn't it time?" He sprays tiny flakes of buttery goodness everywhere from his mouth.

I felt happiness last night. Contentment. Full-on contentment and happiness.

Not a feeling I am accustomed to.

But I feel it with Eva.

It's never felt like that with Tabby. With her, it was just sex. Nothing more.

"Will you stop talking with your mouth full?"

"You need to de-stress. I know the perfect way to do that. Loosen up, Dad." He banters with me in a relaxed manner.

This is the problem when you have a son that is not that much younger than you—familiarity. We're more like best friends than father and son.

Lincoln continues. "So, Tabby. Let's talk about *that*. Did you tell her about your eighty-grand win last night? I reckon she will love those dance lessons. Although, I, personally, would like to dance one-on-one with Eva. Man, she looked hot last night."

He has no idea how hot she really is. *Clit piercing.* Now that was a hotter than hell surprise.

"Do you think I should ask her out on a date?" Lincoln mumbles around his food, considering.

Fuck.

In only my boxers, I feel hot all over suddenly. Guilt, that's what it is, one hundred percent.

I look up to double-check there isn't a flashing neon sign floating above my head with arrows pointing at me with the words *guilty* in giant-sized letters.

Sam saves me from answering by hobbling into the kitchen.

"Hey, buddy." I crouch down, give him a gentle pat, and rub behind his ears.

Lincoln persists with his line of questioning. "Do you think she would say yes to me, though? Am I too young for her?" he asks with wonder as I rise to my full height again.

"Who?" I play dumb.

"Eva, Dad. Eva. Pay attention, old man."

Where is she?

"Right." I clear my throat. "I don't know. How did the refurbishment go last night?" I deflect.

"Good. Great, in fact. But I think they will complete it by Tuesday, not Monday, like we had planned. We changed the shape of the leather seating booths. They started last night, but it will take longer. I think it will look much better, though. We are definitely using the same remodeling team again. They are very meticulous, efficient, and tidy."

I spent months ensuring I chose the right team, and even longer waiting for them. They are highly in demand.

"I'm proud of you, son. You're a real asset to the family business." He really is. He's incredible with the staff. I'm big man, boss man. Lincoln is the more approachable one, ensuring all the staff are happy, and the hotel runs smoothly, whereas I oversee the larger projects, keep the board happy, and do the financials.

The whole good cop, bad cop thing seems to work for us.

I look down at Sam. "You hungry, old boy?" I make my way to the food pantry, around the corner, off the kitchen area.

As I push open the door, I jump.

Startled, I yell out an, "Aw, fuck."

I throw my hand to my chest as I'm shocked to discover Eva, standing nervously, biting the nail of her thumb in the food pantry. She stands in the dark in nothing but my white shirt from last night. She's all sexy and tousled hair like she been freshly fucked. Because she has been.

"You alright?" Lincoln shouts to me.

"Yeah, I stubbed my toe," I lie, *again*.

Eva mouths an *oh my God* as she bugs her eyes out.

I can't hold back my smile. *She's here.*

Relief floods my veins.

I lean in, stealing a quick kiss.

I always want to be kissing her. What the fuck is wrong with me? I feel giddy.

Reaching Sam's food from the top shelf, I hold my hand out and splay my fingers wide and mouth *five minutes*, then swiftly close the door.

I'm a shitty dad with what I am about to do. "Should you

not be getting to bed if you're on the night shift again tonight?" I walk back into the main kitchen, urging Lincoln to leave.

Lincoln licks his fingers, finishing the last of his croissant. "Yeah, good point. I should go. Thanks for the food." He hops off the bar stool and yawns wide, stretching his arms up into the air.

He is a handsome boy, and he's never short of offers from beautiful women. Most of them I see leaving through the side gate of our estate early in the mornings. What a boy.

"You didn't ask for any food. You helped yourself, remember?"

"No food at mine."

What's new?

"Have a great day. Enjoy the weekend off." He grins cheekily. "Have fun with Tabby."

"Get out of here," I urge. "Love you, son." I really love my boy.

Clearly not enough to stop this thing from happening with Eva.

He likes her.

Fuckity, fuckity, fuck.

"Love you too, Dad. See you Monday."

I watch Lincoln saunter out the side door, then hear his noisy Porsche 911 growl down the gravel side road to the west of my house. A few years back, I built him a house at the bottom of my estate. I still can't work out if it was the best or worst decision to do that.

As soon as he's out of earshot, I run to rescue Eva from the pantry. I'm desperate to see her.

I fling open the door. "Coast's clear."

She smiles with relief. "Thank goodness."

"What are you doing in here?" I fold my arms across my chest and lean against the doorjamb.

She pulls the hem of my shirt down her lean thighs. "I came down to grab a bottle of water. Then Lincoln showed up, I grabbed your shirt off the floor and I ran into the first cupboard I could find." She sighs. "That was close. What if he had seen me?" She covers her face. "Oh God. I feel terrible. This is not who I am. I'm a horrible person."

I move toward her, remove her hands, cradle her fresh face, and silence her with my mouth, trying to calm her down. Our slanted mouths fit perfectly together. The kiss is gentle, soft, tender. Everything I never knew I needed. And everything I didn't know I was capable of.

"Stop worrying, and I feel the same too, but I can't resist you. I like you, Eva. I missed you this morning." I actually did. I have clearly taken my talking pills this morning, too.

"What, for all of twenty minutes? You missed me?" She giggles as she wraps her arms around my neck, making my shirt rise, exposing her supple ass, so I give it a firm squeeze. She's got a helluva fine ass.

"Yeah. I thought you'd left without saying goodbye."

"I feel bad about Lincoln. But I also would like to stay here with you again tonight. I like you too." She bites her bottom lip. "Your house is amazing."

She suddenly leans in to kiss me again, teasing me as she bites my bottom lip, then pulls it into her mouth.

Oh, how I love when she does that.

"Only staying for the house. Noted." I tickle her sides as I mumble my words against her mouth.

What is with me? I never do this couple's shit and I am far from the lovey-dovey or touchy-feely type. But Eva makes me feel this way.

She laughs, grabbing my hands to stop me. "Yeah. I'm only here for the house. Oh, and the cooker. I really want to bake on your stove."

Smiling wide, her dimples dent her pale cheeks as she leans out of our close kiss.

"I like having you here, Eva."

"I like being here." Her brows lower. "But tell me. Are you dating Tabitha MacEvoy?"

Joyful feelings blow away in a puff of smoke at the mention of Tabby's name.

I sigh. I didn't want to have this conversation. "I'm not dating Tabitha. We're like friends with benefits." We aren't even friends.

"For three years?" she asks, wide-eyed.

Goddammit. She heard our conversation in the kitchen.

"Yeah."

"Does she know that? Lincoln made it sound more serious. Marriage?" Her furrowed brows deepen as I continue to hold her tight.

"I'm never marrying Tabby. Ever. It's only casual between her and me. Lincoln is talking gibberish."

"I don't think Tabitha knows that, Knox. I don't want to come between you two. Sounds to me like you need to set the record straight with her, if that's how you feel."

Eva's right. I've been avoiding that conversation.

"I will."

"When were you last *with* her? I would never steal someone's boyfriend. That's not my style. Please tell me it was ages ago."

I try to remember. "She's *not* my girlfriend. The last time we were together was about four months ago. I don't sleep around, Eva. I know that's probably not what you've heard about me. But it's the truth." We haven't hooked up for ages. I've been making excuse after excuse not to see Tabby. But I've got to give it to her. She's persistent.

A wave of relief floods Eva's face, and she relaxes in my arms.

"Thank goodness. I've heard nothing about you, Knox. I hardly know anything about you. But you've seriously never brought Tabitha here to your home? Why not?"

"I like to keep my private life private. I've never felt the need to bring her back here." It's not that I don't trust her, but we aren't serious. Bringing her here would imply I want a relationship with her and I don't want that.

Do I want that with Eva?

I've never had a relationship with anyone since Lincoln's mother, and that was a giant-sized mess and not a story I've ever shared with anyone before.

For a moment, we stand together.

I lean my forehead against hers.

"You let me into your sacred space," she whispers.

"Yeah. I did. I want you here."

She smiles and my heart melts.

"I like being here with you."

I don't want her to leave. Forty-eight hours will never be long enough.

"Are you hungry?" I tuck a lock of hair behind her ear.

"Starving."

"Let me call for breakfast to be brought down from the hotel."

"No way. Do you have food in the fridge?"

"Yeah. Always. I keep it stocked for Lincoln."

"Then let me cook for us."

"You sure?"

"Hell yeah. Any excuse to use that cast iron beauty of a cooker you have." She grabs my hand, guiding me out of the pantry.

"I'll help you."

But she doesn't let me. She makes me sit at the kitchen island.

I stare in awe as she weaves her way through my kitchen in nothing but my white dress shirt. Her caramel locks are scooped on top of her head in a giant messy bun. She cooks at the same time as calling her boys to check in with them. Her phone tucked between her ear and shoulder, she giggles and jokes with them as she digs out pots and pans, juggling, making fresh coffee, and mixing up a fresh pancake recipe at the same time. Through her innocent actions, she cheekily flashes her bare pussy and beautiful backside every now and again to me as she bends over and moves around. Eventually, she hangs up before she tells them she loves them. Eva's a remarkable mother—everything Lincoln's mother never was.

Fixated, I can't take my eyes off her. She moves about my kitchen as if she's done this a thousand times, like she belongs here, chatting away to me, firing questions at me a mile a minute as she cooks me the most incredible breakfast of bacon and pancakes with maple syrup. It's divine.

We feed each other, and in what feels like a planetary shift, I feel relaxed. Content.

Happy.

CHAPTER 6

Eva

Staring up at the vaulted glass roof of Knox's swimming pool extension, I float aimlessly in the warm water of the heated pool, unapologetic bliss and relaxation pouring across my aching body. It's a pleasurable pain, in the best possible way, and a reminder of our all-night entanglement.

One thing's for sure, Knox has endurance and stamina. I may sign him up for the Marathon des Sables; he's ultramarathon-worthy.

After I made him breakfast, we showered together. Strike that, after our breakfast, Knox showered me. He washed my hair, then carefully washed every single part of me. He never spoke to me the entire time. He was lost in the moment.

Not once did I feel uncomfortable or shy.

It felt pivotal. Romantic even.

I actually think Knox is a true romantic at heart, but his reinforced walls are firmly held in place. Trusting me will be a big part of tearing them down.

However, I'm not sure he would let me slide a brick out to

allow me even the smallest of peeks. His wall is made of cement. Rock solid.

Tabitha is evidence. Three years and she's never been here.

But you're here, Eva; he let you in.

Maybe he will let me see him, the real him. Another twenty-four hours and I might get a peek through his wall after all. I can live in hope because, on a visceral level, the desire to know everything about him runs deep, and I have so many questions. Most of all about his ex-wife and why he's never remarried.

I'd be overstepping the line, though. I don't want to push him away. The clock is ticking on our time together. I want to hold him close in the confinements of our bubble until I have to pick up my boys tomorrow.

He held me close in the shower, airbrushing kisses over every millimeter of my body. Then, after our shower, Knox made a quick trip out to stock up on condoms.

I have no problems with any of that at all.

More sex? Yes, please. More tender moments? Yup. That too. And the Greek words he whispers to me every time he orgasms. Hell yeah, I want all of that again. I don't understand any of it, but it's incredibly beautiful and makes me feel like he's from another world, which he is. He's a real-life walking, talking, breathing, *fucking* Greek sex God.

I let out a very unladylike snort at my sordid thoughts. Overnight, I've turned into a sex addict.

My phone chimes to life from the poolside, bringing me swiftly out of my dreamy thoughts.

Leisurely, I do the breaststroke over, heave myself out of the pool, and grab my phone off the sun lounger.

Ella.

I roll my eyes at the previewed text and swipe it open.

Ella: Where are you?
Me: Out.

Ella: Out with who?
Me: With Eden.
Ella: Lies, all lies.

Goddammit. I should have said I was out with Beth, my fiery red-headed friend who doesn't work Saturdays.

As the CEO of The Scottish Golf Association, she dictates her own hours and Saturday is a day not worthy of her time. Saturdays are for shopping apparently. I hate the idea of spending all day shopping. Not my idea of fun at all.

"Shit," I hiss as a group chat call comes through between me, my triplet sisters, Ella, Eden, and our lifelong school friends, Toni and Beth.

I pick up the call but decline the video request.

"Put your goddamn video on, Eva," Ella's bossy bitch voice instructs.

"Nope," I answer.

"Why not?" Eden queries.

"Here's a better question," Ella purrs coyly.

"Oh God, what game are we playing today, girls?" Toni asks, then curses in Italian. She's impatient. "My ice cream parlor queue is snaked all the way down the street and around the corner. Be quick."

The lengths people will go to for even a mere tongue dip of Toni's award-winning gelato never ceases to amaze me. And it's November. What are they thinking? Well, I know what they're thinking. It's bloody delicious. I'm grateful we get to sneak through the back door on busy days. Now that's what *I* call friends with benefits.

"Okay, picture this," Ella starts.

Aw, crap, here we go. This can only mean one thing; she knows something already.

Ella continues. "Eva says she's with Eden. When I know for a fact, Eden is with Hunter in Edinburgh today. I'm currently outside Eva's house to drop off the dress I borrowed the other week. Both her car and green passion wagon are in the drive. Her boys are at Mom and Dad's today. Hamish and Archie had a sleepover there last night and another one tonight. She doesn't want to do video chat. If Eva is not with Eden and she's not with me, is she with you, Toni?"

"Nope. I'm too busy for this shit. Hurry up," my exasperating Italian friend replies.

"What about you, Beth? Is she with you?" Ella asks sweetly, knowing the answer already.

"Nope, I'm heading out to the shops. I need a new purse." She laughs at her absurdity. She does not need another purse.

"Great, thanks, girls. So, Eva, I'll ask you again. Where are you?"

"Eh, I'm out. Just out." I sound flustered.

"With?" Eden inquires. God, I love to hate these girls.

"Myself." It's a partial lie by omission.

This doesn't stop her pushing. "Liar. Here's the thing. Fun fact, girls. Eva attended the charity auction last night and in what can only be called a fabulous twist of events where one man laid his cards on the table, Knox Black bid eighty thousand pounds for the private dance lessons we donated. With Eva. Oh, and at one point Lincoln bid twenty-five thousand pounds trying to counterbid his father."

News travels fast. I hate this small town. That's a white lie. I love it really, but sometimes, just sometimes, it would be nice if people learned to keep their mouths shut.

Loud gasps and shrieks whistle through the phone from all four girls.

"Ella!" Forgetting where I am, I scold her, and my voice echoes through the vast swimming pool room.

"Oh, echoes. Clues. All clues." Ella never gives up. She's like a shark with its prey in sight. "Tell us?"

I stay silent.

With bated breath they all wait until Beth pipes up. "You can't leave us hanging, Eva. Is this the first one-night stand you've ever had?"

"Beth, you can't throw me under the bus like this. We're supposed to be friends."

A few curses fly out of my mouth.

"Hey, girl. Listen." Beth uses her calm tone. "This is big. It proves you're moving on. It's great news."

Eden backs her up. "It's brilliant news, Eva. Progress."

"I know," I mutter. "But you know I'm not in love with Ewan anymore, right? I haven't been for a long time. He's the father of my children and he will always have a special place in my heart, but it's not love *love*. When you say progress, it's not like I've been holding out for Ewan or anything. I'm not waiting for him to change. It's been months since I've been on a night out. I've never had the opportunity to meet anyone. I haven't even considered it to be honest. You know this, right, girls?"

"Yeah, we know."

"Of course, we know that."

"Fully aware."

"Yup."

They all speak in harmony. I can see their eye rolls from here.

I wrap the white fluffy towel Knox left me around my cold skin and smile 'cause I know my girls have always got my back.

"I want to know who you're with, though. I'm not serving another customer until I know," Toni says excitedly. She's a sucker for our quintet gossip.

I pinch the bridge of my nose hard. These four always give me headaches. When they push, they push hard. But I love them with all my heart.

"It feels really high school if I tell you who I am with. I've never done this kind of thing before." I haven't.

I have always been very private with my sex life. I dated

Ewan throughout the last year of high school. I'd never been with anyone else. We did the long-distance thing when I went off to study at dance school. As soon as I qualified as a dance instructor, Ewan and I married and I instantly got pregnant with Archie. Marrying young and becoming a mom, my whole life has always been about Ewan, Archie, Hamish, and the dance school.

While I love going out with the girls, two or three nights out a year is more than enough to satisfy my needs. I much prefer meeting them for ice cream in the daytime or for long walks on the beach. I love hearing about the girls' bedroom antics. It's like their thing. It's never been mine. I share my concerns with my girls. "Also, it affects more people. I have to think about the boys if this gets out." *And your dad and Lincoln, Eva.* My inner sass jabs me in the ribs.

"Okay, give us three clues then, and we can work the rest out for ourselves. You don't have to give a specific name," Ella pushes harder. Although I know she's desperate for one.

I think for a minute. Three things. Okay, I can do that. Without being too specific.

"You still with us, Eva?" Eden asks.

"Yeah," I whisper. "Okay, three things. One, I left with him last night. Two, I am currently in his pool. Three, it was the best sex of my life. Oh, and here's a bonus for you. Four, that's how many times we had sex and I lost count how many orgasms I had." I blush berry red in the empty pool room. These are the kinds of conversations I've had with the girls, but from their side of the table. My, how the tables have now turned. "Oh, and he's currently out shopping for more condoms because I'm staying again tonight."

Squeals from the girls pierce the air, vibrating through the high ceiling space.

"And that's all you're getting," I state firmly, all the while smiling.

Ella asks, "Is it Kno—"

I press end, not allowing her to finish, and put my phone in silent mode.

My messages app flashes like a beacon as it notifies me of fourteen new text messages. I tap it open and low and behold. All from Ewan. One pings in from Ella.

Ella: Fair enough. I respect your privacy. ;) But I will find out who you are with! Could you please help me stuff envelopes for my wedding invitations next week? I'm so disorganized and we only have a few weeks to go. Eden was asking if you could do a video on social media promoting our new dance merch? Could you also speak to the printers about the new signage for the studio? It's looking sun-scorched.

I pull out my reminder app and add these to my to-do list for the coming week. There are at least twenty things on it already.

Me: Sure. Consider it done.
Ella: You're a gem. Off to finalize the wedding cake. So exciting.
Me: Have fun and enjoy the planning. Keep the dress you borrowed; it suits you better.
Ella: Thank you. I love it. You have a bridesmaid dress fitting with the girls on Thursday at 6 p.m. at Confetti. I forgot to tell you. Sorry.

Ella is having four bridesmaids—me, Eden, Toni, and Beth. This should be our final fitting.

I'll have to ask Ewan's mom and dad if they can help look after the boys. I add the date and time to my calendar and fire a quick text to Frances, Ewan's mom. She responds instantly with a thumbs-up.

Me: That's fine. I'll be there.
Ella: Thank you! Love you. x.

Closing my phone down, I ignore all of Ewan's messages and dive back into the crystal-clear aqua waves, quickly shooting to the top again to begin my aimless floating I was enjoying so much.

Ella's right on the money if she was about to say Knox.

Knox and I have agreed just this weekend. He's my secret lover, my paramour. I'm not reneging on our promise to one another unless he says otherwise.

Deep contentment threads through my veins as the peaceful water continues to caress my skin.

It confuses me how easy it is to be around him. To be here.

We went from awkward run-ins and conversations over these last few years to ripping each other's clothes off, literally overnight.

I'm still processing the beautiful shift between us. The hypnotizing eye contact. The intimacy. The roughness and the sweetness. I'm filing it all away in my mental storage cabinet under *The Weekend Knox Black Rocked My World*.

It feels nice being with him. He makes me feel like a woman.

A worthy woman. A woman so adored. Worshipped.

I thought Ewan was my everything, and I was his.

I was wrong.

Knox makes me feel like I belong to a different universe and the sex, holy cannoli, the sex is next level. Commanding and at the same time, oh so tender. Not what I expected.

Knox treats me like I'm a goddess.

He calls me Sunshine.

Both Hunter and Fraser have pet names for my sisters; Hunter calls Eden Cupcake and since high school, Fraser has called Ella, Bella. I always thought it was cheesy and cringe, but in the last twelve hours, I now have my own pet name. I love it.

A little giggle leaves my chest and the gentle waves lap against my skin at my sudden vibration.

"What are you giggling at, Sunshine?"

And there it is.

Startled by his unexpected presence, I splash about in the water, flapping about to stop myself from going under.

"Knox! You can't creep up on a woman like that," I splutter. "Not cool, Mr. Black. You startled me."

"You've startled me in that barely-there swimsuit. Very *Baywatch*." He hitches a brow, eyeing me from the side of the pool, trying to see my bright-red one-piece through the busy waves I've created.

My strappy bathing suit has multiple clever waist cutouts to give me the curves I lack. There's not much fabric to it, but it fits where it touches and the perfectly positioned fabric lies exactly where it needs to be, hiding my C-section scar, and the halter neck straps push up my *perfectly sized* boobs. Well, that's how Knox described them.

I glide through the water, over to the edge of the pool in his direction. "Pamela Anderson fan, were you, Mr. Black?"

"Maybe." A secretive smile softens his lips.

"Are you a boob or butt man?"

"Both."

"You're hot out of luck in the boob department with me, then." I'm not kidding.

Knox crouches down to greet me, lazily laying his arms across his dark jean-clad legs. He looks great in a simple white tee shirt and dark jeans.

Sexy.

"I disagree. To be honest, I'm more of a leg man and I'm now adding designer vagina to the list, and clit piercings." He rests his elbow on his knee, cupping his face with his hand.

"Now all three of those I can do." I smile cheekily.

"I like coming home to find you in my pool."

I like being here too.

"Are you enjoying your downtime, Eva?"

"Yeah. Sheer bliss. My boys would love your pool. I have two water babies."

I am missing my crazy boys; it's weird not having them around. There's no noise. It's a lot weirder that I'm not constantly making food for them, picking toys up, or ferrying them around to their various clubs on a Saturday. That's my mom and dad's job today. Like I said, sheer bliss.

His eyes crinkle at the sides. "You should bring them one day."

"Does that not break our two-night rule?" Does he want more nights with me? And time with my boys?

Yikes, introducing my boys to a new man is not something I had given any thought to. Finding a new partner hasn't even been on my radar. I was happy, just me and my boys. Not was, am. I *am* happy. I don't want any more complications in my sons' lives. It's already confusing enough for them, and little Hamish is completely puzzled why his daddy now lives down the road with a new lady.

Knox stares at me for a few seconds longer than I expect him to.

"I suppose it breaks our two-night rule. But do we need rules?" His brows huddle together.

"I don't know, do we?" I reply softly. I am not sure I want rules anymore.

"Stop answering a question with a question."

"Stop asking questions I don't know the answer to," I bite back, grinning.

He eyes me with irritation. I do like playing with him. Testing him.

He's a boss. He gets what he wants. All the time. I've already worked out that he likes direct answers. Be brief. A firm yes or a no. But he's not getting a straight answer from me. Yet.

I'd be very surprised if anyone ever challenges him. Puts him in his place.

Bring it on. I'm more than happy to test his limits.

Knox nods with a deep weighted sigh, moving on by saying, "I have Fredrick coming here at three this afternoon to give you a massage and reflexology. He's our spa manager."

"For me?"

"Yes. For you."

"Won't he say anything about me to the staff?" I crinkle my nose.

"Nope. Not a thing. He's my confidante. Discreet. Plus, he signed a confidentiality agreement with The Sanctuary. It's more than his job's worth to discuss anything outside of work. He's massaged some of the most famous people in the world. Even I don't know who. But the word *presidential* was used."

Oh, Lord.

"Why?"

"Why, what?"

"Why did you organize that?"

"Because you dance every day, teach, school runs, cook, clean, run around all day. You deserve it. You look after your boys and anything else that is thrown at you daily. Who looks after you?"

"You are so thoughtful, Knox. Thank you." I'm a little lost for words. How considerate and caring of him. I can't remember the last time I had a massage *or* reflexology, possibly never.

"Have you tried the sauna and the steam room yet?" He thumbs in their direction.

"No. I was waiting for you." Without warning, I pull myself up on the white-tiled edge of the pool with one arm and grab the neckline of his tee shirt with the other. "Get in here with me, Mr. Black."

He gasps, almost losing his footing as he tips toward me. "I have my phone in my pocket."

"Take off your clothes. Come for a swim. You're the one that needs to loosen up, old man." I smile, teasing him.

"Demanding." He rolls his eyes dramatically.

I steal a quick kiss, planting my wet lips on his, before letting go of him and plunging myself back under the water.

Popping my head back up to the surface, I submerge my face again, just enough to ensure I can still watch Knox on the sidelines as he peels his expensive apparel from his delicious body. My eyes leisurely skate across his taut muscles, taking their time to admire his thick, heavy length between his broad thighs. I love that well-trimmed sprinkle of dark hair from his belly button that heads south.

I internally thank all the Greek gods above and below for creating this fine naked specimen of a man that's slowly walking down the mosaic-patterned blue and white steps into the pool.

He swims toward me with undeniable intention, loops his arms around my waist, and instructs me to hold my breath. I do.

My stomach ties in knots when he drags me under, never letting me go as he holds me perfectly still under the warm water. Our eyes lock.

Reaching up, I thumb his cheek; he rests his hand over mine.

Time stops as the gargle of the waves and bubbles swirl around us.

A few more seconds go by. Something deeper passes between us.

It's tangible. I can feel the buzz of excitement in my heart and soul as I stare at the glorious man before me.

We ascend together. As we breach the surface, catching our breath, we kiss. And kiss.

Our panting breaths, wet skin, and tongues are all I can focus on.

It's so Knox.

Deep.

All-consuming.

Possessive.

I grab on to Knox's face as tight as I can, as if my life depends on it, using him as my breathing aid, and the way he kisses me in response makes my world spin on its axis.

I'm warm in the heated pool, but I shudder as my desire for him deepens. The way Knox kisses me is pure panty-scorching as sparks of joy and electricity jolt through my body. His hands roam my skin under the water.

With every skim, grab, and nip at my skin, he pulls me firmly to him as if trying to glue us together.

He nibbles and bites my lips, then drops his mouth to the spot on my neck he now knows I adore and makes me mewl like a cat in heat.

"You're turning me into a sex addict," he murmurs.

"I think it's the other way around." I laugh, then stroke his growing hard length back and forth beneath the water.

My pulse quickens as our breathing picks up pace.

Knox makes me want to try things I never have. Pushes me. But all the while he's lit up my entire world in less than twenty-four hours, showing me what I needed to see.

That I'm a woman.

A woman with needs.

Who deserves better.

Adored.

Worshipped.

To be taken care of.

And I'm not ashamed to admit that I want someone to take care of me.

For someone to care enough about me again to want to be there for me.

And not just anyone.

I want *him* to take care of me. Well, at least for the next day.

He murmurs a frustrated groan. "I want you."

Now or forever?

He stops kissing me, then leans back slightly, studying me with curiosity.

"Say that again?" he says with a deep rasp.

"Oh, did I say that out loud?"

I have a stupid habit of doing that at the most inappropriate of times. My sister, Eden, does it too.

"You did." His fingers dig into my waist.

I don't respond.

"Well?" he presses me.

I clear my throat. "Forget I said that."

"I don't want to forget. Say it again. I said, I want you."

"I'm not saying it again." Because it slipped out by mistake.

He skims his lips over the shell of my ear. "You know, Sunshine, you can keep denying yourself, keep denying what is happening between you and me, but I know deep down we want the same thing."

"Oh, yeah?" He lifts me up and wraps my legs around his waist. "And what's that?"

"Don't play games, Sunshine."

"I don't play games, Mr. Black." My heart jackhammers in my chest against his. I'm giving nothing away because I've run through every scenario of him and me together. In theory, it might work, but in real terms, there are many other people to consider.

To distract him, I bite the lobe of his ear and he shudders.

"I know what you're doing, Sunshine. Distraction,

avoidance. Believe me, I'm the king of those. I've had enough therapy to recognize both." He gently kisses my shoulder.

Color me curious. "What did you need therapy for, Knox?" I face him, draping my arms over his broad shoulders.

"I don't want to talk about it." He dips his gaze.

"What happened to you, Knox?" I softly ask. I think this is why he's never married again or had a serious relationship with anyone. He's protecting himself from something or *someone*.

"It's a story for another time."

Cradling his face with my hands, I tilt his face back up. "You don't have to tell me anything, Knox. But I'm here if you ever need to talk. Trust me. I would never divulge anything you tell me." I search his deep eyes for answers, but they give nothing away.

"Thank you." He hitches his head up and down quickly in acknowledgement. "Sauna?" He's certainly mastered the art of avoidance, and I allow him to move on because he allowed me too.

"I'd love to."

Knox carries me through the warm water toward the sauna room, where he fucks me like I've never been fucked before. It's relentless and I love every stiflingly steamy minute of it. Steam rooms are supposed to release good feeling endorphins. I don't need a steam or sauna room for that to happen. I only need Knox.

He then takes me again and again on every surface throughout his entire house, only stopping when Fredrick arrives to give me an out-of-this-world massage, leaving me feeling boneless and walking on a rainbow of fluffy clouds.

We spend the evening chatting and stuffing our faces with Chinese takeout. We watch an episode of *The Revamp Champ* on his oversized forest-green leather and walnut sofa, and it's a whole new side of Knox Black that unfolds before me as he jokes, eats with his fingers, and chats with excitement about the on-screen car renovations. I relish in the fact that no one but me gets to see this side of him.

We roll into bed in the wee hours of the morning after chatting about everything and nothing for way too long.

It's the most fun I've had with male company in as long as I can remember.

I wish we had more nights together.

CHAPTER 7

Knox

Slowly waking up from my deep satisfying sleep, my brain can't work out why my bed feels like Satan's anus. I'm hot. Boiling, in fact.

It's then I realize it's because the world's hottest human water bottle has curled herself around my hips, chest, waist, and legs, holding me firmly as if I'm her life buoy.

Fuck me, is she hot. And I don't mean sexy, although there is that too, but she's burning up. It's no wonder she sleeps naked 'cause I'm pretty sure her body heat would burn off the fabric if she did.

Not wanting to wake her up or move, I remain still, only turning my head a fraction to get a good look at her through my lazy squint. I take a mental picture for my memory time capsule.

Her long, wavy caramel locks spread out across my pillow and even when asleep, her dimples give her a mischievous girlish look. My eyes roam down her body. She's got one hell of an incredible body. Combined with an insatiable amount of energy—she's got that in spades—she's a dangerous cocktail of sweet meets spice as she met me thrust upon striking thrust every single time we had sex yesterday.

I think she was testing me or vice versa; maybe we both were.

We went for longer, deeper, and came stronger together with every new connection we made as we tried new positions all over my house. I have never done that before.

Not with anyone.

She's funny, smart, and beautiful. Striking.

We grew closer yesterday. I laughed. Had fun. And fuck, don't get me started on the eye contact. It's unnerving. Like she can see into my soul.

I want to spend more time with her. However, she's never mentioned wanting to spend more time with me, and she avoided the rules question I asked her yesterday.

It's our last day together.

How I'll be able to see her down the beach or out and about now without touching her or kissing her is beyond me.

Clit ring.

Then there's *that.*

It's the ultimate torture.

In addition, I now know what her mouth feels like wrapped around my cock.

Damn, it's going to be harder than ever to be around her. And I mean *hard.*

I run my free hand down my face and release a weighted sigh, then lay my hand over her delicate hand, positioned perfectly over my heavy heart.

I don't like feeling like this.

It's not a feeling I'm familiar with.

Whatever *this* is. It doesn't feel good. Awful, in fact.

After she leaves today, that's it, back to the mundane. Hotel, emails, staff issues, spreadsheets, board meetings, more meetings, and endless problems to solve and then back home again to an empty nest. *Great.* I'm the man who has everything but nothing all at the same time.

I eye the high ceiling of my bedroom.

Since when did this house feel so lonely? So big?

Eva was right about my cooker not living out its purpose, but neither is my house. It's a family home with no family in it anymore, not since my parents gifted it to me and then Lincoln moved out. Leaving only me and Sam. How sad.

Yup, Knox, you're exactly where you want to be in life at forty-three.

Yeah, right.

I read a blog recently that highlighted the top daily habits of successful entrepreneurs. One of them said entrepreneurs, like me, make time to unplug.

It's all lies. Who makes that shit up?

I certainly don't do that. If I do, then all I'm reminded of is exactly what I don't have in my life.

All the things I always wanted.

I wanted the loving wife, the two point four children, more even, more brothers and sisters for Lincoln. I wanted the mess and chaos. Fun, laughter, big family holidays, all of it. There was a time I think I wanted it with Olivia, Lincoln's mother. But it's not what she wanted. So she left me, left Lincoln, left us. And for that, I will never forgive her.

It was always Lincoln and me, and, of course, my parents who helped me raise Linc. I don't know what I would have done without their support. I will forever be grateful to them for picking up the broken pieces of my life when Olivia left us.

And now, I think I'm too old for the extensive family I always dreamed of having.

Newsflash, Knox. You need someone to share your life with and to have that family with in the first place, dumbass.

A soul mate, that's what I want. Something I believe in with epistemic certainty. I truly believe every one of us has a twin heart. Someone who gets you, who understands all your complexities, accepts you as you are, would walk through fire for you and be there, regardless.

I've never experienced that level of romantic connection before. But I crave it. Not that I would ever admit that to anyone because it makes me sound like a soppy asshole.

Both my high school friends, Shane and Corey, have it. I'm the odd man out, the only guy who gets invited to parties and never takes a partner.

Taking Tabby would give off the wrong vibes. Give her the wrong impression. She's already way too keen for my liking, but that spark, that *thing* that everyone speaks about, the connection, it's not there with her and me. It was never there with Olivia, either. I was too young to recognize that. I do now.

It's exactly like me and Tabby too—one-sided.

With Olivia, it was all me who put the effort in, and she gave nothing back. Tabby's the one to pursue, push, text, call, try to arrange meals out and dinner parties, and I do the bare minimum to keep her sweet.

I'm a fucking asshole. I'm calling Tabby to end things once and for all. It's been four months since we fucked, but she needs to be told it's over.

Love everlasting? What a joke. I think that ship sailed for me a very long time ago.

Well, I thought it had. I tilt my head again, shifting my focus to someone that has certainly made my life way more interesting this weekend. I'd take Eva to every wedding, party, and social gathering. I'd be the luckiest guy in the room. I'd shower her with gifts, nights out, nights in, everything. This I know for certain.

Why the hell does she have to be so young, my friend's daughter, *and* Lincoln's new fixation?

"If you keep staring, I might just give you an autograph," Eva grumbles, her morning voice a little scratchy.

Damn, she caught me.

"I'm not staring," I protest.

"Yes, you were." She yawns and her face scrunches up. She's beautiful. Cute too.

I roll over on my side to face her, keeping her lean legs secured firmly around my hips. She nuzzles into my chest.

A man could get used to this. I like it. A lot.

"Who knew? Knox Black is a cuddle fan, after all. Cuddlefest 5000."

I really am. But only with her.

Chuckling, I pull her in close, tickling her bare back with my fingertips.

"I slept like the dead," she mumbles. "This bed is so comfortable. I bet you paid a fortune for it. Did you get your mattress from the *mattresses for rich people* shop?" She rubs her itchy nose on my pec.

"You're funny," I say deadpan.

"I know. I'm hilarious."

"Someone's spicy this morning." I poke her side, making her flinch and squeal.

"Oh, don't do that." She squirms in my arms.

Basking in the warmth of each other, we lie there together, locked in comfortable silence.

Never one to spoil the mood, there's been something I've been desperate to find out. I take a chance while she's relaxed. "Can I ask you something, Eva?"

"Mm-hmm. Ask away." She rests her warm hand on my pec. She's always touching me.

"What happened between you and Ewan?" Her fingers twitch against my skin and her body automatically tenses.

That can't be good. Shit, I should have held my tongue.

Clearing her throat, she tilts her head up and looks me directly in the eye.

"You want to know why we're getting divorced? After the

lovely weekend we've spent together?" She stares hard. "Ewan doesn't deserve my time or energy anymore. He definitely doesn't deserve bursting my happy bubble."

Happy bubble.

"I'm sorry. I didn't mean to upset you. I shouldn't have asked. You don't have to answer."

She stares at me for a bit longer, then shuffles backward out of our embrace, but remains on her side as she pulls the covers up under her chin.

I wasn't expecting her to share her personal circumstances, but she does.

"Things changed when Ewan lost his job and could not find a new one. In fact, I'll rephrase that. He didn't try to find a new one because he was already alcohol dependent. He turned to alcohol. More than usual," she begins softly.

Well, this is news to me.

She continues. "I was too blind to see it before, but it was always there. A little undercurrent of needing to always be out drinking or having to drink before evening meals. Afterward too. His need to drink more than everyone else when we were on nights out is so obvious now. Before he lost his job, the after-work beer turned into three or four beers, then it became more. Nights out with the boys became more frequent. It spiraled out of control.

"Then our sex life became nonexistent. Alcohol became his new addiction. He replaced me and his boys with liquor."

"I'm sorry, Eva."

She shakes her head. "Ewan's drinking became more extreme as the months slowly dragged by. It was gradual. You know, like a roller coaster at the start of the uphill climb, slow, steady, fun to start with and then whoosh, it took hold of him and he became someone I no longer recognized and it no longer became fun through the triple loops and twists. Especially the aftermath of his drinking escapades. He changed. Became someone I no longer recognized. Unacceptable behavior became his default setting, crossing boundaries I still find incomprehensible.

"The part that annoys me the most is that he blamed me for making him turn to drink. Said it was my fault. I made him feel inadequate. 'Emasculated' was how he put it. Apparently, my successful dance school made him feel like he wasn't needed anymore. But his drinking started waaayyyyyy before then. He used that as an excuse."

Motherfucker.

Eva rolls over onto her back and stares straight ahead, eyeballing the ceiling.

Lying motionless, she recounts the sequence of events. "It was like the light went off in his eyes. A simple flick of a switch, and he stopped trying. My teenage sweetheart, the one I dated since I was at high school. The guy who swept me off my feet, whom I could never get enough of, the guy I thought was the love of my life, who treated me like a princess, turned into an egotistical, mean, self-centered, aggressive human being. Although to call him human would be an understatement. He became a zombie.

"His warm eyes turned cold along with his heart. Empty. Just like our marriage. Loveless. He gave up on us. He may have been there physically, but emotionally he left us. The only excitement he showed was first thing in the morning when he could head to the store to buy more alcohol. I knew he was sneakily drinking his purchases along the winding lane behind our house. I walked that lane many times and eventually one day, I found a bush where he was stashing all his empty spirit bottles. It made me sick to my stomach when I saw the quantity and extent of his secret."

I have so many questions but I let her tell her story.

She pushes her fingers into her forehead. "Then his alcohol dependency hit new levels, and I still don't fully understand what happened to us and to him. No matter how many times I suggested he seek help, he refused. Ewan stopped caring about us and himself. He drank his days away and completely gave up trying to have a career. The alcohol poisoned him from the inside out. He lost himself in it. Its venom ran through his veins. I stopped him from attending any of our family events, even Christmas. He couldn't be trusted not to embarrass me or make a fool of himself. As the days and weeks passed, he became vicious with his tongue. Mean to the boys. Hurtful when he played with them, being too rough. He maintained Hamish and Archie were too soft and needed to *man up*. What a prick. But I saw what he was doing. What Ewan deemed as playful toy fighting was, in fact, him being aggressive toward our children. The alcohol skewed his perspective on everything, including his strength, poisoning his soul and good nature. Hurting my boys, *his* boys, physically and mentally, overstepped the mark for me.

"Ewan wore me out. Ground me down. Being around him exhausted me, putting me on edge even having the simplest of conversations. It got to the point where I would make excuses to leave the house to get away from him. I couldn't handle any more of the name-calling. It was too hurtful. The way he lashed hateful words at my already broken heart, he ripped it open and my heart poured out sorrow and sadness, flooding every inch of my body. It was overwhelming, all-consuming, and threatened my own mental well-being. But I was hell-bent on not allowing him to do that to me."

Eva fails to detect my anger that's radiating off my skin. Christ, I might tear Ewan's fucking head off the next time I see him.

Oblivious, Eva's words keep flowing out. "The final nail in the coffin was the day I booked a doctor's appointment. It was my intervention of sorts. When the doctor looked Ewan dead in the eye and asked if he wanted his help to get sober, Ewan flat-out said, 'No, I don't have a drinking problem.' That's the day I knew I had to end our marriage. It would never be the same. I had to protect my boys. And in a way, I was grateful for that day. Ewan's words helped me finally see everything with vivid clarity. That one sentence told me everything I needed to know, that our marriage was not worth saving, that drinking was more important than our little family, our marriage, and he was in denial. He had a problem. And I did something I never thought I could. That same day I asked him to leave. And boy, did he put up a fight." She fake laughs, recalling the events.

"He was roaring throughout the house, scaring my poor kids half to death. The entire street heard him." She turns her head to me. "I'm surprised you don't know this already. No one can keep their mouths shut in Castleview."

"I honestly didn't know any of this, Eva."

She looks away again and starts fiddling with the cover between her fingers. "Well, anyway, I called his parents to come and take him away. Eventually he left, kicking and screaming profanities my way. The words he spat I will never forget. His deplorable tirade of next level verbal abuse will stay with me forever. I can't forgive him. He vowed I would regret what I was doing. Informed me I was making the wrong choice and I would beg him to take me back."

She stops to think for a moment, and I give her the space.

"But something peculiar happened. I didn't feel any pain when he left. Or heartbreak. I felt relieved." She raises her hands to the sky with elation, slapping them back on the bed again. "I changed the locks on the house. We were safe. For the first time in months, I felt like me and my boys could finally thrive again. I knew deep down Ewan's behavior while intoxicated was becoming more and more unacceptable as the weeks went on, and I wasn't sure what he would do next. Forget to pick the boys up from day care and school? Spend all our money on alcohol? Would he drive while under the influence with the boys in the car?" She groans. "I am glad I ended it before I got the chance to find out."

I'm fucking glad she did, too.

Her tone changes to a faint whisper. "When I closed the door on our marriage, I felt light. Calm. Like someone sprinkled solace across my shoulders and my worries floated away. My beautiful, cheerful boys were no longer exposed to Ewan's stumbling throughout the house, calling me names, aggressive outbursts, slurring his words, and saying inappropriate things to them. I could finally breathe again. In an instant, our home life changed."

Her voice becomes stronger with every word she speaks next. "And goddammit, if I have to hug my boys extra tight at night, shower them with kisses and love, explain that it's just us three now, and that we are going to be okay, I will do all of that and more to keep them safe and let them know I love them every single day of every single minute of their lives. I will fight for them."

Her chest heaves up and down at her lengthy recital. She turns back onto her side to face me again, tucking her hands prayer-style under her cheek against the pillow.

"But I'm heartbroken. For my boys. For never getting to know the man I know Ewan once was. Archie at least got a glimmer of him, but little Hamish will never get to see what a fine man his father once was. Funny, smart, handsome. He loved me. Once. I know he did because I felt it. In the beginning, his love was passionate and deep. Ewan always made me his priority.

"I keep wishing that one morning I will wake up to a text message from Ewan that isn't vulgar or gut-wrenching. That he'll stop calling me names, stop shooting small incomprehensible jabs and digs my way. A text that simply says, I'm getting help. That's all I hope for. Not for me. But for my boys. I don't love him anymore. Not romantically."

Automatically I reach out and pull her in close to me, hoping I can pour my feelings into her through my embrace.

My curiosity gets the better of me. "Have you received text messages from Ewan this weekend while you've been here?"

"Yeah. Dozens. It's like his signature thing now. I can't block him because, according to my lawyer, I have to keep the flow of communication open to arrange his visitation times. But it's hard not to read those text messages and not believe them."

"I don't know what he's saying in those text messages, Eva, but you can't let him get to you. You are an excellent mother. One I wished Lincoln had. You are a beautiful woman with a heart of gold. You're remarkable."

Soft sobs break free from Eva's chest.

"Hey, hey, Sunshine. I didn't mean to upset you." I tighten my supportive hug.

She whispers almost inaudibly, "Thank you for that. I feel like I failed, though. More than anything, I wanted us to be a tight family unit, but that was never meant to be. So me, Hamish, and Archie are a newly formed trio powerhouse. Or as me and my sisters would say, *omne trium perfectum*. It means everything that comes in threes is perfect. Archie loves when I say it. He reckons it makes us sound magical, like we are wizards and can achieve anything." She giggles faintly and wipes her tears away with the back of her hand.

"Omne trium perfectum. I like that. I've never heard of that before," I say, kissing the top of her head.

"It's Latin."

After pausing to give her time to recover from her heartbreaking story, I ask, "Are you okay, Eva?"

"Yeah, I will be. I'm mad though. Like inferno-burning, fury mad. I hate the building industry for taking a downturn in our area. I hate that Ewan was one of the hundred men who was laid off. I hate that he gave up and didn't apply for other jobs. I hate that losing his job shone a light on his increasing alcohol dependency. It's me I hate most of all, though. I hate myself for not doing anything about it sooner. Thinking it would stop or go away. That it would get better. But it didn't." She clenches her fist against my chest.

"None of this is your fault, Eva. Have you told your family all of this?" I hope she has.

She sucks in a deep inhale. "No! Please don't say anything. I haven't told them everything. Certainly not about the daily texts. Only a fraction of his drinking problems, too," she says in a trance-like state, lost in her thoughts.

This is a side of Eva I've never seen before. She's always incredibly strong, confident, and a blazing bundle of joy. But she's been dealing with this Ewan shit all by herself. I can't work out why she's protecting him.

"I don't want my family to hate Ewan," she blurts out. "He's the father of my children, after all."

Ah, that's why. Her boys.

She's nice. Too nice.

"Your mom or dad won't think any less of you if you tell them everything, Eva. You need to tell them about the texts. You can't keep putting up with this all by yourself. In fact, I'm pretty sure your lawyer is wrong. What Ewan is doing is harassment, and the police don't take that lightly. You need to file a police report. Enough is enough, Eva."

I'm mad as shit. No way is her lawyer correct.

"Did he ever hit you?" I growl.

Without missing a beat, she answers, "No. Never. But he used to throw things, and I found that terrifying. His aim was getting pretty good, but he never hit me physically."

That's more than I wanted to know.

Fucking Ewan, I hate that guy even more now. I knew there was something super fucking shady about that shithead.

Reassuringly, I find the words I hope she *really* hears. "Divorce doesn't define who you are. It's a lesson. Not a very nice one and one that rarely reveals itself straightaway. But it does eventually. Over time, you'll see. I know from my experience with my ex-wife, the reason she and I met was Lincoln. Lincoln was the reason. He's the best thing to have ever happened to me. When I was seventeen and bringing up a newborn baby by myself with only the help of my parents, I couldn't see it then, but he made me who I am today. He's taught me so much about myself, about others, and he's my proudest moment. And while his mother and I were never meant to be, Lincoln was. Your boys were meant to be. You didn't fail. You brought two incredible boys into this world. You and Ewan, in that moment, throughout those years together, the reason for your marriage was them. You can't change the past. You couldn't have predicted your divorce or stopped Ewan from drinking. It was his choice. Stop beating yourself up because ultimately you can't help someone who doesn't want to be helped."

Without warning, Eva gazes up at me with a full-on beaming smile, fiercely grabs my face, then plants a messy wet, smiling kiss against my lips.

"You are something else, Knox Black. Who are you? Are you some sort of karmic guru?" She weaves her fingers through my hair. "What you said was very sweet and kind. I've never looked at it like that before. You're right. Thank you," she whispers.

Please stay with me.

Eventually, I ask the question I don't want the answer to. "What time do you have to leave today?"

"Around lunchtime. My mom and dad have plans this afternoon. I need to call Eden and get her to come and pick me up as I got a taxi to the auction on Friday evening. I will ask her to meet me over on Castleclay Terrace, pick up my car from my house, and then pick up my boys from mom and dad's."

Christ, she's really serious about no one knowing she was here. Castleclay Terrace is about a mile from here.

I roll over to check the time. "I only have you for another three hours, then?" I want more.

"Yeah." Her dimples pinch deep as she tucks her plump lips into her mouth, her eyes full of...? What? I actually don't know. Sadness? Expectation? Hope?

Fuck if I know, but what I know is I want to see her again. I want to spend more time with this incredible woman who makes me feel things I haven't in a very long time, and who's woken up my deep desire for more. More laughter, more fun, more joy, more sex, 'cause it's as sinful as hell with her.

But she's never mentioned wanting anything further than this weekend. If this is all I get, then I'll make sure I make it memorable for her.

Imprinted in her brain, so she can't think about anything else but me.

Eva's whimpers grow louder as I drive into her hard, striking the exact spot that makes her orgasm fast and furious.

She arches her back as if taken over by the exorcist. Her body tells me everything I need to know. She's close.

"Ah, Knox, please," she begs.

I slide myself out and in, delivering punishing thrusts. I can't fucking get enough of her.

She tilts her hips, playing me at my own game as she takes me deeper and harder. I've been edging her now for the last twenty minutes, teasing her, then pulling out. Kissing her everywhere.

Then the ritual starts all over again.

I guide my cock all the way out, then slam myself back into her. My pulse speeds up, knowing we're about to fall over the edge and beyond together.

"Oh fuck, your pussy feels so fucking good, Sunshine," I growl.

The need to be closer to her makes me lift her legs over my shoulders. I lean down, meeting her eye to eye.

For a moment everything stops, like time doesn't exist 'cause all I see is her. This beautiful woman before me.

"What's happening, Knox?" Her turquoise eyes hold mine.

"The same damn thing that's been happening all fucking weekend, Sunshine. Fate." I punctuate every word with a deep thrust. "Timing. Destiny."

"Destiny," she hisses out loud, arching her neck backwards. "Yes, Knox."

Is she agreeing with me?

She blows my mind.

She clings on to me as I slam into her again and again.

The two opposing forces of us sound across the room, my low groans, her high whimpers.

Our mouths collide and our tongues slide over each other as our orgasms climb together and I can't fucking hold off anymore as the familiar sensation of warmth spreads into my cock.

I'm done teasing.

Undulating my hips in waves, being sure to grind my pelvic bone over her sensitive pierced clit, I drive myself deeper again, knocking all the air out of her lungs.

She suddenly holds her breath. And this is it.

This is when she tries desperately to hold on to that feeling before she detonates.

And she does. Clenching my sensitive cock. Shuddering.

She cries into my mouth and lets out a low moan. I join her. The charge between us reaches its capacity. Like liquid lightning, a flash of heat bolts through us and we come together. Hard.

My heart and balls beat in time with one another.

In this moment, no one can touch us.

It's perfect.

Panting against each other's lips, Eva gently kisses my mouth.

It's so intimate.

And yet contradictory.

It doesn't feel like just for two nights. It feels like she wants more.

"Don't move," she whispers. "Stay here for a bit longer." She continues torturing me with her kisses, moving her legs around my waist to keep me near.

We lay here for a while. Locked together. Neither of us willing to burst what she described as our *happy bubble.*

As if my orgasm cleared away the fog, making me see the brightest and clearest day I've ever seen in my life. I decide. Come hell or high water.

I want this woman.

"So?"

"So," I echo her word, watching her push her overnight bag over her shoulder at the end of my driveway.

She point blank refused to let me drive her home. She was insistent when she called her sister to pick her up over on Castleclay Terrace.

Living on the far parameters of town, you have to walk a fair bit to reach the next street of houses.

She's clearly hell-bent on no one ever finding out who she spent the weekend with.

Folding her arms across her body, she looks down and begins playing with the gravel beneath her black chunky boots.

And we're back to being awkward with one another. *Fucking epic.*

No longer wearing my dress shirt as daywear anymore, she's wearing her statement look of a long black floaty skirt, black chunky ankle-high boots, white vest top, and black leather jacket. The only thing she's missing today is one of her many Fedora hats she wears all the time and a stack of golden bracelets.

She looks effortless. Unique. She pulls off the whole boho chic thing really well, making her look younger than her years.

Shit. She's twenty-eight.

Her words replay in my head from Friday night.

I'll be twenty-nine soon, Knox. There's only fourteen years between us.

What the fuck am I thinking?

Come hell or high water. I want this woman.

I'm clearly fucking thinking with my dick; it's the only explanation for it.

"I guess I'll see you around, Knox Black." She refuses to make eye contact with me.

What the fuck?

After what we just did in my house together for the past two days? No fucking way does she get away with not looking at me.

"Look at me."

She inhales a deep breath before meeting my eyes. I take two steps toward her, but she holds up her hand. "Don't." I stop in my tracks.

Shit.

"Why?"

"Because. I... I, I don't know. But I had a lovely weekend and I think this is where it should end. We agreed. Just two nights." She turns her head away from me.

I hate those words. *Two nights.*

"I know." I don't fucking know or understand, but at the same time I do. "Give me your phone."

"Why?"

"I want to give you my number."

"But..."

"To organize dance lessons, Eva." *Yeah, right.*

Eva pulls her phone out of her pocket. Before she unlocks her phone, she stares at the screen. Shaking her head at her previewed texts, an agonizing frown furrows her brow.

"Ewan?"

She nods her head, then passes me the phone.

He's a fucking asshole.

I quickly type my number into her phone and pass it back.

"Text me, then I'll have yours." *Slick, Knox. Slick.*

She looks down at her screen. "You put a black heart emoji in as your name?" She grins.

Cheekily, I grin back when she looks back at me. Fuck it.

My phone vibrates in the back pocket of my jeans.

Eva: *Sunshine emoji*

"Clever." I save her cherished number, replacing her name with a sunshine emoji instead.

I turn my phone around and show her how I stored her number. "You have your own emoji name now, too."

She bobs her head up and down in acknowledgement. *Too much? Yeah, Knox. Too much.*

"I have to go," she says almost inaudibly.

Yup, definitely too much.

"Okay. Will you text me to let me know when I can have my first dance lesson? Will it be this week?" I'm too damn keen. I don't give a shit about the lessons. All I want to do is spend time with *her.*

"Yeah. I'll check where I slotted those in. But if it's not convenient for you..."

"I'll move things around." Shut up, Knox. You look desperate and she clearly isn't interested.

I'm a fool to think otherwise.

Fuck, this *does* feel awkward. Almost painful.

What a desperate old twat I must look. As if she would ever consider having anything more than this weekend with me.

I really, *really* like this woman before me, but I think she only sees that I'm good for one thing—a weekend fuck.

So I do the one thing I'm an expert at; I close down, walls up.

"I'll let you go." Without another word, I turn on my heel and leave, calling out to Sam to make his way back into the house. I hope he hears me because I don't want to turn back around and watch her leave through my gate.

I noisily stomp back up my long driveway and through my front door, slamming it behind me.

A magnetic pull draws me closer to the front window of my library and I can't help but watch as Eva stares back over her shoulder at the house and me as if she's embedding the memories of this weekend as a bookmark in her life.

'Cause that's all I seem to be. A bookmark, only a mere chapter in someone's life.

I'm never the whole story.

CHAPTER 8

Eva

Bang!

That's the sound of me coming back to reality.

I've been living in cloud cuckoo land all weekend at Knox's place.

Knox.

Wow, what a weekend.

I'm not usually an over-sharer, but I was giddy with excitement after I left Knox's home earlier today and it took everything within me to keep my lips sealed. I haven't told a soul who I was with, not sure I ever will. But I'm desperate to tell someone. Anyone. But I won't. I walked the mile or so down the road to meet my sister, Eden, where I arranged for her to pick me up so she wouldn't find out either.

The wonderful thing about Eden is she didn't push me to disclose who I had spent the weekend with. She knows when I am ready to tell her, I will.

Earlier, in her black Range Rover, she simply looked at me, smiled and resumed our normal conversations—babies, dancing, business, and random crap—as she drove me back to my home.

Before I picked up the boys from my parents' place, I ran about like a crazy woman, cleaning the house, ironing, tidying up the many toys from the back and front garden, then popped a roast dinner in the oven then zoomed over to my parents.

It's been several hours since I left Knox's mansion. I'm back to reality. Back with my boys in my little house.

But my reality is more of a nightmare and that's exactly what's staring me in the face right this very minute, asking me questions I don't think he deserves the answers to.

Ewan. Standing on my doorstep. Or is it *our* doorstep?

Our names are both on the mortgage papers, so I am guessing it's ours, for now. But there is not a chance in hell I am letting him through the front door.

We've been standing here for the last few minutes planning for the boys' school and day care pickup and drop-off times for this coming week. Then he asked me a question I knew he'd been desperate to ask me. "Where have you been all weekend?"

"It's none of your business, Ewan." I wrap my arms around myself.

"It is my fucking business, Eva. You are still my wife," he says, raising his voice, glaring at me with his dark, glazed eyes.

"Oh yeah? Well, if we're playing that game, *husband*, how is your girlfriend? Good? Satisfied? Happy? All the things I wasn't?" Narrowing my eyes, I tilt my head to the side.

"Don't do that."

"Do what?" I say, my voice laced with innocence.

"Turn this back on me."

Ewan has taken no responsibility for his actions throughout this entire breakup, and honestly, I'm too tired to fight anymore.

"Oh, Ewan. Please stop." I pinch my nose, clenching my eyes shut. "I can't keep doing this with you. Sign the divorce papers. Go back to Ruby. Live your life and let me live mine."

"No fucking way."

I snap my head back up. "No fucking way? Are you kidding me right now? It's because of you we are where we are. It's because of you my boys have to live between two homes. It's because of you my boys don't know what dad will show up. Will it be the one that loves them and walks on water for them or the one that hurts, name-calls, and belittles? Do us all a favor and for once do the decent thing because for the last twelve months you haven't made one right move. Just sign the papers. Set me free." I point my finger into his chest. "You are no longer my husband. No longer my Ewan. Standing before me is someone I no longer recognize. When was the last time you had a shower? Because you stink."

At lightning speed, he grabs my wrist and yanks me forward into his chest. I yelp at the unexpectedness of his action.

Unable to look at him, I clench my eyes shut.

Holding my breath, my heart plunges into darkness and suddenly I'm not feeling quite so brave.

I don't like liquor-fueled Ewan. He's petrifying.

Tightening his grip, Ewan snarls close to my lips. "Don't ever speak to me like that again. You are still fucking mine." I lose my footing as he pushes me aggressively out of his hold, having to grab on to the walls on either side of the vestibule to steady me.

His toxic breath reeks of booze and he smells like he hasn't washed in a week. Bile rises in my throat from fear, sadness, and disgust. Heaven knows what Ruby sees in him.

"I have to go," I say in a whispered voice, rubbing my wrist to relieve the dull throb.

On a backward step, I move away from him, being as subtle as I can to retreat slowly into the safety of my home.

Like an angry bull, eyes on me, head bowed, his chest heaves up and down with fury. Nostrils flared. I'm not sure what he'll do next.

He's getting worse. Braver. More aggressive. More everything and I don't like it.

Pushing for information, he asks, "Was it Lincoln Black you were with all weekend? Don't think I didn't see his car here on Friday night. You're a fucking slu—"

Finding my strength, I back into the house and firmly slam, then lock the door in Ewan's face before he calls me any more hate-filled words.

This doesn't stop him, though. He continues his tirade of insults, banging his fists against the closed door. Ranting his dislike at my staying out all weekend.

Staring at the door, I can't help but wonder what I did to deserve this.

Blood jets into my petrified heart, making it pound hard against my chest.

Offering solace, a little hand delicately takes mine. "He's angry, Mommy. I don't like Daddy shouting at you."

I crouch down. "I'm okay, Hamish." I cup my youngest son's face reassuringly, sweep his dark brown locks off his forehead, then give his nose a little bop.

Archie appears by my side. "I don't want him to pick me up from school this week." He shakes his bowed head. "He says not nice things about you. I don't like it."

I loop my arm around Archie's waist. "I know. I'm sorry, Archie."

Knox was right. I have to get a better lawyer. We can't continue like this.

Ewan slams his fists into the door with an almighty thunder, making all three of us jump.

"You're turning my boys against me. You're poisoning them, you bitch," he yells through the door.

He's doing a mighty fine job of that himself.

Desperately, I try to cover the boys' ears, one on each side of my face with my hands over their innocent ears.

"What's a bitch?" Hamish asks.

Epic fail.

"Oh, you can't say that, Hamish," Archie gasps. "That's a bad word. A very bad word."

"But Daddy said it," he says in his sweet voice.

Unable to make words, I remain quiet.

Holding them a couple minutes more, making sure I'm safe to move, I lean out of our three-way hug.

"Daddy's gone now," Archie says. "It's always better when he leaves. Like sunshine after the rain." He fiddles with my dangling gold earring. He's done that since he was a baby. "You're always like sunshine, Mommy. You shine brighter than the sun."

Knox called me Sunshine too.

"A pretty rainbow," Hamish cutely tweets. "I like rainbows."

"Yeah?" I can't hold my emotions in anymore as a couple of lonely tears escape and roll down my cheek. "I love you two boys. Do you know that? With all my heart. I love you both so much. I'm so sorry." I blink over and over, patting my cheeks dry.

My sweet boys.

"What you sorry for, Momma?" Hamish, asks, all wide-eyed and innocent.

Where to begin, baby boy. I have so many regrets.

"That you had to hear that. Daddy's behavior is not good at the moment. But he's not well. We have to remember what he used to be like. Sometimes we make choices in life, some good and some not so good. At the moment, Daddy isn't making very good choices. Remember, the choices we make affect other people."

"Like the cup filling story, Mom?" Archie smiles.

"Yes, Archie, exactly like the cup story. Fill someone's cup up with kindness, joy, and laughter, and what happens?"

"They feel happy." They both raise their hands and smile with glee.

"Yes! But what if we say not nice things and we fill them up with unkindness?"

"They feel blue and sad." They both downturn their mouths, making sad faces.

Finding my strength, I crack a smile. "Exactly. If I tell you I love you, Hamish, how do you feel?"

He giggles when I tickle his sides. "Hap-pee. My cup is full."

"Yay, we have one happy boy. And what about you Archie? If I tell you I love you and I'm so proud of you winning house captain at school this week, how does it make you feel?"

"Double happy."

"Wow, that's a lot of happiness. Annnnd what about if I told you we are having ice cream after dinner? How much happier would that make you?"

"Happy times a gazillion," Archie shouts into the air as Hamish claps his little chubby hands together, getting excited.

"Your cup must be overflowing, Archie." I gaze in awe at my ice-blond-haired boy.

"Did you go to Toni's and get my favorite ice cream?" Archie's striking blue eyes shine back in hope.

"Yes. Mud, with a hint of mushroom and broccoli, that's your favorite, isn't it?" I tease him.

He scrunches his face up. "Noooooo. Argh, yuck. Mom. You should know by now. It's strawberry." He rolls his eyes.

Hamish's dark eyes meet mine. "I like mushrooms." He flings himself into my arms, almost bowling me over.

I kiss his chubby cheeks. "I know you do, baby. And broccoli." He'd eat anything.

"I do, but me not a baby, Momma."

"I know you're not."

He is. He's my baby. As is Archie.

"Right, boys. Shall we serve up dinner? Want to help me set the table?" I ask Archie hopefully.

"Nope. I want to watch *Spiderman*."

"Me too, me too." Hamish wiggles in my arms as he shoots invisible spiderwebs from his wrists. "I put my Spiderman outfit on." He leaps out of my embrace, then dashes up the stairs to his bedroom.

They always have a knack for lifting my mood.

I'm left standing in the hallway by myself again. A gentle ding from my phone alerts me to yet another evening of abusive text messages ahead.

Deep joy.

I make a mental note. Tomorrow. Find a new lawyer.

"Morning. Is this Eva Wallace?"

"Yes," I answer the unknown female voice I've picked up a call from as I zoom about getting ready for school on yet another manic Monday morning.

"This is Veronica Evans. I'm a family lawyer specializing in divorce. Knox Black asked me to call you. I hope you don't mind, but he filled me in regarding the escalating harassing text messages you are receiving from your estranged husband and his reluctance to sign your divorce papers."

I stop picking up the morning towels and pajamas from the bathroom floor.

"Knox?"

"Yes."

"Asked you to call me?"

"Yes, Eva. Knox informed me you're a close family friend. He's very concerned about your ongoing safety."

Is he?

"Right."

"We have grounds to file a police report, but I require more information and I would love for you to meet me today if you're free."

I dump the laundry from my hands into the wash basket in the bathroom corner.

"I will make time," I state firmly.

"Excellent." I can hear her smile down the phone. "One thirty work?"

"Yes. Perfect."

"I look forward to seeing you then, Eva. We've moved. We are now situated at the new office complex off Morrison Way. You know the one?"

"Yes, I do."

"Great. We are the third junction on the left, off the roundabout. You can't miss us. Just look for the big sign that has my name on it." She sounds excited about her new office. "See you at one thirty this afternoon, Eva. Any friend of Knox is a friend of mine. We will look after you."

"Okay." I'm lost for words. "Thank you."

She says a cheerful bye and hangs up.

Removing my phone from my ear, I stare blankly at it.

Knox called a lawyer to help me.

Why would he do that?

Pay attention, Eva. *Family friend.* That's why, and that's all you are. Both Veronica and Knox said it themselves.

I don't want to ask my parents for financial help. I know Veronica's firm incredibly well and how much they charge an hour. Probably as much as Knox Black's fine cut bespoke tailored suits. Also known as fuck tons.

Newsflash. I don't have fuck tons at the moment.

I fan the neck of my vest top back and forth to cool me down as an overwhelming wave of heat flashes over my skin.

The last thing I want to do is sell my collectable

Campervan. I knew it was always going to be a possibility, but now it may be inevitable.

Oh well, let's see what Veronica has to say later. Then I'll have to work out my finances. Juggle a few things to pay for her.

Fuck divorce. This sucks.

I shake my head, bringing me back to the now and back to my Monday morning ritual. "Archie, why is there toothpaste on the mirror in my bedroom?" I shout from the top of the stairs.

Rushing into the boys' bedrooms next, I discover more toothpaste on the wall.

"Boys!"

"It was all Hamish's idea. He painted you a picture on the wall," Archie calls from the bottom of the stairs.

"Was not."

"Was too."

Placing my hands on my hips, I look at the sky as if the heavens above will help me. "Seriously? Enough now, Universe. Stop. No more."

I fling myself back onto Archie's bed and close my eyes.

Give me strength.

Or a vacation.

By myself.

In the Bahamas.

Or back to the safety of Knox's home.

Never. Going. To. Happen.

"I think we've covered everything, Eva. You need to file the police report today. Take your phone with you. That's your evidence. Do not delete a single text. I want you to inform them about last night's events, too. Ewan's physical aggression toward you is escalating. We have to put a stop to this *now*. You telling me today that you are scared, the fear you feel, and feeling threatened is more than enough for us to file a harassment warning. If he breaks that then it will be a harassment injunction we file. It stops today. No more." Veronica cuts an invisible line through the air. "If we do that, I'm certain we will force Ewan's hand to sign the papers. It normally works. Trust me, I have done this hundreds of times."

She slides her reading glasses up into her auburn hair. "My job is to keep you and your family safe. I will do everything in my power to keep a roof over your head. But you will have to buy Ewan out. Or you sell it and split the house profits. It's probably the cleanest path. And the path of least resistance for both of you. Foremost though, we need to get Ewan off your back, keep your boys secure, and ensure we get those divorce papers signed. I will contact Wilbert today to inform him I am taking over your case from here on out."

A giant weight I didn't know was holding me down unhinges itself from my shoulders, making me feel like a helium balloon.

Finally, someone is helping me. Finally, I feel like someone is fighting for me and my boys. I feel lighter. But...

Looking down, I twist my fingers in my lap. I don't want to ask the next question. "There may be a slight problem." I pinch an invisible inch between my fingers in the air. "I'm not sure I have the funds to afford you. How much am I looking at paying for all of this?"

"It's all covered. I owe Knox a favor," she states matter-of-factly as she stacks her notes into a neat pile on her desk.

"Excuse me?" I cough, flabbergasted.

"Whatever you need. Done. I'm here at your disposal. Fees? Covered." She smiles, flashing her white teeth. "Like I said. Knox helped me out a few years ago. I owe him one. This is my repayment. He asked. I said yes." She moves on, unaware of my astonishment. "Okay, great, it's all settled. Drop me an email later. Let me know how it goes with the police. I need to read over your current divorce papers. Make sure they are kosher and you are getting what you are entitled to and if everything goes to plan, I reckon in four to six months, legally, you'll be divorced."

Veronica is nothing but efficient. She stands from her desk.

Four to six months. That's a lot sooner than I expected. Although Ewan is a stubborn asshole.

I'm not convinced an injunction will change anything.

Sensing I'm dismissed, I stand from the black leather armchair, then grab my purse from the wooden oak floor. Everything about this place screams expensive.

It's all covered.

I'm getting the best lawyer in town. For free.

I feel weak at the knees.

Holy shit. No one does this kind of thing for me. I am never lucky and push every hour of every single day at the moment.

"I'm very grateful, Veronica." I feel a bubble of emotion in my throat. "Thank you for helping me." I reach out to shake her hand. But she walks around the desk and encases me in a warm hug.

"You are very welcome, Eva. You're not alone."

Pulling back, I cough, clearing my throat to cover the tears I feel swimming in my eyes, simultaneously nodding my head up and down quickly.

Sensing my *falling off a cliff* state, Veronica says, "I know. There's a lot going on. But I've got you. It's all going to be okay. I promise." She runs her hands up and down the tops of my arms and winks with a warm smile. "Email me later, okay?"

"Yeah." I step toward the door.

Before leaving, I turn around on my heel. "Thank you, Veronica."

She shoos me out the door with the back of hand. "Go on. Skedaddle before you get me started."

I step out into the hallway. For the first time in months, I sense freedom is on its way.

Knox Black. I owe you big-time.

Getting into my new car, I quickly pull out my phone from my purse and write a text.

Me: Thank you for organizing Veronica.

I hum to myself, considering. Do I put a kiss on the end of my text? Nope. Leave it.

I press send.

I'm not sure he'll reply, but I wait in my car, holding on to my phone, staring at it, as if waiting for him to jump through it.

Bubbles bounce across the screen, informing me he's replying.

Excitement threads my veins.

Knox: You're welcome.

Is that it? You're welcome?

Me: I am very grateful.
Knox: I know.

I quickly check my calendar.

Me: I have you booked in for dance lessons on Wednesday evening at 5:30 p.m. Does that suit you?
Knox: Forget the lessons. Thanks though.

Huh?

Me: What do you mean forget the lessons?
Knox: I changed my mind. I don't want them.

I fight hard not to scream out loud in the car. What the hell?

Me: You paid eighty thousand pounds to dance with me. You said that yourself.
Knox: Things change. It was for the hospital.

A wild, low roar leaves my clenched jaw.

My finger hovers over his name to call him. I quickly change my mind.

I furiously push the electronic start button on my sun-yellow Mercedes A-Class and open her up.

Things change. What a dickhead.

CHAPTER 9

Eva

"Eh, excuse me, miss. You can't go in there. Mr. Black is currently on a conference call."

On a mission, I hold up my hand to silence Knox's stuttering secretary. I leave a gust of air behind me as I stomp past at breakneck speed, then grab and twist the door handle before I fly through the door.

Alarmed at my disruptive entry, Knox jolts his head up from his laptop screen.

His mysterious eyes widen, then quickly narrow.

Slamming the door behind me without looking back, I drop my purse on the floor with a *thunk* by my feet, stand wide, and place my hands on my hips.

"Things change? What the hell does that mean, exactly?" I'm stark-raving mad.

"I'll have to call you back, boys." He hovers his finger over the end button on his desk phone.

"Okay. Problems?" a male voice asks through the speakerphone.

"Yeah, eighty-thousand-pound problems," Knox mutters darkly.

"Oh, yikes." Two different snickers sound from the phone.

"Good luck, man."

"Out this weekend though, yeah?" I think that's Corey, Knox's friend. And where there's Corey, there is Shane.

"Hell yeah. First time you've been out in months, big man." Yup, I was right.

"See you Saturday night, boys." Knox stares right at me as he presses the button to hang up his call.

Asshole.

"Conference call, my ass." I stand firm.

He leans back in his black leather chair, then casually rests his elbow on the arm.

Eyeing me suspiciously, painfully slow he brackets his pointer finger against his cheek, places his thumb under his chin, then cushions his middle finger against his lips.

With his other hand, he smooths his tie down over his shirt.

He's divine.

His black eyes impale me, reminding me of the way he looked at me this weekend as he buried himself deep inside me.

His fingers are a gentle nod at the things he did to me as he danced them across my skin. And those lips.

He's a fuckable devil in a suit.

I'm trembling. I'm totally out of my depth.

"Lock the door," he commands.

"Why?"

"Lock. The. Door."

Losing my cool, I do as instructed. Fumbling with the latch, I turn back to face his desk.

I muster all the self-confidence I can. "As I was asking. Things change? What has changed? Why don't you want the lessons?"

His strong features hold firm. "Why does it matter, Eva?"

"It doesn't matter." I struggle for an answer.

"So, why are you here?"

I sift through my jumbled thoughts because, well, now I don't know. His divinely well-cut suit is too distracting. Then there are his exotic features, and that tan, and don't get me started on what his finger is currently doing to his top lip. I know what those lips and fingers can do.

Stop it, stop it, stop it.

Biting my tongue to stop me from saying anything inappropriate, I don't answer.

"Well? I've clearly annoyed you to have you drive all the way up here to my hotel. Railroad my secretary. Fly through my office door like a woman on fire, then force me to end my important call."

"That was Corey and Shane. Hardly important," I snip back and pop a hip.

"Ah, but it was important. They want to set me up on a *date* on Saturday night."

Oh, that stings.

I jut my chin out with determination, trying to show him I'm not bothered. "Great. I'm sure you'll have a *super* time," I mutter through a tight smile.

"I'm sure I will," he says, a glint of humor in his eyes at our verbal combat.

"I bet she'll be all fake tits and ass. Only after your money and likes to be fucked in every orifice."

What the hell am I saying?

Current status: powered by bitch dust.

"Nailed it. That's exactly my type," he says deadpan, then waits for me to continue.

But I don't know what my next move is. I'm lost.

He leans forward, straightening his laptop in front of him. "Are we done here? Because in case you haven't noticed, I have a hotel resort to manage. Plus, I have a date with a woman who's waiting to be fucked in every orifice, apparently. So if you'll excuse me while I do my research to prepare for that, you can show yourself out." He taps on his keyboard.

Aw, screw this. I don't know what I was thinking of coming here.

Mad at myself, I turn around to unlock the door, cursing and muttering to myself through clenched teeth.

On a rampage, I spin back around to face him again. I'm not letting him get away with this. I'm as furious as a trapped wasp in a jam jar.

"You know what, Knox. You said I lit up your soul. I made you feel like a fucking blazing inferno burns inside of you when I'm around. Isn't that what you said? You called me Sunshine. You told me you wanted me and wanted to spend time with me." I'm on a roll now. "That you dreamed about me." I lay my hand over my chest. "That you've been waiting."

I can't stop my bullet train of words. "I did things with you, in your bed this past weekend, that I have never done with anyone, ever. You took me back to your house. You shared a part of you with me. And I shared things with you about my life I have never shared with anyone. Not even my sisters."

I pace back and forth. "And then you organize a new lawyer for me that is *way* out of my price range, but you've covered it all. For me. Because you're worried about my ongoing safety. If I told you what Ewan did to me last night, you wouldn't want to be paying for any of it. Because he's a prize prick. I'm not sure who I am anymore or what my life has become. It feels like such a mess." I continue to stomp back and forth, and my heart picks up pace. "Did you know I've to go to the police station after I leave here and file a police report? A *police* report. Against my husband. Well, ex-husband. For harassment." I shake my head furiously as I push my hands through my hair I took ages straightening earlier.

"Then there's you. You reminded me of who I am again. I felt happy. You made me feel sexy. I had the best weekend of my life. And for two utterly hotter than the devil days I spent with you, I felt special. You made me believe I was worth more than the way I have been treated in the last year. But you are so confusing. You want me? But you don't now? Was it really just for this weekend? Because it sure felt like you wanted more." I finally look at him. I hadn't noticed him moving, but he's now standing on the other side of his desk, his hands clenched by his sides.

"That's what you wanted, Eva. What we agreed."

"Did we though?" Running my hand over my tight brow, I'm confused.

"Eva, as you stood in my driveway, you put your hands up to stop me from touching you. You had your sister pick you up over a mile away from my house. You set the boundaries." His voice is harsh and raw.

He's right. I did.

I lower my defenses. "But you didn't have to cancel our dance lessons. I thought you were still keen. Do you not want to spend time with me?"

I sound desperate.

"You're the one that pushed me away. You and I both know Lincoln likes you. I'm your father's friend. But I asked you by the pool if we needed rules and you didn't answer me. I told you I like you, that I want you." His eyes fill with pain. "I liked having you in my house on the weekend. Watching you cook in my kitchen, swimming in my pool, watching television with me, wearing my shirts. Talking about cars. I loved it all. I've never felt so complete." He tugs the back of his neck. "For fuck's sake, Eva, forget I said all that." His voice dies away as he turns away from me to look out the window at the ocean waves below.

He loved it all.

Complete.

My heart swoons. "Do you want to see me again?" I ask hopefully.

"Forget it. It doesn't matter. Just go." With his back still to me, he pushes his hands into the pockets of his dress pants.

"Of course it matters if it's what you want."

In business, he's ruthless. He gets what he wants. But he's protecting himself and his heart.

All that therapy he paid for was a waste of money. I've figured him out in a few days.

He looks back over his shoulder. "And what about you? What do you want? You're not even divorced yet. You have two young sons. There's your dad, Lincoln. You were adamant we were simply a two-night thing. You should be with someone the same age as you. Less complicated." His shoulders drop in defeat.

He's oblivious to how much I want him. Maybe I didn't realize how much either until right this very minute.

Who am I kidding?

I've wanted Knox since, oh, now I'm not so sure. For as long as I've been available. Maybe sooner. Because Ewan stopped paying me any kind of attention long before our breakup.

I've always felt this magical and appealing pull to Knox. He sucks all the air out of my lungs into his. He consumes me.

He's always *there*. On the fringes.

Entrancing me.

Changing my tone, I confess, "I'm not interested in anyone else. 'Cause you see, I've liked this one guy for a while now. Longer than I've allowed myself to admit."

Knox slowly turns back around, then leans against his desk. I've got his attention.

"He's super smart. Handsome. Phenomenal in the bedroom."

His eyebrows hitch upward in surprise.

"He's funnier than he realizes. He has a hard shell but a beautiful soft heart. He's kind. He's always watching me. I know he's liked me for a while too because I feel it as well as this indescribable connection to him this past weekend that I have never felt with anyone else before." I wiggle my way toward him.

He removes his hands from his pockets, then clenches the edge of his desk.

"It's thrown me for a loop. Perplexing. Complicated. But oh, so beautiful and thrilling."

Continuing my slow pace, he spreads his legs wide, welcoming me.

"He showed me a side of him no one else gets to see. He's pretty wonderful. He also has a secret smile meant only for me."

My confidence grows with every beat of my heart. "And then he has a freaking ace car collection that I just happen to like. He does too. But I know he *likes* me more because he even offered to take me out in the *rain* in his ten-million-pound car."

"That guy's a fool." He struggles to hide his amusement.

Chest to chest, I finally reach him. "Total idiot. A savage."

"Tell me more about this guy," he urges me.

"Well, he wears the sexiest of suits that do things to my lady bits."

He splutters, "Lady bits?"

I nod my head suggestively, flirting with my eyes and I say coyly, "Yes. Lady bits. And my whole body seems to come alive when I'm around him. It's not something I can control." I wrap his navy silk tie around my fist, pulling him to me.

His Adam's apple bobs up, then down. I know I've got him. Pressing myself against his rock-hard chest, I whisper in his ear, "When he calls me Sunshine, my nipples get so hard for him."

He makes a rough, hungry sound from the back of his throat.

Teasing his earlobe between my teeth, I show him my hand. "Can you feel how hard they are through my blouse, Knox?"

He slides his large hand down the soft curves of my ass. His chest rumbles as he explores.

Enjoying what I do to him, I unleash my sex kitten I didn't even know I had within me. "The way he sucked my nipples this weekend made me... wet. And when he played with my clit ring, I've never come so hard."

Knox pulls me into his pelvis, rubbing me against him, showing me what I do to him. "Sunshine," he wisps against my ear.

Pushing him to admit he wants me, I go in for the kill. "His delicious cock was big and so fucking hard for me all weekend. I loved it when he filled me up over and over and over again. He made me feel so fucking good. My tight, hot pussy loved every single... hot... minute. I'm wet right now just thinking about him," I hiss. "My panties are soaked."

His resistance to me dissolves like effervescence.

With firm hands, he cradles my face. "I can't stop thinking about you. You drive me fucking crazy." His desire-filled eyes bounce between mine. "I don't want you just for the weekend. I want more, Eva."

I knew it.

"I do too." My pulse quickens.

It's the invitation he's been waiting for. Leaping into action, he claims me with his ravenous lips.

Our tongues touch each other with reckless abandon. Immersing myself into him, I can't stop the feeling of relief washing over me.

All I want to do is feel good again. To be seen, heard, appreciated, and loved. Nope. Not love. *Smack that thought right of your head, Eva.* Lusted after. To fool around. I've never done the whole friends with benefits thing before.

It sounds like fun.

Doing a happy dance, my heart skips with joy.

Kissing more slowly now, I quickly say, "Knox, as much as I want to continue kissing you, because I've discovered it's my new favorite thing in the world to do, and I would love you to take me on your desk right now, I have to pick up Archie from school, then I have to go file a police report at the station."

His kisses become feathered touches as he cups my face, lingering kisses over my temple and into my hair.

"Family first. Always," he says firmly before leaning his forehead against mine.

We kiss for a few more moments. His kisses are always so consuming. It's easy to get lost in him.

He pulls away. "I have to ask you though; what the fuck do you have on, Sunshine?"

That was not what I was expecting him to ask.

I spin around, showcasing my professional outfit. "What, do you not like my secretary look?"

"It doesn't suit you. I prefer your own unique style. *That...*" He waves a pointer finger up and down in the air, referencing my outfit. "...is not your thing. Although I do like the heels." He hitches a brow.

I'm extremely uncomfortable with what I have on. He's right. It's not me at all.

"I've been to see Veronica. I went for the classic black pencil skirt and blush silk blouse. Professional. Businesslike." I wiggle my hips, smoothing the clothing over my body, wobbling slightly in my black heels. I hate high heels. Give me flat biker boots any day of the week.

Interestingly, he doesn't like this look, but this is how Tabitha dresses all the time. Even when shopping on her days off. I know because Beth talks about her a lot. Being on the Castleview Business Circle together, their paths cross often.

Beth has always maintained Tabitha needs a serious good dicking to help her loosen up.

Tabitha is a bit of a mystery to me. Older, we move in different circles. She's seriously stern and cold. Rigid. Almost rude, in fact, and frigid. I imagine sex with her would be carried out with military precision. Although I could have her completely wrong because Knox fucks like Satan on fire.

Eurgh.

My inner jealous bitch scrapes a finger along the pit of my stomach, making me shudder at the thought of Knox and Tabitha together.

I bet no one would ever place Knox and me together, either.

Who would have thought him, of all people, Mr. Billionaire in a suit, would like me. An ordinary run-of-the-mill, five-foot-ten dance instructor who is barely getting by in life, with two kids, soon to be divorced, and has a love for offbeat bohemian clothes.

It blows my crazy little mind somewhat that he wants me for *more.*

Looking down at my outfit, I say, "You're not into the secretary look. Got it." Realizing I've never been in his office before, I look around the huge, modern space. "The view from up here is spectacular." I gasp at the high cliffs leading down to the pewter sea.

"It is." But he's not looking out the window. He's looking at me. "Come." He holds his hand out for me to take. Pulling me toward him, he nuzzles into my neck. "When can I see you again?"

"Wednesday after dance lessons with you is my next free night. That's if you are still having them." I look at him hopefully and he nods his head.

"I'll be there, Sunshine." He goes back to kissing my neck, leaving a blazing ribbon of heat across my skin.

"Ella is looking after the boys for me in the evening. I can ask her to look after them for longer. She won't mind." Wednesday seems like a lifetime away.

He needs to stop kissing my neck or little Archie will be left standing at the school gates.

"That's too long, but it will have to do, for now." His voice is heavy with disappointment.

I shoot my shot. "If I asked you to cancel your date on Saturday night, would you?" I don't want him to go out with another woman.

He stands tall and studies my face. "There is no date. I was winding you up. Although I was looking forward to fucking my imaginary date in every orifice."

I snort at my in-the-heat-of-the-moment comment. He squeezes my ass.

"You are something else, Eva." He shakes his head in surprise.

I change direction. "What is *more*? This thing, me and you?"

He smiles easily. "I don't know yet. What I know is I want to see you. More time. More of everything."

"Exclusive?"

"Just you, Sunshine."

"Okay. Just checking. Friends with benefits?"

"It's *more* than that, don't you think?"

I'm too surprised to do more than nod.

"But our secret, Eva. For now."

I do not know how we plan on telling my father and Lincoln, *if* we ever do, because even the thought of it makes my chest tighten.

Without realizing, I've placed my hand on my heart.

"What's that?" Knox eyes my bruised wrist.

I quickly cover it with my other hand and look away. "Ewan," I say in my stage voice. "Last night. He asked me where I had been all weekend. I wouldn't tell him."

With his pointer finger under my chin, he turns my face to look at him, his expression now thunderous. "Pick up Archie. Drop him off at your parents. I know Hamish goes there today.

Go straight to the police station. I will meet you there. It stops. Today, Eva. That bastard will not lay another finger on you ever again."

"You don't have to come with me." And how does he know Hamish goes to Mom and Dad's on a Monday?

"I want to. I am. Sergeant Taylor is a good friend of mine."

I'm shocked by the depths of his concern for me.

"Plus, I get to see you again today." He winks suggestively, trying to lighten the mood.

"Okay. I need to go." I check the time on my wristwatch. "I'll meet you at the station in half an hour. Give me time to buffer my parents. I don't want to tell them what I am doing. Not Yet."

As if it's the most natural thing in the world, I push up on my tiptoes and steal a quick goodbye kiss. "Thank you."

"Eva, I want to help you. You're not doing this alone."

Taking my hand, he walks me to the door. "Just to clarify, Sunshine. I make you happy? I'm phenomenal in the bedroom? *And* you had the best weekend of your life?"

A rush of color flushes my cheeks. "Yeah, all true. But it was also the worst." I hesitate.

His questioning narrowed eyes can't hide his confusion.

I put him out of his misery. "Leaving you was the worst part of my weekend." I wished I'd had the ladyballs to tell him that yesterday.

His shoulders grow broader with pride. "Good. Glad I checked." He grins. "You're in a lot of trouble and owe me big time. I now have to come up with a reason for your uninvited barge in. My secretary probably does not know what hit her today. She's of retirement age. You could have given her a heart attack."

Oh, Lord. My mom knows Mrs. Kinnear. "Sorry." My toes curl in my shoes.

"I was maybe too hasty with my choice of nickname for you. Westie may be a more suitable choice."

"Westie?" I tuck a lock of hair behind my ear.

"West Highland Terrier? Little fluffy dog? Looks cute, but fuck me, do they have some sass and their yapping is brutal."

Oh, I like teasing Knox. He's funny.

"Any more of that, and it will be another week before I can fit you in for dance lessons," I drawl. I'm not at all serious. If I could, I'd make plans to see him tonight. I scoop my purse up off the floor.

Unlocking the door, he drops my hand as he swings his office door open wide to discover Lincoln on the other side of it, hand mid-knock.

Oh boy.

Lincoln smiles at me with sparkling eyes. "Ah, Eva, it's lovely to see you. Was my dad filling you in on his idea for our joint venture?" He puts his arms above his head as if he's a ballerina.

Lincoln's default setting is continually set to festive. Such a jovial guy. He doesn't care what anyone thinks about him and was always known as the class clown in his year at school.

Chin up, chest out, fighting desperately to hide my confusion, I summon my inner businesswoman to make an appearance.

"Um, eh..." Mission outcome: fail.

Thankfully, Knox takes over. "Yes. Eva is on board. I need to go over the specifics with her again later this week. We also need the approval from her sisters, but I'm sure they will be more than satisfied with our proposal."

What is he talking about? I haven't got the foggiest. I remain tight-lipped.

"Excellent." Lincoln beams.

"Great." Unable to make eye contact with Lincoln, I bow my head down and make for the lobby. "I have to go. Thanks for, um, a great meeting." I turn slightly to wave back at Knox.

Unblinking, he watches me squirm.

"Eh, Eva," Lincoln addresses me, stopping me in my tracks.

Bugger, bugger, bugger. Not quick enough.

"A few of us are going out on Saturday night. The Vault, then the new wine bar, The Basement. Would you and your sisters be up for it? Maybe Toni and Beth too?"

Eyes wide, Knox folds his arms across his body and stands wide as he waits for my response.

I stall. "Um, Saturday? Hmm, I'm not sure."

"Ask your mom and dad to take the boys, Eva. I know how much your dad loves getting his tractors and quad bikes out for the boys," Knox says, unshaken.

Perplexed at his response, I say, "Oh, um. Well, they had them last weekend. I can't ask them again."

Knox wiggles his eyebrows. "You sure? I'm going out on Saturday night with my friends. To the Vault. Maybe even The Basement." My devil in a suit is playing with me.

"Yeah, right, as if she'd dance with you, old man." Lincoln laughs, patting his dad on the back.

Knox's shoulders droop. It's slight, but I catch it.

Shoulders back with confidence, I say, "You're forgetting your dad has dance lessons booked with me. They also say you're only as old as you feel. If he's dancing with me, I'm knocking several years off his age. After I'm finished with him, he'll have every woman of all ages in this town queuing up to dance with him. You wait and see. You know as well as I do your father is a bit of a legend in this town. You have some major competition, young man."

I sneak a glance at Knox. I spot him wearing an enigmatic smile as Lincoln stands beside him, open-mouthed.

Before Lincoln has the chance to reply, I sashay out of the office, swinging my hips as I tip-tap on my heels down the shiny black and white marble lobby.

"Tabby would go apeshit if she heard Eva say that. Can we swap places? Can I do the dance lessons instead of you? Eva looks sexy as hell in that wiggle skirt she's got on today," I hear Lincoln say to his dad. Moving further down the corridor, I miss Knox's response.

I couldn't give two hoots what Tabitha has to say. Because he's not with her. He's with me. Exclusive.

I do a little internal squee.

Oh, this could be fun.

"See you on Wednesday for dance lessons, Knox, and I'll see you Saturday night, Lincoln," I shout back in their direction.

Looks like I'm going out on Saturday night then.

I like this feeling.

CHAPTER 10

Knox

Foot to floor, I test my Pɪ McLaren, or Raven as I now call her following Eva's naming ceremony.

On a mission to get to my first kizomba dance lesson with Eva tonight, I push Raven around the tight corners of the quiet, winding countryside cliff roads from my hotel down into Castleview Cove.

Deep winter is flirting along the edges of November. It's almost here. It's a stunning time of the year in Castleview; dark, bitter cold, and the sparkling frost that sets in is a gentle welcome to the snow that's about to make its appearance come December and January.

My Mediterranean heritage draws me to summer sun, but of all the seasons, there is something truly special about wintertime in Scotland.

Day-trippers, golfers, vacationists, and locals alike all describe Castleview Cove as magical. It is, and once the glistening frost makes itself at home, it looks and feels even more so.

It's a time when everyone starts layering up and huddling together to seal in and capture the warmth.

My resort is quieter at this time of the year, which pleases me no end, because much like every winter, it's the time when we remodel and upgrade sections of the hotel and spa.

It's all part of our strategy to evolve and improve our guest experience while maintaining our gold five-star rating. It seems to be working so far as we're fully booked from next February onward again.

My father and his father, my grandfather, laid the foundations on our exclusive hotel and spa, and now this is mine and Lincoln's time to build upon and create something truly special.

We are on a mission. We have a goal, a six-star rating. There are only a handful in the world and none in Scotland. We decided we are going to be the first.

Having Lincoln by my side, I know we can do it. He's driven, smart, and he's not afraid to take risks.

That's my boy.

My inner gremlin pokes my sides. I'm going to have to tell Lincoln soon about Eva and me. I'll discuss that with Eva first and she can dictate how we broach that dilemma. She's in control, plus she also has her own sons to consider.

It's been two days since I've seen her. Two painful, long days. Man, have they dragged.

It took every sheer bit of willpower within me not to kiss Eva right there in the parking lot of the police station before she jumped into her canary-yellow car and drove away.

I made a promise to myself not to act too keen, scare her off, or stifle her, but we've been texting back and forth several times a day and I can't get enough of our textual foreplay.

Never one for virtual relationships, now that I have Eva at my fingertips, my phone has been firmly glued to my hand. Checking it every two minutes, waiting for a text, replying straightaway, distracted in meetings. I'm beginning to understand the obsession—to phones and to her.

She makes me feel like a giddy schoolboy. It's a foreign feeling that's new to me.

As if the lights have been switched on again in my life, this *thing* between us, whatever it is, excites me; it feels good, great even.

But it scares me.

More than I care to admit.

I gave myself to Olivia and in the end, it caused cataclysmic heartbreak for me, more for Lincoln than for me. Pain for the absence of a mother in his life.

Thoughts of her have faded to a splintered memory now. It took me a very long time to be able to say her name without it causing somber thoughts.

Letting Eva into my life, both physically *and* emotionally, I'm not prepared.

Eva probably isn't either. Cutting emotional cords with someone you've been with for years isn't easy.

Ewan is finding it hard to let her go, too. That's why he's playing up.

Trust me, I know.

Many years ago, I found it very difficult to let go, and then I couldn't let anyone into my life again. Even now, I still struggle and have reservations.

Following our short three-month marriage, Olivia left, severing all connections to me and Lincoln. She sliced a knife through those ties and never looked back.

Me, on the other hand, I held on to her, emotionally, for longer than necessary.

There were no birthday or Christmas cards. It was as if Lincoln didn't exist to her.

It fucking destroyed me. Made my heart ache for my motherless baby boy.

Lying awake in bed during the nights, I beat myself about it way too much; she fucked us both over and I was a stupid prick for not seeing it sooner.

One of the positives to come from it all; I discovered who my friends were during my time of uncertainty.

My high school friends, Corey and Shane, stood by me and never faltered. Through thick and thin, they were always there for me. Even when they went off to university and medical school, they stayed in touch and visited me as soon as they were home between semesters.

Innocent, wet behind the ears, and still a teenager, I felt like a complete failure before my own life had even begun. It fucking killed me inside. But I grew up fast. It wasn't just me to consider anymore because I had a little person to look after.

While my friends gained their degrees at university, I earned mine at the University of Life.

Juggling a baby, learning the hotel business from my father, as well as navigating being a dad *and* a mother. All the while studying for my hospitality management degree via distance learning.

My long days were consumed with a multitude of weaning, potty training, profit-and-loss sheets, marketing strategy, learning all the roles of each employee in the hotel, and doing them, too. Hospital corners? Nailed those. Towel origami? I'm your man. It was all part of my father's plan—learn the business top to bottom.

Every night I went to bed exhausted, but I lived every day to the fullest and to the best of my ability for my boy.

Over time and with age came enlightenment.

In my twenties, I realized I had no control over Olivia's actions and the decision she made to follow the path she felt called to walk along.

She was chaotic. Obscenely bodacious. She was flamboyant, impulsive, and energetic. It's what drew me to her.

She was everything I wasn't. She was exciting at first. But selfish.

It took me a while, combined with hours of therapy, to figure out that Olivia and I were never a good fit. Not even a smidge.

Olivia wanted to travel, see the world, and explore. Experience life, backpacking and winging every day, never sure of where the next penny or bed would come from.

She sure as hell never wanted to be tied down with a baby.

Our little oopsie in the back of my dad's car inside his garage when we turned seventeen changed the course of both of our lives. Forever.

I always knew I wanted to take over the family business. Go to university. Earn my degree. Settle down with the love of my life and one day have a family. Exactly like my father did.

My father is an incredible man. He and my mother helped me raise Lincoln. They both love him like he's their own. They never judged me or chastised. A parental coax here and there and a slither of advice when I needed it was everything I required. To this day, I am grateful for their love and support.

My mother and father are an inspiration to me.

One summer vacation in Athens, my father fell madly in love with my mom. She's his everything, from sun up to sun down and vice versa. He moved mountains for her and him to be together.

Eventually, she moved to Scotland. My father maintains she teased him, made him work that bit harder to prove his love for her. But we all know the truth; she loved him as much back then as she does now.

My grandfather, her father, was against her leaving Greece. But she stood in her power, followed her heart. She changed her life, forged her own path, and moved to Scotland to be with my dad.

Forty-eight years on, she still complains about the freezing temperatures.

Those were my goals, too. I wanted what my parents had. I still do. It's what bothers me most days.

If I could simply let my guard down. Find my twin soul.

Olivia described Lincoln and me as a burden. That word of hers, *burden*, I've committed to memory, forever.

It hurts knowing me and Lincoln were not a strong enough reason for Olivia to stay in Castleview Cove. She couldn't be tied down. Didn't want to be. Her desire to live a nomadic life was much too strong, so she left me holding the baby. Literally.

I've still, to this day, never wrapped my head around why her maternal instincts never kicked in. Especially when I see Eva with her two boys and Corey and Shane's wives with their children. None of it makes sense to me.

As soon as Lincoln popped out into the world, I instantly fell in love with him. It's a feeling I can't even explain.

The warmth in my heart. A whoosh of emotion.

I felt this overwhelming feeling to protect him with all that I was.

Olivia left me to protect him alone.

And I did.

I made sacrifices.

I did the best I could.

A few years later, after she left, I had a couple of relationships. I was always the careful father; to reduce Lincoln's confusion, I didn't let anyone into our lives who had no intention of sticking around.

None of them did.

No one ever rocked my world.

It never felt right.

Then casual hookups became my thing. Always when my mom took care of Lincoln. I would never do it around him. But I was never the long-term plan for anyone. Always the rebound guy or the guy to fuck with until their forever came along.

'Cause who the hell wanted a guy in his twenties with a toddler?

I sure hope I'm not Eva's rebound. Or that I'm repeating the same cycle again because I suddenly feel like it's my time now. With her.

Nonetheless Eva hasn't been separated from Ewan all that long.

It's possibly too soon.

Not for me. But for her.

I'm ready. I have been for a while.

Wishing and hoping, two of my strongest desires. I believe anything is possible. I wished for Eva to be mine and hoped she would be.

It happened.

Now it's time to make my own destiny. Like my mother and father did.

Challenges have never daunted me, but I have yet to devise a plan on how we tell our loved ones without hurting them.

Like a strategic game of chess, each move we make will have to be tactical, considered with a massive dollop of patience, or its checkmate for us before we even begin.

I for one don't want that to happen.

Lost in my rambled thoughts, I continue to carve my way around the sweeping road. My tires bite harder into the tarmac as I throw my black beauty into the tight corners.

I haven't been able to concentrate for days. Eva has consumed all my thoughts.

Some not-so-great ones too.

That poor girl.

She's been through the mill with Ewan.

I sat by her side in the police interview room as she ran through the text messages Ewan has been sending her.

Sometimes up to twenty times a day. It overwhelmed her with emotion as she explained in vivid detail his escalating aggression. And don't get me started on the name-calling.

The yelling, the insults, and his anger toward her. It's all getting out of hand.

If Ewan is trying to break her, he's doing a good fucking job.

She's been having nightmares, is unable to sleep, and feels terrorized in her own home.

And the worst part. She's scared. Scared to speak to him. Anxious when he drops the boys off. Stressed to the point of developing a skin rash at the base of her hairline on her neck. Something I noticed this weekend but said nothing.

The poor girl is suffering mentally and physically.

After hearing all of Eva's evidence, I was explicit with Sergeant Taylor; proceed with caution, but protect Eva and her boys. Luckily, he's a good friend of mine and knows me as a *family friend* of the Wallace's. I asked him to keep mum on the whole situation. If it remains a secret in Castleview for longer than two days, it will be a world record.

Eva was informed how serious gaslighting was. It's a very serious offense, and they explained at length how they would proceed. First, they would pay Ewan a visit that very night.

I'd never heard of the term before, but apparently, it's a term used when a manipulator tries to confuse someone's perception or manipulate reality.

Sergeant Taylor explained it all to us.

And Ewan sure knows how to take gaslighting to a new level. Telling Eva she's the problem. That she's turning the boys against him and she's the one who turned him to drink.

He's baffled her with words. Mind-bending manipulation at the highest level.

And then there's the aggression. It's escalating.

He grabbed her, leaving his mark on her on Sunday night. I saw those bruises.

My blood boils like a burning inferno in my veins. He's a bastard.

A bastard I'm not sure I'll be able to control my anger around, but I have to stay calm. Be her rock. I want to be.

I want to be everything he's not.

For her.

In addition, per Scots law, Ewan has had a harassment warning filed against him. Something he has had to sign to ensure he understands the severity of his actions.

If Ewan breaks the agreement, the next step is a restraining order or an injunction.

It's a strategic process they have to follow, but the police advised Eva to make sure everything is catalogued legally.

An injunction isn't something Eva wants to pursue, as she doesn't want Ewan blaming her for taking the boys away from him.

She's torn between doing what *is* right and what *feels* right as her boys are at an impressionable age and are fully aware of what's going on. She even made reference to Ewan calling her names in front of Archie. That poor wee mite told Eva he doesn't want Ewan picking him up from school anymore. He's frightened too.

If the same thing had happened to Lincoln when he was younger, I would do anything and everything to protect him. I did.

After hearing Eva read some of Ewan's truly deplorable text messages out loud, I didn't think I could dislike that guy anymore. Junk punching him with a steel glove doesn't feel like enough of a punishment.

My grip tightens around my steering wheel.

Check me out, being all protective and shit with Eva and her boys.

Her boys feel like my responsibility now too.

Her commitments keep us apart in the evenings. Something

she mentioned in a text message today. She said we needed to navigate that together and work out when we can see each other around her boys' schedules and her teaching classes.

That was the one and only good thing about Tabby. No responsibilities and at my beck and call. When I called, she came running. Too easily.

What a schmuck I am. However, I did always make it clear to Tabby that I wasn't interested in anything long term and that I wasn't looking for a serious relationship. But one month led to two, then three, and before we knew it, three years crept up on us in a flash. Three boring-as-fuck years. Sex with Tabitha was always mediocre. Mundane, I suppose. I don't know what the hell I was thinking.

Actually, I know. Easy lay. On tap. Nice legs.

However, the last time we hooked up, four months ago now, I struggled to get hard for her. It was fucking embarrassing.

Since then I've ghosted her. Dodging run-ins if I spot her in the street. Sitting on the other side of the table in Castleview Business Circle meetings. Not replying to texts. Avoiding eye contact at all costs.

I'll say it again. I'm a schmuck.

Although I can pinpoint exactly when I lost interest. It was as soon as Charlie, Eva's father, informed me Eva was getting a divorce.

It was unexpected news. News I relished in. Which was awful of me too, bathing in someone's misery. But I fucking knew she was unhappy. I knew it was only a matter of time before she realized.

And now, well, now she's mine. In private. Our secret.

Despite that, I'll take what she's offering.

She feels like mine. Like this could be *it*.

I run my hand down my tired face. It's been a hell of a long day in finance meetings.

Dance lessons are exactly what I need.

The big-time bonus is wrapping my arms around that sweet woman who *did things with me she never has with anyone else.* And has a fucking clit ring. No matter how many times I say that to myself or think about it, I still can't get over it.

Like the jewel in the crown, it's secretly tucked away. And all mine.

She loves a little sexting too. Teasing me to let me know her pussy piercing tickled when she walked a certain way or was thinking about me.

Eva, my angelic, spicy girl.

She's a fucking dream come true.

How the hell I'm going to get through an entire hour together at her dance studio without kissing her, I have no clue.

Absolutely impossible.

It's a schoolboy error; I should have suggested we conduct the lessons at my house instead because the dance studio, at the back of her parents' sports retreat, is like a lighthouse with its wall of glass and fluorescent strip lighting. You can see that thing from a mile away. Trust me, I know.

I have, occasionally, driven past that way, trying to catch even a mere glimpse of Eva. Or dropping in on Charlie and Edith, Eva's parents, for a *coffee.* The retreat is in the complete opposite direction of my house, and I'm not a fan of coffee either. What a truly sad fuck I am.

I push the pedal to metal. Once the turbo kicks in, she just wants to go—she resembles someone I know.

Only two minutes away now, my heart pumps faster. Surging with excitement and apprehension.

Eva, she's mine for the next few hours.

Just her and me.

CHAPTER 11

Knox

I enter the bright dance studio and I'm greeted by a carnival of noise and vibrant, animated people.

Well, this isn't what I was expecting.

Because of the pulsating music that's vibrating through the black sea of flooring and echoing studio, Eva hasn't noticed my arrival.

I noted from getting out of my car all of the studio blinds were closed so they wouldn't have seen me pulling into the parking lot outside. I wonder if Eva did that to conceal us.

I stand back and take it all in. Eva and her triplet sisters, Eden and Ella; Eden's new husband and pro golfer, Hunter King, alongside Ella's future husband, Fraser Farmer, also a pro golfer, are all huddled together, swaying to music, chatting loudly, and laughing.

Eva, Eden, and Ella each bounce identically dressed babies on their hips, Eden and Hunter's triplet boys.

On the other side of the room, Archie and Hamish spin around on the metal poles the girls use to teach pole dancing classes. I inwardly have a chuckle; it's so many levels of wrong.

It's little Hamish that spots me first. "Knoxy," he calls, running toward me all rubber arms and uncoordinated fast legs.

Instantly, all eyes land on me.

The music is dropped to a faint murmur.

Catching Eva's eyes, she gives me a soft wave and a shy smile.

My Sunshine.

Those fucking dimples get me every time.

It takes everything within me not to run over and take her, show everyone she's mine.

Bending down to catch Hamish, he leaps into my arms and flings his arms around my neck.

I love this kid.

Monday mornings are the day me and Charlie play golf. We played this week.

Conscious-stricken—*I slept with your daughter*—I trudged around eighteen holes with Charlie. He spotted my half-hearted swing and shots. Made fun of my form, mocking my inability to switch off from work. Little did he know it had absolutely zilch to do with work and everything to do with my conflicted thoughts of Eva, his own flesh and blood.

Then she threw me a curveball, catapulting herself through my office door later that day.

Super ballsy.

And now, she and I, we're giving it a shot.

I'm fucked.

So much has happened in the space of a few days.

Mondays are also the day Charlie and Edith look after Hamish for Eva.

He sure loves the sports retreat quad bikes. Exactly like his mom, he's a petrol head and thrill seeker.

Every week before we leave for our game of golf, Hamish likes to race his papa. With me and Hamish in one quad bike and Charlie in the other, we race up and over the big hill to the west of the main mansion house.

The squeals of enjoyment and giggles that little lad produces fill my heart with joy. He's such a happy kid and reminds me of Lincoln when he was younger.

Hamish and I win every week. Charlie lets us. Because who could deprive him of the coveted winner's hot chocolate that's up for grabs? It's the best part of my Monday, hot chocolate with Hamish.

"It's not Monday, Knox."

Moving him to my hip, I carry him toward his family. "I know. Do you know what day it is today?"

"Saturday," he says with confidence.

"Noooooo." I tickle his sides, and he squirms in my arms. "It's Wednesday."

"I have the swimming on Wesnesdays."

"It's Wednesday. With a *D*."

"That's what me said, Knox." He fiddles with the buttons of my white polo shirt.

He's so cute.

"Do you like swimming?"

"Yes. Me swims like a fishy." He grants me a big, cheesy grin.

"So I've heard. Your mommy says you're a water baby."

Whatever I said makes him angrily wiggle out of my arms to the floor.

"Momma, Knox called me a baby. I am not a baby." He stomps his little left foot.

Oh dear.

Eva places her hands on her hips. "Did you call my big grown-up boy a baby, Knox Black?"

Oh, I like this game.

"No. I said you told me Hamish was a water baby and loved swimming. I didn't say he was a baby."

Inquisitively, Ella tilts her head in my direction. "Oh yeah, and when did Eva tell you that, Knox?"

Aw, fuck.

"Do you happen to have a pool in your home?" She continues to bounce her nephew on her hip.

They all wait for me to reply.

Ella turns to look back at Eva, who has her eyes clenched closed and her face scrunched up. She opens one eye, then sucks her lips in between her teeth.

Ella breaks the silence. "Uh-huh."

"I don't have a pool," I lie.

Eva's family eyes me suspiciously. I don't think they believe me.

Inhaling deep, Eva shakes her head, then suddenly, she says, "So, dance lessons, Knox. Everyone was just leaving."

They all laugh.

Goddammit.

"I want to watch you dance, Mom." Archie knee slides across the floor.

"Not tonight, Archie," Eva replies.

"Why not? We haven't danced in forever together." Eden hands their son to Hunter. "One song. Then we'll go." Unladylike Eden hikes her leggings up, forcing them to go almost transparent. Is she not wearing any panties? Oh my God, Knox, stop fucking looking.

I think these Wallace girls are saucier than I first thought.

Eva distracts me by letting out a long groan. "Do we have to? Tonight? C'mon guys."

"Yes, yes, yes, Eva." Ella places her nephew into Fraser's arms. I wish I could tell the babies apart so I knew their names.

Grabbing the last of the triplets out of Eva's arms, Ella thrusts him into mine.

Oh crap, it's been a while since I've held a baby.

"Suits you." Ella pats the top of my arm. "Oh, firm muscles, Knox."

"Stop teasing me, Bella, or you'll end up with a hot ass," Fraser growls.

"Oh, goodie." She goes in for another bicep squeeze.

"You've done it now." He shakes his head.

"I was hoping you'd say that." Ella reaches up on her tiptoes and smacks a loud kiss against Fraser's lips.

Yup, definitely saucy, this lot.

I fumble a bit before finding a comfortable hold and look down at the smiling gummy baby in my arms.

"Hey, wee fella." He grabs my nose firmly. Boy's got some grip.

"That's Lewis in your arms, by the way. And I'm Hunter." Hunter reaches out to shake my hand. "We've met before. A few years ago. I think it was the first time I won the Championship Cup. I stayed at your hotel."

Fraser scoffs. "You always have to rub that in, don't you? Because you've won *twice* now." Fraser rolls his eyes.

Hunter rubs his middle finger up the side of his nose, subtly giving Fraser the bird. "Yeah, man, won the girl and the Cup. *Twice*. And three babies. I have strong aim, powerful shots." He grins wide, then kisses his son's head.

"Fucking prick," Fraser mumbles under his breath. "Next time, King, next time. And you can keep the triplets. Never happening. Nope. No to the triplets." He shudders.

"Keep dreaming," Hunter bites back. "I would laugh my ass off if you had triplets. What we think, we attract." Hunter swallows a laugh.

"Yeah, wow. Triplets." I shudder at that thought, too.

"Over and done with. No more." Hunter cuts an invisible line through the air.

Fraser looks at me. "I'd piss myself laughing if they had another set of triplets. Couldn't happen to a nicer guy."

"Whatever, asshole," Hunter says, making sure Hamish and Archie aren't within earshot.

They both clearly like winding each other up.

Nice guys. I like them.

I know Fraser and his family very well. Fraser's father has carried out some emergency plumbing work for me in the past and his mom works at the local grocery store. I can't remember a time when she didn't work in the checkout there.

"How are you, Knox? And how is Linc? I haven't seen him in a while."

"He's great. Working nights while we remodel over the winter. How's your mom doing? I was sorry to hear about her breast cancer. How is her treatment going?"

"She's better. Well, not better. But better than she was. The treatment is messing with her appetite and has made her feel pretty grim, but she's finished her radiotherapy. Now we wait to see if it worked." A heavy sigh escapes his lips.

"Will you pass on my regards to your mom and dad? They're a great couple, Fraser."

"Sure will. Thanks, Knox. And tell Linc to get in touch. We're due a night out."

"He's out this weekend. Something about old school friends. Let me give you his number." I fish my phone out of my pocket awkwardly. I'd forgotten how difficult it was to juggle a happy bundle of baby and do anything else at the same time.

"I'll AirDrop it to you now."

Fraser quickly saves Linc's contact details. "Cheers for that." Fraser turns to comfort the little squirming bundle in his arms. "C'mon, Lennox. Be good for Uncle Fraser." He snuggles him into his chest. "It's almost your bath, bottle, and bedtime, wee man." Lennox rubs his nose with his chubby hand and gives a big gummy yawn as Fraser smooths his hand down his back.

This family is so in tune with each other.

By process of elimination, it means Hunter has Lachlan in his arms.

Lewis. Lennox. Lachlan. Triplets.

Fuck that. That sounds like many years of sleepless nights.

Poor Hunter and Eden. Although they look happy. They are happy. You can feel it.

"Okay." Eden claps her hands. "Are you ready, Archie? You wanted this." She smiles at her white-blond nephew.

"Yes. Can I join in, Aunty Eden?"

"Of course."

Ella moves into position. "You watch for my signal, Archie. Right girls, let's do this."

"It had better not be a sexy dance, Eden," Hunter warns.

In a private manner, Fraser tilts his head my way and says through the side of his mouth, "He'll come in his pants like a college boy if it's a sexy dance. He can't control himself around Eden."

I snort.

"Oh, fuck off, Fraser." Hunter's brows hunch together. "Who am I kidding? Eden's just too sexy. I mean, look at that bubble butt. No panties. She's fucking teasing me. And then when the boobs jiggle. It's all too much. I can't take it. Dancing's the reason we have three babies," he says with a serious face.

I have to hide my amusement. Hunter is not what I imagined him to be like at all.

He's a great guy. Playful and honest. Way too honest.

I know what he means. I paid eighty thousand pounds to dance with Eva. I've watched Eva dancing. Quite a bit actually. More than I would care to admit to anyone. And I can see how triplet babies would happen.

These girls are sweetness personified but deadly provocative.

Definitely trouble.

Triple shots of trouble.

"This one is for you, Fraser," Ella points at him, then throws a sexy wink his way.

"Oh, yeah?" His brows fly up.

"Yes!" Ella confirms.

Eva laughs, shaking her head. "God, you guys are sickeningly in love."

"Stop the hating, out-of-love Eva. It'll be you again one day. Love will find you." Eden pats her on the shoulder.

Eva glances my way and for a moment I can't fucking think straight.

I repeat Eden's words in my head. *Love will find you.*

Let it go, Knox.

It's only been a few days.

Our secret.

Breaking our gaze, Eva moves beside the girls to form a line.

When Eden instructs the voice activated music system to play, "Single Ladies" by Beyoncé booms across the studio.

Before my very eyes, perfectly in sync with one another, the blond trio dance, landing each move from the infamous music video.

My eyes stay firmly on Eva, following her every move in her figure-kissing white-bleached high-waisted jeans and long-sleeved off-the-shoulder black baggy sweatshirt. The music fades away, and the only thing I see and hear is her.

Every flick, twist, spin, and hip shake. She's the epitome of elegance, precision, and sex on legs.

Hair in a tight, slick bun, her hands roam her body, skimming across the fair skin of her long neck that I've now had the pleasure of tasting and touching myself.

The girls whoop and cheer as they immerse themselves in the practiced routine, the faint smiles and looks of determination evident with every hard beat of the music.

Hunter leans over in front of Fraser and shouts over the

music to me. "So I hear you paid eighty thousand pounds for dance lessons. With Eva."

I nod in agreement. "It was for the hospital," I defend myself. It's the worst thing I could have said. I sound like a bald-faced liar and all it does is spur them on.

"Yeah, right." He laughs out loud.

"Keep telling yourself that, Knox," Fraser joins in, watching Ella the whole time.

Ignoring me, Hunter and Fraser, both face forward and continue a private conversation.

"He's lying."

"He is."

"He's spellbound."

"Yup, totally smitten."

"It's the dancing."

"Sure is."

"He's..."

"Fucked," they both say in unison, then grin at each other.

Assholes.

I look back at Eva. Because I can't stop.

Irritated by her long-sleeved top, in an eye blink, Eva whips it off, revealing a tiny black crop top beneath.

Under the harsh studio lighting, a faint outline of Eva's nipples emboss the thin fabric. Having spent a record number of naked hours with Eva over two days, I now know the color of those pale-pink nipples. How she likes them to be licked, how hard she likes them to be sucked, and what happens when I bite them, hard.

I have to close my eyes.

"Yup, he's a goner," Fraser teases.

"Frat boy style boner," Hunter says as if I'm not here.

I turn away, holding on to Lewis firmly.

Get a grip, Knox. You're a fucking wealthy, successful

businessman. Controlled. You're not at high school. Eva is a normal, average, ordinary woman.

I groan to myself.

But she's not.

She's extraordinary. Sexy, hip swishing, lean, beautiful, leggy, captivating, blond—a fucking delectable woman.

Pussy piercing.

These two jokers beside me are right.

I'm doomed.

Watching again, the girls part ways, breaking their routine.

Ella beckons Archie up as she dances toward Fraser, flashing her engagement ring.

"I put a ring on it, baby," Fraser shouts, puffing out his chest. That guy.

"Yeah, you did." She wiggles her hips, urging Fraser to join her. They dance with Lennox between them, content and happy in their little threesome.

Hunter makes his way over to Eden and shouts something in her ear. Eden grabs Hunter's face and kisses him as she nods her head in agreement. Well, he's getting it tonight then. They aren't afraid of showing their public displays of affection, either. I admire that.

I can't touch Eva in front of them.

I want to.

Eva calls Archie over. "C'mon then, Archie. Let's do this." She urges him to dance.

In time to the music, Archie does the most unexpected thing; he break-dances.

Windmilling to begin his routine, he then moves into hip-hop dance moves I have never seen before. Cheering him on, we circle around him, shouting his name. With confidence and ease, he flourishes before my very eyes. His tiny body goes in for a head spin and almost nails it. He saves it by landing on his side on the floor. With elbow bent, he finishes with his head on his hand as the music comes to an abrupt end.

Unable to clap, we boys whoop instead and the girls clap, cheering their delight. I can't stop smiling.

He's seven.

Eva must have taught him. I'm so proud and he isn't even my boy.

"Archie, you're gonna be a star." She crouches down and gives him a cuddle and then a high five. His beaming smile dazzles us all.

"Aunty Ella is having you tonight, okay?" Eva tries to catch her breath.

"No swimming, Momma?" Hamish launches himself into her arms.

"Nope. Canceled tonight. Next week. But you're going to Aunty Ella and Uncle Fraser's for a sleepover. Mommy is working late this evening, but you get to play with the doggies and the new puppy back at Aunty Ella's new house. Uncle Fraser is taking you both to school and day care tomorrow. I am picking you up, though." She kisses his cheek.

"Yaayyy, I get to play with the new puppy." He bounces over to Ella.

"I love you two," she calls in their direction, but Archie and Hamish have moved on, desperate to play with Ella and Fraser's new fur baby.

Eva stands tall. "Great, now you can all go. Knox has paid for some very expensive lessons to be taught."

"It was for the hospital," Hunter says deadpan.

Then he and Fraser burst out laughing.

"Oh, shut up, you pair of buffoons. What do you two see in those two?" Eva asks her sisters, pointing to Hunter and Fraser.

"Abs," Eden answers without hesitation. "Arm porn."

"Fraser has a massive—"

"Not now, Ella," Eva stops her.

"Oh, that too." Eden raises her finger in the air.

A chuckle leaves my chest.

I love this family.

They're fun.

I think I want to be part of it.

Secret.

"Right, cupcake. Let's get you home." Hunter stalks across the room.

I hadn't even realized Hunter had fastened his three sons into their stroller. When the hell did he take Lewis out of my arms?

Obviously, I was too busy ogling Eva.

"Fraser, would you push the boys out to the car and place them in their seats? I'll be two, maybe five minutes. I have something to check in Eden's old house." Hunter suddenly scoops Eden up over his shoulder and gives her ass a firm slap. She lets out an almighty squeal. Hunter throws Fraser his car keys.

"Checking Eden out more like." Fraser makes his way out of the dance studio. "C'mon, Archie, Hamish, you're with me and Aunty Ella."

Eden raises her head, smiling and double-hand waves back at us as Hunter carries her out of the door. "Have fun. I know I will."

Running past us to catch up with everyone, Ella suddenly circles back. "Eh, Eva, remember to, you know, ask. About the thing." She nudges her head in my direction. "Please." She slaps her hands together, prayer style. "Oh, and next week can you cover four of my classes? I'll send you a text of which ones. Trevor can't cover them as he's on vacation next week."

"Yeah, yeah. Just go." And then there were two.

"Your family is great, Eva. Good fun." I push my hands in my pockets.

I have always known this, but without their mom and dad

around, they let themselves go and I saw a funnier side to them tonight.

"They're a lot."

"I like them."

"Great." She opens her arms wide. "Shall we dance?"

"That's what I'm here for." I walk confidently across the floor and pull her into my arms.

It's fine if anyone sees us touching each other.

Dance lessons.

I've missed touching her.

"I don't have the boys this evening."

"I heard. Stay with me."

"I already have my overnight bag in my car." Tilting her head to the side, she scrunches her nose.

"Presumptuous. I like it."

"I like your house and the cooker, and then there's the pool." She looks upward.

"And me?"

"You're the bonus."

"Keep telling yourself that, Sunshine."

I run my fingers across the inch of exposed skin of her back, making her shiver at my touch.

She rolls her shoulders out. "I can't wait to show you how to dance the kizomba. I love it." Her whole face lights up.

I nod briefly in acknowledgment. I fucking adore it too. Wait till she and I dance it together. I stall. "First, what did Ella want?"

Eva plays with the buttons on my tee shirt, just like Hamish did. "I promise I didn't want to ask you. But she begged me and I'm honestly not trying to take advantage of you."

"Okay?" I frown, waiting for her next words.

"Ella is struggling to find a venue for her wedding. It's currently being held here within the grounds of the sports retreat. But she wants The Sanctuary. She tried calling you directly but was told you were busy. Then Dad forgot to ask you again on Monday. And now the wedding is only three and a half weeks away because Fraser wants to get married, like yesterday. He's already waited too long; you know their story, yadda yadda. He's free now, living back here in Scotland; their history, they split, now they are together and have three dogs and a big fancy house. Anyway, yeah, Ella asked me to ask you, and now I feel like I'm taking liberties," she finishes her long ramble.

"Done. I'll make it happen."

I would do anything for those turquoise eyes. They melt me.

"Do you not need to check the bookings or something?"

"Nope. Consider it done."

"Oh, my God. She will die when I tell her."

"I fucking hope not. No dying brides-to-be."

"Shit, sorry." She flings her hand over her mouth. "Wrong choice of words."

I squeeze her sides. "You have to repay the favor."

Having never done this before, I put all my reservations in the fuck-it bucket.

"Yeah?" She looks at me in wonder.

I lean in close to her ear. "Promise me, tonight, you will suck my cock like the good girl you are. You suck me so fucking good, Sunshine. I want a private lap dance when we return to my house. And then let me play with that pretty little clit ring of yours and in return I'll make you come so fucking hard, all you'll ever hunger will be me. I'll be your earth, your moon, and your stars. I'll be all you ever need. I've made my decision. I want you. All of you."

A bungee cord of silence bounces between us.

She audibly gulps. "You can be quite intense, Knox," she says in a hushed voice. "Yes, to all of that." She clears her throat. "You and me. It's quite sudden. I have to admit, it scares me, but

165

when I'm with you, I feel safe. Like we fit." She pauses before looking me in the eye. "If you're my earth, my moon, and my stars, let me be your Sunshine."

Blood rushes to my cock. Fuck yeah.

She's mine.

"You excite me, Knox. I can't wait to see what happens between us."

"I really want to kiss you right now." I clasp her face in my hands.

Making me jump, Eva projects her voice, saying, "Studio lights off."

As quick as a bullet through the air, we're immersed in a black cloak.

"Clever."

"Stop talking and kiss me, Knox. Make me yours."

For the next few minutes, in the middle of the heavy dark room, we kiss long and leisurely, slow, then hard, soft, then fast.

I can't remember a time when I felt this accepted.

She's got me. I'm hooked.

CHAPTER 12

Eva

Lights back on now, following our passionate make-out session which I find oddly addictive, I begin explaining to Knox the basic moves.

But he stops me mid-sentence with his confession.

With a mixture of admiration and confusion, my peep toe dance stiletto taps a synchronized beat of my heart against the sprung-vinyl dance floor.

To clarify, I ask Knox, "Let me get this straight. You can already dance?"

Innocently, Knox replies with a simple, "Yes."

"Your mother sent you for dance lessons when you were a boy and you can dance the salsa, mambo, and rumba?"

"Yes."

"You went to Greece last year to a dance retreat though, to learn how to dance the kizomba?" I love a man who can dance.

"Yes."

"So, you don't need dance lessons from me?"

"Oh, fuck yeah, I do. You're going to refine my technique."

I rub my head in confusion. "You went to lessons last year?

After you saw me dancing? And you wanted to make sure if we ever danced together, you could impress me?"

"Yes."

"Wow. I don't know if I should admire you for going to lessons when you were on vacation in Greece last year, or be mad you didn't come to learn from me in the first place, or be blown away by your eagerness to please me."

I actually don't.

Or be worried he's a stalker.

He must like me. More than I realized.

His gesture, learning the kizomba, almost seems romantic. It doesn't creep me out or worry me.

He's been pining for me from afar.

Waiting for his chance.

I've yet to see him move, but my excitement picks up pace at the possibility of finally dancing with someone whom I feel connected to.

Kizomba is more than dance.

It's about vulnerability. Trust.

Incredibly sensual.

Knowing he learned the kizomba makes me want to dance with Knox even more.

Ewan never danced with me. Not once. I've had many epiphanies since we split. His lack of interest in my career was always evident. But I was too close to see it. From over here on the bright side now, I've thrown those curtains open wide. They've highlighted everything it was. Vapid, one-sided, laborious.

However, this is new and exciting. Full-on 4D tactile, visual color. Knox is interested in me and my boys. He asked a hell of a lot of questions on the weekend about us all. He cares.

Knox waits for me to say something. He's like decadent chocolate, wrapped in a simple white polo tee shirt, dark jeans, and pristine white leather designer sneakers. Effortless. *I want to eat him.*

"I'll lead then, shall I?" He smirks, stepping forward.

"Sorry, yeah. You're a little distracting. You keep surprising me."

"Says the girl in jeans she must have jumped off the wardrobe to get into, and a tiny black crop top I can see the outline of her nipples through."

Fair point. I smooth my fingers over my tight, slick bun on top of my head, making sure it's firmly in place.

"Keeping you on your toes, Knox." For the first time in my career, I'm nervous about dancing with a partner. "Okay. Let's do this."

Knox hugs us close together, joining our hands in a relaxed ballroom position, elbows bent, below shoulder height.

His strong body locks against mine as he threads his bent knee between my thighs, firmly positioning our hips level. The broadness of his thigh brushes against my pussy.

He wasn't lying. He knows his positioning.

Finding my focus, I say, "There are many takes on this Angolan dance, Knox. There are no hard and fast rules. It's open to interpretation. Depending on who taught you, will depend on your style. I will follow your lead. I can adjust your posture and footwork as we go. How does that sound?"

"Fantastic." His shovel-size hand rests lightly on my back, tickling the space between the waist of my jeans and crop top.

"Head up. Relax your shoulders. Remember to keep your feet close together, and soft knees. Eyes on me to begin. I prefer temple to temple or forehead to forehead depending on the backward and forward movement of our feet. It's entirely up to you."

"I don't mind."

"Think smooth as we move."

"Like your pussy."

My mouth drops open wide. "For the next sixty minutes, Mr. Black, I am your dance teacher, not your..."

We haven't discussed what I am. Lover, lady friend, non-girlfriend, fuck buddy?

"Girl. You're my girl." His deep eyes blaze down on me.

"Right, yes, I knew that." My voice comes out slightly higher than expected.

I'm Knox Black's girl. The most eligible bachelor in Scotland, and I'm his.

My heart does a nervous leap of joy.

I loosen my neck up from side to side. "Ready?"

"I have been for a while."

He's so cool and calm and I'm flapping like a baby bird.

"How long?" Without being specific, he knows what I'm asking. He didn't answer me the first time I asked him on Friday evening.

"Two years. Everything changed for me two years ago."

"Go on."

"That's all you need to know, Sunshine." I crane my neck to meet his excessive height.

Being respectful, I don't push and give him the space he desires. He'll tell me when he's ready.

His eyes hold steady.

"Thank you," I say.

He raises his eyebrows with interest. "For?"

"Being respectful and not pursuing me when I was married."

"Not my style, Sunshine. I did kind of fuck up the night of the Spring Fling Ball last year though. I shouldn't have told you I wanted you. It was deeply inappropriate, and I crossed the line. You were married."

Here we are crossing a new line—my dad and Lincoln.

We have to tell them.

"I forgive you. You made me feel special that evening, Knox.

For the first time in what felt like a decade, someone saw me. *You* saw me. Maybe, deep down, you knew, or detected, I was unhappy."

"I did."

Knew it. I was wearing my unhappiness like a neon-colored flag—very difficult not to notice.

"For the record, I'm not that girl anymore. Ewan drama aside, I feel better than I have in months. I'm optimistic. I've accepted my past is my past. I will not let it shape my future. I'm not a bitter person and I will not allow my broken marriage with Ewan to dictate who I am now. You made me remember who I am. I am not the problem. I simply needed someone to remind me of who I once was—happy, carefree. Eva."

"Dazzling and heartbreakingly beautiful."

His words hula hoop around my heart.

"Let's dance, Sunshine," he says through a burning gaze.

"Alexa, play "Love Nwantinti" by CKay."

The haunting vocals float through the air.

Without instruction, Knox begins confidently swaying his hips in time to the rich guitar strums. Mimicking his movements, I follow him.

When the sensual intro beat drops, he unclasps our hands.

Fascinated, not knowing where he plans on placing his hand, I bathe in his meticulous touch as he glides his fingers up my bare arm, then firmly, predatorily wraps his entire hand lightly around the back of my neck. Between us, I lay my free hand over his heart.

Instinctively, we hip sway together.

Never missing a stride, he matches me beat for beat and step for step. There's no hesitation between our hip bumps. No second-guessing. In harmony, we move.

He's an excellent dancer. Incredible, in fact.

Cheek to cheek, I nestle in, stealing the warmth of his body.

Subtle smooth steps and taps, we follow a repeated foot

pattern back and forth. Wiggling my hips in time with his, his broad thigh traces my clit ring over and over.

If we shuffle together any longer, I may explode right here in the dance studio.

Urgent with need, he pulls me closer and lets out a low groan.

I'm mad with lust, taking anything he'll give me.

Provocatively, his fingers wander into the waistband of my skin-tight jeans.

His heart beats wild and hard in his chest beneath my hand. I remove my hand between us, to relieve the ache to be even closer to him, and place it around his back, hooking my fingertips to the top of his shoulder.

Sealed chest to chest in liberating slow romantic rhythmic movements, we dance.

Never missing a beat, his masculine energy dominates me as he leads me around the dance studio. The close connection I feel is new, scary, and wonderful, and my hula-hooping heart spins faster.

As the mellow song swirls through the air, Knox's knee nudges further in between my thighs. Pressing my hips with intention, he rubs my center against his leg. I jerk unexpectedly as a jolt of desire sparks. My whole body is now alive with unapologetic white-hot need.

The steps in kizomba are fluid and sensual. They're not supposed to be that obvious, and he's doing this on purpose.

Knox whispers in my ear, "How's that pussy feeling?"

"Sooooo good." I let out a breathy sigh against his ear.

The melodic African music continues to envelop us, connecting us as if the world could be on fire and neither of us would care.

With every touch, movement, and hip sway, I imagine myself dancing with Knox for the rest of my life.

He feels like my eternal partner.

All this time, he's been so close. Always around.

Why didn't I see how good we could be together before?

Our temples beat in time, his grip growing firmer with every swish of my hips.

Undeniably, we have intangible chemistry without the need for any verbal communication.

When he does speak, he slays me in unexpected ways with his thoughtful words. But *this*. This is everything I have wanted. Someone who connects, understands, and is in the moment with me.

Another firm brush of his thigh against my jean-clad pussy pulls a deep, raspy moan from my chest. I need to come.

Knox stops dancing, then instructs the lights to go off.

Plummeting us into darkness again, he removes his hand from my waist, unbuttons my jeans with Olympic expertise, thrust his hands down the front of my jeans, and he commands me to come.

With feral groans he smothers my lips with his mouth, attacking me with his tongue and intoxicating, velvety, indefinable scent.

He cocoons my ass cheek with his strong, frantic hand, thrusting my hips into the fingers of his other hand.

With a couple of quick flicks of my clit ring, I come, shattering in his arms as my orgasm cascades in waves. It's violent, soul-shattering, and tender all at once.

Feeling like I've been stripped of all my senses, I can't think straight. Or see, and it's not from the dark; it's the powerful orgasm he pulled from my body. It's too much.

And yet not enough. I want more.

Wobbling on jelly legs, Knox blankets me in his arms, placing hot, gentle kisses down the side of my face and neck as my hard breathing subsides, finding peace in his arms.

"Same time next week," he joshes between peppered kisses.

"I don't think I can take any more. I need time to recover or work on my cardio or I need an energy drink or something," I pant.

"I'll help you with your cardio later tonight. Now button up your jeans, naughty girl."

"So bossy."

"I am the boss."

"Of staff. Not me." With no music on anymore, I fumble in the dark, pushing the metal donut button through the buttonhole of my jeans.

He chuckles in the pitch-black. It's deep and velvety.

"Hello," a voice bellows from the dark. "Eva, are you here?"

Oh, sweet baby Jesus, it's my father.

Shit, shit, shit.

Frantically, I pull myself together, smoothing my clothes out.

What should I do?

Knox grabs me. With an *oomph,* I stumble into his chest, causing my heels to click against the wooden floor. Decision made.

"We're here, Charlie," Knox says in his authoritative tone.

"Eh, yeah, here, Dad," I stammer.

"I knew you were here. Both of your cars are parked outside. Why are you dancing in the dark?"

"Alexa, studio lights on." Thank Christ Knox is in control. I feel totally unhinged.

Squinting and blinking, adjusting to the bright strip lighting overhead, Knox holds me in place.

Knox saves us, he says, "Eva was teaching me how to dance without inhibitions. Building trust with her and using only my senses to lead and follow."

That was too close for comfort.

I'm grateful I didn't apply any lipstick, although my lips feel swollen as I rub my fingers over them nervously.

"Hey, that's pretty cool, Eva. You're such an incredible

teacher." He beams with pride. My dad thinks he's twenty still and uses the word cool, 'cause he thinks he's *cool*.

My dad's curiosity bounces off him. "Is this something new you'll be rolling out to all of your students? Sounds interesting. Is it like bats and how they use their sound senses?"

I've no idea.

"I suppose it's like bats, yeah." I squirm.

Knox squeezes my waist playfully. "But no to rolling it out to everyone. It's something I watched online one day. Won't be trying that again."

"No?" Knox looks down at me.

"No."

"Was I not very good in the dark, Eva?"

Flustered, I move out of the dance position and tuck an invisible hair behind my ear, forgetting my hair is slicked back so tight I have ponytail ache.

I shake my head, screwing up my face, trying to think of what to say. "Mmmm, your footing needs work and your hands move too much."

I'm a big fat fibster.

He's an incredibly sensual dancer. Perfect, in fact.

"Hands or fingers?"

"Sorry, what?" I blink.

Knox looks at me with a mischievous smirk. "Do my hands or fingers move too much, or is it both?"

"Both. Both hands and fingers. Both need work. No moving and wiggling of the fingers or hands. Just waaaayyy too much of the twitching, digging, flicking."

"Flicking?" He tilts his head.

Oh, he really is Lucifer.

Ignoring him, I face my dad again, who's watched our whole weird interaction. "Did you want something?" I feel perspiration bead along my top lip.

"Oh, yes. I came to ask a huge favor, Knox." My dad moves

fully into the studio. "Ella asked me ages ago, then I forgot. She tried calling you and couldn't get you, so now I am in the Guinness Book of Records under The Worst Dad title." My dad runs his hand through his white locks. He's such a handsome man. My mother says he's her silver fox.

He's like her own personal lumberjack Santa. He keeps fit working around the sports retreat all day, every day.

They are very lucky to have found each other. When she was only nineteen, she decided he was *it* for her. She knew he was *the one* despite the ten-year age gap and my gran and grandad forcing them apart.

They didn't listen to anyone.

Their determination to be together almost split them from their families, but now, well, now thirty-plus years later, they still rock each other's world.

My mom still swoons; my dad still kisses and cuddles. They can't stop.

It's admirable. Gorgeous, and it also freaks me out. Their public displays of affection are often a little too much for my stomach.

Gosh, maybe Dad will be more understanding when, *if*, Knox and I tell him about *us*.

"You're not the worst, Dad." I shake my head. He's the furthest thing from it.

But I'm currently the worst daughter, way up in first position.

I'm fucking your friend.

"I feel like it, Eva. Ella is going to make me dress in a bright-pink suit if I don't sort this venue out for her."

"She won't." I chuckle.

"She will. She showed me a picture online." He looks deadly serious.

"Consider it done, Charlie." Knox casually pushes his hands into the pockets of his jeans.

My dad's brow furrows. "I haven't even asked you what I want yet."

"Eva already asked me about Ella and Fraser having the wedding reception at The Sanctuary. It's a firm yes."

"Oh, good grief, Ella is going to love you, Eva. Your mother even more so. The pink suit threat didn't go down very well. Apparently, it would clash with her soft peach mother of the bride outfit." He rolls his eyes, mimicking her high-pitched voice. That poor man is stuck with us four women in his life. We sure do like to mess with him.

"I know. I will give you the honor of telling Ella, though. But remember to tell her it was me that wangled it." I shake my finger at him. "And remember, I saved your backside. No pink suit." I unravel my bun. How Ariana Grande manages a taut, high ponytail all day is beyond me. The top of my head is throbbing like a bitch. And the stress rash I've developed at the back of my neck feels itchy.

"You're a life saver, Eva. And you Knox. Thank you." My dad places his hand over his heart. "Right, I'll be off then and let you get back to your lesson. Remember, Knox, no flicking of your fingers. Hand positioning is everything in dance. Isn't it, Eva? See, I pay attention to your dancing lessons." He winks my way. "And golf on Monday, Knox. And I'll call you to settle the bill for the reception."

If only my dad knew what he was saying; none of my feedback was even dance related. It comprised panicked words of mumbo jumbo.

It's official, I'm going to hell.

Unable to make eye contact with my dad, Knox juts his chin in my dad's direction. "See you Monday, Charlie."

My dad runs over to me, taps a kiss to my forehead, tells me he loves me, then leaves.

I contemplate what to say next as I stare at the empty doorway.

"We have to tell him," Knox says before me.

"We do."

"Lincoln first though, Eva."

"Yeah. When?"

"I'm not sure. Should we see how we get on in the next few weeks? Figure out how we tell people? Plus, we have Ewan to consider and your boys."

Yikes.

I don't want to be the one to tell Ewan, but it's inevitable.

"Maybe we should wait until after Ella and Fraser get married?" he suggests.

That sounds sensible. My family has had enough drama the last eighteen months, what with all of Eden and Ella's ups and downs.

He continues. "Let the dust settle after Ella and Fraser are married, then we can tell everyone."

A mini whirlpool swirls in my stomach at the thought of telling my father.

"Should we have some fun in the meantime?" I throw him a cheeky wink, hiding my nerves.

"I'm counting on it."

Enjoying the relief, I run my fingers through my sensitive scalp as I puff out my hair.

"Let's see what you can do then, Mr. Black. I'm taking the tempo up a notch. No funny business, though. We'll save that for later." I sway myself elegantly toward him. "For now, we dance. I think dancing with you is my new favorite hobby."

He's a confident dance partner. I find that so deeply and consumingly attractive.

"My fingers need adjusting," he says deadpan.

"Oh, stop it. I couldn't think of anything else to say." I lift my shoulder in a lopsided shrug. "I don't have any critique to give you. Your technique is immaculate."

Knox excels at everything in life. He studies. Refines. All with one goal, to be the best.

"It's who I'm dancing with that makes all the difference. Also, my fingers are the best at dancing across that beautiful jeweled bud of yours. My technique is flawless."

Facts.

To my annoyance, I feel myself blush.

I'm certain he says these things to watch my reaction.

A satisfied smirk twitches his mouth.

I knew it.

"No more distractions." I slice a line with my flat hand through the air.

Positioning ourselves again, I inhale to announce the next song when, without notice, a voice whines from the entryway.

"Ah, you *are* here. Lincoln said this is where you would be, but seeing is believing."

Wonderful. Castleview Cove's very own rich girl.

Tabitha MacEvoy.

Loaded. Confident. Connected.

"Tabby?" Knox scowls. "What are you doing here?"

"This place is like a revolving door tonight," I mutter under my breath.

Never letting me go, he grips my waist tightly as if telling me to hold firm.

Tabitha bats her eyelashes, flipping her hair over her shoulder with defiance. "I went up to the hotel to find you. Lincoln checked your online calendar, told me you were here, and you'd bought dance lessons for me and I should be here too."

Bloody Lincoln.

She is undeniably beautiful. From head to toe, Tabitha is immaculate. Every day. There is never an ice-blond hair out of place on her sleek bob. Today is no different. She is wearing a pale-mint button-up silk shirt tucked into a tight racing-green calf-length pencil skirt, and heels. Always heels. There is no way she works on the whisky distillery floor.

She's a paper pusher at best.

"I didn't receive my calendar request like I normally do from you, Knox."

Does he calendar request sex dates?

How impersonal.

Scheduled.

I bet my life on it she's a missionary position woman.

Yuck.

Stop thinking about them together.

"It's my fault." Covering for Knox, I fire out, "I should have sent the request."

"Ah, well, that explains it. Sloppy disorganization." With a judgmental gaze, Tabitha explores our modern dance studio, leaving no inch of the space untouched. "I can't imagine you have systemized processes or a good business head on those artsy-fartsy shoulders of yours for this place," she mumbles under her breath.

She can't seriously be so far out of touch to think I wouldn't hear that?

Bitch.

Through the grapevine, I've heard Tabitha MacEvoy treats her workers like peasants. The local restaurants despair when she makes reservations. I've never had the pleasure of meeting her before. I'm suddenly grateful for that. She's deeply unpleasant and rude.

She may speak to her own personnel in that manner and tone, but I'm not letting her get away with her defamatory comments. "I'll pretend I didn't hear that, Tabitha. Please do not come into my dance studio and criticize my thriving business."

She screws her face up and snaps her neck back as if I slapped her.

Knox bites down on his lip to hide a smile. He's proud of me for sticking up for myself.

I give him a *get this bitch out of my studio* glare.

"You should mind your manners, Tabby, and I didn't invite you because I wanted to take the lessons myself," he says through a tense jaw.

"Ah, were you going to surprise me at The Sanctuary Winter Ball? How romantic."

Looking away, I bow my head and remove myself from Knox's arms. "I think our lesson is over."

"You should leave, Tabby."

I smile inside at Knox's words.

"Don't be like that, Knox. I wanted to speak to you. You've been ignoring me for around four months, and then I find you here. I can't believe you are learning to dance for me. Now this all makes sense," Tabitha gasps with wonder.

She's delusional.

Knox was telling the truth. The last time he and Tabitha were together was months ago.

"I didn't do it for you. I did it for myself. I wanted to learn from the best dance teacher in Scotland. She just so happens to be right on our doorstep. Tonight is my first lesson, Tabby." Knox stands firm.

"Oh, yeah?" Tabitha responds, all wide-eyed and confused.

Well, this is awkward.

"I'll call you tomorrow, Tabby." He turns his back on her, ending the conversation.

Why is he calling her tomorrow?

As if he's thrown her a lifeline, this seems to appease her. She flashes him a dreamy smile. "I'll wait by my phone for you to call, then."

Oh, please get the hell out of my dance studio.

"Speak tomorrow," Knox says back over his shoulder. His cold shoulder.

Rooted to the spot, Tabitha stands in place.

Take the hint, Tabitha. You look pathetic.

"Bye, Eva." She gives me a flirty wave as she skips out of my studio.

Her vibe is off. Way off.

What a weirdo.

Hearing her drive out of the gravel driveway, I wait a beat before I ask Knox, "Sorry, tell me exactly how you ended up sleeping with her for three years." I point in the exit's direction. "She's one crazy-ass woman. Has she got some kind of frontal lobe dysfunction? She didn't even apologize for being rude to me. You and her don't make any sense. Like ketchup and ice cream, you don't go together. She's the ketchup by the way—acidic." I shudder.

I'm completely flabbergasted.

Out of the blue, Knox breaks into deep, spontaneous laughter. His powerful shoulders and chest bounce up and down. "I don't think anyone has told Tabby off in years." His eyes gleam with amusement. He shakes his head. "You are something else, Sunshine."

Am I?

"She was mean about my business. She called me artsy-fartsy," I protest. "It's not funny, Knox." Placing my hands on my waist, I pop a hip.

His bronzed face continues to crease, his olive skin against his chalk-white tee shirt contrasts perfectly.

"Okay, whatever," I mutter. "Yes, hilarious. You know she seems a bit fatal attraction-like. Should I be worried? Hamish has a bunny. A white one."

This sets Knox off again.

What is so funny?

"I should make you one of our security guards at the hotel at the front gate. I was right about the Westie nickname. You are feisty." He strides forward, pulling me into his arms. "Such a surprise."

I can't hold my tongue. "Why are you calling her tomorrow?"

His face drops. "To ensure she knows we are through. Completely finished."

My shoulders slump, relieved.

Knox pulls what looks like a car key fob from his back pocket, placing it in my hand. "This is for you."

I run my finger over the metal and plastic fob.

"That one, lettered *A*." Knox points to the silver shiny button. "That opens the electric gate to my house. And that one." He points to button *B*. "That opens the garage door. Park your car in there tonight. Lincoln is working nights this week. It's precautionary. I will text you the code to the side door that leads through to the main house. The one we went through on Friday evening."

My head bobs nervously.

He's giving me a key to his house. He must trust me.

"I will try not to lose this between now and having to give it back to you later."

"It's yours. For keeps. To come and go as you please. We need to be careful until we tell Lincoln, but that's your own key."

A giggle rises from my belly. "Okay. I might steal your Cobra."

"She has a tracker."

"I don't care. It would be worth it."

"Try it and I may have to handcuff you, Sunshine." His voice turns dark.

"Is that an invitation?"

"Might be. Soft, metal, or leather?"

He's being serious.

Desire mingled with desperation forces me to clench my

fists tight. I want to reach out and kiss him again, but we're forbidden in my giant, brighter than a light box studio.

I must learn to control my carnal urges in public.

Knox doesn't wait for my answer. "We'll buy them together."

"I've never..."

"Me either. It'll be fun. I want to try new things with you."

Ditto.

A powerful, indescribable force passes between us.

What is that?

Whatever it is, I feel it all the way down to my tippy-toes.

He whispers, "I have to go before I fuck you on the dance floor. I'll order takeout and pick it up on the way home. Do what you need to do. Lock up, and I'll see you at the house. You owe me a lap dance."

Aw, crap. The things I do for my sisters. I've never given anyone a lap dance before.

"I would kiss you, but..." Knox waves his hand in an arc, gesturing to the wall-to-wall windows and bright studio lights. "See you at the house, Sunshine."

Every instinct in me wants to kiss him goodbye, too, but I don't.

Knox bounces energetically in the direction of the studio exit. He seems lighter tonight. Happier.

"Hey, Knox," I call after him.

He turns on his heel.

"You've got great moves for an old man. I loved dancing with you this evening."

Delighted, he winks.

Yeah, this man may very well steal my heart.

If he hasn't already.

CHAPTER 13

Eva

I move in time to the mellow music as I dramatically striptease for Knox, peeling my snug jeans from my body.

Circular, slow booty rolls in sexy waves, I tease Knox more.

Like a king, he's sitting on his charcoal-gray button-back sofa positioned next to his lit bedroom fireplace.

Legs spread wide, eyes fixed on me, both arms are draped along the back of the sofa. He stares.

The crackling flames from the roaring fire cast my moving shadow shapes across the vast room as I rotate my body, running my hands down my naked chest, stomach, and thighs.

The sexy, slow pulse of "Purple Rain" by Prince builds with intensity across the room.

His choice.

The meaning of the song is not lost on me. He waited, didn't want to split me and Ewan up, and wants to be more than a part-time lover.

I know this song. It represents a deeper meaning, a new beginning.

A new dawn.

I didn't need to be persuaded. I want this new start.

With him.

Unhurried, I swivel my hips in a figure eight before crawling into his lap to straddle him.

Gripping the back of the sofa, I press my naked chest against his tee shirt, grinding my hips into his crotch.

Our eyes hold steady.

Knox skillfully anchors his hands around my waist and assists as I grind in time to the drums of the orchestral music.

Arching my back, thrusting my breasts into his face, I roll my body around in a semicircle, making my hair fall loose over my shoulders in waves.

Knox takes this as an invitation to suck my nipple into his hot mouth.

Rocking my hips, I grip the back of his neck, urging him for more. He lashes at my hard peak, biting and nipping before he moves to the other, where he gives it even more attention.

He glides his hand down my arched back and into the waistband of my white lace micro thong panties, the only thing I have left on, and pulls me into him, grinding his rock-hard erection against my now soaking wet folds.

Every one of my nerve endings switches on. The thrill of his touch fires rockets of sheer heat across my skin.

I clutch his tee shirt, then clumsily pull it up over his head. "I love your body, Knox. Just look at you." I run my hands over his sculpted chest.

"And here's me thinking you wanted me for my cooker and pool."

"Oh, that too," I coo teasingly as I continue to push my hips into his. "I want to see all of you." I reverse off his lap, then unbutton his fly with speed. He lifts his hips to help me remove his jeans and boxers in one go.

Kneeling between his widened legs, I run my hands up his firm thighs, then take his beautiful cock in my hands.

Who knew men looked like this? Never have I been with a man so utterly captivating.

I only have Ewan to compare him to.

And Ewan doesn't even come close to Knox's solid frame, six-foot-five height or his enormous cock.

Eden and Ella's partners are both buff and drop-dead gorgeous.

To me, Knox is on a different level.

And he's mine.

"Your cock is so big, Knox." My nipples tighten.

"Suck me," he demands.

Gently at first, I stroke him up and down, then circle my thumb around his glistening crown. On the next downward stroke, eager to taste him, I lean in and take him in my mouth.

He hisses, bucking his hips, then grabs on to the back of my head, pushing himself farther into my mouth.

The head of his cock touches the back of my throat and I love the feeling of being in control of his pleasure.

Fisting my silky hair in his hands, he moves me up and down his length.

I continue to move my hand up and down, swirling my tongue around his shaft and create a channel for his dick to slip and slide back and forth in and out of.

He grows harder with every stroke and lick as I worship this incredible man.

With intention, I suck faster. He grows bigger.

"Oh, Sunshine. I'm gonna come if you keep doing that."

Reaching up to grab his free hand, I give it a firm squeeze, informing him that's what I want.

"Look at me."

And I do.

"Make yourself come, Eva. Flick your clit for me," He says, his voice laced with deep urgency.

And I do.

I'd do anything for him.

I lightly tickle his balls before I move my hand from his cock down into my now-soaked panties to my clit ring.

He holds the root of his cock for me.

Moaning around his hard length, I dance my fingers over and over my jewel, rubbing my sensitive nub.

"Put your finger inside yourself, Eva," he pants.

I follow his instruction.

Running my finger down the seam of my lower lips, I thrust my finger into my wet core in and out.

The heat between us rises.

My hand in his. His cock in my mouth. My fingers in my panties.

It's addictive.

"Now flick that ring, Sunshine. Come for me now." His breathing gathers speed.

Coating my swollen bud with my own excitement, it feels like the heat of the sun grows between my thighs and the throbbing crescendos in my lower stomach.

Fingers and eyes locked, we give in to our own release.

Surrendering to the ultimate ecstasy, every muscle of mine clenches as I come hard, my breathing ragged, humming as I purr with unashamed pleasure.

His body bucks at the vibration of my moans around his cock, and his fingers knot into the back of my hair. Within a few more deep-throat strokes, he grunts, then pours himself into my mouth, bellowing my name as he comes.

I hold still as he and I find our own air again, then I clean his cock with my tongue. He twitches at my sensual action.

Knox sits up, pulls out my now limp hand that's still inside my panties, and sucks my fingers into his mouth. Swirling his tongue around, he licks every drop of my orgasm off them.

With superstrength, he scoops me up under my arms and

lifts me into the air. He stands, sealing our slick-from-perspiration bodies together, wraps my legs around his waist, and carries me to bed, caressing my ass and kissing me as he does.

For the next few hours, he fucks me like a madman, clawing at me, devouring me with his hands and mouth.

Finally, we collapse together, panting, totally spent, cocooned in each other's arms.

Never have I felt so alive.

Or so satisfied.

Dopamine is clearly messing with my emotions.

I feel as if I'm floating on air.

I never expected Knox Black.

In every possible way.

I'm screwed.

"What the hell are you doing, Sunshine?" Knox mumbles half-asleep, lying on his stomach.

"Eh, sorry, I didn't mean to wake you up." I continue to pull the corner of the fitted mattress sheet off the bed.

Knox groans. "What time is it?"

"Six in the morning."

"Come back to bed. I don't need to be at the hotel until nine."

"Okay, but just let me..." I continue on my mission.

Curiosity gets the better of him. Knox twists around in the bed to find out what I am doing.

"Are you changing the sheets?" one-eyed, he asks groggily, his face creased with sleep.

"No." I *humph*, with Knox still in the bed, struggling to push the sheet far enough up to find what I'm looking for.

"Ah, gotcha." I dip my head under the Egyptian cotton

fabric and take a quick photo on my phone of the mattress label on the bed with its brand name and model.

"There." I pull it back down, tucking it back in place. "I was taking a picture of your mattress label. I always have a bad lower back with my mattress, but with yours I don't. Where did you get it from?" I lay my phone back down on the nightstand.

"It's too early for questions," he grumbles, closing his eye again.

"I'll just google rich mattresses for rich people shop, see what search results that brings back," I jump back in beside him.

"I hate morning people."

"I'm a morning person," I sing.

"I knew it. You have to leave or be quiet."

With no intention of going, I say, "I'll grab my stuff. Bye." I roll over, pretending to leave Knox's Olympic-sized bed.

Knowing his reaction, he pounces on me, surrounding me with his body heat, hooking his thick thigh around mine to hold me in place.

"Stay where you are. You're my prisoner. I won't see you now until Saturday night. Don't move." He tickles my sides.

He's quite playful when he wants to be.

Squirming and shrieking in his arms, he tells me to be quiet again. I let his large arms calm me.

My back to his chest, he nuzzles into my neck. "That's better."

"I need a cup of tea," I chirp.

"I'll get you one later. Go back to sleep," he mutters.

"I can't. I'm up at this time every day. I have a natural body clock. Two little people in your life will do that to you."

"Argh, I remember those days." He kisses my shoulder tenderly. "Awful."

"Great fun."

"Diaper changes."

"Laughter."

"Bottle feeding."

"Snuggles."

"Everything takes twice as long."

"Best friends for life."

"I'll give you that. But all you do is worry if you're doing everything right."

"Watching them grow and learn is magical."

"Sleepless nights."

"Not as they get older, Knox." I tap his hand that's now squeezing my boob.

"I remember being tired. I juggled Lincoln, distance learning to earn my degree, and working at the hotel. I was constantly tired," he murmurs against my skin. "Why are we still talking? Go back to sleep." He pulls me in tighter.

"I can't." I wait a few minutes. "Did you really raise Lincoln, work, and study simultaneously?" I never knew this.

"Mm-hmm."

"That must have been tough."

"Mm-hmm."

"What happened to Lincoln's mother?" I ask with softness.

Stilling behind me, he holds his breath for a moment.

He didn't expect me to ask. I shouldn't have asked.

"I don't want to talk about it." He moves out of our embrace and jumps out of the bed.

I roll over and watch as he pulls on his snug black trunks.

"Tea?"

I give him a gentle nod. "Yes, please. I can get up and do it myself."

"No. Stay here. I'll make it and let Sam out for his morning bathroom break."

With that, he turns on bare heel and leaves the room.

Goddammit, Eva. Mad at myself, I punch the mattress on either side of me.

Within ten minutes, he's back.

"I'm sorry. I didn't mean to pry," I say with concern as he passes me the steaming mug of tea.

"It's okay. But I don't want to talk about it. Can't."

"Ever?"

She must have really screwed Knox over. Or she died. I can't work it out.

"Maybe one day."

"Okay."

"Whatever happened, Knox, I'm sorry."

Knox scoots back into his bed beside me and takes a sip of his cup of tea, then rests his head against the leather headboard. "It was a long time ago."

A gnawing sensation grinds in my ribs. Is he not over her?

He needs more therapy sessions.

"Tell me what happened with Ewan. Have the texts stopped?" He diverts the conversation.

So, it's okay for me to divulge my life story, but he doesn't want to share his with me?

Double standards.

I'm a girl with very few secrets from him and he already knows my shitstorm of a disaster I'm living through right now.

Before I unfold the last couple of days' revelations to Knox, I sip my morning cup of breakfast tea as I stare out of his bedroom wall of glass overlooking his backyard. He remembered and made the tea just the way I like it—strong with a dash of milk.

I start. "Ewan came to apologize. With Ruby, I might add. He seemed genuinely apologetic, but I don't know how long his sincerity will last. The only text messages I've received from him since then have been about the boys. The police informed me that is all he's allowed to do via text or call. If he breaks the commitment the police made him sign, then..."

I don't know why, but deep in my gut I feel like it was all for show with Ruby around. From his sly smile to his over-the-top apology and promise to be a better dad and man for them.

I'm not sure I believe him.

I've heard it all before.

It never lasts.

"And if he goes back to his old ways?" Knox asks.

"Then I suppose I have to follow the advice of, thanks to you, my new lawyer, Veronica, and the police. Restraining order or an injunction." I let out a long sigh. "I'll feel terrible if it comes to that. All he'll do is blame me for taking the boys away from him."

"You're doing what's right, Eva. Protecting them. But hopefully it won't come to that."

I hope so too.

"Now it's my turn to ask the questions." I turn to face him.

His dark eyes look worried as his brows pinch together.

"First of all. This joint venture thingy. Tell me about that."

On safer topics, his face relaxes. "Okay, hear me out." He places his mug on his nightstand and faces me, tucking the covers around his waist. I find his athletic chest very distracting.

Focus, Eva. Business head on.

He becomes animated. "The reason I learned how to kizomba was a combination of selfish reasons and also research. The dance retreat I attended in Greece was incredible. But what if we offered an all-inclusive dance retreat here in Castleview Cove? It would be a *Dirty Dancing* getaway as such. But exclusive, high-end. We would offer it to everyone of all skill levels. Over five days, lessons in ballroom, the tango, kizomba, Latin, salsa—you and your sisters would decide what to include. And we only run it twice a year. We limit the spaces. They stay with us; you and your sisters teach. We charge ten grand a head."

"Ten grand per person?" I almost spit out my tea.

"Yes," he says seriously. "They get to stay at a five-star hotel, high-end group dance lessons in the ballroom, breakfast and lunch included as well as evening meals. Access to the spa. We always include airport transfers as standard. But yeah, five-day, four-night stay. You girls receive half per head. What do you say?"

"For each person we receive five grand a head?" I ask, shocked at his proposal. This is not what I was expecting.

"Yes. And we would limit numbers to forty people, twenty couples."

I quickly do the math in my head. Two hundred thousand pounds.

See, I'm not flaky; I have a good business head on my *artsy-fartsy* shoulders.

"And you want to run this twice a year?"

"Yes. Maybe three times." He tilts his hand back and forth in the air, considering.

"Can I speak to Eden and Ella first?"

I don't even have to ask my sisters. It'll be a firm yes. It would move us closer to purchasing a new dance studio. Four hundred thousand pounds closer, minus the tax and the cost for our wages to teach, but much closer and quicker. And that would be running it twice a year; three times a year would be a game changer.

"I would expect you to make these decisions together. Also, it's a big ask. Two to possibly three weeks of every year away from your business. Plus, the preparation."

It's not. We have lots of admin staff now and we could hire a few more temporary dance teachers to run the school on those weeks. We know many dance instructors desperate to work with us. They are patiently waiting in the wings.

"Okay. Leave it with me." Inside I'm squealing like a piggy, and I'm finding it really hard to contain myself.

"You're smiling. Like a full beam of sunshine smile."

"I'm happy. Thank you for considering us."

"I won't be making the proposal to anyone else. It's your dance school or no one else and we don't run a dance retreat."

"Wow, no pressure," I scoff.

I can't wait to call Ella and Eden.

"Did you want to ask me something else?" He removes my cup of tea from my hands, rests it on the nightstand beside his, and then straddles me around his waist.

He loves being close to me. I'm not used to someone wanting to be so touchy-feely with me though. But it's nice. I like it.

Tucking a strand of my hair behind my ear, he strokes his thumb across my cheek. I feel his touch all the way into my soul.

"Eva?"

I clear my throat. "Sorry. You made me lose my train of thought. Um, oh, yeah. Why did Hamish ask you if it was Monday? What happens on a Monday? And why was he so excited to see you?"

He dips his gaze from mine as if embarrassed.

I place my forefinger under his chin, forcing him to make eye contact with me.

Surprising me, he eventually says, "Every Monday morning, before your dad and I head out for a game of golf, Hamish and I race your dad in the quad bikes." He cringes through his apprehensive jaw. "I know he shouldn't be on the quad bike. He's only three, I know, but he loves it. And I'm safe. I wrap my arms around him tight and we only do twenty miles per hour, at most. He thinks we are going superfast. Supersonic, actually, but we aren't. Every week, Hamish and I win. Every week, your dad lets us win. Every Monday, Hamish and I win hot chocolate."

With my hands looped around Knox's neck, I look at him with admiration and alarm.

"We've always told Hamish to keep it as our secret because

you would go crazy if you knew we took him on the quads to race."

"He's never told me." My child can't keep a burp in. Gosh knows how he managed to keep this a secret.

"I think he knows he would lose his hot chocolate on a Monday."

"With marshmallows?"

"*And* cream."

"Yeah, that would be why," I whisper softly. "How long have you been doing this for?"

"Since you separated from Ewan. I wanted to cheer him up. He told me one day he missed his daddy."

Astonished, I can't think of anything to say. My heart aches for my sweet boy.

"It's the best part of my week, being with Hamish."

As if I didn't think my heart could take any more, he then says, "He's a lovely kid. And it made me feel closer to you." His voice is calm.

"When did things change, Knox? Your attraction to me? I asked you last night. You said two years ago. But when?"

He's resistant at first, but then he says, "It was one afternoon on the beach. The sun was shining. I was walking Sam. You were alone. Barefoot. You had on a bright-yellow sundress. You stopped, looking out to sea, lost in your thoughts. And for a brief moment, the clouds covered the sun. Everything went gray, and when they finally parted like a ray of light, the sun shone down on you. I can't explain what happened. But I saw you."

He saw me. How incredibly beautiful.

"I wanted you, Eva. I felt a change. Something happened to me. I was so mad at myself."

"Why?"

"Because it was wrong of me to want you. To see you that way. You were, *are*, my friend's daughter. Fourteen years my junior. You're only three years older than Linc. It felt wrong. And you *were* married too."

"So what changed? Why did you ask me to stay with you on the weekend?"

I want to know.

"Impatience. Longing. Deep knowing that you're... I don't know." He runs his lean fingers through his dark hair. "I'm not good at talking about my feelings."

"You're doing a great job so far." I kiss him tenderly. "Can you let me finish for you?"

He nods dubiously. "Yeah."

"Where you struggle to find the words, I don't. When you back off, I lean in. When you push me away, I will gravitate toward you. I'll be the yin to your yang. Because life is full of contrasts, Knox, and that's exactly what you and I are. Opposites. You have to feel pain sometimes to enjoy the pleasure. Other times you have to take a leap of faith to reap the benefits, and sometimes you have to admit, give in to your inner being, listen, and tune in when something feels so aligned, even when you fight with yourself that it feels wrong. Because destiny can't be avoided. Not if you feel a powerful pull toward the unknown and it feels like it's your life path."

Astounded by my words, he remains still.

He eventually says, "Is that how you feel, Eva? Like I'm your destiny?"

This is quite a deep conversation for a Thursday morning before the sun has even risen, but he needs an answer. So do I.

"Answer me first. What I described, is that how you feel?"

He stalls.

"It's okay to admit how you feel, Knox. It's what makes us human. Feeling."

"I do," he says quietly. "I feel a deeper bond with you than I have ever felt with anyone else before."

"It's intense. Instant." I'm not asking a question.

"Yeah."

"Undeniable."

"Yeah."

"Scary as hell."

"Scared shitless."

"It's okay to be scared. I am too."

"Yeah?"

"Yes," I say firmly. "I have played every scenario out in my head of how, when, and what we tell our family and friends, and if I'm not ready, I'm not sure they are." I let out a faint laugh, then squeeze this physically strong man in my arms. Emotionally, he's fragile. Although he would never admit that to anyone.

"You don't have to tell me. For me to know you've had your heart broken, Knox. That you don't trust easily and that you're scared and you hold back. You promised me you would be my earth, moon, and stars. I believe you. I trust you and I will be your sunshine, but you have *got* to let me in. I will never be dishonest. I will never cheat on you, and I will never break your heart. I've never serial dated. I've been with only one other man my whole life and I took a marriage vow *through sickness and health*. I meant those words, but he broke my heart because he didn't love or cherish me as he vowed to do. My love wasn't strong enough to keep us together. We weren't aligned. But you were right." I smile. "My boys were the best thing to ever happen to me. They were the reason Ewan and I married. Like Lincoln was for you and..."

He finishes my sentence. "Olivia. Lincoln's mother is named Olivia."

Olivia. Finally, a name.

"Thank you for sharing that with me," I reassure him with a soft smile.

"I haven't said her name out loud in a very long time," he says with quiet emphasis.

"You don't have to say it again."

"It's okay. It helps. She is Linc's mother, after all."

"Is she still alive, then?"

"Yes."

I don't ask any more. He'll tell me when the timing is right for him.

"You have a kind heart, Eva. I think that's what I like about you the most."

"Not so keen on the early bird part of me, though, right?"

"Honestly, I like every part of you."

"And I like all the parts of you, too. Apart from one thing."

His expression grows serious.

"I don't know what part of you thought it was a good idea to sleep with Tabitha MacEvoy."

"Oh, I do."

"Your dick."

He grimaces. "That sounds so crass."

"I'm right though, aren't I?"

He groans, and his mouth unpleasantly twists. "I'm not proud of myself. But there aren't that many women in Castleview Cove."

"There are hundreds of women passing through your hotel every year. Rich women, socialite women."

"Yeah, but no one I've ever felt attracted to."

"Except me."

"Apart from you, but you were not an option. Married, remember." He squeezes my backside.

"Soon-to-be divorced."

"Couldn't come quick enough."

"Veronica reckons six months."

"Too long." He traces the slight curve of my hips.

"So you're calling Tabitha today?"

"Yes."

"Make it official. No more fuck buddy arrangement. It's over."

"Consider it done."

"You're mine, Knox Black."

"I'm all yours, Sunshine," he confirms.

My heart booms in my chest at his admission.

He's beginning to open up to me.

One slow graceful waltz step at a time.

CHAPTER 14

Eva

Stunned mid-lick, Eden stops lapping at her Scottish Tablet ice cream sundae. "Say that again, Eva?"

Seated round the pastel-lilac and powder-blue semicircle booth of Castle Cones Ice Cream Parlor, for the second time, I repeat Knox's dance retreat proposal to Eden and Ella, and of course, these days, wherever there is Eden and Ella, there is Hunter and Fraser.

Hunter's mathematical sports brain is doing the sums. "Four hundred thousand pounds. That's almost five hundred and fifty thousand dollars," he blurts out.

Hunter always reverts to his American currency. Since he moved to Scotland full-time and married Eden, he can't get used to the British pound. I'm sure he will, eventually.

He continues. "It would be more if you run it three times a year. Do it. It's a smart business move."

It would definitely help me buy Ewan out of the house and maintain some sort of normality for my boys, at the very least.

"One hundred percent. Work out the schedule. Get the

contract signed. It's a no-brainer," Fraser pipes in, drumming his fingers against the tabletop.

Ella still hasn't said anything.

"Helllooooo." I wave my hand in front of Ella's face. "Are you there?" Ella pushes my hand away.

Eden chuckles. "Ella's in shock. So am I. Ten grand a head and we get half? Are you sure?"

"Yeah. Positive. I need the green light from you girls and we'll get a contract prepared and signed. Deal done. Then we need to plan, sort out studio staff coverage. A schedule for the five days. I was thinking we might do a dance-off on the last day or a showcase for each couple. Let everyone shine."

"I love the sound of that, Eva." Eden shovels a heaping spoonful of ice cream into her mouth. That girl sure loves ice cream.

I turn my attention to Ella, who's seated next to me. "What do you think?"

Gobsmacked. She throws her arms around my neck. "I think it's the best day of my life."

"Hey." Fraser points at himself. "I thought the day I showed you our new house was the best day of your life. Or the day I asked you to marry me was the best day of your life."

We know he's kidding.

"Oh yeah, those too." Ella brushes Fraser off as she unwraps herself from my neck. "This is unbelievable. A total game changer for us. Maybe we'll get our new studio sooner than we expected."

"That's what I thought too." It's quite exciting.

"And Knox proposed this to you on Wednesday night and you've waited until Saturday lunchtime to tell us? Here? Now?"

Actually, it was while I was in his lap on Thursday morning in his bed.

But I don't say that. Instead, I say, "I've been busy. I'm sorry."

The rest of my week was taken up with teaching dance

classes, lawyer's phone calls, and then wrestling my boys to and from childcare, school, after-school clubs, bridesmaid dress fittings, and I still found the time to cook, clean, remember to feed myself, and do the ironing. It's amazing what lots of orgasms can do. I feel re-energized.

Plus, all the sexting Knox and I have been sending one another all week. I live my minutes, hours, and days for them.

And of course my boys. They keep me sane.

Speaking of which. "Mommy, look what Toni gave us." Archie floats a gigantic luminous swirled rainbow-colored ice cream into my view. I've had one of those myself before and it tastes like caramel. I turn to discover Hamish has the same size cone but in a bright-blue color; I think that's bubblegum flavor. Those are at least three scoop cones.

"Wow, those cones are almost the same size as your head," I exclaim as they shuffle into the booth beside us.

Oh well, at least it won't be me having to deal with their hyperactivity later.

From three o'clock onward, Mom and Dad are taking the boys for me overnight because we are hitting the town tonight. Knox will be out, too. I can't wait to hit the dance floor with my sisters, Hunter, and Fraser, and no night out would be complete without Toni and Beth.

Beth is, of course, bringing her boyfriend Billy. I think they'll be engaged before the year is through. I hope they will. It's the happiest I've seen Beth.

And Toni's boyfriend, Evan, who's American and Hunter's fitness instructor, is flying in from Florida later this afternoon to spend the next two months training Hunter and Fraser for their upcoming golf tournament in Hawaii at the end of January.

What a life those boys have.

I have a sneaky suspicion Hunter wangled it so Evan could

be here for Ella's wedding and Christmas. Hunter is such a considerate guy.

Toni has been buzzing with excitement for days, waiting for his arrival. And nope, that's not from the vibration of her vibrator. She informed me via text message she's been saving herself, so when they fuck for the first time in months, it will be explosive. Toni always knows how to cheer me up with her silly texts and voice messages.

Ella's heated stare bores into the side of my face. I can hear her thinking. "So let me get this straight."

Oh balls.

"Knox Black paid eighty thousand pounds for dance lessons. With you. You went missing for two days last weekend. You asked him on Wednesday if I could have my wedding reception at his hotel. He said yes, even though it's only three and a half weeks' notice."

"*Our* wedding reception," Fraser interjects.

"Stop interrupting me." Ella points at him, all the while her eyes hold mine.

Rolling my neck to ease the tension I feel building at Ella's interrogation, I suddenly feel hot. Knox is wrong. It's Ella that's the Westie.

Ella pushes. "And then, out of the blue, Knox proposed a dance retreat partnership between his hotel and us."

"It wasn't out of the blue. He thought of it weeks ago. Remember that day on the beach?"

"Oh, I remember that day on the beach, Eva. Vividly." A faint mocking smile edges her lips. "It was as if you and Knox, you know?" She nods her head toward me.

"I like Knoxy," Hamish chimes in with his little voice. "He's nice. We have hot chocolate together." He continues to lick his melting ice cream that's now dripping down over his chubby hands.

Yeah, I like him too, Hamish, *a lot.*

And that's the first time Hamish has ever mentioned Knox before. Bless him.

I grab a couple of large napkins off the table and lay them over Hamish's lap to stop the ice cream from staining his red shorts. Shorts in winter. I know. But it's what he wanted to wear today with flip-flops. He really doesn't care. What a beautiful way to live. Not caring what other people think.

"I don't know what you mean, Ella," I say in a neutral tone, forcing a nervous laugh down that's simmering deep in my belly.

"Oh, yes, you do. You know, like, deep connection. Like you'd... you know?" She makes a fist with one hand and pushes her pointer finger from her other hand into the space between her clenched fist. Then does an in and out motion.

"Oh, my God. Ella!" Eden snorts. "There are children at the table."

"They're too busy eating ice cream," Ella defends her actions.

"Wook at the size of mine, Aunty Ella." Hamish holds his cone up in the air with a giant-sized blue-ice-cream-covered smile. So much mess to clean up before we leave here.

"Mine is yummee," Archie says, entranced with his frozen sweet treat.

"See?" Ella looks at Eden. "They didn't even notice me. So?"

Hunter leans across the table. "Oh, let me explain, Ella."

I love and hate this lot in equal measure.

"For sure, dude's got it bad. I can see it in his eyes," Hunter teases.

"Shut up. It's not like that." My raised voice turns heads.

"It's like that movie *Indecent Proposal*." Eden chips in.

"It's not," I hiss as nerves prickle my skin. "He pays her to sleep with him to pay off their debt."

"Same thing." She gives a one-shouldered shrug.

"Ooooo, defensive." Fraser grins at me.

"The auction money was *for the hospital*.'" Leaning his elbows on top of the table, Hunter does air quotes with his fingers.

Fraser joins in. Leisurely, he places his thick arms along the back edge of the seating booth. "The dance lessons, meant for two people by the way, were a kind gesture, because the money was *for the hospital*.'" Fraser mimics Hunter's air quotes. "Now, here's the kicker. Did you ask Knox about our wedding reception before or after the lights went out in the studio on Wednesday night?"

"Great question, Fraser," Hunter throws in. "Because when Eden and I drove off about ten minutes later, the lights were still off."

These two asshats.

"There was a fault with the lights," I say a little too quickly.

"First I've heard of it." Ella hitches a perfectly preened brow. "Did you report it to Dad to check it out for us, get his maintenance team to have a look?"

"Eh, yeah, I think I did. Maybe I forgot." My new nickname is Fibsterina.

"Ooooo, and what about that echoing on the phone on Saturday? Knox said he doesn't have a pool, but..." Ella holds a manicured finger in the air to make her point. "Dad tells me he does."

"What did you say to Dad?" I gape.

"Uh-huh. And there's all the evidence we needed."

"I'm not sleeping with Knox," I protest.

"No, you're not, because I am," a voice butts in. "And he doesn't take women back to his home. He's very protective of his personal space."

Aw, hell. Just brilliant. Tabitha 'the princess' MacEvoy.

But a nice save.

She stands at the foot of our table, just off to the side of the three-seater stroller where my triplet nephews are all snuggled up, sleeping. So damn cute.

"See? Told you." I point to Tabitha. "Knox and Tabitha are a *thing*," I say, knowing good and well they are not.

"We're more than a thing." Tabitha's tight lips curl. "We'll be getting married. Watch this space. And as if he would go with you, Eva." She looks me up and down like I'm a piece of dog shit on her shoe. "You are way too young for him. And look at the way you dress." She flares her nostrils as if the stench from my outfit offends her. "You are so *not* his type."

I look down and question my vintage dark-green and red leopard print wrap skirt and simple tucked in white tee shirt I am wearing today. I thought I'd matched it perfectly with my forest green Fedora hat with a contrasting white leather band. Clearly not.

I love my outfit today.

"Hey, uptight Tabby. You watch your tongue." Ella squares her shoulders.

"Rude," Eden mutters.

"Do us a favor, Tabitha." Fraser looks at me as he covers Archie's ears. "Cover Hamish's ears, please, Eva." I do. He continues. "Go fuck yourself, sweetheart. If you have nothing nice to say, don't say it all. It's true what they say about you, Tabitha. You're a class A bitch with no class."

Holding my tongue, I maintain my cool and sit up straighter, grateful for Fraser having my back.

"And what they about you is true too, Fraser. A Neanderthal with a filthy mouth. I also read in the papers you'd cheated on your ex-wife. Good luck, Ella." Flashing her wears, she pulls her caramel designer tote bag into the crook of her elbow and leaves on her red-soled heels.

"Motherfucker," Fraser hisses with his hands still over Archie's ears as he continues eating his never-ending ice cream.

"Don't let her upset you, Fraser. She doesn't know the full

story." Comforting him, I remove my hands from Hamish's ears and reach my hand out, gesturing for him to take it. I cover his hand with mine and give it a squeeze. "Thank you for sticking up for me." I like having two big burly brothers-in-law. It's quite nice.

Even when they are teasing me.

"Oh, she will know the full story. Trust me. She knows everything. She's a wind-up merchant." Fraser watches Tabitha's back as she leaves the parlor.

"I know. Seeking Knox out, like she was on some kind of hunting expedition, she turned up at the studio on Wednesday evening and she was mean to me then too. She said I was *artsy-fartsy*. I don't like her."

"*Whoa*, she must be really awful if you don't like her. You girls like everyone." Hunter takes a sip of his soda. "She seems incredibly likeable, too. What's not to love?" he says sarcastically. "And what the hell does Knox see in her?"

"Pussy," Fraser says without thinking.

Argh. I'm jealous of her, knowing what Knox is like in bed. The thought of her even so much as pressing a finger to his skin gives me the collywobbles.

"I would like a pussycat, Momma. Can we get one?" Hamish asks, all sticky fingers and gooey mouth.

"Can we call it Tabby?" Archie chimes in.

We all burst out laughing.

Well, that diverted the conversation from Knox and me.

Thank you, Tabitha, Hamish, and Archie.

Nice diversion.

"Oh, I need your help with the centerpieces for the wedding reception and picking the wedding favors, Eva. Eden isn't free on Monday anymore when I have the appointment. Could you come with me instead, please?"

"Yes, no problem at all."

More to-do list stuff and more childcare to reshuffle.

Great.

"Which one are you fucking?" Beth, my forthright friend, shouts into my ear over the infectious beats of "Tell Me Something Good" by Ewan McVicar.

We're at the Vault. The only nightclub in town. It's beautifully styled in shimmering golds and plush black fabrics. Beth's brother, Roman, manages the venue. She always scores us a VIP spot up the stairs. Tonight is no exception.

Leaning against the glass balcony, I look down at both Lincoln and Knox, who are both propped against the bar. They're both similar, but so very different.

"I'm not telling." I bite my straw seductively.

As if Knox senses me, he looks up and throws me a knowing smile.

"Lincoln's old man is sexy as hell. Fuck me, is he hot. What I wouldn't do to get a taste of his man-meat."

I know what she's doing. Beth's trying to gauge my reaction. But I don't give her what she seeks.

"You're no fun." She nudges my shoulder. I do enjoy the daily sparring between us all.

"What are we looking at?" Ella joins us.

"We're ogling. Billionaire playboys." Beth swirls the ice around in her glass tumbler.

"Oh, now let me see." Ella peers over the balcony. "I knew it. Eden, Toni," Ella calls them both over.

We become a party of five.

"Roulette style, place your bets now, girls. Knox or Lincoln? Who will Eva be going home with tonight? Make your decision now." Mouth drumming, Ella beats invisible drumsticks against the side of the balcony.

Well, that's a given. I already left my stuff there from the other night so I could stay over at Knox's tonight again. I'm loving my newfound freedom and balance in my life again, time with my boys, work, and love life.

Er, not love. Sex. Sex life is what I meant.

Ella points her imaginary drumstick at each of the girls as if it's a microphone and they all say Lincoln, apart from Ella. She's fixated. I need to divert her off the Knox path.

Synchronized Knox, Lincoln, Lincoln's two friends, Jacob and Owen, along with Knox's buddies, Shane and Corey, all look up in our direction.

"Or is it Jacob or Owen?" Eden raises her voice over the music. "Shane and Corey are both married."

"Could be." Toni giggles. "C'mon, Eva, put us out of our misery."

"Okay." I move away from the balcony. The boys below follow my every move as I move along the transparent walkway toward the curving stairs to take me to the floor below.

I take my time down the steps and quickly send Knox a text from my smart watch.

Me: Go with the flow. Trust me.
Knox: Okay. You look incredible tonight.

Being sure not to trip on my black and pink embroidered sheer maxi dress, I hike it up, allowing it to skim the floor no more. I'm wearing a solid black strapless corset bodysuit underneath the soft floaty fabric. It's provocatively boho chic. But classy. I feel like a million dollars. Although I felt like that earlier too before Tabitha rained all over my parade.

Tiptoeing along the outer edge of the bar in my high black multi-strap gladiator heels, I finally reach my destination. I look up one more time, eyeing my line of girls, anticipation written all over their faces. I love those four. I flash them a massive smile, then find my target.

"Hi."

Hyper aware all eyes are on me now. The boys all stop talking.

"Uh, hi, Eva. Would you like a drink?" He gulps.

I move in closer. "I'm good. Would you like to dance, Lincoln?"

"I'm not very good. But okay." He thrusts his bottle of beer into Jacob's chest for him to take.

I shift my focus skyward again to catch Toni, Eden, and Beth clinking their glasses together in celebration while Ella slaps her forehead and I think she mouths, she is lying.

I'm playing a naughty, dangerous game. Using Lincoln as our diversion. It's a necessary evil for the time being to disguise mine and Knoxs' affinity.

I'll tell my friends and family soon about Knox.

Pinky promise.

The entire song, Lincoln, keeps a safe distance between us. But I need this to look real. Looping my arms around his neck, we move together to the happy beat of "Say So" by Doja Cat. Placing his hands on my waist, he moves them down toward my ass, but I instinctively move them back to my waist.

I twirl around and secure eyes with Knox. I jut my chin in recognition as he takes a sip of his amber liquid. He's not happy. I don't blame him.

Fix it, Eva.

I raise my hand in the girls' direction above and summon them down to dance. Within seconds, they're beside me. Lincoln says something to Toni, and she laughs. Owen and Jacob join us too, and before I know it, we've formed a mini circle on the dance floor.

Now that feels better. Less personal.

I continually check Knox, who is still rooted to the spot. Like a stalker, his senses are all tuned into me.

He looks lush in his dark jeans and navy dress shirt, with a tiny white embroidered logo on his chest I can't quite make out. I guarantee he's wearing expensive leather Chelsea boots. It's his statement look when he's out. Which isn't very often, but when he's out, he's always immaculate and expensive-looking.

For the next five songs, our little ennead dance together before the tempo changes and the first mellow piano notes of "Love Nwantinti" flow through the nightclub.

I shift my focus to Knox. It's what we danced to in the studio together. Then he made me come.

He sets his glass on the bar. With intent, he propels toward me.

Corey and Shane shake their heads, laughing. They know.

Unable to move, I stand, waiting to greet him.

He doesn't ask; he simply takes me in his arms, assumes his kizomba dance position, and leads me around the floor.

I tilt my head upward. "Hi."

"Hey, Sunshine."

"I'm sorry."

"I know. It's okay. But I can't stand another minute not being able to touch you." He leans in. I close my eyes. Cheek to cheek we step back and forth together in harmony. God, how I love dancing with this man.

When I open my eyes again, over his shoulder, I see Ella is dancing with Fraser and she mouths, I knew it.

As if from nowhere, Eden taps my shoulder. I lean back to find her hanging off Hunter's neck. She's so short compared to Hunter. But she's not wanting to talk to me. She asks Knox, "Did you learn all of those dance moves in one lesson, Knox?" She calls over the music, puzzled.

"Yes," I answer.

While Knox says, "No."

Flippity flip.

As if the penny drops, Eden's eyes light up and she puts two and two together.

Hunter bursts out laughing and puts his hand out to shake Knox's. "Welcome to the family, man."

Knox doesn't take it. "I don't know what you mean."

"What the fuck ever." Always playful, Hunter spins Eden around. Eden leans to the side, peeking back, and draws a zip over her mouth.

"We are shit at this," I whisper in his ear as we continue to dance.

Running my gaze around the dance floor, no one else is looking at us. Even Lincoln has found a new dance partner.

"Do Corey and Shane know?" I ask him.

"They figured it out. They heard you in my office the other day when they were on speakerphone. And they also heard about my auction bid. They've been making fun of me all night."

"You have to buy me to get me." I poke fun at him.

"Yeah, like *Pretty Woman* apparently."

I step back and place my hands on my hips. "I am not a hooker."

He flings his head back and lets out a rich laugh. I love his laugh.

"You could have fooled me with that barely-there dress you have on. All you need is the thigh-high boots."

I look down at myself. "My whole body is covered up, Knox."

Do I look like a hooker?

"I'm joking." He pulls me into his warm arms again. "You are stunning. I don't know why you never considered modeling. You have this whole glamazon thing going on. You're fucking beautiful, Eva. You dazzle me."

We aren't moving in time to the music anymore. We're just holding one another, gently swaying together.

"You smell nice," I say.

"Tom Ford."

"Knew it. Is it from the same rich people shop you get the mattresses from?"

He's boyishly affectionate when he squeezes my waist.

"The exact same shop, Sunshine. What time are you heading home?"

I'm tired now. I check my wristwatch.

"Now?"

"Do you have your key fob?"

I bob my head.

"I'll see you at home then."

Home.

He steps back and takes a bow. Lifting my hand to his lips, he kisses it gently, then thanks me for the dance.

With that beautiful gesture, I know he's lassoed my heart forever.

Standing tall, he smiles at me, but something catches his eye over my shoulder and his face turns to thunder.

I glance back.

There she is.

Tabitha.

CHAPTER 15

Knox

Fuck.

Me.

To.

Hell.

"You didn't call me, Knox." Tabitha smiles through innocent words. But it's laced with a deep unpleasant gaze in Eva's direction.

What the fuck made me wet my dick inside her I have yet to figure out.

My inner devil screams the word *convenience* in my ear.

Eva and Tabby couldn't be more different. My free-spirited Eva, all lush, ethereal, and kindhearted.

Looking at Tabby with a new perspective, all she needs is the leather belt to complete her outfit, and she's one step away from looking like Miss Trunchbull. Forced and uncomfortable, exactly what sex felt like with her, too.

Eva looks at me with a tilted head as if to say *you're kidding me, you still haven't broken up with her?*

Keeping my distance, I shout over to Tabby. "I forgot. There was a fire in the spa. I've had a busy week."

"What?" Eva exclaims as her eyebrows shoot into her hairline. "Was anyone hurt?" She cares.

I brush it off. "No. It happens all the time. Essential oils mix in with the fabric. You wash them, put them in the dryer, and *boom*." Stop waffling on the dance floor, Knox.

I rub my forehead. "I'm sorry. I forgot, Tabby." I look back at her stern face.

"It's okay. Do you want to dance?"

"I was leaving."

"Should I come back to the hotel with you?"

"No." Never again. "Can we meet this week instead?"

"Yes. Your hotel suite?"

"No," I say firmly. "I was thinking of meeting elsewhere."

"Oh?" She blinks, wide-eyed and confused.

"What about Wee Oscars? For a meal."

Eva observes our interaction.

Tabby turns her head slowly in Eva's direction. "You're like a bad smell, Eva. You keep showing up. Why are you still here? And why are you dressed as if you're about to hit the center stage of a hippie festival?"

Eva's eyebrows dip and she squeezes her eyes closed as if in pain.

Ewan has done enough name-calling toward that girl to last a lifetime. No way will I allow Tabby to verbally abuse her too.

"Tabby! That is enough. You know what? Fuck this." I stalk toward her. "I didn't want to do this here, but you've left me no other option. Me and you. Over. We have been for four months. Not that we were anything much to begin with. You are not my girlfriend. Please stop telling everyone that. I am not marrying you. I would never marry someone so rude, so out of touch with reality or entitled. You have never worked a hard day in your life, Tabby. Don't you ever, and I mean this *ever*, speak to Eva like that again. In fact, don't even so much as look at her."

Did the music get turned down?

I look up. At least thirty sets of eyes are all on me with Lincoln at the forefront of the crowd, staring at me in a *what the fuck* way.

Shit.

"Or anyone else, for that matter. Your manners need addressing. As does your attitude."

"Right. Seems like you've made up your mind." Tabby looks around. She's loving the attention. Then she drops a bombshell. "Your son was a better fuck than you, anyway."

A wave of gasps and soft laughter breaks out.

"*Buuurn,*" I hear someone say.

Lincoln steps forward urgently. "I never slept with her. No way. She's seventeen years older than me. She's lying."

I eye Tabby, who's wearing a smug face.

"I swear on YaYa's life, Dad. I never slept with her. She's deranged."

He's telling the truth. No way would he ever swear on his grandmother's life. He's a sucker for the truth, and the bond he has with my mother is extremely special. She's been more like his mother than a grandmother.

Tabby lets out a maniacal laugh and then says, "Ha, gotcha."

Fucking.

Crazy.

Bitch.

"I think you just showed your true colors, Tabby." Lincoln flares his nostrils. "Thank goodness my dad isn't marrying you. You'd make a shitty stepmom. What a horrific thing to say." With that, he weaves around Tabby's stoic frame and disappears into the crowd.

Low whispers trickle everywhere.

Why would she say that?

That's a low blow.

No way is that hunk of a man bad in bed. Look at him.

Imagine saying you'd slept with his son. What a terrible lie to tell.

"See you around, Tabby. Preferably not." I turn my back on her.

"I'm still on the Castleview Business Circle. I'll see you then," she shouts out to me.

Superb.

I make my way toward Shane and Corey through the thick sea of nightclubbers. On my arrival Corey hands me a whisky.

"You need that. Lucky escape." Corey's green eyes glow. "What the fuck happened to Tabby? Since when did she become so fucking unhinged?"

I tilt my head up and scan the room for Eva.

"I stopped seeing her four months ago. She's been obsessively calling me, texting me. Turning up at the hotel at random times. I told her we are nothing more than friends anymore, but she's been oddly persistent." I shudder.

"You're wise to move on. Stay away from her." Corey leans against the bar. "Fucking bunny boiler, that one."

Eva said the same.

I down the entire glass of oak-flavored liquid. It burns as it goes down. "Fuck. I'm too old for this shit."

"It's like high school all over again." Shane pauses. "Remember Melanie Forrester? She was obsessed with you." He shakes his head, chuckling to himself.

"She had a screen-printed picture of you on her pillow. She mailed it to you in pieces when you split up with her." Corey laughs, winding a finger around in the air at his temple. "Cuckoo. You're a magnet for the crazies."

Then after that was Olivia.

I've never been lucky with women.

"Eva's gone, by the way," Shane informs me.

"Gone?"

"Yeah. With her usual crew. And your son and his buddies."

A twinge of jealousy snowballs in my chest.

"Linc said they were off to try the new wine bar," Corey adds. "Here's a word of advice, take or leave it. But... you could make it easy for yourselves. Tell Charlie. He'll understand. As will Linc."

"Charlie trusts me. He confides in me about his business and life. His daughters. I can't; it's too soon. I've only been seeing her since last Friday. We don't even know where this, *us* thing, is going." I hunch my shoulders and fold my arms over the bar.

"And yearning for her for how long? Two years? I think you've waited long enough, Knox. Tell everyone. If you don't, it will only manifest into something bigger. And not in a good way."

Maybe he's right.

I push myself off the bar and shove my hands into my jeans pockets. "I'm going home."

"We are staying out." Shane smiles mischievously. "Free pass."

"You'll last two more drinks. Maybe one at most."

"Yeah, you're right. I'm on a promise with Alice tonight if I get home before midnight and in one piece." Corey stands wide, then runs his hands through his wild blond hair. It never looks tidy.

Alice and Corey met at university and have been together ever since.

It's admirable.

Shane jumps in. "I should do the same. I hesitated the other day when Emma asked me if her new dress was nice so I'm on a blow job ban for a month. But maybe, just maybe, if I get home at a reasonable time tonight, she might reduce it."

"You're an asshole." I chuckle.

They're both pussywhipped, Shane, more so. He and Emma

have been together since high school. Sickly sweet together and more in love than they have ever been.

I'm disappointed in myself for never finding what they both have.

It sucks.

Shane's eyes fill with wanderlust. "She gives the best fucking head, man. Porn star status blow jobs. It's the fucking eye contact and the deep throating. Honestly, man, she's the fucking best. I would say you should try it, but I can't allow that. Especially if she got her hands on you, you handsome rake." He punches my arm.

"Fuck off." Although I know what he means. Eva sucked me like a fucking porn star on Wednesday night. My cock twitches at the memory.

"I saw that too in *Scottish Entrepreneur* magazine. You're officially the most sought-after bachelor in all of Scotland," Corey confirms.

"What a pile of shit. I'm taken." I think.

"Yeah, but they don't know that. I don't think anyone will touch you now; they all know your unhinged ex-girlfriend slept with your son."

"Fuck, that'll be in the paper tomorrow if word gets out. She wasn't my girlfriend."

They both laugh out loud.

"If you want that blow job, Shane, and if you want to get your brains fucked out tonight, Corey, then less of the lip. I can call my driver now and take you home to your good women."

"Fuck it. He's right. Let's go home." Corey downs the last of his beer.

We move to the exit. "Come on, then, dumb and dumber. I'll text my driver."

"Eh, we're not the dumb ones. Mr. I Fucked Your Son." Shane throws his head back with laughter.

Bastards. I am never living this one down.

"Better still, I'm fucking your daughter. You like living dangerously, Knox. What's the fucking sex like with a younger woman anyway these days? I bet she can go all night." Shane pushes the gigantic nightclub door open for us. "Your dick might fall off."

"I'm surprised it hasn't already. He's been single for so long." Corey begins banter ping-pong with Shane as if I'm not here. It's their favorite game.

And so it begins.

"He should have married his hand."

"Being a doctor, I can prescribe you Viagra."

I stop listening as they continue mocking me.

My phone buzzes in my back pocket. Pulling it into my hand, I'm instantly relieved to see a sunshine emoji smiling back at me.

Eva: Didn't want to hang around. Left with Lincoln. Divergence! Off to The Basement.

I quickly send a text to my driver.
He replies he's already outside.
Good man.
I send Eva a reply.

Me: Are you still staying with me tonight?
Eva: Of course I am. I'm just having one drink. I have to sneak away from Lincoln, though.

Thank God, Tabby didn't scare her away.

Olivia ran at the first hurdle. I want Eva to stick around. For good.

Me: I can send my driver for you once he drops me at the house.

221

Eva: Great idea. As long as he keeps his lips shut about us. Tell him to meet me on the corner of Elmwood Place.

Me: He's not allowed to talk about anything involving my life. He's contracted. I'm sorry about Tabby.

Eva: You should have told her this week you were through. Properly. Then she wouldn't have caused a scene tonight. We need to tread carefully with her.

Me: You're right. I should have. I didn't like the way she spoke to you.

Eva: Thank you for sticking up for me. She's a very rude woman.

Me: See you at home, Sunshine.

Eva: Can't wait Mr. *black heart emoji* xoxo

She put kisses and cuddles on the end of her text.

"What the fuck are you smiling at you lovesick fool?" Shane pushes my shoulder, making me stumble as we stride out into the freezing cobbled street.

"I'm not," I protest.

"You are," Corey says adamantly.

"I'm not."

"You fucking are," they both say in unison.

I am.

Eva

"Where are you going, Eva?"

Lincoln.

Aw, damn it all to hell. I turn back around on my sky-high heels on the steep steps.

I announced I was going to use the bathroom, but really I was secretly sneaking away.

The Basement wine bar is situated below street level inside

an old brewery. It's actually pretty cool and I'll definitely be coming back. As much as I want to stay, I want to go *home* to Knox. It's going to be Wednesday again before I see him.

I already despise this sneaky stuff, and it's only been a week.

Lincoln casually glides up the stairs.

One step down from me, we're the same height.

"I'm going home. Gotta get back for the boys."

"Eden mentioned all the kids are at your mom and dad's tonight, though," he says, confused, his forehead wrinkling.

"Yeah, but early morning pickup." I start to get flustered.

He thumbs over his shoulder back in the direction of the wine bar. "But Eden and Hunter said you're not picking them all up until later tomorrow afternoon."

Christ sakes, Eden.

"Oh, yeah, right. I forgot." I'm not keen on how close Lincoln is. "I best get going, anyway." I go to take a backward step up the ascending stairs.

"Eva." Lincoln gently grasps my elbow. "I like you."

Oh, not good. Time-out. I call time-out.

"And I would like to take you out sometime."

"I'm not sure that's a good idea, Lincoln."

"Why? Am I too young? Is that what it is? 'Cause I'm only three years younger than you."

"Nope. No. It's not that. It's..."

"I want to kiss you."

"That's definitely not a good idea," I whisper, not sounding quite so confident.

A couple leaving the bar step into the small hallway below and I have to shuffle across to one side to make space for them to pass.

"Oh, hey, Eva," Matthew greets me as he slowly ascends the steps with his new wife, Tiff. He eyes Lincoln and me standing on the stairs as he passes.

Matthew was Ewan's best man at our wedding. His best

friend. I'm unaware of how close they are these days. I certainly haven't seen Matthew since Tiff and he tied the knot last year, before Ewan and I officially split up. It was another evening I spent watching every drink Ewan drank, every interaction, apologizing on his behalf when Ewan said something rude. It. Was. Not. Fun.

"How are you? You are looking great," Tiff says with a genuine smile.

"Oh, thank you. I'm good. Better." I roll my eyes. "Sorry, I shouldn't say that. I know you and Ewan are friends."

"No need to apologize, Eva. I haven't spoken with Ewan since he took a voluntary layoff. He's never been in touch."

Did I hear that correctly?

"Voluntary layoff?" I'm baffled.

"Yeah. He should have stayed on. It was a foolish move in my opinion. Is he still out of work?"

"He is, yes. He told me he was laid off. *Made* to take it."

Tiff slaps Matthew's jean-clad backside. "Matthew!"

"Shit. I may have put my foot in that one. Did he not tell you?"

I shake my head in dismay.

"Fuck. Look, please don't tell him I told you."

"We don't speak anymore."

"Is it that bad?"

"Yes." They have no idea. "He would have gotten severance pay if he took a voluntary layoff?" He worked there from leaving school, so almost ten years' worth of pay.

Matthew nods.

That scheming son of a bitch.

Forcing my confusion and anger into a neat pile, I straighten myself out with dignity.

"Well, it was nice to see you both again. I'm just saying goodbye to Lincoln." They know I've dismissed them.

"It was good to see you too." Tiff lays a gentle hand on my bare arm. "Take care, Eva."

"Thanks." I suck my lips into my mouth.

Lincoln nods, informing me they've gone. I let out a huge breath.

"He lied to you."

"He did. He's been lying to me for years. There's so much I can't tell you."

"I understand. Will you be okay getting home?"

Your dad's driver is here to pick me up.

"I will be. Thank you." I give him a grateful smile.

Without notice, Lincoln leans in for a kiss, but I pull back and raise my hand in the air just in time. His lips smack against my hand as they make contact.

"We can't happen, Lincoln," I say softly.

"Shit. Now or ever?" He looks embarrassed.

"Ever."

"Okay. I think you and I could be something special. You're not like other girls, Eva. You're pretty remarkable. Unique."

Knox said the exact same words.

"I'm sorry. I don't see you in a romantic way."

He shrugs to hide his embarrassment.

"I get it. I tried though, huh?"

"You did." I rub his shoulder. "You'll meet someone soon, Lincoln. I promise. And she'll blow you out of the water. You'll feel it so deep. It'll be instalove."

"I doubt that. Here, in Castleview Cove?"

"It will happen. The perfect girl is waiting for you. Be patient. She's coming."

I want to tell him it's how I feel about his dad, but I can't, *yet.*

Instalove?

Whoa.

That's not what I meant about Knox and me.

Is it?

"Okay, good chat, Dr. Phil." Lincoln turns away from me.

"Night, Lincoln."

He doesn't turn back.

"Night, Eva."

I look directly down at my feet and mutter to myself, "I know my space is already reserved for me down there in hell. I can hear you making my bed."

Shoulders back, deep breath in, I shake my head.

Time to go home. A tornado of butterflies dances in my lower belly. I can't wait to see Knox and spend the night with him.

Wait till I tell Knox about the Ewan voluntary layoff revelation.

What a douche canoe.

And me? I feel like such a fool.

I must have been the ultimate pushover wife.

Not anymore.

Wait until my lawyer finds out about this too.

Our girl group chat texts appear on my phone screen

Eden: Where are you?

Ella: Are you fucking Knox?

Beth: I thought it was Lincoln?

Ella: It's not Lincoln! He's still here in the bar.

Eden: Did you go home by yourself?

Ella: Tell us, Eva!

Beth: She's not giving anything away.

Toni: Will you clowns shut up. I left the bar 'cause I am trying to get some sexy time in with my man. I haven't seen him in weeks. I'm turning my phone off. I still want to know if you are fucking Knox though, Eva. ;)

Beth: Does he make you call him daddy?

Me: *laughing emoji*

Eden: Text us when you get home to let us know you're safe.
Me: Will do.
Ella: Eva Wallace! You are deeper than the ocean.
Beth: She's never going to confirm or deny.

"Then Matthew told me it was voluntary layoff he took. He wasn't forced," I say through a contented wide morning yawn.

Having slept on Matthew's surprising fact, I don't feel so shocked about it.

"Which means he would have received a payout," Knox says matter-of-factly.

"Yeah, but where is it? It never came into our bank account. He never mentioned money. His explanation was very different. Compulsory layoff, the firm had no money, so no payout. It makes no sense."

It certainly doesn't make a blind bit of difference to my current situation. Screw Ewan and his conniving ways. I will teach my sons to be wonderful humans. Unlike their father.

I turn from my side onto my back, stretching out.

I'm sore from our evening of bedroom gymnastics. It was so worth it. Knox can keep me up all night, anytime of the week. I don't know where he gets his never-ending supply of zest from. Not that I'm complaining.

Returning to Knox's house last night, he'd already popped open a bottle of champagne. We chatted for a while, stuffed our faces with finger food from the refrigerator we could easily shovel into our mouths, then he piped Bastille's "Shut Off The Lights" on repeat through his integrated multiroom sound system, and we danced barefoot in his kitchen in the dark with only the moonlight shining through to keep us company.

Eros, the Greek god of love, doesn't stand a chance. He's so romantic.

Knox has already speared my heart with his golden arrow. I'm smitten.

Falling into bed later than expected, Knox worshipped my body. He kissed every millimeter of me.

Each one seeped deep into my soul.

He held on to me for dear life as he thrust into me with almost brutal passion, staring deep into my eyes as he entered me.

He wasn't subtle. Throwing me into different positions.

The way he sucked on my clit ring like I was the best meal he'd had all day.

I loved every single minute of it.

He made me feel so sexy, so loved, so adored as he whispered how beautiful I am and how he loves my body as he ran his hands over my skin.

It was different from last weekend. Deeper, more emotional.

He's even figured out what makes me come quickly and often, aligning his pelvic bone with my clit ring while raising my hips. He is a phenomenal lover.

The secrecy of our relationship appears to be increasing the intensity between us due to the excitement of being forced to play it cool by day and getting deep down and dirty at night as we share our shady hookups.

Or maybe it's because of him. My very own filthy Greek talking lothario.

I'd love to know what he's saying to me.

With his head in his hand for support, Knox props himself up on his side against the mattress.

"I feel like such a fool. I didn't question Ewan at the time."

"Because you trusted him, Eva." Knox traces his fingertips over the skin of my arm.

"I did. Once."

"It will all work out. Stop worrying."

"You don't know that, Knox. And I am worried. If I have to buy Ewan out of the house, then it will be a lot for me to take on. Ewan no longer contributes, I have many bills to pay for by myself." I'm currently walking a fine line juggling my household bills.

Proportionally, there is enough money coming in to cover my outgoings every month. Fractionally. But we refinanced my mortgage several years ago when I invested in the dance studio. It almost broke us then. We managed with two incomes, and the dance studio started gaining traction and performing financially well, but my wages haven't increased by that much. Our profits have but so have our staff costs and outgoings too.

My concerns keep on flowing. "What's worse, if I have to sell, which Veronica said would be easier to facilitate the divorce because we simply cut the profits down the middle, then it will leave my boys with none of the familiarity or stability I want them to have. I'd need to rent."

"And what about the dance studio? Have you protected it to ensure Ewan doesn't receive a penny of your business?"

"Well, now I never even thought about that."

"Is your business set up as a partnership between you and your sisters?"

"Yes, it is."

"He can't get his hands on it then. You've inadvertently locked him out of your business, so to speak. Your business is safe, Eva."

I may as well ask Knox as he seems to know.

"Okay, what if, hypothetically, someone refinances their house mortgage to invest in a business at the start? And they are married and the couple both contributed toward the mortgage payments that increased because of the refinance. Let's say years later, they get divorced. Would that mean one of the parties involved could potentially stake a claim to the future profits of the business they took the money out of the house for?"

"I am assuming you are talking about yourself, Eva? You don't have to be embarrassed about your income and outgoings."

I twiddle my fingers. "Yeah. I took a chunk of money out of the house to invest in the business. I wish I hadn't now."

"We all have to start somewhere, Eva."

"Give it to me. Where does this leave me?"

"Your business is protected with your sisters. He can't come after that. But he could, however, come after your profits in what is called ownership interest. But he may not know this stuff. Let's assume he doesn't. If I were you, I would buy him out on a property settlement note where you pay him back over a longer period of time, with interest, but it would keep a roof over your head and maintain the stability and familiarity for your boys. The last thing you want is to confuse or unsettle them further."

"And if he knows about ownership interest?"

"Then I would suggest you give him the house in full. Keep him happy. You walk away empty-handed, homeless, but your business would be safe. He doesn't receive any of the profits. It would be a new start for you."

"I could rent somewhere new. I hate that house now. Too many shitty memories." I feel more positive as I say that.

I continue. "I will speak with Veronica this week. See what she says. Form a plan." Then I change the subject. "I have something to tell you. Two things actually. The first one." I hold my finger up in the air. "My sisters said yes to the dance retreat."

"Excellent. Smart business move. I knew you girls would make the right decision. I will ask Veronica to advise who is best in her practice to draft the contracts. I'll do that Monday morning."

"That simple?"

"Yes."

He's a smooth operator in business. He moves fast like a panther.

"Okay. That was easy. Second thing. Now you can't get mad."

"Tell me."

Pulling the cotton sheet over my exposed breasts, I turn onto my side and prop myself up on my elbow to face him.

"Lincoln tried to kiss me last night."

His eyes crinkle at the sides.

"Continue."

"He also asked me out on a date."

"And?"

"I turned him down as gently as I could, stopped him from kissing me, and told him he would find his true flame soon. I think I called it instalove or something. Like us. But not like us. Not love," I blabber, regretting my choice of words. "But what I mean is, someone most unexpected will come along, maybe on your doorstep, around the corner, someone you'll feel a deep connection to. Yeah. That. I think that's what I said." I bite my bottom lip.

"Three weeks," he says.

"What do you mean?"

"That's all we have to wait. Ella and Fraser get married in three weeks. Then we can tell Linc and your family. Three weeks, with a couple of days for them to decompress from the wedding."

"Okay." Yikes. Will Knox and I tell them together or individually?

Hell if I know.

"Ella and Eden have their suspicions. When they saw us dancing, they think they figured it out. I didn't confirm or deny when they text me late last night. But they won't say anything if they do know."

"Hold tight, Sunshine."

"I am."

"It will be worth it."

"I know."

I cup his chin tenderly in my hand, running my thumb over his dark scruff. "You mentioned a swim session before I have to leave. Can we do that now?"

"Yes, but first I need breakfast."

"Oh, me too." Flipping the cover off to shift out of the bed, I'm stopped by Knox. His strong body jumps on top of me.

"That's not what I meant," He says, his voice dark and playful.

Heading south, he pushes my legs open, disappears between them, spreads my soft lips wide, then sinks his thumb deep into my already wet center, making my back arch off the mattress.

"You're always ready for me, Sunshine."

I hook my fingers into his hair and push his mouth over my clit ring.

As the commander of my satisfaction, there's no two ways about it. Knox will never leave me disappointed.

He delivers the best lip service.

It's five star; he knows his customer, responds quickly, listens, and he's exceptionally thorough.

With his clever tongue and hungry mouth, he eats me out until we're both satisfied and I'm thrashing and moaning his name as he catapults me into erotic oblivion.

He ushers me back down from my high, I smile down at him.

"It will be lunchtime soon." He kisses my inner thigh.

And there it is; that's what makes him so much better than a five star because he relentlessly follows up.

He's a five star with distinction.

An award-winning clit champion.

I want more.

Every day won't be enough.

Although every day isn't an option.

For now, I'll have to make do with these little snippets of time and our private stolen moments.

"Fuck me, Knox," I say breathlessly.

"Oh, baby, that was the plan." He pulls out a condom from the nightstand.

"I have an implant. I trust you."

He frowns.

"Are you sure?"

"Never been so certain. I want to feel you."

He groans at this revelation, then settles between my thighs. In one truly dominating deep thrust into me, he bottoms out.

Overwhelming excitement fills my body with his bare, thick length.

I urge him to move.

He flips me over, sits up, and shuffles us over to the edge of the bed to position us perfectly in front of his freestanding ornate mirror leaning against the wall.

He lifts me off his hard cock, sits me on the bed, and commands me to stay exactly where I am.

I can't take my eyes off his incredibly athletic body as he moves over to his chest of drawers and pulls out one of his ties and what I believe to be a bottle of lube. Holy shit, what are his plans?

His thick and ready-for-me length bobs in the air. Knox fists his cock up and down as he makes his way back to me. *I would like to be that hand.*

"Stand up," he instructs, and I do as he requests.

He can be quite intense when he's in full-on sex mode.

From over my shoulder, he says, "Do you trust me,

Sunshine?"

"Yes." I'm excited about what he's about to do.

"Hands behind your back."

Securing my wrists with his silk tie, he then sits on the edge of his giant bed. I turn to face him, but he stops me.

"Uh-uh. Face the mirror. You're gonna ride me reverse cowgirl. Spread those legs wide for me."

Backing onto him, I bend my legs and lower myself. Knox holds the root of his cock and guides me, aligning his cock with my wet flesh. I slide myself down until I'm fully seated.

Knox kisses my shoulder and locks eyes with me in the mirror.

"Fucking beautiful."

He disappears from sight as he lies back. "Now fuck me, Eva."

Using the floor to give me leverage, I bounce up and down. With my hands tied behind my back, I find it difficult at first to find my balance. But then Knox grips on to my hips to help steady me.

He grows harder as I undulate my hips, presenting my derriere to him, or more obviously, my puckered hole. His hands leave my hips, and through the mirror, I watch him pump lube onto his fingers.

Shuffling behind me, his breath becomes labored, then I feel him circle his slick finger around my back entrance.

We've never done this before. He's explored a little but nothing like this.

"Relax, Sunshine."

I continue bouncing up and down for him and I let out a low moan at the stretching sensation I feel as he pushes a finger in. It's strange at first, but then it begins to feel good as he moves his finger in and out of my tight hole.

"Oh, baby, you take me so good," Knox whispers.

It begins to feel even nicer and it's an odd pleasure I want more of. "Deeper, Knox."

He pushes in further.

"You like that, Sunshine."

"Oh God, yeah," I gasp and throw my head back.

Knox pushes in further yet again and I'm on the edge, hanging on to that feeling I love. The heat and sound of our bodies getting off on the pleasure of it all. The frantic ecstasy we both chase, we are so in sync with one another. The heat and throbbing feeling building in my core, him growing bigger inside of me, I love it all.

Knox sits up, wraps his other arm around my waist, and continues to finger fuck my back entrance.

"Your fucking pussy is dripping for me."

He slides his hand from my waist to my neck, wraps his fingers around it, and gives it a squeeze.

"Ah, Knox," I hiss. I love his crass mouth. I tilt my neck to the side and lean back against him to give me better leverage. Spreading my legs wider, I show him what he does to me.

"Look at that pretty pierced swollen pussy. Look at yourself and don't stop fucking me."

Our eyes meet in the reflection.

"Now, Sunshine." His hot breath douses the skin on my neck. "You're gonna have to come quick 'cause you are the sexiest fucking thing I have ever seen and you turn me on so bad. So be a good girl and come for me." I can only nod in agreement.

Painfully slow, he moves his hand over my skin from my neck down my stomach to my jeweled pussy.

His dark eyes turn black as he expertly parts my lower lips and with his middle finger, he circles my clit.

I can't take it anymore. His finger in my back entrance, his cock teasing me and filling me up so good, and his finger playing with my piercing, I let out a low guttural groan that even surprises me. I need to come now.

"Keep your eyes open. Watch," he whispers.

He slaps my clit and it takes my breath away. It's sensational. My pussy pulses in agreement at how lovely it feels.

I pick up the pace, fucking him frantically as he continues to push his finger in out of my behind. He slaps my clit over and over, and when he bites down on the skin of my shoulder, I come. And it's not like anything I have ever felt before.

"There you fucking go. That's my girl," he mumbles against my nape.

My inner walls pulsate, teasing him to come with me on this extraordinary never-felt-before feeling.

My orgasm continues to tear through me as Knox quickly pushes us up from the edge of the bed, ensuring he's still inside of me, and tells me to kneel on the bed.

Pushing my shoulders and face down into the mattress, he then holds on to my tied hands with the other and thrusts in and out of me from behind. I push back, fucking him in return, and I scream into the bed as he pulls another orgasm from my body.

Spilling himself inside of me. He grunts, then stills behind me.

Panting, he finally says, "Fucking hell, Sunshine." He slaps my ass playfully.

"That was unreal," I say, muffled by the mattress.

He pulls me up by my tied hands, then loosens his tie, releasing me. I raise my hand up and thread my fingers around the back of his neck, then I tilt my head and find his lips. He rubs my shoulders tenderly.

"You were fucking incredible, Sunshine."

This is exactly where I should be.

Skin to skin.

With him.

Always.

CHAPTER 16

Eva

I give my stiff front door a good shoulder shove as I unlock it.

Which reminds me, I must call a carpenter to come and fix it.

The beep of a horn signifies my dad leaving. I raise my hand and give him a wave goodbye.

From Knox's, I went straight to Mom and Dad's in a taxi to pick up the kids. Dad insisted I go in for a cup of tea, and then he would drive me home.

I lied again. I told them both I stayed overnight at Beth's place last night, hence the reason for no car. They'll never know, and they have no reason to doubt me. But I feel shitty about it.

On the drive back to my house, my dad was so nice to me, informing me how happy I looked and how he and Mom loved the fact I was having fun and enjoying my life again.

What a crappy daughter I am.

"Okay, you crazy boys, in you go." I hold the door open

wide. Hamish and Archie sprint past me, jumping over the threshold.

The low winter sun catches my attention as it bounces off something metal lying on the mat.

It's my spare door key.

What's that doing there?

I eye it suspiciously.

"Where's the television gone, Mom?" Archie shouts from the living room. Shouting. It's one of my biggest pet peeves, especially when it's between rooms. Drives me nuts. Archie dashes up the stairs.

"What do you mean?" I struggle to lug the boys' and my overnight bags into the hall. Dropping them all on the floor with a *thump*, I lay Hamish's giant teddy he sleeps with every night on top of our mountain of luggage. The boys do not travel light.

Kicking my foot behind me to close the door, it shuts with an almighty clatter. It needs superstrength and force to open and shut that thing these days. Winter is making it worse.

Tomorrow, Eva. Get it sorted tomorrow.

Hamish enters the hallway. "A magician has been here."

"What?" I shake my head, confused. "What do you mean, wee man?" I ruffle his hair, laughing at his silliness as I turn the corner into the living room.

"Wook, it's all gone." He spread his arms wide as if he's *The Greatest Showman*. He adores that film.

He's right. Where has all my furniture gone?

Where my television once lived, there's only an aerial cable dangling from the wall. The cabinet has gone too.

It's all gone—everything. My couch, coffee table.

Only a couple of lamps and soft furnishings remain.

Archie runs down the stairs noisily.

"Where is my bed, Mom?"

I whip around.

"What?"

"My bed has vanished."

"Huh?"

Have I been burglarized?

Hitching up my skirt, I hurriedly run up the stairs, taking two steps at a time in a panic.

Scurrying between rooms, I see Archie's correct.

I look around the rooms in disbelief.

The kids' beds are gone as well as their bedside tables. Frantically opening the integrated wardrobes in Archie's room, I discover all his clothes are still hanging in place.

I inspect his room as I run my hands through my hair. Hamish's is the same.

What happened here?

Confused, I wander around the room. My pulse is spinning; my heart is bouncing in my chest, and I unexpectedly feel like I've been sucked into a parallel universe where nothing makes sense.

Making a mental inventory, I keep looking around. Not only are both the boys' beds gone, as well as their nightstands and their drawers, but someone has dumped the toys onto the floor and removed the toy box.

Entering my bedroom, everything except for my clothes has disappeared. Even my bedside lamps, cushions, and the bedding. All my clothes have been removed from my integrated wardrobes and left in a strategic giant heap in the middle of the floor.

I eye the mound.

Carefully positioned on top of the pile is my vibrator, along with my wedding and engagement ring.

There's an envelope.

What the hell?

I tentatively pick it up. With a shaky hand, I rip it open.

"I guess you won't be needing these anymore. Whore."

It's Ewan's handwriting.

I fall to the floor.

How could he do this to me? And his boys.

They've no beds to sleep in tonight.

I knew he was too nice to me with Ruby when he apologized the other night.

Drops of salty water fall onto the note I can't stop staring at, blurring the words behind my eyes. Diluting Ewan's nasty words, the ink grows, veining tendrils across the page.

Raw emotion burns in my chest, and I breathe in shallow, quick breaths.

Upset is replaced with scattered thoughts and contempt for Ewan.

My fury mounts; my blood rushes through my chest, making my heart race, and a full-on cloak of rage wraps itself around me.

I've reached my boiling point.

Pulling my phone out of my jacket pocket, I clench my teeth as I hit the FaceTime button on my screen and wipe my eyes with the back of my hand, not caring if I've smudged my dark eyeliner and mascara all to hell.

Looking around, I can't believe what I am seeing, or not seeing. The bastard took everything.

A low hum alerts me to his pickup.

"Sunshine?"

"He took everything," I blurt out and stare at Knox through the phone.

"Have you been crying? What happened? He? As in Ewan?" He fires questions at me in a panic.

"Look." I turn the camera viewpoint around and stand up. I then show him around, up and then downstairs. I showcase the carnage Ewan left behind. My home is a mess.

Although it doesn't feel like home anymore.

Knox stays deathly quiet as I present my empty home.

Heading into the kitchen, which appears to be untouched apart from a space where the dining table and chairs used to be, I spot Hamish and Archie through the kitchen window, outside playing in the garden with Crystal, Hamish's white rabbit. They seem unfazed by the lack of furniture in the house.

Kids. They go into fight-or-flight mode. Adaptable.

It's just as well 'cause if they weren't here right now, I would have lost it. For them, I need to remain calm.

I flip the camera focus back to me.

"He took all my furniture," I whisper. I can't believe it.

"You have to call the police, Eva. How do you know it was him?"

"He left me a note. He called me a whore. It's his handwriting."

"Motherfucker. He knew you were out last night."

I take a deep breath in.

"I can't call the police, Knox. There's no break-in. He stole my spare key. As if to rub it in my face, he had the audacity to push it back through the letterbox after he'd finished taking what he wanted."

"Do you know when he took your key? That's theft, Eva."

I close my eyes, trying to recall the threads of memories from the last week.

"He was here Friday morning. I was upstairs in the bathroom when he arrived to take the kids to school and day care."

It must have been then. The key box is inside one of the kitchen cupboards. I never thought to relocate it. But I never expected Ewan to do anything like *this*.

"Did he ask you if you were going out this weekend?"

"Yes. I told him where the kids would be on Saturday night.

I keep him informed about their whereabouts. He's their father, Knox."

"It's okay. You don't have to justify yourself. I'm only asking. I'm trying to help. Paint a picture of events. I'm on your side, Eva."

"I know." I let out a frustrated breath. "I can't believe he did this. My boys have no beds, Knox. He took their beds!" I cover my hand over my mouth and cry. I can't believe I'm letting Knox see me like this.

My home is a mess. My life is a mess. My ex-husband is on the warpath to hurt me as much as humanly possible. It's all drama Knox could do without.

Why would Knox want to continue to see me after this? I'm a calamity.

"Hey, hey. Eva, baby. C'mon. You're alright. Look at me, Sunshine," he coos, calming me down.

I sniff.

"You still have a house. That roof over your head keeps you safe and warm. You're all unharmed. Where are your boys?"

"Outside playing."

"Take photos of every room, including the letter. If you don't want the police involved, that's fair enough. I think you're wrong, but if you change your mind, you have the evidence. Although I think you should share this information with Veronica. In divorce, every piece of information and evidence will assist your case. Plus, he broke his harassment agreement with the police. You should call them. But I will not push you. In the meantime, I want you to tidy up as best you can. Put all your clothes back into your wardrobe, Eva. Will you do that?"

I pull a piece of kitchen towel off the roll and wipe my nose and face. I'm a snotty mess. So unattractive. No way would he want to continue a relationship with me after this.

"Will you?" he presses.

"I can do that." My shoulders drop with a sigh. "I will have to stay with my mom tonight. Or Ella." I groan. "I don't want any of them to know." My words trail off.

I'm so embarrassed.

"Stay put. Not happening. Do you trust me?"

My head dips a quick nod.

"Give me an hour or two."

"To do what?"

"Just trust me. And Sunshine?"

"Yeah?"

"Smile, baby. It's gonna be okay." He shoots me a dazzling smile, which I can't help but mirror.

"Thank you, Knox."

I don't know what I'm thanking him for yet, but combined with his gentle aura and calming words, I feel like he's wrapped me in a cozy blanket of calm.

"Go." He tilts his head to the side. "Tidy with newfound purpose. Out with the old, in with the new, Eva. Let it go. Let him have it."

He's right.

"I'll call you soon."

Through the camera I blow him a teary kiss goodbye. In return, he throws me one of his cheeky winks I love.

The phone makes a disconnect tone as I hang up.

So much for my fun and relaxing movie afternoon on the couch with my boys.

Pulling my arms out of my black leather jacket, I fling it on top of the kitchen countertop because I no longer have a dining table.

I call out the back door, instructing the boys in the back yard to play nice together. I'm asking for a miracle. I eagerly toe off my black ankle boots at the back door and roll up the sleeves of my white boho-style shirt.

Tidy up time.

Oh well, at least this gives me the opportunity to declutter and keep only what we need.

I've said it before and I'll say it again.

Fuck. My. Life.

A firm double tap at my front door breaks me out of my daydream.

I've had a fairly productive two hours.

Looking down at the black trash bags now lining my hallway full of old clothes, toys, and ornaments I should have parted ways with months ago, I feel a sense of release.

Knox was right. It was the cleaning ritual I needed.

Next job was to load the car up so I can drop them off at the thrift store tomorrow morning. But first up answer the front door.

I hope Knox ordered me food. I'm guessing that's what he had planned, so I didn't have to cook after my laborious task of tidying up.

We're all set for nighttime. I made me and the boys a gang hut in my bedroom so we can all sleep together tonight.

I'm desperately trying to salvage my day and make it an adventure for us.

I checked my online credit card balance ten minutes ago. I've figured out I can afford three new beds, then that card is at its limit.

Once we sign Knox's dance retreat contract, I can clear that card off.

Hopefully. For now, needs come before wants. I have to sacrifice a sofa and television.

I tug the door and swing it open to find a member of Knox's staff dressed in a black suit. It's embroidered with the hotel and spa logo in sparkling gold thread.

Knox's staff are always immaculate.

His level of detail doesn't go unnoticed by me. Or anyone else, for that matter.

Parked outside near my door is a black van with the gold Sanctuary logo branded across the side.

I was right. I'm pretty sure that is their catering van. Food. My stomach rumbles in appreciation.

Then another identical van pulls up. Two vans for food?

"Afternoon, Ms. Wallace. We have your delivery. I'm Robert. Please call me Rob." The distinctively handsome guy reaches out to shake my hand. "I will oversee the safe arrival of your new furniture for you. Mr. Black has asked me to assure you we will take extra special care with your paintwork and decor."

I pinch my brows.

I beg your pardon?

"Can you show me where your living area is situated and I am guessing the beds and bedroom furniture are to go up the stairs, correct?"

"Beds?" I choke.

"Yes." He gestures for me to take the crisp white envelope he's holding out of his hand.

"Check your order over, Ms. Wallace, and I will organize my team. Then you can show me where to position your sofas." He strides back down the path to manage the group of men who have appeared as if magically from nowhere, each wearing a Sanctuary uniform.

Say what now?

"A couch?" I whisper to myself.

Ripping open the envelope, I unfold the single piece of textured paper within. I read each line.

Three-seater forest-green leather sofa x 1 (walnut backed)
Two-seater forest-green leather sofa x 1 (walnut backed)

Walnut television unit x 1 (please ensure you take the glass toppers with cable cutouts to top the unit)
48 inch television x 1 (one of the new ones please)
Walnut coffee table x 1 (please include green painted glass to top the table)
Black Gloss dining Table x 1 (from top floor champagne bar)
Black Leather Dining Chairs to match table x 4
White leather button-back king-sized bed frame x 1 (the same one in the spare bedrooms in the penthouse)
King-sized mattress x 1 (same as penthouse)
White nightstand with metal crossed legs x 2 (again same as penthouse)
White matching bedroom dressing table with metal crossed legs (again same as penthouse)
White leather button-back singles bed frame x 2 (same as penthouse)
Single mattress x 2 (same as penthouse)
Two-drawer white nightstand with metal handles x 2 (same as those in the adjoining children's suites)
Four-drawer white side units with metal handles x 2 (same as those in the adjoining children's suites)
And what do we have in the way of white boxes? Toy box similar—please find two. Do we have any from the recent crèche refurb?
Bedding and pillows for all beds.

At the bottom is an inked personal message from Knox.

Your order as requested. Paid in full.

There's no embellishments or frills. But he's covering for me. Implying I bought this from the hotel directly.

Feeling hysterical, I don't know whether to laugh or cry. I keep staring at the list and reading it over again. This is no ordinary list of furniture. It's contract furniture standard—gold standard. Heavy, high quality, *expensive*.

"Do you want those sacks taken off your hands, Ms. Wallace?" Rob snaps me out of staring at the list. When I look up, he's pointing at my ready-to-part with donations.

"I was going to drop them off at the thrift shop tomorrow."

"We'll do that for you. Save you. You have little ones to get to school tomorrow." He winks with a kind smile.

I feel tears tickle my eyes.

No one has ever treated me so kindly. Knox. Rob. Fredrick with the massage.

I am being well and truly spoiled.

"Are all the rooms clear enough for us to unload the vans and position your furniture, Ms. Wallace?"

I can't quite believe this.

"Ms. Wallace?"

"Sorry." I shake my head, astounded. "Yes. Thank you. C'mon, I will show you." I indicate he should come inside.

It takes the six men no time at all to deliver, unwrap, and position all of *my* new furniture. They even helped me make the beds up and connect the new television, stopping to play with Hamish and Archie every now and again.

Knox guessed all my colors and sizes correctly. Everything is perfect.

He's perfect.

Two hours later, I'm now weaving myself in a dreamlike daze from room to room, running my hands over the exquisite glossy furniture. My house smells like a newly built home. My heart's about to burst. How generous of *him*.

Compared to how I felt a few hours ago, Knox has reinstated my happiness and joy.

My house looks beautiful. Better than it did. My old furniture was tired and in desperate need of replacing.

It's out with the old and in with the new, alright.

I throw myself onto my new green leather couch, smoothing my fingertips across the expensive fabric. It's what I have always fantasized about owning. My budget never stretched this far.

The boys have loved the last few hours and enjoyed finding old toys they had forgotten about, too. Content in the sanctuary of their rooms, they've both been busy playing. I'm grateful for the peace.

A gentle chime sounds from my phone, and I smile at the black heart appearing on my screen.

Knox: Did everything fit?
Me: Everything is perfect. So are you. I should start calling you Mr. Perfect. There are no words to describe how grateful I am.
Knox: Call me anything you want, Sunshine.
Me: Please let me know how much I owe you.

There's no way I can afford it but I have to pay him back.

Knox: Nothing. All that matters is your happiness. Is my cloudy girl a sunshine happy one again?
Me: More than happy. I'm ecstatic. You've blown me away with your generosity and kindness. Thank you so much.
Knox: You are very welcome. You do not deserve to be treated the way you have.
Me: Ewan saw the vans at the front door.
Knox: I hope you didn't let him see you when you were upset.
Me: No way. I waved down the street at him with a smile.
Knox: Good girl. Rise above.

I was super proud of myself for my ballsy move. Even from my front door, I could see his clenched, twitchy jaw and fierce fists.

He's not a happy man.

Little did he know his act of stupidity would upgrade my life.

Me: We now have matching sofas.
Knox: We do. And mattresses. It's the same one as mine but smaller.
Me: What size is yours? My king is huge. It just fits.
Knox: I did wonder. Mine is Alaskan King.
Me: Wow. Big in every way, right?
Knox: You got it, Sunshine ;)
Me: I would love to see you tonight. To thank you properly.
Knox: Wednesday. And only for dance lessons. I wish it was longer.
Me: Me too.
Knox: What if I was to schedule in a 'lunch meeting' with you? My office. To discuss the dance retreat contract. Would that work?
Me: I can only do Friday.

He takes a moment to reply. He's probably checking his schedule.

Knox: Works for me.
Me: Please promise you won't send me a calendar request like you did with Tabitha :(And I never want to see inside your hotel suite.
Knox: Wouldn't dream of it. Come to my office anytime between noon and two.
Me: That works for me. Thank you.
Knox: A locksmith is on his way to replace your locks back and front.
Me: But Ewan gave me the key back.
Knox: He had more than enough time while it was in his possession to have copies made.

Gosh. That never crossed my mind.

Me: Thank you. Again. Oh. Gotta go. That's my doorbell.

Knox: It's food. I ordered from Wee Oscars. I hope the boys like pasta.

Me: They do! I don't know what I did without you in my life before. I keep saying it. But THANK YOU.

Knox: See you Wednesday.

Me: And again Friday. Can't wait to see you. I'll take photos of my new furniture and send them to you. My house looks incredible :)

Knox: Look forward to it.

Me: I appreciate you. For today. For everything. xoxo

Knox: :) xoxo

I swoon at his kisses and cuddles sign-off.

Can a girl die from a burst lust-filled heart?

It might be possible because mine is beating out of my chest.

It feels full of jumping beans.

What a day.

What a week.

It's only been a week.

I can't believe it.

Knox Black.

The man's my new obsession.

I'm almost asleep.

Encapsulated in the world's most comfortable memory foam bed I have ever slept on.

I'm lying in one seriously blissful bed.

My old lumpy, sagging mattress was dead.

But this one contours my body perfectly.

Unlike my old mattress, it's completely silent. Not a squeak or creak to be heard in this bedroom anymore.

Hugging the surrounding comforter, my body sighs into the deep molded layers.

My boys went to sleep straightaway, too. Ewan is a genius for stealing their beds.

A genius and a fool. What a douchebag.

On silent mode, my phone vibrates, alerting me to a text. Considering if I should answer, I flip my phone over to see who it is first.

I roll my eyes and sit up in the dark.

Ewan: I'll pick up Archie from school tomorrow.
Me: As planned. Yes. Thank you. Drop him off at my mom and dad's, please. Hamish is staying at Mom's until late too. I'm helping Ella with wedding plans tomorrow night after classes.
Ewan: Okay. Did you have a good weekend?
Me: Yes.
Ewan: What was happening at the house today?
Me: I upgraded the furniture.
Ewan: Why?
Me: A new fresh start. Getting rid of what no longer serves me and the boys. The old furniture was reeking of self-pity and bad memories.

That's a low blow, Eva.

Ewan: You don't have to be such a callous bitch all the time. How can you afford that?
Me: Oh. My dad pulled a favor.
Ewan: From the Blacks?
Me: Yes.
Ewan: You appear to be awfully close with them recently.

Me: Dad has been friends with the family for years. Not new.
Ewan: I heard a rumor.
Me: Oh yeah?
Ewan: That you were seen dancing with Lincoln last night at The Vault.

Matthew wasn't in The Vault last night. It must have been someone else. News travels fast.

Me: Nice guy.
Ewan: Why?
Me: Why, what?
Ewan: Why were you dancing with him?
Me: He invited us to the new wine bar. We had a dance at The Vault before we went. You're probably already on first name terms with the bar staff at the new place.
Ewan: Fuck off. Who's we?
Me: Sisters, Toni, Beth, their respective partners. The usual.
Ewan: And Lincoln.
Me: Yes.
Ewan: Convenient, you just happened to be the odd one out with no partner and Lincoln was there.
Me: So were Owen and Jacob.
Ewan: Oh really. Which one did you stay with last night?
Me: All of them. I had all of them at once :)

I'm skating on thin ice. But I'm holding steady.

Ewan: Whore.
Me: Oh, I know. You said in the letter you kindly left me. I heard a rumor too.
Ewan: About?
Me: VOLUNTARY...
Me: LAYOFF!

I don't get a response.

A few more minutes pass and still nothing.

I slide my phone back onto my nightstand, immerse myself back into the bed, and make myself comfortable again. Once settled, I'm drawn to what sounds like a scrambling noise at my front door.

I reach for my phone, and it vibrates again, making me jump.

Ewan: Open up. You bitch. Why the fuck does my key not fit?

Knox was right. Changing the door locks was a smart move. He made a copy. Sneaky shithead.

Me: I had the locks changed. AGAIN. You can't be trusted. You will not be allowed in my home ever again. It is not your key. This is my home.

Ewan: It's still mine, too. My name is on the papers.

Me: It won't be when I buy you out. Or how much exactly did you receive on your payout from your old job? Maybe it's me that should ask for more. My new lawyer will be on that in the morning.

Ewan: I don't know what the fuck I ever saw in you.

Me: Ditto.

Ewan: You wait, Eva.

Me: For what exactly? Good night, Ewan. Until the morning. Lawyer—informed. Police—informed. I think we're done here.

Screw Ewan. I'm going to the police station first thing in the morning.

Despite my new comfortable bed and new locks, I toss and turn. Ewan scares me and he always finds a way in. I don't think I can take it anymore.

The rash on my neck prickles with heat. I give it a good scratch to relieve the itch. I grab my phone.

Me: I've decided to file a police report.

I get an instant response.

Knox: Wise decision.
Me: Ewan tried to get in the house tonight. You were right.
Knox: Are you okay? The boys?
Me: Yes, they are sound asleep. Oblivious. Would you come with me tomorrow?
Knox: I'll meet you in the station car park at 9:10 a.m. after school drop-off.

He remembers all the details of my daily routine. It's very sweet.

Me: Thank you.
Knox: I might even bring you a tea and some breakfast.
Me: That would be lovely. We need to be careful, though. I hope no one sees us.
Knox: I'll say I was there about hotel business.
Me: Good plan. See you tomorrow.

If only for a couple of minutes, I'll cherish those.

Knox: Good night, baby. Call me if Ewan acts up before sunrise. I am here for you. xoxo
Me: I promise I will. xoxo

This is too hard. I want to show him off. Show the world he's mine. Share him with my friends and family.

Disclose how utterly smitten I am with him.

Ella and Eden can't keep their hands off their men. I want that too.

Crave it.

Three weeks feels like an eternity.

But with Ella's wedding to help plan, the boys to juggle, meetings with my lawyer, and instructing dance classes too, the weeks will fly by.

Let's hope they do.

CHAPTER 17

Knox

As if the time-space continuum is doing everything to mess with me, the last couple of weeks appear to be the longest on record.

Eva and I have only seen each other a handful of times, twice for dance lessons and twice in my office, because she doesn't want to take advantage of her parents. Plus, she loves her boys and likes her downtime on the weekends with them.

She's a great mother.

The sooner we tell everyone, the sooner we can all spend more time together.

Our secret lunchtime trysts are fun, especially when Eva has to be gagged with my tie to keep her quiet. Yup, she's my ultimate fantasy come true and Eva's pierced pussy for lunch on my desk was the highlight of my week; it was the fucking best.

I have to rub myself under the desk to readjust my twitching cock at that memory.

This is not the time nor the place, Knox.

Eva and her sisters signed the contract to seal our deal for our dance retreat partnership, too. *Enjoying* Eva for *lunch* was a celebration of sorts.

And then of course there was filing the police report for Eva's disappearing furniture and Ewan's continued threats. Conveniently, I found myself at the police station following the vandalization of my P1 McLaren. From front to back, someone kindly keyed the entire driver's side of my car.

Fucking asshole.

Lincoln had borrowed it the day before and neither of us can remember if it was there already or keyed when he or I used it.

Being extremely particular where we park the car, it was most unexpected and baffled the pair of us.

Lincoln recalled parking it in the town center when he ran into the local bakery, so it may have happened then, but the CCTV showed nothing either. It's currently in the shop being repainted and should be ready today. It will never be the same. I'm tempted to sell it.

Following Eva's explained situation to the police about her missing furniture and the text messaging evidence, an injunction was issued by the court against Ewan.

Veronica moved swiftly and within forty-eight hours he was no longer allowed to enter or be near her home.

She's finally protected.

He was forced to move out of his girlfriend, Ruby's, house and move back in with his parents.

The only slight kick in the teeth for Eva is that Ewan is forbidden to pick up the children from school, making her life even more hectic.

Being the kindhearted soul Eva is, she agreed to Ewan having access to the boys on the condition Ewan's parents were present at all times.

I'm proud of how strong she is. She's a warrior.

I could do without this duller than dishwater Castleview

Business Circle meeting today. Neither Beth or Toni can make it today, which I am gutted about. They both have a way of lightening these meetings. We always hold them here at my hotel. We have the best facilities around and it makes sense. Bimonthly, twenty of us, along with the governing body for Scottish tourism, meet to discuss the promotion of our unique town.

We may be small, but the championship golf courses set us apart from all the other seaside towns around.

With the winter wind down, like us at the hotel, it's a time for many businesses in Castleview to revamp and remodel, and today's meeting is more of a catch-up than a strategy plan, which suits me just fine.

I look around the table, and my eyes land on Tabby. She did as I asked; she stayed away. Thank fuck.

Sensing her desperation to ask me something, she keeps flitting her eyes in my direction.

There are two sides to Tabby and most days, you're never sure which version you'll get. The uptight one or the bitchy one. Neither are great options.

I wonder which version we will get today.

I can't be fucked with either.

Between the daily hotel administration, juggling time with Eva, the refurb of the members' bar, and a Winter Ball to prepare for, something I am actively involved with every year, I'm done. I need a break. Like yesterday.

I give my neck a roll from side to side to stretch out the tension.

Toward the middle of January, The Sanctuary holds the finest Winter Ball for miles around; however, this year is different. Because this coming January, The Sanctuary is celebrating sixty years in business. We are commemorating my father's and grandfather's legacy.

It's going to be big, over the top, a festival of sorts. Ice sculptures, photo booths, blackjack tables, bombastic bands, secret operatic singers disguised as servers who will pop up from time to time, designed to amaze guests. It will be grandiose and an event people will talk about for years to come. That's the plan, anyway.

My secretary, Mrs. Kinnear, is also retiring and we will also honor her at the event. Something she doesn't know about. She's been my father's and my right-hand woman for decades and we are struggling to find a replacement.

Only six people who applied have potential.

The interviewing process begins in two weeks. Hopefully, we find a suitable candidate to enable them to work alongside Mrs. Kinnear. I want a smooth handover and transition and someone who can jump straight into our demanding fast-paced schedule.

I'm going to miss Mrs. Kinnear. Even her plant talking, which I have become accustomed to.

There is so much to do in only a few weeks. Plus, the added pressure of Ella and Fraser's wedding.

We normally try to block off weeks before the Winter Ball to prepare for it and a last-minute wedding booking was not planned for.

My bad.

Our preference has always been to have the ballroom fully stripped, cleaned, and ready for party preparations. But of course I said yes because I couldn't resist Eva's plea for help.

Who could say no to those dimples, anyway?

And now my staff hate me because we have little time, especially as most places close for a week over Christmas. We are on a tighter than tight schedule.

Yikes, what was I thinking?

Dimples. It's always the dimples.

Lincoln is the one who has been keeping order and maintaining calm. He's restructured our normal timetable.

One of his lifeline suggestions was to install the forty-foot indoor stage and white LED dance floor to prepare for our seventeen-piece band for Ella and Fraser's wedding, meaning it will already be in place for the ball and they are getting one helluva wedding.

It takes a crew of ten men to install over five days, so this has saved us a week already; my boy is an organizational genius.

Lost in my thoughts, Tabitha breaks me from my mental list making. "How have you been, Knox?"

"Good. And you, Tabitha?" I loosen my tie.

"Oh, it's Tabitha now, is it? No longer Tabby," she huffs.

That woman is a child.

Eva may be fourteen years younger than her, but she has more maturity in her pinky finger than Tabitha has in her whole body.

A gentle knock on the boardroom door is a welcome distraction.

It opens, and a blond-haired beauty pops her head around the gap in the door.

"Hi, hey. I'm not sure I'm in the correct place. Is this the Castleview Business Circle meeting?" she says in a gentle tone.

Like a missile seeking its target, her eyes meet mine.

Eva.

What's she doing here?

I sit up straighter.

"Yes, it is. Professional business owners only, Eva," Tabitha dismisses her.

Eva holds her ground and dazzles me with a smile. "I'm in the correct room, then. My father asked me to attend in his place today."

"Perfect. We were looking for someone to take the minutes." Tabitha grins wickedly.

"Mrs. Kinnear has offered to take them today." I pull out my phone, write a quick email with praying hands emoji begging Mrs. Kinnear to help us in the boardroom, with the returned promise to water her plants for a week. She instantly replies with a hands off my plants email, informing me she's on her way.

She's saved my backside an infinite amount of times.

"Take a seat, Eva." Excited at the prospect of spending the next hour in her company, I pull out the second-to-last available seat on my right-hand side.

Eva elegantly glides around the table, removing her camel Fedora hat as she bounces closer to me.

She gracefully hooks it on the coat stand in the corner of the room along with her long toffee-colored belted wool coat and multicolored tartan scarf. Unwrapping herself, she reveals her knockout dance outfit—sculpted black leggings, oversized black jumper that says Addicted to Dance on the front with the girls' dance school name T3SDS in teal in giant letters arched across the back, and black jeweled high-top sneakers.

She's a clashing cacophony of styles and colors, but like everything Eva wears and does, she pulls it off.

"Nice outfit," Tabitha mutters under her breath. The entire table hears. Some of the Circle members *tut*, shaking their heads in disapproval. Some of them are too scared to say anything, or even breathe around Tabitha.

Tabitha is not well liked within the business community. Thankfully, her father is a sterling bloke and upholds the MacEvoy brand name. Tabitha is here simply to appease her father. Nothing more. And then there's keeping her busy to keep her away from the office; her staff are not the biggest fans of daddy's little princess either.

Eva casually slides her notepad she's taken out of her purse onto the ebony table. Slowly she sits down, then fluffs out her hair. Leaning over the table, she threads her hands together. "Thanks, Tabitha. Hip-hop lessons today. You should join a class. Might loosen you up a bit. Remove the stick that's permanently stuck up your ass."

She said ass in our meeting.

My polite sweet-dimpled goddess, gone bad.

Without meaning to, I snort. I love how fierce my woman is and how she's growing in confidence again, since Ewan is no longer pestering her.

"And I will say this one last time. If you have nothing nice to say to me, then move on, Tabitha." Eva looks around the table. "Hi, I'm Eva, Charlie's daughter. Most of you know me, anyway. I'm sorry about that, but I've had enough of Tabitha's new sport of name-calling and belittling me in front of everyone. I'm here to help my dad out this week. I'll hold my tongue from here on in."

Like a fish out of water, Tabby's mouth opens and shuts as if expecting someone to jump in to defend her.

But that doesn't happen.

I pull my chair in and give Eva's knee a reassuring squeeze under the table discreetly.

Atta girl. Rise above.

As Mrs. Kinnear appears to complete the full list of attendees, I address the room. "Shall we begin?"

Well, this afternoon just got interesting.

Eva

Fucking Tabitha MacEvoy.

Who the hell does she think she is?

Talking to me like that.

No more.

Whatever I said, I can't even remember now. It appears to have silenced her during the entire meeting.

Dad and Mom are away today to view new chalets for the

sports retreat. I assumed they would scale down the business or hold it steady, but nope, they are off to choose four new log cabins for the retreat, allowing them to expand.

Even though they could, my parents have no intention of retiring anytime soon. They love what they do, and it shines through in every way. Hence the reason for their success too. It's no coincidence.

Knowing Knox would be here today, I offered to stand in for Dad, even though Eden was keen.

She's got a great business head on her and thrives in marketing, promotion, and strategy meetings, but I thought I would leap in first when Dad asked one of us to take his place.

It gives me more time with Knox, even if we can't speak to each other properly.

Simply orbiting around him feels comforting.

The meeting has been boring as hell, but he's here, squeezing my knee from time to time.

My gentle but powerful and reassuring Greek god in a suit.

As I doodle in my notepad, I listen to the business circle members saying that mail drops and advertising is the way to increase more tourists in quieter times. It is a false economy in my opinion.

You're all wrong.

I continue making blue ink star shapes on the outer edges of my notepaper.

After a few seconds, I realize how quiet the room became and look up.

Everyone is looking at me.

Oh damn, did I say that out loud?

"We're wrong? And I suppose you have a better idea?" Tabitha challenges me.

I shuffle in my seat and sit up straighter. "Eh, no. I'm only here to take notes for my father."

"Oh no. If you think you know better than we do, then

please proceed." She interlaces her fingers against her mouth, except her index fingers in a handgun steeple.

She thinks she's got me.

Well, screw you, Tabitha MacEvoy.

Challenge accepted.

I managed our business when Eden took a sabbatical after she had her car crash last year, and I loved every single minute of it. It's me that introduced paid-for partnership ideas on our social media. We're now flooded with daily requests. Our social media is flawless. And of course it helps to have triplet babies and golfing champion daddy Hunter with abs for days, partaking in all the silly online challenges. Eden and Hunter have helped us gain thousands of followers in the last six months. Plus Archie pulls in the views. People sure do love watching my seven year old break dancing. He's so cool.

"Okay." I clear my throat.

"You don't have to, Eva." Knox lays his hand on my arm and it dawns on him what he's done. He removes it as if I scorched his skin.

I wish it didn't have to be like this.

"No. I'm good," I reply. "So..." I clap my hands together. "You want consistent income. You want consistency in sales or tourists staying longer than one night or day? Then from my experience and what we have found at the dance studio, there are a couple of things that work. For us, day-trippers aren't an issue as they don't factor into our business model, but what we found, painfully so at the beginning, is running classes on a pay as you go is a surefire way to fail. That's why we offer blocks of classes. People pay up front for blocks. Take Cupcakes and Castles." I point to Gemma, who owns the local cupcake shop. It's my sister Eden's favorite place in town. "You could offer subscription boxes. Reaching far and wide. You can't expect all the customers to come to you; you need to go to the customer. Every time a day-tripper comes in, push that subscription service, offer a discount. Market it like, oh, I don't know, they get a taste of Castleview even when they aren't here. Offer a digital cupcake making class too; you send them all of the ingredients as part of the subscription. And you all are missing a trick with social media. A simple photo doesn't cut it anymore. You have to tell your brand story. People love stories."

I'm on a roll now.

"Who are you? What's your history? Your business backstory? How are your cupcakes baked? What makes them special, nut-free, allergy-free, flavors? Meet the team, people love that. Video will sell your business more than any other type of media. What's worked for us is that we are consistent with our content. We let potential customers see us, our lives, who we are, our transformations, daily routines. I even did a video this morning of me opening the studio for the day. Turning on the studio lights, pumping the music up, and all I said on the video was, 'Good morning, are you ready to dance?' It's already received..."

I open my phone and check the analytics. "Over twenty thousand views. People want to know everything. Let them in. Show them around the castle, Angus. The dungeons. Share the tales of old or ask a question and get them so intrigued they have to come and visit. Captivate them. Then the tourists will still show up. But you have to let them know the castle is open all year round because you have lighting that paves the way. You have tour guides. And why don't you hook up with Toni at Castleview Cones and Gemma. Call it the Castle, Cones, and Cupcake tour. Join partnerships together. The old meets new. Tours of the town, the more the merrier."

I point to Tabitha. "I know your whisky is world-famous, Tabitha, but whisky tasting tours during the week would be perfect for you guys, not just on the weekends. Charge a premium price, approach all the little quaint bed-and-breakfast establishments around town, have them do a midweek special, whisky tasting days and food provided by Wee Oscars for lunch. It's a perfect partnership. As well as sending business to the taxi services who could ferry them around town, as you know, they are very quiet in the wintertime. It would keep them busy. Market them as, oh, I don't know, The Winter Whisky Staycation, that's just off the top of my head."

I press my hand to my chest. "I for one want to know about the copper stills you distill the whisky in. What does it do? Why do you still use them? Who are the men and women on the floor every day? Your business is steeped in history, Tabitha. It's oozing traditions that haven't changed for the last one hundred years. Tourists love that. You could create at least one video a day showcasing all the beautiful aspects of whisky making, the bottling, and the intricate hand-labeling you guys are famously known for. Show them. You should also consider speaking to Toni about making a MacEvoy whisky ice cream."

"She already has one," she butts in.

"Yes, because you dismissed her idea, so she created one herself. But you could sell that far and wide. Not only here in Castleview Cove. Do you follow her on social media?"

I look around the table and the circle members shake their heads.

"Then start. Today. Study what she does. Learn from her. Toni shows her customers exactly how she makes the ice cream. The flavors. The samples she trials too. Even the ones that don't work; those get the best reach and views because they taste vile and it's funny to watch the taste testers. She talks about the history of her ice cream parlor. She shares the length of the queues on a daily basis. She shares every part of her day. Even the refurbishment. She let her customers on social media choose the colors of the banquette seating. Then those people from social media flocked to them on opening day and they felt part of the story. She has her own unique hashtag; she encourages every customer to share it on social media. You could do the same, Knox."

I turn to face him.

"What makes your hotel different? Details. Your hotel stands out because of the immaculate level of detail you put into every part of the customer experience. Choose a member of staff and do A Day in the Life of. Media train them. They can document their day. A Day in the Life of a masseuse. A Day in the Life of a concierge. An event coordinator. The stage being erected for the upcoming Winter Ball. Everything. It's interesting. Video is where it's at. Think tour guide Barbie and bingo you got it. Take part in the silly social media challenges. I would advise ones that apply to your business, though. And not for you, Knox; those are not appropriate for your five-star hotel, but for the rest of you, it would work. Challenge customers to come and do the same at your shops. Eat a cupcake in ten seconds and you can have yours for free. That's a silly example." I swat my hand in the air. "But it will draw people in. Make them come to you. But you all have to think outside the box. Advertising and mail drops will not cut it. People spend more time on social media than ever. Get in front of them.

"Set up Castleview Cove accounts across social media. Each of you takes a day or a week where you take over. It's super simple and I could train you. Collaboration is key. We are not individuals here. What sets Castleview apart is community and heritage. Show people what makes us unique and that will bring the tourists in."

I fold my arms across my body and rest back in my seat.

"You're a marketing genius, Eva," Gemma says through a head shake. "We all need to up our game. I'm in." She raises her hand. "Who else is?"

One by one, they all raise their hands. Reluctantly, Tabitha puts hers up last.

"That settles it then. When can you train us, Eva?" Gemma asks expectantly.

"I could train you all at the same time. They have this clever piece of software you can screencast from your phone to your computer screen. If you guys buy it, I will train you all at next month's meeting. In the meantime, you need to set up new social accounts for Castleview. You all need access to the usernames and passwords, but only one person should be responsible for the email address so they can reset it if ever one of you locks yourself out of the accounts."

"I'll get my head of tech to set that up. Can you minute that, Mrs. Kinnear, to ensure I remember?" Knox says, deep in thought as he sweeps his fingertips back and forth across the shiny tabletop, the other on the arm of his chair. "And I think that's us finished for the day. This room is booked out in five minutes time." He checks the wall clock.

"What about you, Knox? Eva never had any joint ventures for your hotel. What would you do for him? Running out of ideas?" Tabitha says through barbed words.

Knox answers her before I do.

"Not true," he says. "Eva and her sisters signed a contract with The Sanctuary. We are setting up a dance retreat. We've already sold twenty places for the spring intake and the summer intake is full."

Is it? Holy moly.

Shit just got real.

Tabitha pushes her seat back to escape the answers we have for everything. "You've kept that quiet, Knox."

"It's on the website and has been for two weeks. Plus, it was emailed out to our customers, too," he replies sharply. "Enough now, Tabitha. You've made your point."

Head down, Tabitha throws yet another designer bag back over her shoulder, draping her expensive-looking red cashmere coat over her bent forearm. It probably cost more than my entire wardrobe. I love shopping at thrift shops and secondhand vintage stores. The only designer items I own are branded sneakers. Like the ones I have on today. They are sparkly as hell, and I love them.

She looks back over her shoulder at Knox and me, bouncing her eyes left and right between the both of us, then she leaves.

What is she up to?

As the final few stragglers depart too, Knox asks the last person to close the door as he needs to discuss some finer details of the dance retreat with me.

Minutes pass before he says, "You're a smart girl, Eva. You fucking rocked today."

I beam. "Yeah?"

"Yeah, you did." With his clenched fist, he shakes it, then punches it in the air. "I'm so proud of you. I should hire you as my marketing assistant."

"Thank you."

"You keep surprising me."

"Do I, how come?"

"Well, one minute I think I've got you all figured out, and then the next thing you blow me away with something new and unexpected."

"There is still so much to learn about each other. We've only been seeing each other since the auction."

Next Saturday is Ella's wedding. Only a few more days to tell everyone.

"Feels like longer."

"Feels like it's not long enough."

"Feels like I have known you my whole life."

"Almost."

"True. But not like this." He gestures between us.

"I like us."

"I like us too."

"I have something else to surprise you with."

"Yeah, what's that?"

I lean in close to him, stare deep into his eyes, and whisper, "I changed the jewel on my clit ring yesterday. Want to see?"

Turning darker than ever, his eyes dilate.

It's incredible how much control that tiny little jewel has over this powerful, strong man.

I sense his brain emptying of thoughts as the hunger in his eyes glows.

"Yes," he whispers back.

"Too bad. You'll have to wait until tomorrow afternoon." I push my seat backward.

Making me giggle, he groans, then bangs his head against the edge of the tabletop.

"You drive me crazy. Now I have to spend the rest of the afternoon working with a fucking hard-on."

I push my arms into my caramel coat and belt it up, then secure my scarf around my neck. It's minus one outside today. Winter has arrived.

"I've heard cold showers work wonders. Or you could dip your dick in the frost outside or skinny dip. The cove is lovely this time of year." I place my hat on top of my head.

"He would shrivel up to a pressed stud if I did that." He shivers at the thought.

"I'd pay good money to see it."

Knox lifts his forehead off the table. "You wouldn't. No woman ever needs to see that. And Ms. Wallace, from what I've witnessed, you prefer the opposite." He accordions his hands out in front of him, then pulls them apart to make the gap wider and wider. Yup, he is a big man.

"I do. Do you know where I can find such a thing?"

"My house. Tomorrow afternoon."

"Great. Who are you inviting?" I tease.

"Ha ha, very funny. If you're not careful, young lady. I will skinny dip before you arrive."

"I'll see your pressed stud then, Mr. Black." I tip my hat. "It's been a pleasure doing business with you."

"It will be even more pleasurable tomorrow, Sunshine."

"Can't wait. Oh, and Knox." I turn back around before opening the door. "My new clit ring has a little black heart at the top, just for you." I wink. "When I swapped it over, I was thinking about you and made myself come. I was so wet for you." I draw out the last words slowly, then suck my finger into my mouth.

"Get out." He rubs his cock over his dress pants, then drops his head back on the table. "Wicked woman," he mumbles.

"Bye, Mr. Black."

"Go," he groans. "You look like an angel, but really, you're an evil enchantress in disguise."

"Mrs. Kinnear is on her way back along the corridor," I whisper back into the room.

He snaps up, pulls his chair under the table to hide his erection, and sits up straight.

"Just kidding." I don't wait for his reaction but hear him moan out loud as I close the door behind me.

I feel like I've taken heaps of liberties recently, but I asked Mom and Dad to take the kids for me tonight. They love helping me out and the boys love going there too. Plus, they are always informing me I haven't been asking for enough help. So I did.

Knox doesn't know this, of course.

I'm surprising him later.

How exciting.

CHAPTER 18

Eva

I punch the code into the keypad on the wall.

Granting me access, the side door leading into Knox's home *clicks* open for me.

I never considered how dayglow my bright-yellow car was until I had to sneak around. I'm far from inconspicuous. It's just as well Knox has a multicar garage for me to hide it in. And a house that sits on the outer edges of town. Hardly anyone comes this way. Plus, the houses in Cherry Gardens Lane are strategically placed far apart from one another so technically Knox has no neighbors.

I'm parked right next to his P1 McLaren, which he must have gotten back from the body shop today. The police still have yet to find out who scratched it. If they ever do.

The two cars are an accurate reflection of us—yellow and black, blond and dark. I've heard of owners looking like their dogs but never looking like their cars.

I stifle a giggle and tiptoe into the dark hall.

He must have gone to bed. But it's still early. I tap my

fingertip against my smartwatch to check the time. Ten o'clock. I left it long enough for me to be unsuspecting.

Softly closing the heavy door behind me, I hold on to my overnight bag and teeter up the sweeping staircase. Making sure my sky-high heels don't clack against the marble flooring, I creep stealthily along the long hallway until I reach his bedroom.

I carefully place my weekend bag on the floor, then remove my raincoat as quietly as I can, scooping up the metal buckle of my belt to ensuring it doesn't clatter against the floor.

Craning my neck around the slightly open door, I sneak through the small gap and make my way across the deep carpeted room on my tippy-toes.

Eyeing the outline of his body in the sheets, excitement flutters in my belly as it backflips like an Olympian gymnast.

He's going to love what I have planned.

Standing at the end of the bed, I position my knee at the edge and crawl slowly toward him.

"Hey, baby," I whisper. He rustles in the bed.

I move closer.

"Come on, sleepyhead. I have a surprise for you," I sing softly.

He groans.

On hands and knees, I bracket his body.

He turns around, placing his arm over his eyes, and moans again.

"Would you like to see my pretty pussy piercing now? You don't have to wait until tomorrow."

With one hand, he reaches down and cups my face.

"I must be dreaming," he mumble-whispers in a strange voice.

I move closer again.

"You're not dreaming, baby. I'm here. And I brought some

handcuffs. I thought you might like to experiment." I giggle softly.

My chuckle is stopped in its tracks as the room is suddenly flooded in dazzling light and the bedroom door flies open.

I snap my face in the intruder's direction.

"Eva?" Knox exclaims from the doorway.

"Knox!" I gasp.

Oh.

My.

God.

I snap my attention back to the person lying in the bed.

"Lincoln?" I shout, leaping backward off the bed.

"What the fuck?" Lincoln catapults up.

CHAPTER 19

Knox

"What the hell is going on?" I bellow.

"I could ask you the same thing." Linc points to Eva who's standing awkwardly in the middle of my room looking like a fucking wet dream in the tiniest canary yellow string panties and matching peephole bra.

Fucking peephole bra.

And is she wearing a set of handcuffs like a bangle and pole dancing shoes?

Oh, dear fuck.

Immediately aware of her state of undress, she grabs the sheet off the bed to cover herself with.

Through no fault of her own, she uncovers Lincoln's naked body.

"Oh, my God. What the fuck is going on?" She squeezes her eyes shut.

"You're supposed to be on nights covering my shift." Lincoln points at me.

"And you're supposed to be in your own house," I counter.

"And what are you doing here?" I ask Eva, but she can't see

me looking at her because she still has her eyes clenched closed. "Eva?"

"My mom and dad took the boys. I wanted to surprise you," she whispers.

"You've done that alright. You've surprised me too," Lincoln interjects. "Are you two fucking?"

"Are you two fucking?" I direct my question wide-eyed at Lincoln.

"Oh, fuck to the no. She won't have me. Now I know why."

"I *am* still in the room you know," Eva says through pained words. "And I would never cheat on you, Knox. I can't believe you would think that of me."

Aw, shit.

"I'm sorry, Sunshine. I didn't mean it. I wasn't thinking."

"Sunshine?" Lincoln frowns.

"Put some goddamn clothes on Lincoln, and we'll meet you in the kitchen." I go over to Eva, wrap my arm around her, and guide her out of the room.

Once out in the hallway, she opens her eyes.

"You thought I would cheat on you?" She looks sad. I've disappointed her. Disappointed myself.

"No, never. It was a heat of the moment, asshole thing to say. I have never doubted you. Not even for a minute. I'm sorry. Please forgive me." I cup her face. I don't want to lose her.

"I would nev—"

I cover her mouth with mine and kiss her tenderly, trying to pour my apology into her skin.

"Please forgive me." I kiss her again. "Please don't leave." Another kiss. "I'm sorry. I didn't mean it." I kiss her urgently now.

She pulls back, her brilliant blue eyes twinkle in the low light. "I'm not leaving you, Knox." Her voice is low and deliberate. "Whatever happened in your past is your past, but you can't tar me with the same brush. And I would *never* sleep with your son. That's low."

"I'm an asshole."

"You're not. But you are damaged by your past, and it makes you insecure sometimes. You pretend to be this big, strong guy, but you've been hurt. It's stuck with you and it takes time to heal. And I don't know the full story between Olivia and you. But I am not leaving you, Knox. Because I'm a talker. I like to talk things through. And that's exactly what we will do. It's called being in a re-la-tion-ship. We work things out together. But after we've spoken to Lincoln."

She knows me so well. Better than I know myself.

"He saw you. You're practically naked."

She pulls the cover up to hide her face. "How embarrassing. I need to change. I wanted to surprise you."

"You did that, alright. You look sexy as fuck. Are you wearing handcuffs like a bangle?"

"I am." She groans. "Lincoln saw everything."

"He did. C'mon, Sunshine." I scoop her bag off the floor. "Change in there." I point to the master bathroom, turn on the light, and place her bag inside the door. "See you in the kitchen."

"Okay. How did you not know I was here? My car is in the garage," she asks, frowning.

"Lincoln picked up my car today from the body shop. I brought his car home and parked it outside his house. I haven't been in the garage."

"Why is he in your bed?"

"That I am yet to find out. Get dressed, Sunshine."

What a fucking mess.

Lincoln enters the kitchen first in a pair of gray sweatpants and a white tee.

"So?"

"So," I repeat back.

Opening the fridge, he grabs a bottle of water. Unscrewing the top, he downs half the bottle, then sits down at the breakfast bar.

Leaning back against the bar stool, he folds his arms, making his vast biceps expand.

I gear myself up for one of the most uncomfortable conversations I have ever had with my son.

I sit down next to him, unknot my tie, and lay it on the marble countertop.

Deep breath in, I begin. "Eva and I are—"

"Sleeping together. Yeah, memo received," he says deadpan.

"It's more than that."

"Is it? Because I distinctly remember telling you I liked Eva. When was that? Three weeks ago?"

"Yes. It was the night of the auction. She came home with me that night."

"Here?" He points downward, gesturing to the house.

"Yes. She stayed that entire weekend."

He looks upward as if trying to recall.

"But I was here on Saturday morning, Dad. I sat in this exact spot. I asked you about Tabby. You said she was here. But you're telling me it wasn't her?"

I shake my head.

"It was Eva?"

I nod.

"And it was her panties hanging on the door handle and her bag?"

"I'm not proud about lying to you, son."

"You shouldn't be. You've always brought me up to tell the truth. No lies. That has always been your biggest house rule."

"I know. I am sorry. We were going to tell you after Ella and Fraser's wedding that's next weekend."

"Why wait?"

"Because the Wallaces have lots going on right now and the last thing Charlie needs is me telling him I am seeing his daughter."

"Oh, my God." Lincoln's lips twist into a cynical smile. "Well, that's going to go down like a fart in an elevator. You lied to me? I can't believe you." He pushes his chair back, preparing to leave.

"Please stay and talk to me, Linc."

"I don't want to."

"Please, son."

"Don't call me that." He moves across the room.

"Don't call you that? Are you for real right now?"

"Yes. I am. I am pissed at you for not being straight up with me about Eva. I like her. I actually *really* like her."

"Do you though? 'Cause I've seen at least five girls leave your house these past four weeks alone, Linc."

He shoots his head back as if I slapped him across the face.

"What the fuck does that mean?"

"It means you aren't exactly picky. And do you have a fascination with Eva, simply because she's not into you, making it all the more challenging for you? I know you. I see you with girls. It's not cool. I've been your age myself."

"Is that what it's like with Eva for you too, then?"

I stand up, frustrated by his arrogance, and slap my palm against the cool marble. "It's nothing like that. Eva is *it* for me."

"And does she feel the same way? You're fourteen years older than her. She has two young kids. Are you going to bring them up now, too? Move them in, live like one big fucking happy family? Get the thing you want the most. A wife who doesn't take off at the drop of a hat. Because Eva is stuck here.

She has her business, her family. She's a sure thing. Is that what it is? Security?"

"It's not like that."

"Are you sure? 'Cause it sure seems like that." He sneers at me.

I have never argued with Lincoln like this before. This is unknown land I've discovered and I don't like it. Not one bit.

"You're a sucker for orphans. You brought me up after all."

"Now that is enough," I roar. "Your mother may have left you. But I never did. You are far from an orphan. And she was selfish and inconsiderate. And when was the last time you heard from her, by the way? Ten years ago? She's not fucking interested, Linc. But I am. I love you so much."

"Doesn't seem like it to me. You went behind my back and slept with someone I had a mad crush on."

How fucking dare he.

"Had?"

"Have," he fiercely says, frowning.

"You know what, Linc? Be mad at me. Be mad at me for loving you. Protecting you. Waiting to tell you. We waited because Eva and I were waiting for the timing to be right. So we didn't cause upset with Eva's father either. They have a big wedding coming up. We were going to sit down together and tell you all together. And I have been patient my entire life. But finally, after all these years, I feel happy.

"When I was seventeen and you entered my life, you changed everything. I fell in love with you instantly and did everything to protect you. Your mother left three months after we got married. I was eighteen. And since then, you have been my priority.

"When my friends were out partying, I was in the house reading books about weaning and diaper rashes. When they were graduating, I was attending hospital appointments with you for the hernia you had. When they started their first week at their new jobs, I was taking you to your first day of school."

I pull out my wallet from my inside jacket pocket. "I carry that picture of you on your first day with me everywhere I go because it was my best and worst day. You grew up too fast. I wanted to look after you all the time. I worried about you going to school. What would the other kids say to you when they found out you didn't have a mom like they did? Would they tease you? I worried about you every day of my life and I still do.

"I juggled studying and learning the ropes at the hotel around your routine. Every day was scheduled so that I could be there for you. I had dreams too, Linc. I wanted to go to university. Go to parties. Have my own adventures. But I didn't."

He pushes his hands into his sweatpants pockets and hangs his head.

"And I never once, not once, introduced you to the women I dated, not that I dated many. Because again, I protected you. I kept you safe, warm, happy. Those were the only things that mattered to me.

"Raising you was never a chore to me. From the minute you were born, I was consumed with love for you. And I may have hurt you by dating Eva behind your back and you might think I don't love you, but I do. I have always put you first. When your mother left us, it fucking broke my heart, and I lay awake most nights trying to figure out what I did wrong. It's taken me all this time to realize that I was never the problem. As hard as this might be to hear, son, she didn't want us. She called us a burden."

Lincoln flinches. I've never disclosed that information to him before.

"You were never a burden to me."

I take a step closer to him.

"I have no regrets. You are the best thing to ever happen to me. Your mother and I didn't fit together right. We weren't meant to be. But you, you were."

I place my hand on his shoulder.

"You are the magic that kept me going and the biggest surprise of my life. Every day you blow me away with your witty banter, your clever mind, and phenomenal business head on your shoulders. You're kind, smart, annoyingly cheerful, and so freakin' handsome. It's painful. It's no wonder the women come and go like buses."

He chuckles.

"And I may have sacrificed a massive chunk of my life to care for you, but I don't have any regrets, Linc. And I do love you and there is no way I would intentionally hurt you. I like Eva so much it's painful to think about her not being in my life anymore. I'm putting myself first for a change."

Giving him time to digest, silence stretches like an elastic band between us.

"I think I found my person, Lincoln. After all this time. This isn't a game I'm playing. I'm serious about Eva."

Feeling brave, I confess, "I wasn't exactly truthful on the night of the auction. But I have liked her for two years."

"Two years?" he exclaims.

"Yeah."

"Man, you are patient."

"I think I've waited long enough to find happiness, don't you? You said it yourself before. It's my time, Linc. But not with Tabitha. With Eva. The way I feel about you is the same way I feel about Eva and her boys. I want to protect her and it's killing me. I can't show her off to the world. Show everyone she's mine. She's so beautiful, Lincoln. Kind. Warm. I care about her. A lot. You think I like sneaking around with her? 'Cause I don't. I'm so desperate to be with her properly. Officially. And it's not because she's convenient. She's special. Different."

"You're serious about her." It's not a question. "Are you in love with her?" he asks, unblinking.

"I don't know, but it feels real and pretty epic. Is that the word you and your friends use? Epic?"

He nods, smirking.

"But I am so scared. I've never been lucky in love. It feels like if I say I am or confess how I feel about her, then I'll push her away and everything will fall to shit if I do. Like it did before."

"That won't happen, Dad. If what you say is true and if you feel strongly about her, I'm sure she feels the same way. You let her into your home. That's a big deal for you. I know what she must mean to you. I'm sorry for the things I said. I didn't mean it."

"We all say things in the heat of the moment."

"What, like, are you sleeping with my girlfriend? Those kinds of things?"

Chuckling at my stupidity, my shoulders shake up and down.

"Yeah. See, I'm a dipshit. I mess everything up before it begins. I'm not very good at this relationship stuff."

"You're better than you think. And I don't feel the same way about her as you feel. What you describe is next level. I've never felt like that about anyone before. I'm happy for you, Dad."

Lincoln pulls me into a fierce hug.

In the middle of the kitchen, we have our moment.

"Thank you for everything." He squeezes me. "Mom hasn't been in touch for twelve years. It's been twelve years this Christmas. I don't need her. I never have because you were everything I needed and more. You were the best dad. You always made my football matches, my school shows, parent-teacher nights. You were always there for me. And you can move Eva and her boys in. I didn't mean any of that orphan shit. It might actually be quite nice having little brothers. I love you, Dad."

"I know you do, son." I double pat his back. "Eva's not moving in with me. She's going through a shitty divorce and Ewan is being a prick." We continue to hug each other. I love this boy.

"I would move her in straightaway. She's got a banging body. Holy shit, man, you hit the jackpot. Shane and Corey are gonna be so jealous of you. A younger woman. Wow. You know I've heard you can buy Viagra over the counter now."

I push him out of my arms, laughing.

"Okay, very funny, Linc." I don't tell him Corey said the same or that he and Shane knew about us before he did.

He throws his head back and gives a hearty laugh. "Christ, your face tonight up the stairs."

I point at my chest. "My face. What about yours? What the hell were you doing in my bed, anyway?"

"I always sleep in your bed when you're on nights. Your bed is epic."

"That stops tonight."

"Yup, I agree with you. Never again. Although pole dancing shoes, handcuffs, and what else... Oh, yeah." He holds his finger up in the air, then whispers, "Clit ring. I could be tempted."

"How the hell did you see that?" I gasp in horror.

"I thought I heard Eva say she was going to show you her new jewel. I was half asleep. But thanks for the confirmation."

Holy shit. This is not how I saw my evening panning out.

"Please don't mention this evening ever again," I plead.

"Consider it forgotten."

He won't forget that. Ever.

He thumbs over his shoulder in the direction of the stairs. "I'll just go grab my house keys and get out of here."

"Okay."

Linc walks backward out of the kitchen. "It makes a lot of sense now, though."

"Does it?"

"Yeah. Ewan has been hanging about the side entrance of my house since the auction. I couldn't work out why he would venture this far out to Cherry Gardens Lane. He must think it's me Eva is seeing."

"He must."

"Do you think he scratched the car?"

Of course he fucking did. That guy is really starting to annoy me.

"Don't worry. I would never disclose anything about you and Eva. Your secret's safe with me until you tell her family. I've always got your back, Dad."

"I know." He's a good kid.

What is holding Eva up?

I suddenly feel extremely tired. I slump my heavy frame back onto one of the breakfast bar chairs and pull at the back of my neck. I need a stiff drink.

"Have you been sitting there this whole time?" I hear Lincoln say in the hallway.

I look up and sure enough, through the doorway, fully clothed now, Eva is huddled up on the bottom step of the stair.

I've never disclosed anything to anyone about Olivia.

She heard everything about my runaway ex-wife.

And I answered Lincoln when he asked me if I was in love with her.

It feels real.

How the heck do I explain that?

CHAPTER 20

Eva

Sitting sideways on the sofa in Knox's living room, I listen intently to Knox as he unfolds his life story.

I pay attention to every heartbreaking word as he leaves no stone left unturned and pours his heart out to me.

He fills me in on the events that led up to Olivia's departure, then the events following.

She left her baby.

I can't wrap my head around that.

I could never imagine leaving my boys.

Come hell or high water, I would do everything in my power to keep them.

How could she have left Lincoln and Knox?

I'm not sure my father knows this version of events, either.

Knox bends his head over the back of the sofa. "And there you have it. My sorry-ass tale." He rolls his head to the side. "I should have told you sooner, but I find it incredibly difficult to speak about." He runs his hands down his face. He looks tired.

"Timing, Knox. It was perfect timing. You didn't need to tell me sooner. Synergy is everything. Maybe it was better Lincoln found out about us this way, too."

His eyebrows shoot up in surprise. "You reckon?"

"I do." I lean back against the couch next to him.

Taking my time, I slide my feet on top of the solid walnut coffee table and cross my ankles. "Synergy is when two or more things come together to produce something for the greater good. Lincoln is on our side. He admitted it himself. I think deep down he wants us to be a family, too. Your little heart-to-heart interaction made him see and appreciate you all the more. You weren't just his dad; you were greater than that. His security, his protector, his friend, and more importantly, you gave him the confidence and the ability to see past the lack of having his mother around while he helped you focus your attention on becoming an incredible businessman, growing the business for his future. You're the best dad and the best teacher. You taught him how to be a good human, Knox. You were a perfectly paired team. And in return, he taught you how to love unconditionally. Without prejudice. You show no hate toward Olivia in his presence. You ultimately allowed him to make up his own mind about her. When Olivia left, you could have very well given up your responsibilities and let your parents raise him. But you didn't." I roll my head to the side to face him. "Now, that's pretty special. Admirable, actually."

"It didn't stop me from thinking badly of her, though."

"Yeah. But you didn't think it out loud." It was so long ago now, but I am keen to know. "Did you love her?" I ask softly.

He fills his cheeks with air and blows out a long breath. "She fascinated me. She was this breath of fresh air. Light. Fun. She never took anything seriously. She lived life day to day. She wasn't concerned about her education. She had no plans. But me? I had a plan—university, work for my dad, take over the hotel. I was born and raised in that hotel. It's ingrained in my soul. I found it fascinating. The busy back lobbies, the staff, the people, their lifestyles. I took note and was desperate to be part of that massive moving machine. My goal never changed. Olivia and I were a high school thing. Growing up, experimenting. She made me feel like anything was possible. I expected us to part as soon as high school was over. But the universe had other plans. I did the honorable thing by marrying her. I did think I was in love with her, but I was young. We both were. My parents let us live in their home because Olivia's parents didn't have the space. We were good for a while. When we both turned eighteen, I married her, but it drove a giant wedge between us. She felt trapped. As soon as we were married, I knew she had doubts. Sensed it. Three months later, she left a note. There were no frills. It was a simple goodbye. *I can't do this. You can look after him better than I can.* No apology. Several months later, my father eventually hired a private investigator. He found her in France. I've never told anyone this before." He clears his throat. "But I hand-delivered the divorce papers myself to make sure she signed them. I took Dad's lawyer with me. It was the last time I saw her."

"That must have been hard."

"It had been a year by that point, so I had already given up hope. She was living with about eight other people in this run-down apartment. Stoned off her face. New boyfriend, sleeping by day, partying every night. Not my scene."

"And she signed the papers?"

"Oh yeah. At the drop of a hat, she signed. She asked for nothing in return. No money, no property, no access to Linc. Nothing. She didn't even ask about his well-being."

"How peculiar."

"She wasn't fit to be a mother. She made the right choice for her, for Linc, and for me. I see it now."

"You didn't answer my question."

"Didn't I?"

"Nope. Did you love her?" I ask again.

"Fascinated and infatuated to begin with, yes. Love? No. Her disregard for Linc, lack of love and care for him, and sheer lack of consideration for anyone else but herself exposed her ugly traits, and there was no way I could have loved her. Like nature, as we get older, wiser, we change, transform, but she never did."

"I'm guessing you don't speak to her anymore. I overheard Lincoln say it's been twelve years since he's heard from her."

"No."

"That's a long time."

"She's not interested."

"I personally don't understand that. But I have never been in Olivia's position. I miss my boys, even now. I like knowing everything about them. I even texted my mom when I was in the bathroom getting changed to make sure they went to sleep early."

"Did they?"

"Did they hell. My dad bought a candy floss making machine."

"Bouncing off the ceiling?" His eyes are full of amusement.

"If my dad wants to be up all night with them, he only has himself to blame." I giggle, lacing my fingers together, resting them against my belly. I go back to Olivia. I find the whole thing intriguing. Baffling, actually.

"Do you know where Olivia is now?" I twiddle my thumbs.

"I don't. No."

How well this will go down, I don't know, but I say it anyway. "Have you ever considered that she wasn't running away from you but running toward something else because she couldn't face the enormity of being a teenage mother? She was a baby herself, too. And we all handle life in different ways. Look at Ewan and me, for instance. Our lives couldn't be more different. We both made different choices. I think Olivia's choices were fear, Knox. It's what drove her away. Not you. Or Linc. Does she move frequently?"

"Yeah."

"Classic fear-based behavior. She avoids life. Responsibilities. Looking on, watching others, seeking what others have and thinking that will make her happy, when in fact what she already had was what would have made her happy all along. If she'd stayed put, she may have seen that. But hindsight is a wonderful thing."

"I love the way you look at things. You look at everything from a different perspective. You should have been a counselor." He takes my hand in his and threads our fingers together.

"I've read a lot since me and Ewan separated. Olivia said yes to fear and no to love. It sounds simple, but we all do it. We make choices based on fear or love."

"I think I've done that in the past."

"Yeah?" I smirk.

He nods.

"And now?" I quiz.

"Still shitting myself about what your father will say. One hundred percent fearful."

That's not what I was asking him.

His default emotional setting is fear. Not expressing himself or telling people how he feels. Or me how he feels.

It feels real is what he told Lincoln. He's scared to tell me, afraid of old pain.

Regardless of him not saying the words, I feel it. I feel the same way he does.

It feels real to me too.

But he needs more time.

"How would you feel if maybe we wait until after the wedding to tell everyone about us? Tell everyone, including Ella, so I don't have to tell her over the phone. Ella and Fraser come back from their honeymoon a few days before Christmas, then it's New Year's. It's a busy time of year."

"If that's what you want." He blinks. "I have the Winter Ball coming up. I will not be able to see you much either. We have the members' only bar on the top floor being remodeled too. After the ball would work. We could maybe go away on vacation together."

We do need more time. I want more sacred time with him, to show him I'm not going anywhere.

And I love the sound of a vacation.

"Great idea. When do you ever relax, Mr. Black?"

"I'm relaxing now."

"This evening has been stressful, Knox. Hardly relaxing."

"True. My heart can't take another evening of my son seeing my girlfriend in her underwear."

I throw my hands over my face, then fall sideways into him. "I will *never* live that down." My words are muffled by his shoulder. "I nearly died of embarrassment."

"Or hypothermia. Your nipples looked cold. Or were they happy to see me?"

I squeal. "Stop it."

Knox lets out a deep, rich laugh and swaddles me in his giant arms.

"You looked sexy as fuck in that getup. Promise me you will dress up for me another night. And planned. No more surprises." He kisses the top of my head.

"Deal," I mumble, cuddling up to him.

"Lincoln said Ewan has been hanging around outside the side entrance of his house. He thinks you're seeing Linc."

"He does. He's already mentioned it a couple of times." I never told Knox that, though.

"Let him think whatever the hell he wants to. For now."

"Okay." Sounds like a good plan.

For the next hour, we lie together on the sofa and watch an episode of our favorite car restoration show.

"I'm done in. C'mon, let's go to bed, Sunshine." He yawns, stretching his arms above his head.

Tidying up, we slowly make our way up the elegant sweeping staircase.

Exhausted, we both fall into the bed, and Knox spoons himself against me.

"I need to sleep." He lets out a tired sigh.

"Me too." But my brain is wired to the moon.

A few minutes pass and I whisper in the dark, "It feels real for me, too. Epic."

My heart misses a beat when he doesn't respond.

His lips graze my back. He props himself up and leans over my shoulder.

I turn my head in his direction. "I mean it. I'm not going anywhere. As screwed up as Ewan makes it, I love my life. I like everything about this town. My sisters. My boys. My family. My business. I couldn't imagine my life anywhere else. I am happy. But much happier with you in it. I'll always be here for you."

I turn onto my back. I can only make out the faint shape of his silhouette in the dark and reach up to cup his face.

"Your confession to Lincoln about me didn't scare me and you aren't pushing me away. You don't have to tell me with words how you feel about me because I already feel it," I say softly. "In every cell of my body, I feel how much I mean to you. You're the one for me, too. It seems crazy when I say that. But in three short weeks, I know."

I pull his head down to kiss him.

My fingers clench the back of his neck as I hold him against my lips.

When our tongues connect, we moan together. He moves on top of me and my legs part for him.

"Make love to me, Knox."

Kissing me slowly, tenderly, and deeply, he grinds against me.

As he grows harder by the minute, I reach down to guide him into my wet center.

Between featherlike kisses, he lets out a low groan.

I completely surrender myself to him, giving him all of me, showing him I trust him, letting him know he can trust me with his heart.

He pushes his cock into me, deliciously stretching me, filling me completely. My back arches off the bed, and my lips leave his mouth at the invasion of his thick length.

I grab on to his solid back and run my nails down his skin as he moves in and out.

"Do you mean everything you said?" His voice is filled with raw emotion.

"Everything," I gasp.

His lips devour me, then he rests his forehead against mine.

Breathing deep together, against each other's lips, this feels different from all the times we've had sex before. This isn't sex. It's precious. Meaningful. Connecting us in a way we haven't before.

It feels profound as we find our slow pace together. He goes slightly deeper as I lift my leg, wrapping it around his waist. He grabs my ass cheek, dips his head, then sucks my nipple into his mouth. Softly, he swirls his tongue around my pebbled peak.

Heading north again, he nuzzles into my neck as he fucks me painfully slow, ensuring every hip thrust hits me deep within. The tip of his cock teases my G-spot over and over.

Hip to hip, we grind together, seeking our own release to officially unify us.

Heat builds between my thighs and core, and a flood of powerful sensations sizzle through my body.

We continue to kiss. Calming, dreamy kisses.

Pulling him into me, I seal our hot bodies together, knowing how right we are together.

Mouths sealed, our kissing turns red hot. Knox grows frantic. Muscular arms on either side of my head, he hammers into me repeatedly.

Licking, kissing, and breathing hard against my open mouth, he cries out, urging me to come.

He works me hard. He tilts my hips and his cock hits me so deep, blistering heat explodes in my core and I come. My walls tightly flutter around him. He joins me, his cock pulsing into me as he whispers foreign words against my lips.

The only distinguishable sound I make out is *Se'agapó*.

My body still shaking, he nibbles on my bottom lip.

Every nerve ending is alive now with certainty that I am so deeply in love with this beautiful, kind, and powerful man.

Possessively, he wraps his arms around me and rolls us onto our sides. As he caresses the contours of my body, he scatters kisses across my face, forehead, temples, and nape.

He worships every part of me.

No words are needed. I burrow myself into his chest and give him a little squeeze to let him know I'm his. I'm here.

Locked together, I drift off, safe in the knowledge that my heart is safe with him, and his with me.

And it feels *epic*.

CHAPTER 21

Eva

"I don't think he's coming today." Archie tilts his head sideways and leans it against the wall, staring at the front door.

I sit down on the stair below his.

My heart hurts for him. Archie has been sitting on the bottom stair for over an hour, waiting for Ewan to pick up him and Hamish.

"I think he may have forgotten, baby." I rub his little leg.

"We were supposed to be going to the zoo today." His big disappointed blue eyes stare straight ahead.

"I know." I look at the front door with a sigh too, as if magically Ewan will appear through it.

Ewan is only allowed to pick up and drop off at the house on allocated days as long as he's accompanied by his parents. Today is that day.

Today, Saturday, Ewan was supposed to be taking them from ten a.m. until six p.m., but it doesn't look like that's going to happen.

Having stayed over at Knox's place last night, and following our extremely intense lovemaking session, I reluctantly left his place, picked up the boys, then came home just in time for Ewan to pick up our sons. It's the first full day he's planned to take them in weeks.

I pull my phone out of my pocket and dial Ewan.

No answer.

I drop a quick text to Knox.

Me: Ewan didn't pick the boys up today :(Archie is so sad.

Knox: That's not cool. Poor wee guy.

Me: I know and he was so excited. He promised to take them to the zoo.

Knox: In Edinburgh?

Me: Yeah. I can't see you this afternoon like we planned. Sorry.

Knox: Takes an hour to get there. Twenty minutes to sort yourself out. Get the car packed up. Be there by 1 p.m.

Me: Yeah. I could take them.

Knox: WE will take them. Get them ready. I'll meet you at the parking lot on the south side of town. The old one they don't use anymore. We'll take my estate car.

What?

Me: Are you sure? What if someone sees us?

Knox: They won't. The zoo is huge. Miles away too.

Me: Oh my goodness. You are some kind of wonderful.

Knox: I know. ;)

Me: Thank you.

Knox: Go... See you in twenty minutes. Wrap them up. It's cold outside today. I'll be waiting. xoxo

Eeeek, we get to spend the day together, all of us.

I look at my little brokenhearted boy. "Hey. What if *we* go to the zoo?"

Hamish bounces into the hallway, oblivious to his brother's disappointment.

His eyes light up. "Really? With Dad?"

"Nope, me, you, Hamish, and Knox."

"I like Knox. Hot chocolate?" Hamish plays with the laces on my black boots.

"Why is Knox taking us?" Archie screws his face up.

"Eh, because he has a car to take us in."

"We have a car." His cute face searches mine.

"His is bigger, more comfortable. It's a long way to the zoo. We need a bigger car for that."

"Yaayyyyyy." Hamish squeals with excitement. "I want to see the hellefants."

Archie and I giggle at Hamish.

"What would you like to see, Archie?"

"The reptiles. They have a reticulated python. It can stretch its mouth up to four times the size of its body. It could eat Hamish." He stretches his arms out in the air.

Archie has been a very articulate speaker since he was five years old. Ewan and I were both astonished when he could say more complex words like Tyrannosaurus Rex with no problems. He's a clever cookie.

Hamish gasps. "Oh no, Momma. Don't let it eat me." I tickle his sides and he breaks into a peel of laughter.

"Mr. Snake will eat you too, Archie." And I tickle him too and he squirms around, sliding down the last two steps on the stairs and landing in a heap on the floor.

I clap my hands together. "Okay, boys. Let's go."

When we jumped in the car to come here, Frances, Ewan's mom, texted me to say that they wouldn't be picking up our boys today because Ewan had been out on a bender and was in no fit state to see them. She apologized for her delayed text, but Ewan was in a bad way and needed to be cleaned up.

My boys definitely don't need to see that. I feel sorry for his parents too.

She promised she would take them another day but I'm not holding my breath.

I drive into the abandoned parking lot on the far outskirts of town and there he is.

Knox.

Arms folded, ankle crossed, leaning confidently against his dynamic Audi RS6 Avant. Casually dressed in black jeans, pure white tennis shoes, a white tee, and a black insulated jacket. Dripping in designer apparel. He's the sexiest man I know.

He pushes himself off his metallic blue car as I pull up beside him.

I click open my door, pull myself out, and look over the roof of my daffodil-colored car. I can't hide my smile.

"Hello."

"Hey, Sunshine."

"We're doing this today?"

I close my door gently and walk around the back of the car.

"Yes, we are. I thought our kids could bond. I brought mine."

Knox opens his rear door of his car. And right enough, perched in the middle of the back seat, is Lincoln.

"We're having a family day out, apparently." He rolls his eyes. "And I've promised to be a good boy today and that every time I close my eyes, I won't imagine you in your under—"

Knox closes the car door before he finishes his final word.

"See, child," he mutters under his breath.

I pull my lips into my mouth. I am never living that down.

"We're really doing this?" I ask him again, crossing my arms across my body.

"Yes, we are. We can try to integrate them slowly. My child is around the same mental age as your two. They'll get along great." He grins.

He's not wrong.

I swing open the back door of my car, revealing my two rascals.

"Knoxy." Hamish beams and throws his little hand out to him.

"Hey, boys." Knox crouches down, peering into the car. "Ready for the zoo?"

Archie side-eyes Knox suspiciously around the headrest of his car seat while Hamish yells an enthusiastic yes.

"I know what animal I want to see today." Knox tries to get Archie's attention.

I mutter snakes under my breath.

"Snakes. I hope they have snakes," he says.

Archie points at Knox, getting excited. "They do. They have them. A python one."

"A python. Oh my goodness, Archie. I can't wait. You'll have to show me what it looks like. They have so many different colors and sizes."

"They are called species."

"Wow. Let's get this show on the road then, shall we? Let's go see all the different species."

Yep, it's official. I've died and gone to heaven.

Died and gone to *swoony billionaire, furniture-buying, snake-loving, fast-car-driving, loves my sons and would do anything to appease them* heaven.

"I want that one. That gonna be mine one." Hamish points into the elephant enclosure.

Knox laughs. "I don't think it will fit in the car."

"We can leave Hamish here. In the monkey enclosure. We'd have space then," Lincoln chimes in.

"No, me come home," Hamish says defensively.

"Leave him here," Archie shouts, clapping his hands as if it's the best idea.

My boys love each other, but my God they love winding each other up.

I look up.

Knox is carrying Hamish on his shoulders and Lincoln has Archie on his. It's been a brilliant day. It's almost closing time and we are visiting the last enclosure before we leave. The elephants, Hamish's favorite.

This is what we needed. Knox was right. Family time.

Lincoln has chased the boys around the entire visit. Running to each animal attraction. Reading out the fact sheets. Sharing the scariest parts of information about the venomous snakes and spiders.

When he mimicked the penguins waddling during the penguin parade, Hamish and Archie thought it was hilarious. What made it extra funny was the silly faces Lincoln made. My boys love him.

Lincoln joked with them the entire journey here, too. Teasing them, they were squashing him and going to squeeze out all his farts as he sat between their child safety seats in the back. He did kind of look ridiculous and it felt weird at first with my high school friend in the back—my stepson.

Holy shit. I can't think about that.

"He's pooping," Archie yells.

"That is a big poop," Lincoln says. "It's about the same size as you, Hamish."

"My hellefant do a poop," he cheeses down at me.

"He did. I bet that stinks. Poo-wee." I swipe my hand back and forth in front of my nose.

Knox turns around and looks my way. "You okay? Have you had a good day?"

"The best. We will have to do more of these."

"We will." He winks sexily.

"Ewwwwww. My hellefant is eating his poo. Me don't want that one, Momma." Hamish sticks his tongue out, pretending to be sick while he holds his stomach.

"He is definitely not coming home with us in the car now, boys," Knox says to us all as we stand in a line watching poop-gate. "Right. Time to go."

"Me down, Knox." Knox lifts Hamish in the air off his shoulders and plonks him onto the ground. Lincoln mirrors his actions, doing the same with Archie.

"I'll race you to the gift shop, Knox." Archie runs. So does Hamish.

Knox groans. "You're cheating." He runs after them. "You started running before me."

And they're off.

"I've never seen him so happy, you know." Lincoln bumps my shoulder as we meander down the gray path leading to the entrance. "You're good for him."

"Thank you," I say softly. I'm still embarrassed about last night and this is all very odd.

"Is this weird? Me, you, your dad, the boys? It is, isn't it?"

"Kinda." He shakes his head back and forth. "But fun. Your boys are great. And I have a sneaky suspicion my dad might be a little bit in love with you. I don't think that's weird at all. It's understandable. You're pretty cool."

"You think?" I squeak.

"Yup. He's smitten. He's never introduced me to any of his previous girlfriends before. I actually don't think he's had any. And Tabitha doesn't count." He screws his face up, trying to recall. "*This* is a first. He even made me leave my shift at the hotel today to come here. Pigs may fly this evening." He sticks his hands into the pockets of his black insulated jacket. It's getting cold now as the sun fades.

Wow. This *is* a big deal for Knox.

I clear my throat. "So, last night."

"Don't mention it. I was kidding earlier. And eh, I tried to kiss my dad's girlfriend."

"Oh God, yeah." I snort, then cover my hand over my mouth.

"I think we're even."

"We are." I put my hand out, and he shakes it.

"Let's never mention either of those things again."

"Deal."

We saunter down the steep path.

"Oh, hi, Eva," a voice sings from my left.

I snap my head toward the familiar voice and there, standing to the side of me, is Nicole, Ewan's sister.

My soon-to-be ex-sister-in-law, along with her husband and two kids.

Shit. Shit. Shit.

"Oh, hi."

Lincoln senses my awkwardness and keeps on walking down the path. I'm sure he's off to do some damage control up ahead and make sure the boys and Knox are out of the gift shop and in the car before Ewan's family gets that far.

But they saw Lincoln; handsome is hard to miss.

"Are the boys here?"

"Yeah. Up ahead with my... friends."

"Here with a group of *friends,* then?"

"Yeah," I lie through my teeth.

"Ewan was supposed to come with us today with the boys. But Mom texted me to say they couldn't make it."

Ah, I didn't know they were all coming together. Aw, crap.

"Your mom texted me too. I brought them instead."

"With your *friends*?" She tilts her head forward, eyeing me as if peering over the top of a pair of spectacles.

"Yes."

She knows. She saw Lincoln. She thinks I'm dating Lincoln. *Abort. Abort. Abort.*

"Which reminds me. I must go catch up with them." I rush down the path. "Have a great day," I call back over my shoulder.

"The place is closed. We're going home," Nicole calls.

"Safe journey home then."

Aw, shit.

Once out of sight, I run through the shop, out the exit, through the narrow lane toward the parking lot, and as if he's my savior in shiny metal, Knox is already waiting for me. Window rolled down, he shouts, "Get in, Sunshine."

As soon as I'm in the safety of the car, he takes off.

I'm internally praying to the heavens above that Ewan's family didn't see Knox's car.

"Wook. I got a hellefant. Knox get me it." Hamish waves a bright-blue plushie about in the air.

"I got a snake." Archie shoves his green fluffy toy in my face from behind me. "Hisssssssssssss."

"Oh, wow. You two are lucky boys. I hope you said thank you." I try to catch my breath.

"Yesssss," they both ring out.

Knox pats my knee. "It'll be okay, Sunshine. Don't worry."

"They think you're dating me," Lincoln says.

I rest my head against the headrest.

"They do. They'll tell Ewan," I confirm my greatest worry.

"I hope so," he joshes.

"Lincoln. This is serious," Knox scowls.

"Oh, I know. But life is too short to worry about it. Everyone will know after the Winter Ball, anyway. Just chill. If Ewan asks me, I'll deny it."

Knox looks in his rearview mirror and nods in acknowledgement.

"There is no way anyone will believe me, anyway. I'd be seriously leveling up on the girlfriend front if we were dating. And if I'm punching, then you are punching way above your belt, you old fart." Lincoln slaps the top of his dad's arm. "You're probably still trying to upload images to Bebo."

"You are so mean, Linc." Then I decide to join in. "He probably still has a MySpace account."

"Ha ha, very funny. Let's all pick on Knox." He rolls his eyes.

"He called you a fart, Knox. That is bad," Archie tattles.

"Knox is a farrrrt. Knox is a farrrtt," Lincoln chimes under his breath, then Hamish and Archie join in. They get louder and louder.

I laugh. Knox does too.

"Welcome to our new dysfunctional family, Sunshine." He squeezes my knee.

"Blended."

"It couldn't be more perfect," he says over our three boys in the back.

Three boys.

How the hell did this happen?

"This is for you." Knox pulls a small yellow jellyfish plushie from the side pocket on the driver's side.

I hold it up. "Cute."

"Aw, why didn't I get a plushie too, Dad?" Linc says, sulking.

"You can share mine." Hamish offers his toy to Linc.

Yeah, our family is awesome. I sigh with happiness.

We drive home singing and joking with one another, our worries parked for another few days.

Once back on the outskirts of Castleview, I pick up my car. Kindly, Lincoln distracts the boys so Knox and I can have a sneaky kiss goodbye.

Tired out from our adventurous day, the boys didn't eat very much for dinner and pass out in their beds instantly.

Watching television on my new leather sofa, a text drops into my phone. Knox.

Knox: I had a great day today. The boys will sleep tonight.
Me: They will. They are already sleeping soundly. Thank you for my jellyfish plushie. :)
Knox: It's how you make me feel.
Me: I don't understand.
Knox: You turn my legs to jelly. Night, Sunshine. xoxo

He doesn't just turn my legs to jelly. He melts my whole body.

Can a woman die of happiness?

I pick up my phone to Google it.

I think it might be possible.

CHAPTER 22

Knox - Three and a half weeks later - two days before Christmas

"When will I see you again?"

"Boxing Day. Ewan is taking the boys. Or so he says. It's all arranged with Frances."

I spin my spaghetti around my fork. "If he doesn't, we will all spend the day together." I clatter my fork against my white plate and push it away from me. I'm not hungry.

I can't eat. Can't sleep either.

Stretching my back, I reach up.

I need a massage. My back is so stiff these days.

"You need sunshine." Eva watches me wince.

"I have sunshine, right here."

She gifts me a smile.

Beautiful.

Throughout everything, Eva has maintained her calm. She's such a breath of fresh air when I need it most. She has this ability to detect what I need when I need it.

She has lots of her own shit going on too and she never complains.

Veronica was unable to find out where Ewan's severance pay disappeared to. However much it was, it's vanished. Just like her furniture.

Ewan has yet to sign the divorce papers. Our only saving grace is he has continued to keep his distance.

He's been deadly silent. Worryingly so.

If he would just sign the papers and set her free, I think Eva would sleep better at night, too.

Although the stress rash on the back of her neck has almost gone, which is a great sign.

I'm grateful for the small things.

She nailed the Castleview Business Circle social media training too and some of the businesses have embraced their newfound addiction; others not so much.

At the hotel, finally, the members' bar has been fully remodeled. What a nightmare that was. The bar stools arrived in the incorrect finish. We asked for all white and what did we get? Black with red leather seat pads—someone else's order.

That set us back by a week, delaying the members' only opening party. But I let Linc handle that too.

Over time, he'll be running the place.

That's the plan, anyway.

Then there is the Winter Ball. The white LED dance floor has given us nothing but issues. It flashes on and off sporadically. We're going to get sued for causing seizures if it isn't replaced. Luckily, our trial run at Ella and Fraser's wedding highlighted the problem and a new floor is being laid the week after the New Year's celebrations.

I had to threaten to pull our three-year equipment hire contract with them. Miraculously, within an hour, they'd found a replacement.

Then some dipshit—me—thought it was a great idea to over-invite people in the hope some wouldn't make it, but I fucked up. We are now seventy-three people over our ballroom capacity, forcing us to open the adjoining function suite, that's only used for smaller parties, to redistribute people.

Lincoln assures me it's going to be just fine. I trust him.

With every day that passes, Eva and I are getting closer to telling our friends and families about our relationship.

I'm excited but so fucking nervous.

I'm also preparing myself for the many questions my own parents will have, too. Then there are my staff, my friends' wives, and the town. The gossip.

Always the fucking gossip.

My chest feels tight.

I'm going to give myself a heart attack if I keep worrying about what other people think.

Eva takes a sip of the crisp apple juice. Lunch today in my office is the only time I get to see her this week. Christmas is in two days, meaning she has a full schedule with the boys.

In the last three weeks, we've only snuck in a couple of nights here and there—not enough.

I miss her.

"I have something for you." I pull out the elegant white-wrapped slim square box from the inside pocket of my suit jacket. I hope she likes it. "Merry Christmas."

"Oh, my goodness. It's too beautiful to open." She plays with the dark-red ribbon. "I bought you something too." Dipping into her purse, she pulls out a similar-sized black-wrapped box with a bouncy gold bow.

"You didn't have to get me anything." I shake my head.

"I know we never spoke about getting each other gifts. But I saw this." She taps her gift for me. "And thought of you, and you got me one too, so you can't be mad at me," she says coyly.

"Is it a new clit jewel?" I reply, laughing.

"Noooooo." She hits me playfully on the shoulder.

I point to her box. "You go first."

"Nope. You first." She bobs her head toward my present.

"I've never had a woman buy me a gift before." I untie the silk bow.

"No?" she asks, full of surprise. "Massive pressure on me, then?"

Unwrapping the paper reveals a black leather pouch. I open the gold pouch popper and pull out a shiny brass object.

"It's a pocket sundial compass." Sounding nervous, she points at it. "It's antique. The man in the shop was very helpful and said it allows you to tell the time and find directions or something. You can look it up. And I had it engraved. See?" She flips it over in my hand.

So you can always find your way back to me. Just follow the Sunshine x

I'm lost for words. I run my thumb over the intricate detailing and the sentiment she's lovingly etched into the truly beautiful golden instrument.

Feeling emotional, I utter in a gruff voice, "I wasn't expecting this."

She picks it out of my hand and starts repacking it. "It's okay if you don't like it. Who uses a sundial these days? Duh. You have that fancy watch on your wrist that probably cost the price of my car. I know, it's cool. I get it. It's a stupid gift."

Clasping her wrist to stop her fumbling around, I say, "That's not what I meant at all. It's the most thoughtful present anyone has ever bought me."

She looks at me suspiciously. "You're not just saying that?"

"No. Never. I love it."

"Yeah?" She throws her hand to her heart. "Well, that's okay then. I thought with the story you told me about the day on the beach, you saw me, the clouds, the sun, your pet name for me." She waves her hands about. "All of those things. You know?" She bites her bottom lip.

She's nervous.

"It's perfect. I will carry it with me always." I place it into the palm of my hand again, examining the fine brass cogs and dials.

"You don't have to," she squeaks and pulls her shoulders up, thrilled I'll be carrying a dollop of her with me everywhere I go. *Sunshine.*

"I will. I want to."

"Okay. Should I open mine now?"

"Please do."

With bated breath, she slowly takes her time to pull apart the thin ribbon and then the white gift wrap.

She lets out a little squeal of excitement. "This is exciting. Oooo, a red box. What's inside?" she whispers to herself with glee.

She gasps when she flips the top open. "Oh, my goodness. That is beautiful. Can I put it on?"

That was the plan.

She rests the red and gold box on my desk.

I point to it. "Do you know what it is?"

"A bracelet." She looks at me, confused.

"Do you know what kind of bracelet it is?"

"A gold one?" she says slowly.

"Smart-ass." We both laugh, then I explain. "This is a super special bracelet." I carefully lift it out of the molded box. "An Italian jeweler invented it in the sixties. He grew up in Rome." I tilt the bracelet. "You see that there?" I point to the screw lock.

"Yeah." She's fascinated. I've got her.

"Well, the only way to get it on and off is with this special little tool here." I remove the tiny gold screwdriver from the velvet-lined box. I don't think she saw that in there.

"Now, that is cute. Look at the size of it." She goes all girly.

"Can I put it on you?"

"Why are you asking me that? Of course."

"Well, because this is more than a bracelet. This is called a Love Bangle."

She stills as if frozen in time.

"This bangle symbolizes something much deeper. Once locked on your wrist, it doesn't slip off, and the only way to remove it is with this."

I hold the screwdriver up to my face so she's forced to make eye contact with me. "It's a permanent symbol of love."

I pause, letting that sink in.

"If I lock the bracelet on your wrist, I'm keeping you forever."

Her sapphire eyes glaze over. When she finally blinks, fat teardrops plop onto her top, disappearing into the fabric.

Unexpectedly, she says, "This sucks."

Fuck. I've read the signs all wrong.

"I'm sorry." I lay the bracelet back into the box. "I have to get back to work."

"What?" She sits with her mouth agape. "You will do no such thing, Mr. Black. You pick that bracelet up and lock that bad boy on my wrist right this very minute."

"But you just said this sucks." I'm confused.

"Yes, because your gift trumps mine by a gazillion times. This is a *huge* deal." She looks into my eyes and cups my face. "A Love Bangle?" She thumbs my cheek with a goofy grin on her face, her eyes watery.

I nod nervously.

"You love me?" she asks quietly, her eyes searching mine for an answer.

"I do. I've fallen for you."

"You love me." She sighs as if the weight of the moon lifted off her shoulders. "I know how hard you find it to express yourself, but you have never needed to tell me. You care for me and my boys in ways a girl only dreams about. I've felt your love for me since I met you. All the way down into my tippy-toes, I feel it."

She plants the softest kiss on my lips and looks deep into my eyes. "I love you, Knox. I love you more than the rays of the sun."

"That's not a thing."

"It could be. I love you more than the waves in the sea."

"That's better."

"And I love you more than all the stars in the night sky."

"That works."

"It does."

My heart does an Olympic backflip, it's so fucking happy.

I'm happy.

We kiss for what feels like a lifetime. It's slow and pure. Deep and sensual. She teases me with her tongue and our kiss turns erotic. Full of hope. Full of heat and passion. Adventures we've still to discover together.

She directs her kisses to the side of my lip. "I love you," she whispers.

Then my cheek. "I love you."

Then my eyelid. "I love you."

Then my forehead. "I love you."

Branding me as hers, weaving all the little cobwebs of doubt I ever had together, as if turning them into pure spun golden love.

"You might find it difficult to say those words. But I don't. I will keep on telling you. Me and you are meant for a reason. Our souls met in this lifetime, but I think we've met before. I feel drawn to you." She carefully scrambles onto my lap. "I have never told you this before, but I've always liked watching you walk on the beach with Sam. Loved it when you came to our events at the sports retreat. I treasured our slithers of conversations and fateful interactions. I found you fascinating.

I still do. More than before. I love your heart, your never-ending kindness. I love how you love me."

She loves how I love her.

"Now chastity belt me up, Mr. Black." She holds out her wrist, breaking her sentimental speech.

She makes me laugh. "It's not a chastity belt."

"It is, or is it more like a fancy handcuff? Kinky." She's fucking teasing me.

Pulling off her length of bracelets, making space for her new one, the dozens of thin bangles she wears tinkle against the desk as she disposes of them.

"You can leave the others on."

"No way. Those are fashion jewelry bangles. This one is so special it has to be the only one I wear from now on. I should have bought you one too. Ensure no one touches my man. Or I might make you wear a sandwich board with a big sign that says, *Hands off, he's mine.*" She splays her hands across the space in front of her.

"We're having a special moment and you are spoiling it by being silly. Now give me your wrist and let me chastity belt you up."

She watches me intently as I lock her bracelet in place on her tiny wrist. "There, done. It's official. Never coming off."

"Never. And you can keep that little screwdriver tool thingy. You, kind sir, have been betrothed with the taking careth of the keyth," she says in a fake stiff upper lip British accent.

"I think I changed my mind." I pretend to unlock it. "You are not taking this seriously enough. I announced my undying love for you and there is too much tomfoolery going on. There is no place here for that today."

"You love it really." Wrapping her arms around my neck, she pushes me back against my office chair. "You love me, remember?" She nods her head up and down, instructing me to agree with her. "Plus, I suck you so fucking good." Her voice drops an octave. "At least that's what you told me the other night." She slides her hand down my chest. "And I make you so hard because I have the best. Tight. Wet. Pussy." She punctuates every word as she grinds herself against my cock.

Fuck, I could come like this.

"It's all yours." Kissing the shell of my ear, she gently licks it, then bites my lobe. "Forever."

My breathing becomes ragged.

Hot breath floods the skin of my neck. "But not today. 'Cause I have to go." She springs off my lap. "I have a class to teach in..." She taps her smartwatch. "Eeeek. Ten minutes. I gotta go."

Palming my cock through my suit pants, she assures me she will help me with my *problem* on Boxing Day.

"Too long." I let out a frustrated sigh.

"Oh, it's long alright. Very impressive. I gotta go." She lands a wet, messy kiss on my lips. "I love you. I'll text you."

I'll never tire of hearing her say that.

"I wish we could spend Christmas Day together."

"Next year," she assures me, shouting back over her shoulder as she piles her coat, purse, and hat into her arms.

Next year.

Eva: Merry Christmas! I will call you later when I leave Mom and Dad's. I'm the designated driver and I'm ferrying everyone around today. Deep joy!

Me: Merry Christmas, Sunshine. In the campervan?

Eva: Yes and... Ella and Fraser are having a baby! They've just told us. We are multiplying. Like Gremlins. :)

Me: That's great news.

Eva: She has no idea what she's in for.

Me: She doesn't.

Eva: Watermelons out of lemons. Ouch.

Me: I wouldn't know.

Eva: You would have seen. You know exactly what I'm talking about. :) Never again.

Me: Never?

Eva: Nope.

Me: Why not?

Eva: Stretch marks, pain, and no more designer vagina!

Me: That wouldn't bother me.

Eva: You don't have to worry about it. 'Cause that's never happening again, anyway.

Me: I would have liked more. Had a big family. I still would.

The little text message bubbles dance across my screen. Then stop. Then start again. She takes another few minutes to reply.

Eva: With me?

Me: Only you.

Eva: I'll call you later. xoxo

CHAPTER 23

Knox

She didn't call.

I freaked her out with the baby comment. I won't ever mention it again.

We have three boys between us. That's more than enough to keep us busy.

Having spent all day eating, playing games, and watching crap on the television at my parents' house with Lincoln, we then dropped into the hotel to hand out Christmas gifts for the staff working today. That was Mrs. Kinnear's idea several years ago, so she runs with it every year, scouring for gifts that suit everyone. She insists Lincoln and I hand-deliver them before the night shift starts.

She's a dreamboat.

Today is a day of celebration and families; however, many of my staff are younger in age, with no kids, and the lure of triple pay on Christmas Day is a big bonus for them; therefore, finding people to work Christmas Day has never been an issue.

Christmas dinner at the hotel was another fully booked event. Apparently, everything went to plan except for McLeish, the farmer, who felt up several of the waitresses and was politely asked to leave. His wife was mortified. Not so mortified, she continues to stay with him year after year. *Fucking pervert.*

I pour myself a nightcap and look out into the dark backyard of my house. My reflection stares back at me in the window.

Alone again.

Lincoln stayed at the hotel to organize the New Year's roster. I urged him to come home with me, but he insisted he wanted to get ahead of the game so he can have New Year's off.

I wish he would find a girlfriend and settle down. It would stop him working ungodly hours. Been there, done that.

Sensing my melancholy mood, Sam settles beside me. "Hey, old pal. Just me and you again?"

I'm about to switch the lights off when I hear Eva call out, "Knox! Are you home?"

My excitement at her being here kicks up a gear.

She came to see me.

Her hushed tones and gentle coos, as if she is talking to Archie and Hamish, wisp through the echoing hall.

"Knox! Please be here," she wails.

Why is she shouting?

I dash out of the living room; my emotions derail in a flash.

My whole world shifts.

Standing in my hall is my beautiful girl. Her two boys. One on her hip. The other holding her hand. They're all in their pajamas. Disheveled.

Everything is wrong with this picture.

Hamish is sound asleep in her arms. Archie's been crying, and Eva's face tells the whole story.

I don't wait another second. I run to her and inspect her face.

"Ewan?"

"Yes."

Motherfucker.

The entire left side of her face is swollen to double its size and bruising has already begun. Purple and deep red in places. Blotches scatter her skin from crying, and a small cut at the top of her cheekbone oozes fresh droplets of sticky red blood.

"What happened?" Boiling with fury, I grind my teeth.

"Not now." Clenching her eyes shut, silent tears roll down her swollen cheeks.

I pull her into my arms and kiss the top of her head. "Hey. You're safe now."

Eva allows me to scoop a sleeping Hamish out of her arms.

Bending down to greet Archie, he hides shyly behind the protection of Eva's legs. "Hey, wee guy." I ruffle his hair softly. Archie sucks on his finger, his head tilted down, unable to make eye contact with me. "Fancy a sleepover?"

"My daddy, not nice. He hurt my momma."

My heart breaks into a million fragments as my veins boil with raging heat. No little boy should ever witness whatever happened tonight. Christmas fucking night.

And my girl's face. I almost whimper with the pain I feel for her.

"You are safe here. You see that camera there?" I point to the CCTV camera in the hall. "That sees everything. We have cameras everywhere. Plus, we have an attack dog. My dog, Sam, is here to protect us."

"I like doggies," he mumbles.

"He'll love you. Want to come see him?"

He takes my hand and I usher them into my home. Where it's safe.

Half an hour later, Eva and I are in my bedroom. The boys are settled into their room next door.

Sensing Hamish and Archie's sadness, Sam lies down by their bed, standing guard. He'll stay there all night. He used to do the same with Lincoln when he was unwell as a teenager, too.

Eva pulls herself up and leans back against the headboard, takes the two painkillers from my hand, and swallows them down slowly with the glass of cool water I left on her side of the bed.

Sitting sideways on the edge of the mattress, I squeeze the warm water out of the soft warm cloth and pat it lightly against her cut, trying to clean it as best I can.

She hisses.

"I'm sorry."

"It stings."

A few more light dabs and I can finally see what damage he's caused. It's a small cut with lots of deep bruising.

"What happened, baby?"

I take her hand in mine.

She takes a deep breath in and exposes Ewan in all his fine fucked-up glory. "We'd had such a lovely day with all of us at Mom and Dad's. The boys had great fun playing with the chocolate fountain Dad bought. He's a big kid at heart. Christmas dinner was the best."

She shuffles down the bed. "By eight o'clock everyone wanted to go home so, acting as everyone's taxi service, we all bundled into my campervan. I dropped everyone off and went home myself with the boys. It had been a long day. The boys woke me up at five o'clock, excited to see if Santa had been there."

"I would have liked to be there to see that."

"You wouldn't. I'm so tired." She tries to hide her yawn with the back of her hand. "I was keen to get them to bed. I dumped my bags and all our presents from everyone at the front door. We ran straight up the stairs."

Eva looks deflated.

"The boys brushed their teeth, hopped into bed, and I got myself ready for bed too. I feel like such a fool."

"You are not, Eva. No way." I push her hair off her forehead. "And then what happened?"

"I must not have closed the door properly when we went into the house. It's so stiff with it being winter; I need to get it fixed. I keep forgetting to call a carpenter. When I went back down the stairs an hour or so later to grab my phone from my purse, Ewan was standing in the hallway with my phone in his hand. He became frantic, unintelligible ramblings, kicking the presents. I ran down, urged him to get out of the house, but he wouldn't listen. It all got out of hand.

"He pinned me against the wall, shouting in my face, screaming at me to tell him what the passcode was for my phone. But I wouldn't give it to him and kept hiding my face so the facial recognition wouldn't work. He mentioned something about Lincoln. His family saw us. I'm a bitch. I caused this mess. Same old, same old. Threatening to hunt Lincoln down."

"Intoxicated?"

"Heavily. And he was dirty and unwashed." She screws her face up, forgetting about her bruised skin. "Ow, that is sore."

"It's gonna hurt like a bitch tomorrow."

"Difficult to hide." She forces a smile.

"And then?" I keep pushing. I need to know what that bastard did to her.

"I got away from him. Somehow. He was so strong, Knox. He chased after me. Into the kitchen. Around the dining table. I've never been so scared. I don't know what he planned to do to me. He picked up the kettle and threw it at me. Then the toaster and anything else he could find. I dodged them all. I don't remember what happened next, but I think he turned his back, and I made a run for it to the living room to get to the house phone. He was on me so fast. My heart was racing. I tried to slam the living room door shut, but he pushed me through it and I fell to the floor and smacked my face on the edge of the coffee table. He was straight on top of me and I did everything I could to get him off, but he was so heavy." She cups her mouth with her hand. "What if the neighbors hadn't called the police? Oh my God, Knox. I might not have been here tonight. And my boys. Archie heard everything."

Her chest heaves in deep waves of audible gasps. Her tears flow and I let her get it all out as I move up onto the bed and cradle her in my arms, making sure I don't make her injuries any worse.

Rocking her back and forth, I coo, "Hey, that didn't happen. You are here now. Safe. Your boys are safe. They are sound asleep. You're okay."

"He was going to hit me with my phone in his hand." She howls. "I should have given him the passcode."

Fucking bastard. I'm going to make sure he pays for this.

"He's no longer entitled to be near you. Or dictate who you see or what you do. He overstepped the mark tonight. Way over the fucking boundary and beyond. What he did was completely unacceptable, Eva."

She takes a few minutes to gather herself before she continues. This is not my usual solid, in control girl. He fucking broke her tonight.

"It all happened so fast. The next thing I knew, the police were there. They caught him midair. He didn't get a chance to hit me. But he was going to. The police arrested him. He didn't go easy. There was lots of shouting and they had to wrestle him out of the house. Archie was crying. Luckily, Charlotte from next door sat with him in his bedroom, comforting him while the paramedics checked me over. Hamish slept through the entire thing. The police took my statement and now here we are. My kitchen is a mess. My walls have massive dents in them. They'll need to be plastered. I left everything. I didn't want to stay there tonight. I wanted you." She hugs me tighter. "I was so frightened."

"What did the paramedics say? Your cheek is very swollen. How do they know your cheekbone isn't broken?"

"I don't know. But I didn't want to go to the hospital. Not on Christmas night."

"Then we will go to the hospital tomorrow. Get you checked over."

"Oh no, I don't want anyone seeing me like this," she gasps.

"Corey is a doctor, Eva. He will see you privately."

"It's Boxing Day tomorrow. I can't take him away from his family."

"That man would walk through fire for me. It will take him half an hour, an hour tops to see you. No arguing." I continue to rub her back.

"Okay. Thank you. I don't want to tell my sisters. I'm so ashamed."

"You have nothing to be ashamed of."

"I still don't want them to know. Look at my face. What if my dad and mom find out? I want to tell them about Ewan on my own terms. But after the divorce. I don't want them worrying about me."

It's going to be very hard to keep this quiet and people do like to talk in Castleview. Especially Mrs. Mitchell, the leader of the gossip patrol.

Eva is fiercely independent in every way.

"Forget that for the moment. Okay. You need to rest. C'mon. Let's get you comfortable."

Tucking her in for the night, I run my fingers through her hair and plant a soft kiss against her lips.

With everything I am, I'm going to protect this girl and her boys.

I pull out my phone and drop Corey a text. He instantly replies.

Appointment made for tomorrow at four in the afternoon.

Checking on the boys before I head to bed myself, I stand in their bedroom doorway and I decide that's it. We tell everyone after the Winter Ball, and then they're moving in with me.

Decision made.

CHAPTER 24

Eva

I roll over in Knox's bed and pick up my smartwatch from the nightstand.

Ten a.m.

I shake my head, unable to recall the last time I slept this late.

Tapping my face with my fingertips, I explore my swollen skin.

I roll over onto my back; I realize I'm alone in Knox's giant bed. No wonder half the day is gone. The boys must surely be up too. There is no way they slept this long.

Pushing the covers back, I pull my weary body out of the bed.

I feel sore all over.

Stepping in front of the oversized bronze ornate mirror Knox has leaned against the wall, I examine my swollen cheek.

It doesn't look like me.

Tracing my fingers across my purple skin, I let out a sigh at the realization my poor boys have to see me like this.

It's now or never.

I make my way down to the kitchen. The sound of laughter drifts into the hallway.

Tying Knox's robe around me, I decide to listen to what they are giggling at.

"There is no poop in the pool. I promise." *Knox.*

"There is!" shouts Archie.

"There isn't. Now stop being silly and tell me what would make the coolest pool party on the planet?"

My boys make a list.

"A slide."

"A lilo."

"A ball."

"A mingo."

"A what?" I sense the confusion in his voice. Hamish means flamingo. I hold in my chuckle.

Archie helps Knox out. "He means a flamingo. Oh, oh, oh, a unicorn."

Knox lets out an exaggerated sigh. "A flamingo *and* a unicorn. You two are demanding. Okay, I think we have enough on the list."

He's up to something. Knox always is.

"Next thing. Can you help me? I need two strong boys. Do you know of any?"

"Me, me, me."

"Me too. Oh, me too," Hamish joins in eventually.

"Of course. Why didn't I think of that? I have something important I need help with. Are you strong boys up for the challenge?"

They both squeal yes.

I lean against the wall outside the kitchen, listening with wonder.

"At the bottom of the garden, I have a pond, and in that pond are some special fish. They are magic."

"Ooooooo," the boys gasp.

"The fish are called koi. Have you heard of them?"

"Nope." Archie pops the *P*.

"A tale from lots and lots of years ago said that one golden koi fish took over one hundred years to swim up this huge stream and then swam up a waterfall."

"No waaaaay. Water goes down, not up, Knox." Archie thinks he's right about everything. He's a sponge for this stuff.

"Waaaaaaaay," Knox says, shocked. "And once he reached the top because he was so brave, the waterfall God turned him into a golden dragon."

"Wow. A dragon?"

"Yeah."

"Do you have fishy dragons?" Hamish is curious.

"Not yet, but if we make them strong enough, maybe one day one of them will swim upstream and they'll turn into a golden dragon, and this is why we have to feed them and build up their strength first. That's where you two boys come in. Do you think you could help me feed them today?"

"Yes!"

"Great. Fist pumps all round."

I get the overwhelming urge to cry. With joy. Not sadness.

Knox may be a sex god in the bedroom, but he's also a gorgeous man with a heart made of twenty-four-karat gold.

I walk into the kitchen. Draped over the high bar stools is a white sheet. He's made them a tent.

Aw. God, my full heart can't take anymore.

Walking around to the *entrance* of it, I poke my head in.

"Hey, whatcha doin'?" I ask.

Knox's face twitches when he sees my face. Not drawing attention to it, he simply states what they've done. "We made a den."

Looking at my three boys lying on their backs, looking up at me, I smile. I can't help it.

"Are girls allowed?"

"I don't know. What do you think, lads?" Knox looks left and right. "Should we let this pretty lady into our den?"

"Yes." Hamish punches the air.

"Okay. The boss says yes." Knox grins at me.

I lie down beside them. Hamish rolls over and touches my face. "What happened, Momma? You have an ouchie."

"I do. I'm okay though. Mommy fell."

"Like Mr. Bump?"

"Yes, exactly like him."

Archie sits up and looks at me. "You okay, baby? Will we have a little chat later, you and me?" Clarifying what Archie witnessed last night will help me gauge how I approach the explanation for last night's events.

He nods his blond-covered head slowly, his eyes full of concern.

"I'm okay. I promise." He takes hold of my hand and I squeeze it.

"Me magic." Hamish looks as shocked about that statement as I am.

"Are you?"

"Yes. I sleeped in my bed. Then I woked up here in this big house." Hamish's big brown eyes go wide and he splays his hands out in the air.

"Wow, you are. Like the fish?"

He nods his head enthusiastically.

"Magic." Knox turns his head to the side and grins. "So cute," he mouths.

He loves them.

I put my head back to center and frown. "Why is there a broom handle with bananas hanging from pieces of string above our heads?"

"Decoration. Hamish's idea," Knox says as if it's the most normal thing in the world.

I fall asleep after lunch. My body is exhausted.

Stress from last night, the run up to Christmas, dance classes, sneaking away to see Knox. The list goes on and on and on.

Outcome: I'm shattered.

It turns out Archie didn't see the scuffle between Ewan and me. He heard it, though. Which was more than enough to frighten him. We talked it out. I covered for Ewan, told Archie his daddy isn't well and he is going to get some help.

If only that were true.

I want to keep his innocent mind exactly that, pure and innocent.

I also had a little conversation with them both, which I have had before, but it felt right to do again, about how Mommy and Daddy still cared for each other, but we didn't live together anymore.

Knox and I also put the feelers out and asked the boys about him and me being a couple. How they felt about us being together maybe and would it be okay if Knox maybe cuddled me from time to time.

Hamish asked if it meant he could now have more hot chocolate with Knox and Archie asked if he could stay in the big bedroom he slept in last night again. Our reply of yes to both of those requests appeased the boys and they didn't ask anything else after that.

My boys astonish me at times. I've gone over that scenario in my head a countless number of times and none of them played out as easily as it did.

Archie did, however, mention how cool it was that he now had three houses, more than anyone else in his class.

Little minds always amuse me.

I yawn and stretch as I enter the kitchen.

So much noise. The television is so loud.

I stop in my tracks, as does everyone else.

I can't believe what I am seeing. It's not the television.

Knox appears by my side and blankets me with his warm body. "I called Linc. Who called Fraser. Who called Hunter. You need your family. You need your sisters, Eva. You cannot keep doing this by yourself." I stare into his big brown eyes.

He cradles my face and plants a soft kiss on my forehead.

When I turn my head around, Eden and Ella are by my side.

Ella's eyes fill with tears.

Eden tilts my chin to inspect my injuries.

Neither of them say anything.

I tilt my head back to stop myself from crying. I do need them.

"Omne trium perfectum," I whisper. *Everything in threes is perfect.*

The three of us join hands, and then we wrap our arms around each other.

"We will do this together," Ella mumbles.

"Help you. Help with the boys. Anything." Eden rubs my back.

"I don't want Mom and Dad to know yet. Please don't say anything."

They both agree to keep quiet.

"But why?" Ella quizzes.

"The last few years have been crazy. What with Eden, then triplet baby Hunter drama, and then you and Fraser and the papers, career, wife scandal, and everything. Can we not give them at least one hassle-free, stress-free year?"

Eden chuckles. "You have a point."

I confess, "I wanted more time with Knox. Just the two of us. But then things went south with Ewan. You are all so busy.

Then the wedding, Christmas, and now your baby news, and Knox has the Winter Ball coming up. It's a lot to deal with."

"I suppose that makes sense," Ella agrees.

Fraser and Hunter make their way over to us.

"Thank you for being here," I direct my words to both of them.

Instinctively, they join our threesome.

Fraser lays a kiss on the top of my head. "You are not my sister-in-law, Eva. You're my sister. We are family. I have known you my whole life. We share each other's burdens. You were all there for me when I needed you the most. Now it's our time to be here for you. No more going it alone."

Sobs leave my chest, then Eden's, then Ella's.

"We have to stop this or I will end up a blubbering mess on this kitchen floor. Baby hormones are so unattractive." Ella sniffs.

We break out of our hug.

Eden uses her pointer fingers to swipe away her tears under her eyes. "We are staying here for dinner. You have an appointment with Corey at the hospital. Hunter is taking you. When you come back, we will order takeout. It will be the best Boxing Day ever." Eden loves organization. "Plus, Knox has had all these cool inflatables arrive from the hotel. We are having a pool party later too. Knox has a pool. Funny that, huh?"

I knew he was up to something.

And she's playing with me about the pool. I smile shyly.

"Knox built us a treehouse, Mom," Archie shouts with glee as he bounds through the backdoor, bringing in the cold with him. Lincoln and Hamish trail behind.

"It has a huge slide." Hamish is full of smiles.

"Christmas present." Knox blushes.

Actually blushes.

I love this man.

Ella can't hold her tongue any longer. "I knew it." She

bounces on her toes, looking between me and Knox. "That bangle. I saw it yesterday." She points to my wrist, excited now. "I know what that is."

"What is it?" Eden's brows pull together.

"It's a Love Bangle," Ella confirms.

She knows everything.

Eden's mouth drops open. Hunter closes it with his pointer finger under her chin.

"Those things cost thousands of—" Fraser covers Ella's mouth with his hand.

Thousands?

Really?

"Welcome to the family." Hunter holds his hand out for Knox to shake it.

This time he does.

CHAPTER 25

Knox - Three weeks later

"We are all set. Have a great night, everybody." I clap and rub my hands together, dismissing our team of one hundred staff for this evening's Winter Ball. "And George. Please keep your phone number to yourself this evening," I shout across the room.

"Oh, very good," my cousin from Greece counters. He joined our team two months ago and his lothario ways have not gone unnoticed by me.

"Does that go for me too?" Lincoln chuckles by my side.

"Yes. You even more so."

I look at him dressed in his black tux.

"You look very dashing this evening, Linc."

"Not so bad yourself, Dad." He straightens my bow tie.

"Let's have a run through the schedule, then you two are free to go for the night." Our event coordinator, Sophia, lays the plan on the table at the side of the room.

An hour later, I'm happy with the schedule changes she made.

"You know where I am if you have any drama." I button up

my tuxedo jacket. "Our work here is done, Linc. Thank you, Sophia, for all your hard work. You can have tomorrow off."

She gasps as if offended. "Tomorrow is my day off, anyway."

Linc chuckles.

"The night shift cleanup team will be all over this place like an army of ants. It will be spick-and-span in no time. They know the drill," she assures me.

"Right, Linc. Let's do this." I look at him.

"The giant light-up letters look incredible in the ballroom. I'm happy we went with THE SANCTUARY and not 60 YEARS," he says as we walk across the staff room.

"Me too. Do you know if my mother and father have arrived yet?" I ask Sophia

"Yes. Already mingling. Got a heads-up from the concierge." She waves her phone side to side.

"Fantastic. C'mon. Let's party, Linc."

I'm excited about tonight. Months' worth of planning. Weeks and hours of fine details. Bar staff, waiters, menus, table plans, entertainers.

It all comes together tonight.

"Have fun, Dad."

"You too."

We walk into the lobby and Lincoln heads off in his own direction.

I hit the main event and make my way through the crowd in search of one person in particular.

Shaking hands with our guests congratulating us on our sixty-year milestone, I weave myself through the endless sea of black tuxedos and evening gowns.

What a magnificent turn out.

Laughter, chatter, and music cloud the air.

Cheers from the roulette tables increase the excitement and, all in all, I am so proud of tonight.

Since Christmas night, Eva has spent many nights and days

at my house. She excused herself from the New Year events she had planned with her family. Hiding away from her parents, allowing her face to heal. Instead we spent it together snuggled up on the sofa together. It was perfect.

It made sense for her to take a two-week vacation from the dance studio too. Luckily her parents never heard about Ewan's dreadful assault. They've been so busy installing new log cabins at the retreat I haven't even golfed with Charlie either.

Eva has been religiously rubbing Arnica cream on her cheek to reduce the swelling and bruising. Something Corey suggested, and it's worked wonders. She still has a touch of light bruising, but you really have to look for it.

I have every day.

Checking in, looking after her.

She's started calling me Nurse Knox. I informed her I'm up for a little game of doctor and nurse if she is.

She said she is, once she's healed. *Naughty girl.*

Luckily, her cheekbone wasn't broken or it would have been a much longer healing time of six weeks.

Her sisters and their husbands took Archie to and from school.

Making life as easy as possible for her, she kept Hamish out of day care for a few weeks too.

I had a new front door installed at Eva's house. The plasters and decorators finished this week, erasing any reminders of that dreadful evening.

I also ordered her a new kettle and toaster.

She doesn't need the daily reminder of the old ones being thrown at her.

No one deserves that.

Ewan was charged with common assault. However, as this is his first serious offense, it looks like the courts will decide to fine him. He deserves harsher consequences.

On the plus side, he has all visitation rights to Hamish and

Archie withdrawn. I feel sad for those wee dudes who've captured my heart. They need a dad. But one that is fit to parent, and right now, Ewan isn't in any position to do that.

I can't understand why Ewan would jeopardize his time with them.

Veronica pushed for a quick divorce. She threatened no visitation rights, no future hope, and finally Ewan signed the divorce papers.

His parents forced him. I know this because I was there when Ewan's parents called Eva to apologize for the upset he has caused in her life.

They are trying desperately to get him a place in rehab but are struggling due to him being reluctant and the lack of vacant spaces in any of the county run facilities. He's been allocated a waiting list position, but that's the best they can do.

In sixteen weeks. Springtime. That's when my girl will be free from him.

Finally.

With the turning of the seasons, I have plans for change too. Big plans. I can't wait to tell her.

With each passing day, I fall more in love with her and her boys—more deeply, more madly.

I'm crazy in love and I want to shout it from the rooftops.

But I can't.

Not yet.

Just a couple more days.

It's exciting.

I stop and have a quick chat with my mom and dad. They love what we did. My dad informed me I had created a hotel not even he could have imagined. When I told him about my plans to win us a six-star title, he tried to hide his emotion, but I could see it. He's proud.

I'll die a happy man knowing that.

Everything feels like it's falling into alignment.

I reach for a glass of fizzy champagne from one of the waiters and as if by magic, the crowd in front of me parts and there in all her golden glory is the most beautiful woman on planet Earth.

Eva.

She's changed me. For the better.

I feel lighter, brighter. Happier.

She's surrounded by her family. I slowly take her in as I walk to her.

Wrapped in pale-lemon-yellow chiffon, her one-shoulder dress drapes across the floor behind her.

The sparkling lights above bounce off her two simple gold accessories; a Grecian style gold leaf hair band and my bangle.

Both private messages meant only for me.

Simply beautiful.

Approaching her tight family circle, I greet her parents first.

"Charlie." He shakes my outstretched hand. "Edith, you look beautiful this evening." I kiss her cheek hello.

"Thank you." She flushes. "I found this old thing at the back of the wardrobe." She fans out her black silk evening gown.

"Along with all the others with labels on, no doubt," Charlie mutters. That triggers their own private teasing conversation.

"Evening, everyone. You all look very dashing." I eye the circle of beautiful people. The Wallace sisters and their partners are arguably the poster children for attractive and distinguishable families.

I welcome everyone except Eva, wishing them all a great evening.

As they are all distracted by the entertainment around, I eventually bow a nod in Eva's direction.

In return, she teases me, "Good evening, Mr. Black."

"Eva."

"No date for this evening?"

"Oh, she's around. And yourself?"

"Stood up."

"Fool."

"I know."

"What fool would stand you up?"

I look at her across my glass as I take a sip.

"An old one."

I move to stand beside her. "Very good."

I turn my back to everyone, pretending to look around the room. "You look beautiful," I say quietly.

"Thank you for my dress." Looking up at me, she bats her eyelashes.

"You're welcome." I lean down and kiss her cheek as if saying goodbye, but I whisper in her ear, "To replace the one I ripped off of you the first time I licked your pretty pussy." She sucks in a breath.

I turn around. "Have a great night, guys." I wave and leave her family circle I desperately want to be a part of.

I would love to stay but it's time to work the room and her simply being here soothes my bones. Plus, she's staying at my place tonight, so I will see her later, anyway.

Hunter's parents are here on a visit from America and are looking after Eden and Hunter's sons, as well as Hamish and Archie, this evening.

It all worked out perfectly.

On her way back from the restrooms, quickly checking no one is around, I grab her by the hand and pull her into the empty photo booth.

She lets out a little yelp as she *thumps* into my chest.

I close the floor-length black curtain, shielding us from passersby.

"Hello." I look down at her.

"You almost gave me a heart attack," she pants.

"Sorry. Everyone is watching the fire-eaters. They're distracted. I wanted to steal a kiss."

"Oh, did you now, Mr. Black?"

She pulls me toward her by the collars of my dress jacket.

"You look super handsome in this tux. I could eat you."

Her sparkle has returned since the incident with Ewan; her big blue eyes are shining again.

"I always knew you had a slither of cannibal in you."

She giggles.

I love it when she giggles. "Should we get a photo of us?" She asks.

"Need to be careful when we leave."

"Easy." She turns around to face the camera. "Right. How does this thingy work?"

She sticks her tongue out as she concentrates, reading the instructions on the panel. Archie does the same when he's reading his schoolbooks too.

Adorable.

"Okay, stand there." She moves me back a step onto a white cross on the floor. "We press that big red button there." She points. "We get a five-second countdown between each photo it takes, and we get four. Ready?" She cranes her neck up.

"Ready."

I push the button and the countdown starts.

We do three silly poses, but on the final countdown, I pull her into my arms and kiss her.

Pushing my tongue into her mouth, I lose myself in her touch, her taste, and her little moans I've become addicted to.

The photo booth flashes, but we keep on kissing and kissing and I can't stop.

She entwines her fingers into the hair on the back of my neck, pressing me hard against her pouty lips.

"I'll never grow tired of kissing you," she breathes.

"Me either." I groan and rub my erection against her hip. She fucking drives me wild.

"But we have to stop 'cause I have a speech to make in..." I eye my wristwatch over her shoulder. "Shit. Five minutes. I gotta go, Sunshine."

I cup her face and plant five soft kisses one after the other on her swollen mouth.

"Not fair." She pouts.

"I know. I'll come find you after the speech and Mrs. Kinnear's presentation."

"Can't wait. And I want a dance. Just one."

"I promise I will. I have a fucking hard-on." I adjust myself.

She looks down and laughs.

"Well, now you do have a problem. I know what will help. Think about licking my pussy."

"Not helping."

"Sucking my nipples?"

I growl.

"Flicking my—"

I place my finger over her mouth and take a deep breath. "You. Are. Evil."

She looks back at me with her big blue doe eyes.

I remove my finger. She snaps and snarls at it, pretending to bite it.

"And vicious."

"You have somewhere to be, Mr. Black. Now go."

I nod my head up and down. I do.

Christ.

This woman is going to get me into trouble. I'm acting like a teenager. It's how she makes me feel—young and alive.

I poke my head out of the curtain. There are a couple of stragglers, but they aren't paying attention.

Straightening myself up, I give her the thumbs-up and step into the lobby, but I quickly pop my head back into the booth.

"I love you, by the way. And you look beautiful tonight, although I can't wait to get you out of that dress later."

"Love you." She smiles and tilts her head to the side. "Go do your thing, Mr. Big Bossy Bossman."

"That's not a thing." I grin.

"It is now."

"Pick up the photos?"

"Yes."

Then I leave her.

I run down to the lobby, pulling my speech notes from my inside jacket pocket.

This should be fun.

Eva

Taking my time, I reapply my lipstick in the photo booth mirror, drop it into my clutch, and snap it shut.

I'm excited about having a photo of Knox and me together.

It's been years since I've had any of the images on my phone printed out. I've been thinking about making separate photo albums—one for Hamish, one for Archie.

My parents have dozens of photos of me and my sisters. I barely have a handful printed of the boys; they are all on my phone.

That will be my new project this year; find an app I can print photos directly from my phone with. I make a mental note.

I draw back the curtain and stand and wait for the machine to process our photos.

Another few minutes pass.

Ah! It dawns on me. When Knox asked me to "Pick up the photos?" he must have meant he'll pick them up, it wasn't a question.

Silly Eva.

Knox

"Without further ado and before I cry—yes, people, this blackhearted fool will cry like a baby if I don't stop speaking now—because without Mrs. Kinnear in my life I will have to water the plants, organize my own email folders, and change the printer cartridges myself if her replacement doesn't turn up this coming week."

That gets a laugh from the three-hundred-strong crowd.

"Would Mrs. Kinnear please join me on stage here in this very hotel she has spent the last forty years working in? And would you all please give a round of applause for the most dedicated, highly valued, and respected member of The Sanctuary Hotel."

I raise my hands in the air to clap, and an explosion of whoops and cheers of appreciation break out.

She is loved in the hotel and will be sorely missed.

Embarrassed at the surprise long service award, she only says a few short words of thanks and leaves the stage.

I wrap the evening up with my thanks of appreciation, informing everyone to have a great night. As I'm about to say my final thanks, in front of everyone, I'm rudely interrupted by Tabitha.

"I would like to say something."

Regardless of her shortcomings, her family is a huge part of Castleview, and Lincoln informed me we had to do the right thing by inviting her family and *her*. I reluctantly agreed.

In a hideous pink ruffle dress, she walks toward the stage. Regardless of how much that fucking designer dress costs, she looks like a neon blancmange—ugly and tasteless. Like her.

I fiddle with my speech notes.

All eyes are on her as she makes her way onto the stage. She sure knows how to make an entrance.

Dumbfounded, I lean down and over the mic, I say, "Eh, so not planned for. But apparently Tabitha here from MacEvoy Distillery would like to say something."

A few people limply clap. Tabitha is not a well-liked woman in this town.

I cover the microphone with my hand. "Don't fucking embarrass me."

She sneers back. "Oh, I wouldn't dream of it. I think you are very good at doing that yourself."

What the fuck is she playing at?

She takes her place, relishing in the limelight. "Thank you, Knox. Good evening, everyone. I actually don't have much to say, and please forgive me if I stumble or go too fast; I'm not accustomed to talking to large crowds such as this."

She clears her throat. "First of all, I would like to say a huge congratulations to the Black family this evening on the sixty-year milestone. You are catching up with us at MacEvoy Distillery. As you are all aware, Knox and his family play a key role in this community. Upholding standards, donating to charities, they are a huge part of putting Castleview Cove on the map."

Oh, thank God. My shoulders sigh with relief. She's doing a congratulatory speech.

"Respect, trust, friendship, and reputation are the four values Knox ingrains through his staff training and the daily running of the hotel. Which is funny because those four values are something Knox has failed to live by himself of late. Isn't that right, Knox?"

Oh, no, what is she doing?

CHAPTER 26

Knox

"Funny story. You see, the girl he dumped me for is also one of his best friend's daughters, someone who is fourteen years younger than him. Knox Black is an unfaithful, disrespectful old pervert." She pauses for effect. "Charlie Wallace, Knox Black is *not* your friend, because for the last few months, he's been screwing your daughter. Sneaking around behind your back. Isn't that correct, Eva? And I have the evidence right here." Tabitha holds up our photo booth strip.

Oh.

My.

Fucking.

God.

Audible gasps of shock sound out across the room. The mutterings begin.

I leap forward and unplug the microphone.

"What the fuck are you doing?"

Tabitha sneers. "Payback. You used me. You're a prick, Knox Black. You kicked me to the curb like I was a useless piece of meat." She's shouting now. "I loved you and you broke my heart. To go with her." She points out into the sea of tables. I follow her finger and sure enough, she knows exactly where Eva is seated.

Oh fuck. Eva.

Open-mouthed, she stares at the stage, watching the drama and our secret unfold in front of everyone.

A brief look in Charlie's direction, even from here, it's as clear as day, his jaw is clenched, his veins pulsating in his temple.

I'm a dead man.

"She's a child," Tabitha roars.

Lincoln appears with two security guards. He wraps his arms around Tabitha's waist. She continues to scream profanities at me. I can't hear her 'cause the ringing in my ears is so loud. My heart is thumping in my chest and my pulse is banging in my temples. All I can do is stand here because I appear to have forgotten how to make words or move.

Legs and arms everywhere, Tabitha rips the photos up and throws them at me. Lincoln and the guards struggle to get her off the stage.

I watch the fragments of Eva and I drift to the floor, like leaves on an autumn day. Falling. Like my heart is doing.

How did she get the photos of us? I asked Eva to pick up the photos. Did she not?

In one last-ditch attempt to shame me, Tabitha screams at the top of her voice, "Good luck with your new whore. She's the same age as your son."

She's not. *Well, almost.*

I drag my hand through my hair and look out into the crowd.

The staff at the back of the room are ushering everyone out into the foyer.

Lincoln appears back on the stage.

As if in slow motion, over the mic, he announces for

everyone to make their way to the top-floor balcony for the fireworks display.

I can't move. Can't speak. Can't do anything.

What the fuck just happened?

I watch everyone leave the room until it's only me and Lincoln standing on the stage.

Eva's family are still all seated around their table, and my mom and dad are seated like statues in their seats three tables away.

Throwing his napkin down, Charlie stands up from his seat and storms in my direction.

I mutter my last will and testament to myself and step slowly down the side steps of the stage to meet my maker.

"Is this true?"

"We were going to tell you."

Smack. His punch crashes into my face. My head catapults back and I stumble.

Shattering pain shoots through my nose. I think he broke my fucking nose.

I tilt forward and cup my face. Fuck, that hurts.

Gold specks of powdered dust burst behind my eyes.

I hear screams of horror from her sisters and mom, and Eva shouting in anguish, "Don't touch him."

Warm liquid bubbles in my nose. I feel it cover my hand and flow down my face.

Opening my eyes, I take in the whole sorry situation.

Charlie launches for me and shoves me.

I stumble again, trying to find my feet.

I will not fight him.

Hunter and Fraser grab him, pulling him back from me.

"You touched my daughter, you filthy son of a bitch. She is too young for you. I will never forgive you for this," he roars, scrambling about, trying to tear himself out of his son-in-law's firm grasp.

Charlie is a big guy, but Hunter and especially Fraser are both built like tanks.

"You are supposed to be my friend. Are there not enough women your own age to satisfy you? So you saw an opportunity in my daughter? Is vulnerability what you prey on?" His words are laced with hate.

I stand tall. Fuck this.

"Don't speak about Eva that way. She's a grown woman with a strong mind." I wipe the blood from under my nose that's now dripping down my mouth and chin, seeping into my white dress shirt.

"I will speak about her however I want." Ashamed with me, he shakes his head back and forth. "You touched my daughter," he bellows. "With your hands. Are you sleeping with Tabitha too?"

"No. Never. I would never cheat on Eva."

"You did with Olivia. Isn't that why she left you?" He flares his nostrils, clenching his fists in the air.

I feel like he punched me in the gut. "What?"

"Charlie, that's enough!" Edith bellows.

Lincoln shuts Charlie down. "That is not why my mother left."

"No!" We hit him with both barrels, and I shout at Charlie too. "Never. That never happened. I have never cheated on anyone in my entire life."

Why would Charlie think those things about me?

"Olivia gave me full custody of Lincoln. She left us. Lincoln has seen the divorce papers and read her reasons. You are wrong, Charlie." I stare at him, angry at him for even suggesting such a thing. "How dare you say such lies in front of my son. You are completely out of order."

"And so are you with my daughter. I don't like the things I heard from Tabitha about you earlier this evening, Knox, and the way you treat women. Tabitha confirmed it again on the stage too, right here in front of everyone." He points in the direction of the stage. "We've been friends for over a decade. All that time, all those conversations together, shared secrets. I told you things about the girls and what, were you just waiting for one of them to look your way?"

"Charlie, what are you saying?" Edith cries.

"It was never like that." Denial flies from my lips because it's the truth. I waited for her to be free.

"The famous Knox *bachelor of the year* Black. Tabitha told me Olivia left because you were sleeping with her friend behind her back."

"That's a lie! Tabitha doesn't know anything about Olivia. She's doing this on purpose. She is jealous because I am with Eva. Can't you see that? I broke up with her. After three years, I might add. I never once went with anyone else. She's doing this to get back at me." I spit particles of blood everywhere. "She's a nasty piece of work and she has been horrible to Eva. You should hear the things she says about your daughter. To her face, too. She's bold. Far too bold."

This is unbelievable.

I'm going to bury Tabitha alive if I get my hands on her.

"You clearly know nothing about me after all, Charlie. Olivia left because she was too young and scared to be a mother, didn't want to be stuck in Castleview Cove. She was a free spirit; she wanted to travel, and it had nothing to do with anyone cheating. I don't talk about Olivia. Not only is it not fair to Lincoln, but to Olivia either. I don't trash-talk the mother of my son. I am better than that. But if you had asked, I would have told you the truth."

My face continues to throb. "Did you ever think to ask me about Olivia? Is this really what you think of me, after all of these years of being friends? Or is this a new thing since Tabitha told such sordid lies about me tonight? You made unjustified assumptions about me based on Tabitha's revenge scheme. You played right into her hands. Look at us fighting! You know me." I gesture to the space between us.

"When you drove home after our rounds of golf, did you laugh all the way home 'cause you were going with my daughter behind my back? I hate you," he growls as Hunter and Fraser continue to hold him back as he scrambles about like a ravenous dog.

He's not listening to me.

"Enough!" Holding her own, Eva stands between us.

I keep defending myself. "You're not listening to me, Charlie. I am not the man Tabitha has told you I am. Listen to *me*. Not her."

"She's too young for you. It's wrong. She's my baby girl. My Eva."

"You are ten years older than your wife. Is that wrong too? You're a hypocrite," I spit back.

"That's different. Let me go." He looks left and right at Hunter and Fraser. "I won't touch him again."

"There is no difference. But I don't think our age difference has anything to do with it. I know you. You're a proud man, a man of honor. But you're too proud to back down now. Because you stupidly believe the lies you've been told. I am truly sorry we didn't tell you sooner. I'm sorry for hiding our relationship from you. But I am not a cheat. Or a liar or a skirt-chaser or a playboy or Christ knows what else Tabitha said about me. I am dedicated to your daughter. I'm a good man."

Charlie shrugs his dinner jacket back in place on his shoulders. "You betrayed me!"

He makes a run for me. Eva screams and I hear Edith shouting for him to stop.

Pushing me to the ground, I land with a *thump*. He jumps on top of my chest, crushing my ribs. He swipes his fists left and right. I try to protect myself with my forearms, but then I give in and let him take whatever hate he has for me out on my face.

"I'm not fighting you, Charlie," I say through his punches.

Charlie is pulled off me.

Eva is by my side in an instant.

"What have you done?" she sobs.

I reach up and cup her face, unintentionally painting her cheek with my blood.

"I'm sorry, Sunshine. We should have told him earlier."

Eva's face turns dark. She swivels around on her feet.

"Look at what you did, Dad. Look at what you did to your friend." She turns back to me. Dazed and confused, I try to sit up.

"Get away from him, Eva," Charlie commands.

"No. I will not."

"Yes, you will. You are not to speak to him ever again. Do you hear me?"

"What the hell are you saying, Charlie? You are making this worse," Edith shrills.

Eva continues to look into my eyes. Charlie and I love Eva equally, and there can only be one winner from this. I know it won't be me.

It never crossed my mind Charlie would fight me the way he has this evening. I don't stand a chance.

"I will do no such thing." She's adamant.

"Fine. I am cutting you off. Don't ever speak to me again, Eva," he says flippantly. He's not thinking straight.

Her sisters and mother gasp in horror. I look over and Edith's jaw is grinding together. "Charlie, you take that back right now!"

Eva whips around. "What?"

"You're an embarrassment to me. You have brought deep shame on this family in front of the whole town this evening. I'm blaming him, though, not you. He's brainwashed you. Seduced you with his flashy cars and money."

Eva stands to her full height. "You are the one that is

embarrassing yourself. Knox is right. This isn't about the age difference between us. It's because of the lies Tabitha fed you and how she humiliated you, us, exposed our secret. Because you didn't know. It bruised your ego. I know you're upset because we kept us a secret from you. I know we lied to you, but we had our reasons." Her voice turns soft. "As a family, we have had so much going on, what with Eden and Hunter, then the babies, and then Ella and Fraser, with the media and Fraser's contract scandal, then the wedding, and then Christmas. I was giving you time to recover from all the drama. I knew the relationship between us was always going to be a shock, not to this extent, but I waited to give you breathing space. We were thinking about you.

"Knox has been busy with the ball, which has been completely ruined by Tabitha. She's a spoiled girl who enjoys getting her own way. She did this tonight. To get back at Knox. She succeeded." Eva presses a hand to her chest. "We planned to tell you on Monday. Knox and me together. We were waiting. We were being considerate. You can't even admit you are wrong about Knox. You stubborn old fool. You can't even apologize for believing Tabitha's shameful lies. He's your friend, Dad. Deep down you know the truth." She bows her head.

"He's no friend of mine," he sputters.

I try to stand up. Lincoln helps me. My vision is blurry and I can barely see out of one eye. My skull feels like it's been rattled about in a blender.

"Are you saying that if I don't break up with Knox, then you won't speak to me anymore? You don't want to see my boys? I can't be part of this family?" She begins to wilt. I've witnessed this before. Ewan made her feel the same way.

And I don't fucking like it.

"That will *never* happen, Eva." Edith steps forward.

"That's exactly what I am saying. You girls can rip up that dance retreat contract, too. You are not fulfilling that contract.

He'll be after you two next." He looks at Ella and Eden, who look lost and don't have a clue what to do or say.

"Charlie, that is enough now. You are walking on dangerous ground." Hunter's voice is low and steady.

"Hunter, you can't possibly think this is okay. He's fourteen years older than her. He's warped her mind. Surely you are all as shocked about this as I am?" He looks at everyone. Then it dawns on him.

"You knew. All of you knew. He sucked you all in."

I can't win. He thinks I'm the devil.

He'll never believe anything I say.

"Did you know?" he asks Edith.

She shakes her head no with a saddened face. "Calm down, Charlie. You are out of line tonight. Knox is your friend. The things Tabitha has told you, those are all lies. I am friends with Knox's mother. What Knox says is true. And do you not remember what happened between us? I was almost a decade younger than Eva when we met. Remember how we fought for one another? Because our families didn't want us to be together? You can't make her pick, Charlie. You, of all people, should know what this is like. You are tearing us apart. What has gotten into you this evening? It's not right. This is not right."

"You're correct, Edith. This thing between them is not right."

That's not what Edith meant.

"You're a hypocrite, Charlie Wallace. You cannot make Eva pick. You are not being fair." Edith pulls his shoulder to try make eye contact with him. "Please don't do this. You can't. You will lose us all."

He's adamant and stands tall. "You choose, Eva. Us or him?" He turns to face his daughter.

What a stubborn bastard.

"You can't do this," she stutters.

"Oh, I can."

"But I love him."

"You think you do."

"I do."

"How long have you been together for? A few weeks?"

"Since the auction," she whispers.

Charlie roars, "The night he paid eighty thousand pounds for dance lessons? I was right. He bought you like some kind of prostitute!"

"That's not true!" she bawls.

Charlie's face remains rigid and angry.

"End this now, Knox." He spits venom in my direction.

I have no power here.

"Sunshine." I gently take her elbow. "He's not listening. He doesn't believe me or you. Go. Be with them. Be with your family. I won't allow him to make you choose. I am choosing for you."

Charlie's eyes are full of disdain. "See, he's pushing you away. He doesn't want you, Eva."

I look into her eyes. "That's the furthest thing from the truth."

She sobs.

"You have to choose your family, Eva. Family first."

"But I love you. You love me. It feels so right." She weeps. "You've liked me for two years and you're not going to fight for me?"

She whimpers and my heart beats fast with apprehension at what I know is about to unfold.

"It gets worse. He liked you when you were a married woman?" Charlie puts his hand on his forehead. "You make me sick." His eyes bore through me.

I feel the anger from him bouncing across the room.

My father stands from the seat he's been watching from the whole time. He gives me a gentle nod; he's telling me to let her go. Supporting his advice, my mom reaches out to hold his hand.

I step back.

Sensing my defeat, Lincoln stands between us and takes over.

"Turn around and go, Eva. It's for the best," Lincoln says. "Your father is wrong about us and my dad. He'll step aside. You must choose your family. Those are bonds that can never be broken."

"What? No! No. Please, can we all sit down and talk about this. Please?" She really starts to cry.

"No. I am done here." Charlie puts his hand out for Eva to take.

She turns back around to look at me and I do the thing that Charlie wants me to do; I end it.

I walk through the side entrance of the ballroom.

"I trusted you," Charlie shouts after me.

I can hear Eva howling behind me, begging me to come back.

"I will never forgive you for this, Charlie. What have you done?" Edith wails.

I'm in so much pain and it's not my broken nose or my eye that hurts. It's my fucking heart.

Without sunshine, without her, there is only darkness.

Maybe this is the way it should be.

Destined to be alone.

I wanted to create an evening no one would ever forget.

We certainly did that.

Epic. Fuck, is it ever.

CHAPTER 27

Eva - Two weeks after the ball

"Step back, forward, hop-hop-hop," I shout over the loud music. "Faster now, step back, forward, small hop-hop-hop. Same again." I clap in time to my instructions.

"Looking great, Frank and Ivy. Shake those hips, Brian. Fabulous," I encourage my over-sixties ballroom dancers.

"Big finish. Annnnnnnnd hold! Well done." I give them a larger-than-life fake smile.

I don't want to be here.

I have to pick up the boys from my next door neighbor first. Charlotte has been incredible and helped me out these past few weeks with the boys. Then I am having an early night. That's if I can sleep. I'm surviving on three hours of sleep a night at the moment.

My body and mind are exhausted, but for the life of me I can't sleep, even with my comfortable mattress.

I can't stop thinking about him. *Knox.*

It's difficult to forget when I'm surrounded by all the furniture he bought me.

Constant reminders of *him*. His kindness. His heart. His love for me I no longer feel.

Absent.

It hurts. Deep.

Tears threaten to choke me, but I will not let them do that to me. I am stronger than that. I'm determined to keep pushing through. I did it with Ewan and I will do it again.

But it doesn't feel the way it did with Ewan.

This. This feels more painful. My heart squeezes in response to my thoughts.

Yeah, I know, broken heart; I feel the same.

As the last person leaves the studio, I sit down on the bench, remove my ballroom shoes, and change into my sneakers.

Ewan is still waiting for a place in rehab. It will be next year before he gets one, I reckon.

Until then, another year of drama, heartache, and headaches for us all.

Although he has kept to his agreement, and he's finally left me alone. He's been warned. Another slipup and it's a prison sentence.

Although it would actually be the wake-up call he needs. It would give him the opportunity to dry out, too.

I sigh.

I'm miserable.

Lost.

I feel alone.

I'm utterly devastated.

In my head, I had it all figured out. Me and Knox were going to tell my parents and friends. I was expecting some upset and a little drama, but they'd get over it in time, then we'd book a family vacation together. Knox even hinted at moving us into his place.

The possibilities were endless.

Spending more time with him was a mere dream. A fantasy.

Intentionally staying away from the beach, I haven't seen Knox. He hasn't replied to my texts or my phone calls. So I stopped.

I've given up. He did what my dad asked; he stepped back.

To be fair, I've kept my head down.

I've stayed away from the town center. Had my groceries delivered to the house. Internet shopping has been my savior.

I've been trying to avoid Mom. But she's been dropping into the studio every day to check on me. She's upset I canceled her taking Hamish for me on Mondays.

She informed me she and Dad are barely on speaking terms and she's been trying to talk some sense into him.

It hasn't worked.

Hunter and Fraser returned yesterday from a week-long golf tournament in Hawaii and they promised they could help me out with the boys now too, so that helps me to avoid people.

I don't want to speak to anyone.

Ella and Eden assured me no one has said anything, but I know they are protecting me. There is no way what happened between me and Knox isn't still being gossiped about.

And Tabitha got off scot-free.

Great.

I spot Eden's phone beside the sound system.

There's another thing for me to do before I go home—drop off Eden's phone.

Closing Eden's oversized front door of her modern glass house, I slip off my sneakers and walk down the polished concrete corridor.

Such a cool house. I might stay for a cup of tea. Although

I've heard snow is on its way tonight and I would like to get home and settled for the evening before it hits.

It's been a particularly cold winter. If we have a snow day tomorrow, that will suit me. Another day in hiding.

As always, the noise levels in Eden's house are set to loud.

Entering the huge open-spaced living area, I stop in my tracks.

Mom is here and Ella with Fraser, who's looking all freshly tanned. As is Hunter.

And *he's* here.

My dad.

We haven't spoken since the evening of the ball. I added an extra day onto Hamish's day care package and he hasn't been to my parents' on a Monday for the last two weeks.

I have nothing to say to him.

I have never felt such deep hurt, and he has yet to apologize to me.

Looking around, I realize everyone is here, except for me and my boys.

That hurts.

Eden runs down the stairs. "Oh, hi." She halts halfway on the steps.

I wasn't supposed to be here.

I wasn't invited.

Yeah, that hurts a lot.

The noise level drops slightly and everyone stops chatting. The low chatter from the television is the only sound now.

"You forgot your phone at the studio." I lay it down on the mirrored console table.

"Thanks."

"I'll go then." God, this is awkward.

It didn't have to be like this.

How Tabitha went about outing me and Knox ruined everything and caused this giant wedge between me and my family. Then there's Dad's stubbornness for not admitting he was wrong about Knox.

I'm responsible too. But I don't know how many times I need to apologize.

I should have been honest from the beginning. They say hindsight is twenty-twenty.

"Do you want to stay?" Eden asks.

I look around and make eye contact with my dad.

"No."

"Eva, please, baby," Mom coos.

A giant ball of emotion gets stuck in my throat and I suddenly feel like it's choking me.

Sensing I'm about to cry, I turn around on the balls of my feet and make a fast beeline back down the corridor.

"Eva, please stay," my dad calls out to me.

I stop, but don't turn back. "Are you going to apologize?"

No response.

My temper flares, and adrenaline takes over.

"You know what?" I say, stomping back up the corridor in his direction. "Screw you. I didn't do anything wrong here. Yes, I kept Knox and me a secret. I said I'm sorry a hundred times. But are you going to punish me forever for it? And I don't get invited to our family gatherings anymore? Because if I had known that when you gave me an option to pick him or you, I would have chosen him. But Knox made me choose you. You didn't give him a fair choice, and you still cut me out. Nobody wins. He said family first and you guys are all here. I'm family too."

"It's not like that, Eva. You cut us out too. You stopped bringing the boys." My dad says, sounding pained.

"To teach you a lesson, Dad. It's been two weeks and still you haven't spoken to me. Why the hell would I want to bring my boys into your home when you said all those nasty things about me and Knox? Especially about Knox. You can't even admit that you are wrong."

I pace back and forth.

"We explained everything to you that night. Our reasons. And still here we are." I throw my hands out to the side.

"Have Eden and Ella explained to you what Knox did for me?"

"No?" He looks confused.

"Do you know what has been happening in my life for the last three to four months, longer, but worse in the last three? A complete car crash is what it has been. Do you know any of what I have been going through?"

I don't wait for him to reply.

"Ewan assaulted me. I have an injunction against him for that now."

My dad stands up and tries to come to me. "Eva." He sounds shocked.

"I don't need your compassion. Please sit down. Do you know who went with me to the police station to file a harassment report? Who sat with me for three hours, going through every single threatening text from Ewan? Knox did. He paid for a new divorce lawyer for me, too. And do you know I came home one day to no furniture in my house? Ewan let himself into my house. He removed all my furniture from my home. I stayed at Knox's house one night and I came home to nothing. No sofa. No television. He even took the boys' beds. And do you know what Knox did? He had a full house of furniture delivered to my house so my boys had somewhere to sleep that night. He sent food to my house the same evening because he knew I would be tired and not want to cook. But you wouldn't know this because you never visit me. None of you do. You simply pick up and drop off at the door. I can't remember any of you dropping in for a chat to see me. And this is another reason I didn't tell you about Knox,

Ewan, all of it, because you're all so wrapped up in your own little bubbles, and I understand, I really do. You have your busy lives to get on with. I am not saying you are wrong. Not even close. But we are all busy. However, I make time for you all. I cover classes even when I'm stretched to my time limits. I stayed up until two in the morning to stuff wedding invitations into envelopes for you, Ella. I sorted out the accounts when our assistant was off the other week. I have created something close to one hundred social media videos over the last month. I interviewed the new dance tutors when you two"—I point to Eden and Ella—"went off to pick out nursery furniture for the new baby. You didn't ask me if I wanted to come. I covered for you when you couldn't make the Castleview Business Circle." I look at my dad. "Knox was so proud of the social media training I did for them."

I speak with force. "When Ewan didn't turn up to take my boys to the zoo, Knox took us. When Ewan assaulted me on Christmas night, he took me in. He looked after me and my boys. Fed us, clothed us. Called my sisters to come and carry the burden because he knew I needed them. He built a den in his kitchen for my boys. He organized a truck of inflatables for the boys so they could have a pool party in his house, distracting them from the fact their mother had been attacked by their father the night before."

Sobs leave my heavy chest. "He built them a treehouse in his backyard." I cover my mouth to conceal my sobs. "Hamish loved it. It even has a slide." I laugh, remembering how happy they were that day. I feel slightly hysterical.

"He gave me this bracelet." I hold up my wrist. "It's called a Love Bangle or some stupid shit. It seals a bond between two people. Everlasting love. And it's here every day on my wrist as a constant reminder of what that felt like because I can't take the friggin' thing off because it needs some fancy bloody tool to unlock it." I pull at it, trying to tear it off. "And I want so much to take the goddamn thing off, but I can't.

"And it hurts so bad. In here." I point at my chest. "Because he loved me like no one else has ever loved me. I don't know how we happened. But we did. I fell in love with him, and it was all so unexpected. But so beautiful. It's deeper than anything I have ever felt. He even knows how I like my cup of tea. And he cared for me and my boys. He loves them so much. We were going to be a family. But that's not going to happen anymore because you forced me and him to choose. You made him choose, and he chose you for me, but you didn't choose me back. You chose not to say sorry. Not to tell me you still loved me, regardless of what happened between us. You walked away from me. We are supposed to love each other unconditionally for all our flaws. You stood by Ella and Fraser when it all went to crap last year. But what about me?"

I wipe my nose and eyes on the sleeve of my coat.

"And you made us cancel the dance retreat contract, which was going to be a lifeline for me. I needed that money so bad. But now I have to sell the house to buy Ewan out. Do you know why? Because he gambled all of his severance pay away. And in addition, I have only found this out in the last couple of days, he's racked up three credit cards, in *my* name." Hurting myself, I point at my chest forcefully. "I have had to put my campervan up for sale. I am drowning and still you don't see me. I am dealing with everything by myself, but Knox helped me. He saw everything. He paid attention. Even when I didn't tell him what I needed, he knew."

My anguish shatters into a thousand pieces.

I've been keeping all of this in since the ball.

"Did you consider any of this, or were you only thinking of your reputation, Charlie?"

"Don't call me that," he says through pained words.

"I will. You are not my father. Where is the person who taught us to be compassionate, kind, thoughtful? And this." I motion to my family. "This just drives the nail further into the coffin." I shake my head. "Not being invited. I didn't do anything wrong. Loving someone is not a crime. But you are punishing me. I made a simple mistake of keeping Knox and me a secret for longer than expected to give you more time to deal with our family dramas. Because there is always something.

"But I am done with it all. I can't do it anymore." I make a decision I know I will regret for the rest of my life, but I say it anyway. It's the only way I will survive. "I don't want to be part of the dance school anymore. Buy me out. I need the money."

"No!" Eden runs across the kitchen floor. "That will never happen."

"I don't care." I shrug my shoulders. "Buy me out. You have four weeks to make it happen. I don't want to do any more classes either. I quit."

I pull my studio keys out of my wool coat and throw them on the counter.

"This way I won't have to teach all the people who have done nothing but talk about me for the last two weeks. I fell in love with a man you don't approve of, Dad. Your friend. That was all. And I kept it from you. I'm so sorry. I never meant to hurt you. I still love you, but I can't pretend to like what you did. Knox didn't push me away. He did what you asked him to do. He's a selfless man. You see what a great guy Lincoln is. It's because of Knox. Knox sacrificed everything for Lincoln. He's a true family man, and he believes this is where I should be. With you. You all think you know what is right for me, but you don't. I love him more than anything and now I have no one. Not even you guys. He wasn't just a chapter in my life. He was rewriting my story. Our story."

My dad looks defeated, immobile. He stares at me.

"This town is toxic. I'm selling the house and moving a few towns over. Bayview is beautiful. And I'll rent. Start again. And Tabitha can continue talking crap about me, destroy other people's lives with her ugly lies, and she gets to carry on as normal. But I'll rebuild. I'll be fine. I have my boys. And you can all have each other. So you stand there, Charlie Wallace. Stand there and be too proud to admit you messed up. But I'm not. I messed up and my life is a mess, but I'm not ashamed or too proud to admit those things. Because you brought me up better than that. You taught me how to be independent and strong. So that's what I will be."

My tears haven't stopped, and neither Ella nor my mom can say anything as their emotions reflect mine. Ella is sobbing in Fraser's arms and my mom's hand is over her heart.

"I have to go fetch the boys. Have a nice night. Have your lawyer get in touch with mine about the studio. It's Veronica Evans that is dealing with my divorce. And Mom." I turn to her. "Thank you for taking the boys for sleepovers the past few months. I am very grateful."

I have nothing left to say.

I leave.

And I feel worse than ever.

Raw grief floods my body.

Our family motto is right. Everything in threes is perfect. *Omne trium perfectum.*

Now it's just me, Archie, and Hamish.

CHAPTER 28

Eva - Nine Hours Later

"Eva, Ewan's been in a car crash. He's in the hospital" It's Ewan's mother, Frances.

Instantly awake, I flip the bed covers off me and leap out of the side of the bed.

"What happened? Is he okay?" I ask and tuck my phone between my ear and shoulder.

Scrambling about in the dark, I grab my yoga pants and hoodie off the bedroom chair.

"They found his car flipped upside down in the field on the bad bends at McGregor's fruit farm. We don't know any more than that. It's been snowing tonight."

"What was he doing out at this time of the night?" I pull my phone away from my ear to check the time. Three a.m.

"We don't know."

"Was he drinking?"

She doesn't say anything.

"Frances?"

"Yes. His blood alcohol level is three times over the limit."

I fall onto the edge of the bed. This is bad.

My pulse spins.

"How is he?"

"Can you come to the hospital?"

That's not a good sign.

"I'm getting dressed. I will need to get Charlotte from next door to come and look after the boys. I'll be ten minutes."

I tap the speakerphone button on my screen, allowing me to flip my hoodie over my head.

"Thank you, Eva. I know you don't have to come."

"He's the father of my children and we are still married, Frances." Propelling myself off the bed, I grab my phone and run down the stairs. "I'll see you in ten."

"Please be careful. The roads are dangerous. We've had a few inches of snow."

I hang up.

"Ewan, please be okay. Our boys need a father."

"He has three broken ribs. His scaphoid bone in his hand is also broken. His shoulder was dislocated. We have popped that back into place. The lacerations and bruising on his head and face are superficial. The CT scan showed no signs of bleeding on his brain. He's going to be okay. He was very lucky." The doctor gives us a rundown of Ewan's injuries. "The police are in there talking to him, but as soon as they are finished, you can see him. Cubicle five."

"Thank you, Doctor."

I walk to cubicle five to wait. Frances grabs the top of my arm. "You go first, Eva. We'll see him after you."

"Are you sure?"

"Yes. I know you won't believe me when I say this, but he still loves you."

"He's got a funny way of showing it. What about Ruby?"

"She split up with him. I think that's why he went out for a bit of a session tonight. I'm sorry for the hurt and pain he has caused you."

"Hey, this is not your fault. None of it. We need to work together to get him the help he needs or he's going to end up killing himself or someone else. This is serious, Frances."

She takes my hand in hers and pats it. "You're a lovely girl, Eva. Thank you for being here." I smile gratefully.

"That means a lot to me."

She tilts her chin up. "The police officers are leaving. I want to speak to them. You go see Ewan."

I turn around and head for cubicle five.

"I'm not allowed to be near you. You shouldn't be here," he says gruffly as I enter. I notice he's handcuffed to the bed by his good hand.

"I don't care about that."

"The police will charge me with breach of the injunction if I break the terms and I am already in deep shit. I don't want you here. Please go." He closes his eyes, turns his head away from me, and rests it on the pillow.

"Well, I'm here and I'm staying. What did the police say?"

He ignores me.

"What were you doing out so late?"

No answer.

"I'm going to sit here until you tell me." I drop down into the chair by his hospital bed. This gives me a chance to examine his injuries.

His face is bruised. He looks thin. Ragged. Not himself. Not the handsome man I married, that's for certain.

I feel sorry for him.

His arm is in a sling and his hand looks swollen.

His hand and ribs are broken. So is he.

Broken emotionally and physically.

"Will your hand need a cast?"

Still no answer.

"So you're not going to speak to me at all?"

"No."

"Okay. Well, you can listen to me instead then. I came here tonight because I still care about you, Ewan. I know you don't think I do, but I do. We have two beautiful boys together and I think it's about time we worked together to make sure they have a father in their lives, don't you? They need a dad. They need you. But the old Ewan. Not this one. What happened to you? You are heading down a dangerous path. You could have killed yourself tonight or someone else. Did you even think about that?"

"Stop talking."

"No, I will not. You have dictated the last year of my life and I will not put up with it anymore. It's time to hear a few home truths."

And I do. I tell him everything about his credit cards, forcing us to sell my campervan. I inform him I am selling the house because I can't afford to keep it myself. I lay all my cards on the table. It's neither the time nor the place but I don't care. He needs to hear it all.

"You will go to jail for this. Did the police tell you that tonight? It's six months imprisonment. I looked it up."

His face scrunches up. I have never seen Ewan cry before, but he has a complete emotional breakdown.

"Oh God, what have I done?"

His chest heaves in and out, and he grimaces with pain from his ribs.

I stand up and lean over the bed.

"Look at me."

He does.

His eyes are bloodshot. The fumes of his alcohol addiction puncture the air.

He needs help.

I thumb his cheek.

"You should fuck off back to Knox Black. I heard you were with him now." He sneers.

"Don't do this, Ewan. Don't be that guy. I'm not with Knox anymore. My father saw to that." I didn't realize Ewan knew. Of course he knew. The whole of Castleview Cove knows.

He pulls in a shallow breath. "He's a fool to let you go. He should have fought for you. *I* should have fought for you. Please forgive me?"

"Deep down, I know you are a good man. He is in there somewhere. I knew him once. I would never have married you if you weren't. Even though you gave up on us, I am still here for you. But you need to get professional help, Ewan. If you go to prison. Go. Take your punishment. Get better. I'll be always here for you and so will the boys. They need their father. We need to be a family. For them. I forgive you for everything. I know this isn't you."

He can't look at me and I know he's ashamed of himself.

"Okay," he says. I rest my forehead against his. "I'm so sorry, Eva."

"I know."

Being a partnership for our boys is essential. He needs to work with me in order to bring up two healthy boys, mentally and physically.

After the things that have happened between us, we will never be the same.

However, taking a higher path for my boys and showing them what a healthy divorced couple looks like? I will do that for them.

To keep the peace and to keep my sanity.

Every day, I will stand tall and wear my crown from my boys.

I've said it a bazillion times before. Divorce sucks.

Knox

I can't listen to this. She says she wants to be a family with him.

She's right. The boys do need their father.

Their real one.

I push myself off the wall outside Ewan's cubicle. Shoving my hands into the pockets of my jeans, I drop my head to my chest and drag my lead-weight body down the hospital corridor, step by heavy step.

Heading out of the hospital entrance, I pull my padded jacket around me. The first snow of winter. There will be a few more weeks of it now.

It's bitter tonight. Or morning. Or whatever the hell time it is.

"What are you doing here?"

Charlie.

That's a weighted question, because now I don't know.

"Sergeant Taylor called me to let me know Ewan had been in an accident. He helped with Eva's injunction against him. I wanted to check on Eva. Make sure she isn't upset. Or needed help with the boys," I trail off.

She's not upset. She's getting back together with him.

I replay her words she said to Ewan in my head. *We need to be a family.*

"Don't worry. I was leaving." I side-eye him.

I haven't seen him since our fight. My nose has almost healed; another week and it should be good. I was right. He broke it. But the bruising around my eye has taken longer to disappear. There are still some yellow remnants.

I trudge back to my car across the snow-ridden parking lot.

The delicate snowflakes hit me like mini meteorites, each one burning a hole in my heart.

"I was wrong about you, Knox," he shouts into the space between us.

I stop in my tracks.

"I'm sorry. Eva told me everything tonight. The things you did for her. I am very grateful for what you have done for my daughter and her boys. You were there for her."

Not anymore.

"I wasn't. I've been selfish and narrow-minded, and I am truly sorry. I know I ruined our friendship and I will never forgive myself for that. Eva told me I was a stubborn old fool, and I have been. She's not speaking to me. She quit the dance studio. She's selling her house. Ewan has racked up three credit cards in her name. He's the gift that keeps on giving. My poor girl is broken. She said she's moving to Bayview."

I fly around to face him.

What?

"She's leaving, Knox. Starting again."

Ah, with Ewan. A fresh beginning. That makes sense.

I walk back in Charlie's direction. "Will you give her this, please?" I pull my wallet from the inside pocket of my jacket. From the depth of the coin section, I fish out what I'm looking for.

"I hope Ewan recovers and gets the help he needs." I place the miniscule gold screwdriver into Charlie's hand.

"You should give it to her yourself."

"I don't think it's right for me to do that anymore."

Not if she is getting back with her husband.

"Good night, Charlie."

"Do you love her?" he calls across the echoing parking lot.

My hand stalls on the door handle of my car. "More than you can ever imagine," I respond.

I don't look back.

CHAPTER 29

Eva

"You shouldn't be here." I turn away from my father.

"Yes, I should. You are my daughter, and you need your family right now."

"Please go." I stab the buttons on the hospital coffee machine. I hate coffee, but I'll take caffeine any way I can get it right now.

"No. I'm staying. And your mother will be here with Ella and Eden any minute."

"Ella should be in bed resting. She has the baby to think about."

"She's tough, our Ella. You know that. Nothing will stop her from coming."

"Stop speaking to me. I am mad at you. Why is this not working?" I bend down to have a look at the nozzle on the machine.

"Here, let me do it." Dad moves me aside.

Whatever he does, he gets it working and hands me my hot coffee in a plastic cup.

"I hate hospitals. And the coffee. That is truly vile." I screw up my face at the bitter liquid.

My dad chuckles.

"You know, when you were born, right here in this very hospital, you three girls were like the most magical thing to have ever happened in Castleview." He makes himself a coffee too. "Triplets. There had never been triplets born here until you three girls. You were special. You were even in the newspaper. Front page. I have a shoebox filled with all the little things you used to make me. Including the newspaper article. I treasure those."

He blows the top of his coffee cup.

"You changed my life. For the better. And your mom. She changed me too. She hates me right now and isn't talking to me. I've been a fool." He lets out a big, heavy sigh. "But you four girls made my life complete. Although it was awful when you were all on your periods at the same time of the month together. That's why I took up golf."

I snort over my coffee. *Yeah. Not so good.*

"But you four girls complete me. And that is why you will not call me Charlie. I am your dad, then, now, and forever. And I love you, Eva. Please forgive me for being a hypocrite, a dumb fool, and an asshole."

I've never heard my dad swear before. He's a true gentleman.

Until he punched my boyfriend, that is.

"Can we please be friends again? I promise I will do better, be a better dad, and visit you more. Just please promise you will make better coffee than this. Christ, that is bitter." He puckers his lips together, scrunching his nose.

"I never meant to hurt you." He puts his cup on the chair. "But you are my baby. You will always be my baby. All three of you. I thought what I was doing was protecting you and I didn't. I hurt you and that makes me one truly terrible father." He cups my face. "I should never have said or done the things I did. Should never have made you choose. I feel awful. And I should have seen how badly you were hurting. I messed up. Not you. Me. Please forgive me?"

"I'm sorry I didn't tell you sooner about me and Knox."

"It doesn't matter now. What's done is done." He pulls me into a hug. "I broke his nose."

"You did."

"It's still bruised."

I lean back. "You've seen him?"

He looks like he wants to say something, but he bites his cheek.

"Dad?"

"He was here. About ten minutes ago. Sergeant Taylor called him to inform him about Ewan. He came to make sure you were okay."

He came to see me?

"He asked me to give you this. I was going to give it to you later." My father gently places a tiny golden instrument into the palm of my hand.

Any hope I had of Knox and me evaporates into the air.

"Oh." I don't know what to say. I know what that means.

Unlock it. Break our bond.

Set him free.

"I need the bathroom."

"Eva."

"Nope." I hold my finger in the air. "Don't say anything. Just —" I shake my head urging him to stop. "Not now."

"He said he—"

I run to the restroom.

I don't want to hear.

I roll the beautiful little tool between my fingers. Back and forth and back and forth. The fluorescent restroom light above hits it every now and again, making it glint.

"She's in here."

Aw, crap. Eden. And where there is one, there are two.

"Eva?" Bingo. Ella.

"Open the door."

"No."

"C'mon. We've been shitty sisters, but I don't want to be a shitty sister in a shithouse. This hospital bathroom stinks. Baby hormones are making me feel sick all the time. Come out." She gags.

I silently chuckle at Ella.

"I don't want to." Or they will see I've been crying again.

"Okay, well, we will come to you." Eden's voice is full of determination.

A few clatters and bangs and Ella appears over the top of the bathroom stall on my right.

Then Eden appears underneath from my left and she shuffles into my stall on her back, her legs hidden from sight by my bathroom stall wall.

"Oh, my God. The floor is covered in germs. Get out. Or up or something. Please don't lie on the floor. There will be pee on the floor. Geriatric lady pee."

"I don't care." She smiles.

"And you should get down from there, too. You are pregnant." I look up.

"It's like two steps high. Get a grip."

"Are you going to take it off?" Eden eyes the gold tool between my fingers.

I sigh.

"I can't bring myself to. I love him."

"Then leave it on. Give it to me." Eden puts her hand out, and she takes it.

"Next decision. The house," Ella says above me. "You are moving into Eden's old place. It's sitting empty. It has three bedrooms. Perfect for you, Hamish, and Archie. Modern. Beautiful. Sell your house. You have wanted a new house forever, anyway. You will live in Eden's place rent free. Save some pennies and buy one you want. That is gonna be your fresh start."

What?

Eden goes next. "The credit cards? How much is it?"

"Over thirty thousand pounds."

Ella whistles. "Wow."

"You will not sell the campervan to pay those off. As an act of goodwill for you. *Not* for Ewan. Hunter is going to pay off those credit card bills."

I open my mouth to say that's not happening, but Eden pushes on. "He won five hundred thousand pounds the other week in Hawaii at his last golf championship. He can afford it. He offered. It's happening. I love my husband. He loves us all." She does a little squee.

"And another thing." She continues, "The reason we didn't tell dad about all the incredible things Knox did for you is because it was not our story to tell. And every time we did try to speak to him about you and Knox, he wouldn't listen. But you did a great job earlier of laying it all out for him. He feels terrible Eva. We do too. From this moment on we will do better."

"We promise." Ella says from above me.

Eden clears her throat. "Now the dance studio. Ella and I went back to the studio after you left our house and we are upping the cost of classes. We aren't charging enough. Then we can afford to increase our own wages too. You are not leaving us. You love teaching dance. You love the business. You are so freakin' good at the social media side of it. So you're staying? Great. Okay. Sorted. Now get your ass out here now."

What just happened?

"Ella Farmer, get your pregnant backside down from there right this very minute."

Mom.

"And what are you doing on the floor? That's disgusting, Eden."

Eden smiles at me and mouths, "We're in trouble."

Always triple trouble.

"And you, Eva Wallace. Open this door. We need to talk."

Told you. Triple doses of trouble.

I take my time to unlock the door, revealing my mom and both my sisters standing on either side of her.

"Eva, darling. My beautiful girl." She wraps me in a strong embrace. "I have let you down. Your father and I have been busy at the retreat. Then Ella's wedding, the triplet juggling, planning and building the new cabin installations at the retreat. And you're right, we are all busy, but you are the only one that makes time for us all. I will make this up to you. Your father and I have barely spoken since the ball. I am mad at him for the things he has said and done."

She leans back to face me.

"Your dad and I, we love you. I thought you were okay. I thought you were doing fine. I made assumptions. You've always been this level headed happy girl. But you've been hiding from us. Hiding your pain and the truth about Ewan. I trusted him to look after you. He didn't just fail you and the boys; he failed us too. You are our prized possession; all three of you are." She pulls me into another hug. "My precious cargo. Since you were a little girl, you were always so strong and annoyingly independent—Archie gets that from you too. And you still are. And I am so sorry that I haven't been paying attention. I feel terrible. Your father and I had a one-sided conversation after you left Eden's and I told him some home truths, but he didn't just fail you; so did I and I'm sorry, Eva. But

I am here for you now; however, you have got to let us in. Tell us, share with us, or how do we know? Your dad actually couldn't give a rat's ass about the age difference between you and Knox. It's because you kept you two a secret."

She cradles my face. "He's a proud man. You dented his trust and violated his relationship with Knox. He feels betrayed and humiliated. The way Tabitha embarrassed us all."

"I know. I feel awful, Mom." My emotional cauldron bubbles over and I begin to cry again.

"But here's the thing, Eva. We are family; that's a bond that will never be broken, and you, me, and Dad will sort this out, okay?" Her hopeful eyes shine back at me. "Just not tonight because there is Ewan to focus on this evening. I hear he's broken a few bones, but he's going to be okay."

I nod my head.

"Your father and I are leaving now. I don't care what time it is, but we are going to your house. Frances tells me Charlotte is looking after the boys right now. So we will go back and relieve Charlotte of her duties. Bundle up the boys and we will take care of them for a few days. Dad will bring them back. You need to sleep, rest, have a day off. Until then, know that I love you. I have kicked your dad's backside and my own too. We've been terrible parents. I should have kicked his ass on the night of the ball as well. I think I was in so much shock from it all; I don't know what I was thinking either." She clears her throat. "Also know this, I lost sight of you, but I *see* you." Her eyes begin to swim. "I see you and I am here for you. We all are."

My family is going to piece me back together again.

But there's part of me that's missing.

Him.

CHAPTER 30

Knox - Two days later

"I'll be back in three weeks. You have my number if anything, and I mean it, Linc, if anything happens or goes wrong, you call me."

"You're supposed to be going on vacation, and not a working vacation." He pulls my suitcase out of the back of my estate car. The last time I used this car was for our trip to the zoo.

It's the perfect family car and I have no little family to put in it anymore.

It sucks.

Three weeks in Athens should sort me out. Rest. Visit family.

Clear my head. Come back with new determination.

I hope I do anyway because my drive and focus have disappeared and left me too.

The New Year was supposed to be a new start, a new beginning. Instead, I am barely hanging on by my fingertips. I have no plans. Nothing to get excited about or aim for.

Lincoln has taken over everything for me. Handling finance meetings and anything else I had in my schedule this year.

He even attended the meeting with Tabitha's father as requested. Alone. I didn't want him apologizing on behalf of his daughter. She ruined everything—the ball, my reputation, my fucking nose, and I lost the girl I love.

We don't even have a photograph of us together; Tabitha tore them up.

The only evidence of us together is the sundial I've been clenching in my hand for the last two weeks.

So you can always find your way back to me. Just follow the Sunshine x

I know where she is. But I'm not allowed to go to her.

Forbidden. By Charlie.

She's texted, left voice messages. I can't bring myself to listen or read.

Like a beacon, the two red dot notifications on my text message and calls icon glare back at me with the number of unanswered calls and texts I've ignored from her; it's dozens.

I've never had a heart attack; however, I'm pretty sure the uncomfortable pressure in my chest is similar.

Apparently, Tabitha has been sent away to the family's apartment in New York on half of her allowance to give her time to think about what she did. Oh, boo-fucking-hoo.

And for the first time in my life, I don't care about the hotel.

We eventually hired a new personal assistant. I'm yet to determine if she's any good 'cause I've only been in the office a handful of times.

I'm hiding. From staff. From reality.

Moping about my house watching shitty television programs. Aimlessly walking around the house, remembering her.

Her smile.

Her laugh.

All of her.

She went back to him.

Olivia left me.

Eva left me too.

I give Linc a tight hug goodbye then roll my suitcase into the airport.

Athens isn't exactly going to be hot but it'll be warmer than Scotland. I don't care where I go as long as it's away from Castleview Cove. Although, she won't be there soon, anyway. She's moving to Bayview.

"Is it just you checking in today, sir?" The friendly first-class check-in officer takes my ticket and passport from my hand.

"Yes. Just me."

A vacation alone. Again.

How pathetic.

My phone vibrates in my pocket. It's Corey.

Corey: You know where I am if you need me. Call me anytime.

Me: Thanks, man.

Corey: Shane suggested a night out when you come back.

Me: I think I'll pass. Come to my place?

Corey: You can't hide away forever.

Me: I'm not hiding.

Corey: Yes, you are.

Me: About to board my flight.

Corey: Sure you are. In case you haven't heard. The gossips have moved on to something else. You're old news. Apparently, there's a sex video going around of Tabitha and McLeish, the farmer. Unbeknownst to her, he recorded her and sent it to his friend.

Me: What the hell? He's married!

Corey: And really fucking old. You have nothing to worry about, my friend. His wife is taking him for everything.

Me: He's a sleazebag. Felt up several of my staff on Christmas Day and was asked to leave.

Corey: I heard. Go. Enjoy your time away. I'm sure it will all work out.

Me: It won't, but thank you anyway.

Corey: FYI. Hate to tell you, man. That sex tape was from a year ago.

Me: Cheers for the heads-up.

This year keeps getting better and better. Tabby was fucking a crusty old perv at the same time as seeing me.

I have to get out of here.

Eva

"Can we please talk about Knox?" My dad sits down beside me on my sofa.

He promised me he would come for coffee. He did. He showed up for me, and my family has been incredible the last two days.

"Not now."

Ewan's injunction doesn't allow me to speak to him but Frances has been keeping me updated.

He has deep remorse for his actions and I believe him when he says he wants to get help. His lawyer has said if he agrees to rehab, he may avoid a prison sentence.

He's no longer my responsibility, but I want him to get better for our boys because regardless of our divorce, which should be finalized in fourteen weeks time, we will always be family. We need to act as a partnership. A united front. Mature adults for our sons. The boys connect us to each other. That will never change. We have to learn how to be civil to one another and navigate that. Over time, I have no doubt we will.

His mom and dad have taken him back to their house and they are going to do their best to wean him off the alcohol.

They met with addiction services in the hospital and they now have a plan.

I explained to Frances that I cannot allow Ewan to see the boys again until he is clean. So, right now, the injunction is in place indefinitely.

I explained everything my sisters have done for us.

Surprisingly, and I think Frances had something to do with it, Ewan agreed to take the money for the credit cards off his profits from the house to pay Hunter back.

It's all legally binding now. I organized that straightaway with my lawyer before he could change his mind.

I feel somewhat settled.

"We need to talk about Knox. I cannot have my happy girl dragging her sad backside about anymore. It's too painful to watch."

"I know you said you believe Knox now. But he never made any advances on me when I was married, Dad. He told me over a year ago that he liked me. But he was deeply apologetic and hardly spoke to me after that. It was never our intention to hurt you or betray you, humiliate you—none of those things. And we never laughed at you behind your back. I promise." I let out a huge breath. I have so many regrets.

"I believe you. You told me you love him?"

"Yes."

"Is that why you can't take off your bracelet?"

"Yes."

"Chatty." He chuckles. "Next question. If I told you he told me he loved you two nights ago when we were standing in the hospital parking lot, would you believe me?"

"He still loves me?"

"His exact words were, 'More than you can ever imagine.'"

"But he gave you the tool to unlock my bracelet."

"I do know Knox, Eva. He thinks he's doing the right thing by setting you free. Letting you go."

Dad holds his clenched hand out and turns it over. He spreads his fingers and there in the palm of his hand is that tiny tool.

"Eden gave me this. She told me she would kick my backside if I didn't fix you and Knox."

"I don't want to be free from him. I don't want to take it off." I begin panicking at the prospect of having to remove my bracelet.

"That's not what I am saying at all. I'm giving you my blessing."

My dad takes a sip of his coffee and winks at me across the top of his coffee cup.

I whip my phone off the cushion on the couch so fast I almost fling it across the room. My hands shake at the enormity of what I'm about to do.

We can be together.

We have my father's blessing.

My call goes straight to voicemail.

"Knox, if you get this, *please* call me. I love you."

I have to find him. I hang up and call his direct number at the hotel.

"Good morn—"

"Knox!"

"No, Lincoln. Eva?"

"Yes. Where is your dad?"

"Athens."

"Athens!"

"Yeah, for three weeks."

"Three weeks?"

"Are we having a copycat conversation where you repeat everything I say?"

"No."

"You sure?"

"Yes."

"Okay, just checking. He flew out on the six a.m. flight this morning."

"This morning?"

"Are you certain we aren't playing a game of copycat?"

"Oh, shut up, Linc."

He laughs.

"Athens for three weeks. That's too long," I say softly, almost whispering to myself. "I can't wait. I need to see him or speak to him *now*."

"Finally! It's taken you long enough to come to your senses." He lets out a sigh of relief.

"I know." I sigh too.

"Trust me, *I* know. He didn't shower for three days. He didn't change his boxers for those three days, either. Disgusting. And he even watched an entire season of *Emily in Paris* on Netflix, because apparently that's what you watch. He's not well. He's a man who normally showers two to three times a day. He's broken. He needs his Eva back. To reprogram him."

"I want to make it right."

"Well, you know what you need to do then, don't you?"

CHAPTER 31

Knox - Later that night

"*Efharisto.*" I thank the waiter who slides my drink across the marble bar. I sit back in the high stool and rub my temples.

My lovely Greek family insisted I stay with them, but I turned down their kind offer. Fourteen of them live in a four-story home plus they have no pool so I decided to stay at a hotel for the next three weeks.

That's my excuse and I am sticking to it. I just want to be alone.

I reluctantly switch my phone on.

I had a relaxing afternoon wandering through the busy streets of Athens, had a bit of a siesta, swim, food, more food, and now drinks.

Same again tomorrow.

My phone goes into notification overload. Dings, beeps, pings, whooshes.

I idly scroll through them, spinning the ice around the amber liquid in my glass with my other hand. Nothing important I need to get back to straightaway. Then one catches my eye.

Sunshine Emoji Left a voice message

Eva.

My thumb hovers over the screen. Conflicted. I want to hear her voice, but don't want to at the same time.

"Are you going to listen to that?"

I must be hearing things.

I slap my phone face down on the bartop and look up.

I'm hallucinating.

Looking right at me in the mirror backed bar.

It's her. All fresh-faced, blond hair, and dimples.

I am definitely going fucking crazy. I rub my eyes and scratch my hands over the scruff on my face.

I look back up again.

She's still there.

And she's wearing the same yellow sundress I saw her in on the beach a little over two years ago. The moment I *saw* her.

A devastatingly beautiful smile spreads across her face and I about melt in my seat.

"Hi," she says softly, and the glow of her smile warms my soul.

"Hi." I can't stop staring.

She's here.

"I have something that belongs to you. I wanted to hand-deliver it. Personally."

I frown.

Is she really here?

"This." She holds up a tiny gold screwdriver. "It's yours."

She moves to my side and lays the screwdriver on the bar in front of me; it makes a *tink* sound as she does.

My eyes follow the path of hand, her still bangled wrist, her arm, her shoulder, her neck until they reach her face.

She's wearing my bracelet.

With a slow, sexy grin, she says, "I'm yours."

"You're not back with Ewan?"

She's alarmed at my question. "What! No way. What made you think that?"

"I overheard you at the hospital. You said you needed to be a family."

"Yes, we do. Put on a united front for my boys. Work in harmony together. Not get back together. Did you actually think I would go back with him?"

"I don't know. I don't know anything anymore." I'm so fucking confused and lost.

Lonely.

"I came for you, Knox. I love you. And you made me a promise. You made a bond with me."

She came for me.

She holds up her wrist. "And I will never, ever break it. Or your heart. I will always run *to* you, not from you."

"What about your dad?"

"He paid for my ticket to come here. We have his blessing."

My eyebrows fly up to my hairline.

"He knows how I feel about you. He knows how you feel about me. And my boys. This is real, Knox. Real, deep, everlasting love. The sun, me, needs to move around the Earth, which is you, and I can't shine without you. I want to go to bed every night with you, under the shine of the moon and under the stars."

My girl slays me with her words.

She loops her arms around my neck.

"Your nose and eye look sore. I want to make you better." She rubs a thumb across my eyebrow.

"Your dad broke my nose, but after all the things you've just said, I can't tell the difference between my nose and my toes."

"I love you."

"You're here."

"I'm here. You will never get rid of me. Wherever you go, I will follow."

"I love you so much."

"I know you do. I've always known."

And then she kisses me with such heartfelt tenderness. My heart basks in her sunshine. It's safe with her.

She softly kisses away the pain, heartache, and the uneasiness I've felt for the past two weeks.

She turns me to mush. Every. Single. Time.

"I have a proposal for you."

"An indecent one?" I cradle her face in my hands. I can't believe she's here.

"Later." She kisses my lips. "I don't have eighty thousand pounds, but I will give you every beat of my heart for the rest of my life."

"Sold. But everything I have is yours."

"All I want is you. Oh, and your Cobra."

"You only want me and my ten-million-pound car."

"I changed my mind. Just the car. Oh, and one more thing. The dance retreat contract reinstated."

"I never canceled it or the bookings. I couldn't bring myself to."

I press my lips against hers. She can have anything she wants.

"Take me to your room and make me yours again," she whispers.

I don't have to be asked twice.

I pull her into a fierce deep hug, squeeze her tightly to me and bury my face into her neck.

She came for me.

Eva

"Fucking look at you. Just beautiful."

Knox's eyes turn dark as I watch him fucking me from behind in the mirror.

"Hands on the wall, Sunshine."

I brace myself on either side of the mirror.

"You belong to me," he growls, digging his fingers into my hips.

"I do."

"Don't ever leave me."

"Never," I cry out as he fucks me so deep I stretch up onto my tiptoes.

He reaches around and rubs my clit. It's delicious in every way.

He flicks my ring over and over again, rendering me speechless. He pulls and pinches my clit as he strikes into me from behind.

"Push back and fuck me, baby."

I rock my hips, fucking him, moving back and forth with the need to find my release.

He slides his finger down my backside and he slips his thumb into my tight, puckered hole.

He hammers into me faster. I push back again, meeting every punishing thrust.

"It's too much," I cry.

"It's not enough," he growls.

He spanks my clit, once, then again, as he pushes his thumb deeper into my back entrance, and with one more strike, I let go, giving him what he wants and come. Releasing all the hurt and pain from the last two weeks.

So does he.

Gentle waves of happy pleasure hum across my skin.

We are perfectly in sync with one another.

He moves in and out of my body slowly, emptying himself

inside of me, escorting me out of my fizzy ecstasy. He looks at me in the mirror over my shoulder.

"Se'agapó," I whisper to him. *I love you.*

His eyes go wide with amusement.

He knows I figured out what he was saying to me all those weeks ago. Well, I Googled it. He was hiding from me. Too scared to share his true feelings for me. Protecting himself.

He doesn't have to anymore.

"You speak Greek now?" His deep chocolate eyes meet my blue ones.

"When in Rome and all that."

He kisses me softly on my shoulder. "We're in Greece."

"I know that."

"Se'agapó." He smiles back at me in the mirror.

CHAPTER 32

Knox

The next morning, I still can't believe she came to me. In Athens.

I didn't need a sundial compass to find her. She found me.

"What are we doing today?" She stretches out her beautiful body in the bed.

I can't take my eyes off her.

"Anything you want. I'm not sure you're ready to meet my crazy, loud family. Maybe save that for another day."

"Do they have food?" She shifts onto her side, moves in close, and lifts her leg up onto my hip.

"Lots, and it's the best in Athens. They have a restaurant." I kiss her softly.

"Then we will go to see them today. I want to meet them."

"Are you sure?"

"Yes. If they are all as handsome as you, I'm in for a great day of perving."

I pull her into me and squeeze her backside.

"You should only have eyes for me."

"I do. But behind my sunglasses, anything could happen."

She's always teasing me.

"When are the boys arriving?"

"Later this afternoon with Mom and Dad." We are moving to a family suite later today. I also booked Charlie and Edith a separate suite too, there are staying for a few days. Which can only be a good sign.

"Your father and I need to talk. I'm not looking forward to the conversation with him." I groan.

"He feels bad about your face and about his behavior." She kisses my eyelid. "The bruising looks better than it did yesterday."

"It needed sunshine to heal."

She exhales a long sigh of contentment.

She's happy.

Me too.

I sit back in my chair around the poolside.

"One, two, three, jump, Hamish!" Eva stands in the pool, arms outstretched as Hamish leaps into her arms, and he squeals in delight as he hits the heated water, splashing it everywhere.

It's not warm today. February in Athens is much milder than their searing heat of summer. When I get in that water later, I will be grateful for choosing a hotel that heats their outdoor pool over the cooler months.

Eva's water babies. I class those boys as my own. They've scooped out a piece of my heart, then replaced and repacked themselves inside of it.

I'm not complaining.

I like this feeling. Contentment.

"You love her?"

"I do, Charlie." I run my finger around the rim of my glass.

Charlie and Edith arrived in Athens with them last night. They left me, Eva, and the boys to spend the evening together.

Hamish and Archie were excited to see me. They even brought the toys I bought for them at the zoo, waving them about as they ran into my arms.

I haven't seen Hamish and Archie for over two weeks. I missed them. I think Archie has sprouted again. He's going to be tall, I reckon.

Edith and Charlie asked to speak with me first thing in the morning. Thinking about how this morning would pan out, I didn't sleep very well last night.

I feel like the worst guy in the world for keeping my relationship with their daughter a secret and at the same time the luckiest, because she's here with me now and we're having a three-week family vacation together.

Family vacation. I couldn't be happier.

I had an epiphany last night. It was like I could see everything as clear as crystal.

As soon as it came to me, I called Lincoln. He is joining us today, within the next couple of hours. It's what we need. To bond us together as a new fivesome. I booked his flight and hotel. He was under strict instructions to come.

Fuck the hotel. My managers are awesome. It's time Linc and I enjoyed a bit more leisure time. All I've done is work my whole life. I've had three vacations since I took over from my father ten years ago. And the dance retreat vacation I came for doesn't count as it was a research business trip. I have to learn how to switch off, or as Eva says, *chill out*.

I'm not setting a good example for my son if I don't show him there is much more to life than the hotel and spa.

I want him to travel and forge his own path. He assures me he loves the hotel, but I want him to take some time out to see the world. I know he'll come back to me.

But I need to let him explore his own options, too.

VH NICOLSON

"I've been an asshole, Knox. I am genuinely sorry about everything. I don't know what came over me the night of the ball." He sighs.

"Stupidity. That's what it was," Edith states firmly. "Keep going, Charlie Wallace."

He clears his throat. "It was wrong of me to believe the things Tabitha said. I think, combined with her lies about you still fresh in mind on that night and then her announcement of you two secretly seeing each other behind my back, in front of everyone and the way she said it." He cringes. "I put two and two together and got one hundred. I thought you had taken advantage of her. I know that's not what happened." He shakes his head.

"And you'd had one too many whiskies," Edith mutters.

Charlie keeps going. "It was not a good combination and I take full responsibility for my actions. My reaction was uncalled for and I am deeply ashamed of myself for my behavior. I should have welcomed you into the family, Knox. I know you. I know what an incredible father you are, and I know you will take care of my grandsons and my daughter. I feel terrible about the things I said. I see the sacrifices you made for Lincoln and I never appreciated it until recently. You're a selfless man. Will you ever forgive me? For the sake of my daughter?"

Wow, this is not what I was expecting. I thought this would be a one-way street where I would have to do all the apologizing.

"I forgive you."

"Oh, thank God." He reaches for his chest.

"But only on one condition."

His eyes search mine.

"What's that?"

"You forgive me too. I wasn't honest and upfront with you either. I could have handled this better myself. Been a good friend and told you how I felt about Eva from the start. I genuinely thought it would be better if you didn't know, until me and Eva knew ourselves where we were headed as a couple. I never made any previous advances on her, and I never bought her like a prostitute."

"That was an awful thing for me to say." He breaks eye contact with me. "She told me you didn't. She also told me you learned to dance to impress her."

I can't look at him. Fuck, that's embarrassing. "Yeah."

"You're a big old romantic fool at heart."

"Less of the old, thank you." I chuckle, then go all in. "I think I have loved Eva for longer than I have allowed myself to admit. I can't explain it."

"I know what you mean." He takes Edith's hand in his. "I forgive you, Knox. What you and Eva have is not sordid or forbidden; it's just different. We're the same." He points to Edith and himself.

"It's never felt more perfect."

"You have my full blessing, Knox. My grandsons idolize you. They love Lincoln. Hunter and Fraser and my girls think you are an upstanding guy. We think you are too. And our daughter loves you."

"That's all that matters." Edith smiles across the table at me.

Charlie has made me feel incredibly emotional with his kind words. Hearing things like that about yourself and about what others think of you, especially Eva's family, is a lot to take in. They accept me. He stopped my heart in its tracks for a brief moment.

Charlie rises from the table and open his arms wide. "Can we hug it out? My girls inform me it makes everything better."

I stand up and embrace my friend and if I have anything to do with it, my father-in-law. He pats me on the back and we sit back down.

"I'm sorry about your nose," he says sheepishly.

"Hurt like hell."

"I've got good swing."

"It's all the golf."

We all laugh.

"Can I ask you two something?" I wipe the palm of my hands down the fabric of my swim shorts. I'm so nervous.

"Yes, anything." Edith nods and takes a sip of her water.

"If I was to ask Eva to marry me, once her divorce and everything is settled, not now, but in the future, would I have your permission?"

Charlie gives an outright. "No!"

Shit. They don't want her to get hurt again. I slip my sunglasses back on. Yeah, thought as much.

Then he says, "I'm not ready to have a grandson almost the same age as my daughter." He and Edith burst out laughing.

"He's joking," Edith says. "It'll be wonderful having another grandson. Six grandsons? Where are all the girls?"

"When the time comes, you have my permission, Knox. You don't have to ask me. Welcome to the family." Charlie holds his hand out for me to shake.

What a rush.

Those divorce papers can't come quick enough.

For the next few hours, I play in the pool with Hamish and Archie and we come out like wrinkly piglets.

That's what Archie called us.

"Did you sort everything out?" Eva looks nervous.

I pull her into my arms and give her a soft kiss.

"Yeah. We are good."

"I don't know how long it's going to take for me to get used to seeing you kiss my daughter," Charlie pipes up from his shady spot under the canopy. I chuckle against Eva's lips.

Never thought about that.

Archie pretends to puke. "Argh, Mom and Knox are kissing."

"Can I have a kissy?" Hamish arrives by my side, looking up at me with his big, hopeful eyes.

I drop down and lift him up and plant a big kiss on his chubby cheek. Eva wraps her arms around us both.

"I would like one." Getting jealous, Archie appears too.

I pass Hamish to Eva, and I lift Archie into my arms and kiss his cheek. We all hug again.

"Awwwww, family hug! Me too."

Lincoln.

I roll my eyes as he appears and flings his arms around all of us.

Eva giggles. "I have three children."

"So do I."

"Yeah. Winc is here," Hamish screams with glee.

"Aren't we just the cutest?" Linc jests. "Have we found any poos in the pool yet?"

The boys say no in unison. Linc figured out weeks ago the boys like nothing better than toilet talk, and he supplies it in droves.

"Let's go hunting then, boys, shall we?" Linc cajoles them, getting them all excited.

"Will you ever grow up, Linc?" I sigh. He loves being silly with Eva's lovable rascals.

"No plans for that anytime soon." He squeezes us together tighter.

And just like that we become a little family.

"I love you." I slide slow, deep thrusts in and out of Eva's wet heat.

I cup her face with tender hands.

Showing her, meaning it all.

"I love you," I breathe against her lips.

I can't stop telling her.

Eva gently traces her fingertips across the skin on my back, tickling me with her tenderness.

Our tongues delicately twist and touch one another.

Forehead to forehead, our hot breath ghosts each other's lips as our mutual pleasure builds. Needing more, she whimpers.

Needing me to go fast but I don't. In a slow rhythmic pace, I take it easy, leisurely rocking together, going deep in and out, simultaneously teasing her clit with my pelvic bone and gently provoking her orgasm.

"Ah, Knox," she mewls.

I slide my hand up her thigh, over her hip, cup her ass, and lift her leg around my waist, pulling her even closer to me.

Eyes locked, inch by slow inch, we move together. I take my time between careful thrusts, circling my hips.

She blinks slowly. She sees me.

"I love you," she whispers and lets out a long moan.

Smooth and steady, I push my hips further into her and hold myself deep, barely moving but hitting all of her pleasure spots.

My cock swells; the throb in the base of my spine and in my balls builds.

Climbing together, she pushes her hips into mine. Rubbing herself against me. Chasing her release.

I kiss her deep and we come undone together and it's so fucking beautiful.

It takes my breath away.

I kiss her temple, her cheek, slowing bringing her back down.

We freefall together.

Not moving from where we are.

I take my shot.

"Will you move in with me? With the boys?"

She looks at me with dazed, dreamy eyes. "I'm supposed to be moving into Eden's old place once the house is sold," she says quietly.

I kiss her lips. "You will move in with me eventually anyway. It will save you two house moves."

"Do you mean it?" she whispers.

"Yes. Archie and Hamish can pick their bedrooms. Boy's choice." I smile down at her.

She gasps. "You really are something kind of wonderful, Knox Black. Completely unexpected."

"You are unexpected to me too. Never in a million years did I think you would be mine."

"But I am."

She is, and she's not just my sunshine, she's my universe.

THE END

EPILOGUE

Knox - Two years later

"How are you feeling?"

"Great. Perfect. Totally dandy." Eva nervously picks at her nail.

"You sure?"

"Yes. Oh, do me a favor. Can you pull over here for a minute?" She points to the side of the road.

Confused, I agree.

"Why are we pulling over?

"Just because."

Okaaaaaay.

I slow our new seven-seater Range Rover Sport down and pull into the turnout.

As soon as I've stopped, she hastily unhooks her seat belt, opens the car door, and unladylike in every way, steps out of the high car.

"Wait, let me help you."

"No stay in the car."

Faster than a whippet, she turns around.

"Great thanks for that. Now you can go." She slams the door

shut.

What?

I unclick my seat belt and bolt out of the car.

"Why are you still here?" She paces back and forth, hands cradled into the base of her back.

"Eh, because we are on our way to the hospital."

"Ohhhhhhhhhhhhhh. Yeah, about that. I'm not going. Ooooooohhhhh." She pants in and out, fanning her face with her hand. She's freaking out.

She's scared.

"Hey, c'mon, Sunshi—"

"Don't call me Sunshine. It's because of your sexy mouth that I am in this situation. Look at me."

I am and she's gorgeous.

My wife. Mrs. Black.

All big, pouty pregnancy mouth, big boobs, and bum. I can't get enough. Her swollen belly looks like someone stuck a bicycle pump into her tummy button and pumped her up to the size of a hopper ball.

Perfect.

I sealed the deal and made her my wife as soon as humanly possible and proposed at the following year's Winter Ball. Now that did give the gossips something to talk about.

Carefully, trying hard not to upset her, I move slowly in her direction. The last thing I want to do is poke the bear.

Still pacing, she breathes in and out fast.

"Breathe baby. It's going to be okay. Can we get back in the car? The sooner we get to the hospital, the sooner we'll meet our little girl."

Eva's whole family is excited. Eva is the only one of the girls to have a baby girl herself. So far, anyway.

Our girl is special, like her.

"She's not coming out. No way. Nope. Not happening."

"You know that's not how this works?"

She walks over to the car, braces her hands on the hood. "Oh boy. I'm not prepared for this scheduled C-section nonsense. Did we remember everything? Is everything in the bag? Did you bring her clothes to leave the hospital in?"

I walk over to her and rub her back gently.

"Eva. Look at me."

She tilts her head sideways to meet my eyes.

"It's time."

"I don't think I'm ready," she whimpers.

"You are. And I will be with you every step of the way."

"You have to promise not to peek over the screen, okay?"

"Okay."

"You do not need to see what is going on when they cut me open and when she is coming out. It's not right for you to see that," she mutters.

"I promise." She's mentioned this a few times.

"And as soon as she is born, we have to call our boys on FaceTime. Lincoln is waiting with Hamish and Archie."

Our boys.

"Yes. I am under strict orders."

Our three boys have gelled together as if they are real blood brothers. It's a wonderful thing to watch Lincoln with them. Archie and Hamish adore him. They all love each other.

It's a goddamn sin Ewan never took the first steps to get his drinking addiction under control. He hasn't seen his boys since his car crash. If he had, he would see how funny, smart, and kind they are. I see them, see everything they are, every single day and I provide for them emotionally and physically.

My sons.

With a daughter on her way.

Our life is a fusion of noise, laughter, and shouting with an extra dollop of mayhem. The dance studio never lets up and is busy all year round; the hotel is booked out continually; we are still working toward our six-star goal, and our dance retreat has a waiting list.

Eva's family drops in sporadically and our noise levels in the house are off the scale. I love it. Fraser and Hunter have become firm friends and they trust me to look after their girls when they are away on golfing championships. Eden and Ella always seem to be visiting or on the phone or just around us.

There is never a dull moment. Especially now that we have two new Labrador puppies. My old friend Sam sadly passed away not long after Eva and the boys moved in. It was as if he knew I was going to be okay and had a new family to keep me company.

I still miss him.

Charlie and Edith visit faithfully every week on a Wednesday evening for supper and quite often they take Hamish and Archie for a sleepover to help us out.

My life has rotated a full three hundred and sixty degrees. From calm to chaos.

One thing I've realised is love doesn't come in a neatly bowed package. It comes in all shapes, sizes and shades. It comes with many ups and downs. It comes in the form of two little boys, I am proud to call my sons. It comes with an instant family of nephews, two sisters-in-law and two seriously talented sportsmen brothers-in-law. And a man who is one of my closest friends who I am now honored to call my father-in-law. It comes with Eva's estranged husband who I will never let near my beautiful girl ever again. It comes with a warrior woman. My sunshine goddess.

And it smells like sunshine too—fresh, sparkling and invigorating—I bathe in it, *her*, daily.

"Should we go? The hospital staff are waiting for us. I have organised the best team for you, Eva. You are safe and they will look after you. I've got you, Sunshine."

Eventually she agrees to get back in the car.

Four hours later our big, beautiful butterball baby girl is born into the world. All chubby cheeks and dimples like her mom. Eva was a champion and she was so brave.

Rocking my daughter gently back and forth in my arms, I lower her down for Eva to get a good look at her.

"What are we calling her?" Eva looks up at me, flushed and tired.

I was given the honor of naming our little girl.

It was easy. And given her fuzzy blond hair, now it makes it even more perfect.

"Thea." I smile down at my two girls. "It means goddess of the sun, dawn, and the moon."

"That's beautiful." Eva sighs.

"So are you, Eva. You've changed my life."

Eva reaches out and takes my hand.

"You changed my life too, Knox." She rubs her thumb back and forth across my skin.

In this moment, I realize I got the family I always dreamed of.

It was all so unexpected.

But I should have known, because after the rain always comes sunshine.

And where there is sunshine and rain, there are rainbows.

And my life is now full of color and hope.

And it feels completely and utterly *epic*.

Lincoln is getting his happy ever after in The Boys of Castleview Cove Series... he deserves it...

 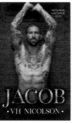

Lincoln's Story: mybook.to/LincolnVHNicolson
Jacob's Story: mybook.to/Jacob_VHNicolson
Owen: mybook.to/OwenVHNicolson (Early 2023)

IN CASE YOU HAVEN'T READ THE OTHER BOOKS IN THE TRIPLE TROUBLE SERIES

Eden's Story: mybook.to/huntingeden_VHNicolson (Book 1)
Ella's Story: mybook.to/inevitableella_VHN (Book 2)

ACKNOWLEDGMENTS

We got there. Can you believe it? We reached the final love story in The Triple Trouble Series and I am so sad to have to let them go. I love them all. Eva really does hold a special place in my heart for many personal reasons and her story was a difficult one to write at times but my gosh did Knox pull through for her.

This book would not be possible without the incredible support network I am surrounded by.

To my incredibly supportive husband, Paul, thank you for your never-ending belief in me. For checking in every day with me on my word count, keeping me accountable and supplying endless cups of tea. I need to book the teeth whitening to deal with that now.

Thank you to Kimberly, my editor, who continues to puts up with all of my strange queries converting British English to American English. I adore having you on my team, without you I couldn't do this.

To my mum, dad, and sister... yet again, thanks for all the little messages of encouragement and sharing.

I will be forever grateful to the Queen of all Swans, TL Swan, who without, I would never have written another book. Her group of Cygnet Authors really is something special. Tee encourages us every single day to keep chasing our dreams, to stand in our power, follow our own path and to write the book we wanted to read. Without her stream of knowledge and without that group of beautiful Cygnets I would not be here now writing the acknowledgement for my third book. Thank you Tee and all you talented Cygnets for your guidance, advice, sharing, cheerleading, and virtual hugs.

I want to give a HUGE shout out to my girl, and super talented author friend, Esme Taylor, who supported me in ways I can not even begin to explain throughout the writing of this book. Esme, I am so grateful you alpha read for me. You truly are extraordinary.

To my beautiful author friends, Elle Nicoll and Sadie Kincaid, there are not enough words to thank you for always being there when I need you most. I love you girls. Keep on shining.

And to JC Hawke who keeps on sharing her words of TikTok wisdom with me. I am very grateful, thank you.

Rosie, Carolann, Patricia and Alison... my enthusiastic beta readers... thank you for taking the time out of your days and nights to read for me. Your constant messages of encouragement, feedback and excitement gave me the energy to keep on writing every single day. You are a huge part of this journey and I love having each and every one of you in my world.

To all of the book bloggers, bookstagrammers and booktokers - a huge thank you for all of your support and the beautiful graphics and videos you create, every day you blow me away.

And to you, the spicy book reader, thank you for taking a leap of faith on a new author, you have no idea how much that means to me, I am eternally grateful. THANK YOU! Mwah x

ALSO BY VH NICOLSON

The Triple Trouble Series

Hunting Eden - The Triple Trouble Series (Book 1):
mybook.to/huntingeden_VHNicolson

Inevitable Ella - The Triple Trouble Series (Book 2):
mybook.to/inevitableella_VHN

The Boys of Castleview Cove

Lincoln - The Boys of Castleview Cove (Book 1):

mybook.to/LincolnVHNicolson

Jacob - The Boys of Castleview Cove (Book 2):

mybook.to/Jacob_VHNicolson

Owen - The Boys of Castleview Cove (Book 3):

mybook.to/OwenVHNicolson

COMING SPRING 2023

ABOUT THE AUTHOR

Since writing her first contemporary romance novel over lockdown, Vicki is now completely smitten with writing love stories with happily ever afters. VH Nicolson was born and raised along the breathtaking coastline in North East Fife in Scotland. For more than two decades she's worked throughout the UK and abroad within the creative marketing and design industry, as a branding strategist and stylist, editor of a magazine and sub-editor of a newspaper. Married to her soul mate, they have one son. She has a weakness for buying too many quirky sparkly jumpers, eating Belgium buns, and walking the endless beaches that surround her beautiful Scottish hometown she's now moved back to.

Website: vhnicolsonauthor.com
Facebook Group:
bit.ly/VHNicolsonFacebookReaderGroup

Printed in Poland
by Amazon Fulfillment
Poland Sp. z o.o., Wrocław
30 October 2023

93aa5c64-7e57-41f8-a7ef-507f18262abeR01